Mr. Darcy

AND THE

SECRET OF BECOMING A GENTLEMAN

MARIA HAMILTON

sourcebooks
landmark

Published by Sourcebooks Landmark, an imprint of Sourcebooks, Inc.
P.O. Box 4410, Naperville, Illinois 60567-4410
(630) 961-3900
FAX: (630) 961-2168
www.sourcebooks.com

Library of Congress Cataloging-in-Publication Data

Hamilton, Maria
  Mr. Darcy and the secret of becoming a gentleman / by Maria Hamilton.
     p. cm.
  1. Darcy, Fitzwilliam (Fictitious character)—Fiction. 2. Bennet, Elizabeth (Fictitious
character)—Fiction. 3. Gentry—England—Fiction. I. Austen, Jane, 1775–1817. Pride
and prejudice. II. Title.
  PS3608.A689M7 2011
  813'.6—dc22
                                    2010041901

Printed and bound in the United States of America.
               VP 10 9 8 7 6 5 4 3 2 1

*To my father, who taught me to believe
that all of life's choices were mine to make;
to my mother, who ensured that my opportunities became reality;
to my children, Max and Victoria, who always make me proud;
and most importantly to my husband, Russell,
whose support and sense of humor would make
Elizabeth Bennet envious.*

Contents

LEAVING HUNSFORD BEHIND

FITZWILLIAM DARCY RESTED HIS head against the seat of his well-appointed coach, relieved that he was at last leaving the outer boundary of Kent. He hoped that the physical distance between himself and the scene of his recent disgrace would allow him to put his humiliation and loss aside, even for just a little while. The next half hour of failed sleep, however, proved his supposition foolish. Regardless of time or distance, he could scarcely meditate on any subject without it reflexively leading back to Elizabeth Bennet's rejection of his marriage proposal at Hunsford.

With a contemptuous laugh and a sad shake of his head, he recalled his emotions before he had entered the parsonage. He was sure that Elizabeth Bennet would be expecting his addresses. He had envisioned her acceptance and his rapture. His optimism now seemed ridiculous. His misjudgment of the situation was another sin to add to the list that Elizabeth had catalogued. His mind jumped to his letter. Surely, in it he had explained himself. Not that it mattered now. He would never see her again, and even if he did, she could never love him. She had made that quite clear. He closed his eyes and took a long deep breath, trying to quell the enveloping despair.

He had to take control. He could not continue this way. He incessantly replayed his failed interaction with Elizabeth, and it always led to the same conclusion. She did not love him and never would. The question was whether she was justified in her opinion of him. Yes, she had been wrong about Wickham, but what of her other complaints? Was he arrogant and selfish? He had to admit that his conduct toward her could be considered arrogant. How else could he explain his misjudgment regarding her opinion of him? During the many weeks that he conducted his internal debate as to her worthiness to be his wife, he had never once considered that his regard for her was not returned. He simply assumed his position and fortune would be sufficient inducement. But, in hindsight, was that really what he hoped would persuade Elizabeth to accept his hand? Oh, if only he had truly considered her reaction. He still would not have her, but the horrible humiliation of his proposal would have been avoided.

In the end though, what did it matter? The results were the same. He had not only lost her, but he now knew that she held him in contempt. That she was alive in the world and thinking so poorly of him caused him a level of despair that he could never imagine overcoming.

But he knew he must. People relied upon him, and not just his younger sister Georgiana. Yet he was about to prove Elizabeth's reproof as to his selfishness true by embarking on a sustained plan of self-pity. In an attempt to steel himself, he thought of the grief he had endured over his parents' passing and how he had eventually picked himself up to tend to his responsibilities. He knew that in this new despair, he would also have to learn to carry on. In the past, he had thrown himself into the management of Pemberley and the care of Georgiana, but now he questioned his own judgment. How could he be trusted to know the right course of action for others when he had failed himself?

He knew he had to plan a path to a future that did not include her. But he could not envision it. Her rejection threatened to indefinitely cast a pall over everything he did. How could he return to Pemberley after he had spent so many nights fantasizing about arriving there with her on his arm—bringing her into his bed? London held nothing for him. Bingley was there, but he could hardly face him now that he knew that in addition to his own remorse, he was responsible for causing his friend's misery.

As his ruminations swirled, self-doubt quickly turned to self-loathing.

Darcy was finally roused from his torment by the voice of his cousin and traveling companion, Colonel Fitzwilliam. "Darcy, what are you thinking of? I have been watching you for the last few miles, and the dark clouds that pass over your countenance are disturbing to say the least. Surely, you do not regret your removal from our aunt?"

"No, not really," muttered Darcy.

"Has Lady Catherine's obvious references to the unification of your families become too heavy-handed for even you to bear? Because, otherwise, I thought the visit far more enjoyable than usual. The frequent inclusion of some of the Hunsford party was an unexpected pleasure."

Choosing to ignore the oblique reference to Miss Bennet,

Darcy simply replied, "Our aunt's comments were no more than I expected. Although I think the situation she refers to is just one more area of my life where I fear I have not behaved as well as I could."

"What is this, cousin?" exclaimed the colonel amiably. "Critical introspection? That is a trait I was not aware you possessed. I have always admired your decisive confidence. If I were in your shoes, I would not begin to know how to handle our aunt. I think your studious avoidance of the topic borders on tactical genius."

"Perhaps," replied Darcy, "but I have of late come to realize that I look on all my interactions solely from my own selfish perspective. The other side of decisive confidence is arrogance. I have never considered how my actions affect others. For instance, I have never thought of whether my avoidance of the topic of Cousin Anne gives pain to Anne or not. It is clear that my disinterest in her as a wife will grievously injure our aunt, but I am content to take the coward's way out and never convey my thoughts on the subject. It seems obvious now that the whole situation is but another example of my selfish disdain for the feeling of others."

"Darcy, what are you saying? Why this melancholy? You have always acted honorably. You know our aunt is impossible and that she has unfairly cast you into this situation with Cousin Anne. What is this really about?"

"You are right in one respect, Fitzwilliam; it is not the situation with Cousin Anne that is disturbing me. In fact, perhaps I have been too hasty in regard to her. Perhaps I should consider her as a mistress for Pemberley. I see no other suitable prospects on the horizon who would have me."

"That, sir, is hardly likely," Colonel Fitzwilliam said evenly, suspecting that his aunt's endless prattle could not induce this mood in Darcy. "I am more interested in knowing what has gotten you into this state."

Darcy knew that brooding alone was not the answer, and he did trust his cousin implicitly. But then again, he did not think he could speak plainly about Elizabeth so soon after the disastrous events in Kent and retain his composure. His pride may have been his worst enemy, but it was all he had left, and he could not bear the thought of lamenting the loss of Elizabeth in front of anyone, even one of his closest relatives. So he responded in a quiet tone by simply saying, "I recently had the opportunity to see myself through someone else's eyes, and I am not pleased with the result."

"Of whose eyes are we speaking?" the colonel asked, his curiosity piqued.

"It does not matter. The important thing is that it has awakened me to my many failings and my selfish nature."

"What failings, Darcy? What selfishness? You are a good man, a loving brother, a fine and fair master to many servants and tenants, and a good friend to me and to others."

"I thank you for the effort, but I believe you are taking the bare requisites of civility that I occasionally exhibit and exaggerating them into virtues. It would be more honest to admit that I am basically a selfish and self-absorbed man who only interacts generously with others when the dictates of duty demand it."

"Darcy, come now, you are not selfish. You are generous in both material matters and in spirit. Did you not recently tell me of the service you provided a friend in need? Is that not evidence of your concern for others?"

"A service I provided!" Darcy spat contemptuously. "That, my dear cousin, is exactly what I am talking about. In this very carriage I boasted to you about my behavior toward Bingley last fall, and now I realize that I may have committed a grave injustice. In retrospect I cannot believe how officiously I acted—all because I hold my own opinions in such high regard that I convinced Bingley to rely upon them above his own. If this is not a failing, then I know not what is."

Looking at Darcy with great remorse, Colonel Fitzwilliam confessed that he had concluded that it was Bingley whom Darcy had spoken of on their earlier journey and had stated as much to Miss Bennet in Kent. "Darcy, I am so sorry for my lack of discretion in this matter; in an attempt to defend your character, I let it slip to Miss Bennet that you had recently protected a friend from an unfortunate alliance. Did I put you in an awkward situation?"

"No more than I deserved, Fitzwilliam, and defending my character to Miss Bennet is an undertaking no mortal could accomplish."

"Then you two spoke of it?" the colonel inquired. "Does she know the family involved?"

"Fitzwilliam, she is a member of the family involved! Bingley was taken with Miss Elizabeth's oldest sister, Jane Bennet. I believed, it now seems erroneously, that Miss Bennet had no real regard for Bingley and was accepting his overtures out of deference to his position and fortune. Bingley trusted in my estimation of her regard above all others and quit Hertfordshire indefinitely without even extending her a proper good-bye."

"Darcy! This is entirely my fault," exclaimed Colonel

Fitzwilliam. "I must make amends. What have I done? I need to speak…"

Darcy held up his hand to silence his cousin. "Do not trouble yourself about it any further, Fitzwilliam. If my actions cannot withstand the light of day, then they do not deserve protection. Miss Elizabeth Bennet is a very astute young woman and no doubt suspected my interference without your accidental intelligence. We had an opportunity to… discuss the matter, and I confessed my involvement to her. She led me to understand that I was wrong about her sister's affections, and through that and other circumstances, I have come to see my behavior for what it was."

"Knowing you as I do, and considering Miss Bennet's forthright disposition, I can only imagine that your discussion was a lively one."

"Yes," Darcy muttered, "that is an understatement."

"So that explains the tension I thought existed between the two of you whenever I saw you together in Kent," surmised Colonel Fitzwilliam. "You always seemed so uncomfortable around her. I even wondered at one point if you preferred her, but I thought it unlikely given her connections."

"Yes, Fitzwilliam, you know me well enough to know I would measure at a woman's value by first appraising her financial status and her family's position in society."

"Darcy, I implied no such thing. How singularly you are behaving. Let me help. I could endeavor to further my acquaintance with Miss Elizabeth and then explain your motives to her."

Gazing out the window, Darcy said resolutely, "There is no point in discussing how I could change Miss Elizabeth Bennet's estimation of me. I have attempted to justify my conduct to her already, and I feel fairly certain there is nothing more to be gained in that regard. The question is, what do I do about Bingley?"

"I suppose, Darcy, you must tell him what you now know or, at least, talk him into returning to Hertfordshire so he can find out on his own."

"But what if that would only make matters worse? I have already jeopardized their happiness by my presumptuous interference. What if I excite Bingley's hopes and she no longer has affections for him or cannot forgive him for his seemingly thoughtless treatment this fall? In the same vein, if I induce Bingley to return to Hertfordshire and he has finally gotten over his attachment for Miss Bennet, his return will excite unwarranted hope on Miss Bennet's part, given that her sister will undoubtedly have told her of my interference."

Knitting his brow, Colonel Fitzwilliam replied, "I guess then you must be surer of your facts before you act. I understand that you feel guilty about your mistake, Darcy, but I do not quite comprehend the level of distress this is causing you. It was an innocent error on your part. Even with your interference, they are both adults and can figure this out themselves. Besides, now that Miss Elizabeth knows the truth, she may be able to resolve the problem herself."

Darcy took his time to respond and eventually said, "I do not think Miss Elizabeth would be in a position to effect much of a change to the situation, and in any regard, I would rather not impose upon her any further."

"Well," inquired the colonel, "then what is your plan?"

"I will visit Bingley in London and determine where his affections lie. From there, I will just have to see."

Suspecting that there was more to the story than Darcy was

admitting, the colonel added, "That seems prudent, and I hope you are able to resolve the situation to everyone's benefit, not only for their sake but for your own. If this is the cause of your dark mood since our departure from Kent, it is affecting you more than it should. I believe you take too much upon yourself."

Darcy failed to respond and instead continued to gaze out the window. Despite the length of the journey, sleep never found him.

Chapter 2

THE TRUE MEANING OF HEARTACHE

DARCY RETURNED TO HIS London home carrying the same despair that had been his constant companion since his disastrous proposal at Hunsford. His lament took two distinct forms: regret over the loss of the one woman he could ever imagine loving and obsession over whether her opinion of him was justified. His mood swung from anger at Elizabeth for her shortsightedness and unwarranted cruelty to remorse and mortification over his own misdeeds and failings.

In moments of weakness, he would imagine Elizabeth regretting her decision. He would envision her mourning all that she had given up, contrite over her misjudgment of Wickham's character. His fantasy would give him temporary relief from his self-reproach, but other thoughts always intruded. He would remember that both his father and sister had also been deceived by Wickham and that he himself had trusted him far longer than he should have. These sober thoughts would ultimately remind him of Elizabeth's other criticism and the mistakes he had made. They were legion. He began to realize that, regardless of whether he would ever have Elizabeth's love or respect, he had to come to terms with his own behavior. He knew in his heart that he had not been totally honest about all that had transpired. It was true that when he initially decided to intervene in Bingley's affairs, he had misunderstood the state of Miss Bennet's regard. But when he saw Miss Bennet in London, he had nagging doubts about her reason for coming. He told himself that his subsequent inaction was designed to spare Bingley needless distress, but he also realized that it was in his own self-interest to keep Bingley away from Miss Bennet if he was going to succeed in his poorly conceived plan to put Elizabeth out of his mind. Had he remained silent simply to protect his friend, or had he deliberately sacrificed Bingley's happiness to suit his own needs? While his failure to court Elizabeth in a civil manner ultimately destroyed his chances to win her, at least he was his own victim. His actions toward Bingley were another matter, and in hindsight they now appeared enormously selfish.

Regardless of whether Elizabeth's overall criticism was warranted, he knew if he continued to ignore the damage he had caused Bingley and Miss Bennet, her reproof would ultimately be justified. Darcy therefore resolved to see Bingley to determine if he still had feelings for Miss Bennet. If he did, he would talk Bingley into returning to Netherfield. Once there, he would observe Miss Bennet to see whether she still held Bingley in high regard. If she did, he would tell Bingley of his sisters' interference and his own deception. Darcy recognized that his plan would most likely force him to face both the mortification of seeing Elizabeth again and Bingley's wrath, but he knew it was a penance he deserved. His only hope was that his interaction with Elizabeth would be brief. He toyed with the idea of telling Bingley the truth before he could ascertain whether Miss Bennet would accept Bingley's renewed addresses, but he could not help but believe it was the coward's way out. He knew the only advantage to that plan was that it would allow him to avoid returning to Netherfield. Darcy vowed that in this endeavor he would not put his own comfort before others.

To that end, Darcy went to see Bingley the day after he arrived in London. Upon his arrival in Bingley's library, his host bounded forward, smiling, to clasp Darcy's hand. For a moment, Darcy was relieved. Bingley appeared to be in his usual spirits. Perchance he had gotten over Miss Bennet after all. After some initial small talk, however, Darcy knew better. Bingley appeared listless, and as they continued to talk, Darcy noticed his inattentiveness and his underlying somber air. Bingley attempted to appear happy and engaged, but his posture showed he was actually patiently waiting for the visit to be done so he could retreat to his own thoughts once more. Given Darcy's new familiarity with heartache, he immediately understood Bingley's frame of mind. It was clear that Bingley was still in love with Miss Bennet and had most likely been suffering from his loss since their departure from Hertfordshire. After a lengthy pause in conversation, Darcy decided to address the question of Miss Bennet in a roundabout manner. Changing the subject more abruptly than he had hoped, he asked, "Bingley, last fall when we were in Hertfordshire, do you remember meeting a land agent by the name of Mr. Briggs?"

Bingley, who started at the mention of Hertfordshire, regained his composure and feebly replied, "Yes, I think I recall him."

"Well," continued Darcy, "he had some very interesting

ideas on crop rotation. Do you remember, we talked to him about it at some length?"

"I suppose I do recall it, but not much of the particulars."

"Well," began Darcy cautiously, "I thought I might call on him. I have been thinking about some of his ideas for Pemberley. Have you given any thought to returning to Hertfordshire at any time in the near future? I could accompany you, and while we were there, I could speak with Briggs. It would give you an opportunity to check on Netherfield and see how the planting is going. Or, if you like, we could look in on some of your acquaintances."

Bingley was silent for a long time. Darcy hoped he would take the bait.

Looking grave, Bingley replied in a measured tone, "Of late I have been giving the subject of Netherfield much thought, and I believe I was mistaken in taking the place. I acted too impulsively. I will not be renewing the lease, and as such, I see no reason to return. I did enjoy having it for a while, but I would prefer to just let it go. The sooner I cut the ties, the better. Darcy, maybe if you are truly intent on going there, you could do me a favor. I could make the place available to you so that you could conduct your business, and while you are there, you could see if there are any eligible purchase offers to be had."

Darcy noted the change in Bingley's demeanor. His cheerful mask was gone and the pain that the mention of Netherfield—and, by implication, Miss Bennet—caused was evident. In an attempt to get his friend to reconsider, Darcy tentatively replied, "Well, of course, Bingley, I would be more than happy to help you, but do you not think that perhaps you have been too hasty in rejecting the place out of hand? When you were there in the fall, you seemed take pleasure in it."

"Yes," responded Bingley in a decisive tone that was unusual for him, "I am quite sure I do not want to return. It has taken me a great deal of time to come to the conclusion that I am better off without the place. If I returned there, it would only reopen the debate, and I would rather not go over that territory again."

Darcy sat dumbfounded. The depth of Bingley's resistance startled him. The self-doubt that Darcy had experienced over his recent mistakes overwhelmed him, and he felt he could not trust his own judgment. He knew that he had reached a crossroad and that he had to make a decision, but he had been wrong so often lately that he no longer had any faith in his ability to choose correctly. In the end, he decided the most prudent course would be best.

After a pause, Darcy finally responded, "Certainly, Bingley. I understand. I will go there on my own then. I can handle any decisions regarding Netherfield. I will visit just long enough to see Mr. Briggs and to inquire after any purchasers. But, Bingley, do give me leave to put off the sale of the property if I believe it is in your best interest. Sometimes, in such a delicate matter as the sale of an estate, timing is everything."

"Darcy, you know I will always defer to your judgment in such matters."

Darcy replied in a resolute voice, "Yes, Bingley, I do."

The rest of the afternoon was spent on much more mundane matters. Bingley agreed to send an express to Netherfield to prepare for Darcy's arrival at the end of the week. He, in turn, promised Bingley that he would see him directly upon his return. Darcy then took his leave upon learning that Bingley's sisters were expected for dinner.

During the carriage ride back to his townhouse, Darcy

reflected on the events of the day. His decision to return to Netherfield seemed impetuous, but all that was left for him to do was determine if Miss Bennet's feelings for Bingley had remained unchanged. Surely, the opportunity to do so would somehow arise. Once it did, he would confess all to Bingley and force his return.

The idea of returning to Hertfordshire, where he would certainly encounter Elizabeth, filled him with dread, embarrassment, and a level of nervousness he had not thought possible. He knew how it would look, as if he were begging for her to reconsider. But it could not be helped. He would have to be careful to make it clear to her that he was not attempting to importune her any further. Hopefully their interaction could be kept to a minimum.

At the same time, he wanted to act in a manner that would make her realize she had been wrong about him. Not to win her back, but perhaps just to make her rethink her harshest judgments. If he was honest, on some level he wanted her to feel regret. Whether or not he could accept all of her criticism, he did regret his treatment of her in so many ways. It would be a small but important victory if she could at least repent some of her behavior. He therefore prepared for his trip to Hertfordshire with two avowed goals. He would attempt to repair the damage he had caused Bingley, and he would use every civility in his power to improve his reputation in the neighborhood so that Elizabeth might view him in a different light.

BACK TO HERTFORDSHIRE

ELIZABETH RETURNED TO HERTFORDSHIRE via London, happy to be leaving behind all that had occurred in Kent. She was only truly comforted, however, when she and Jane were reunited at Longbourn. Elizabeth had longed to tell Jane of what had transpired between herself and Mr. Darcy in Kent. Her eagerness to share all with Jane, however, was tempered by her fear that once she entered the subject, she might repeat something of Bingley that would grieve her sister unnecessarily.

The ladies of Longbourn were assembled in the front parlor when they heard a rider approach. Kitty looked out the window to discover who it was.

"La!" exclaimed Kitty. "It looks just like that man that used to be with Mr. Bingley before. Mr. What's-his-name. That tall, proud man."

"Good gracious! Mr. Darcy!—and so it does, I vow. Well, any friend of Mr. Bingley's will always be welcome here, to be sure, but else I must say that I hate the very sight of him."

Jane looked at Elizabeth with surprise and concern. She

knew the awkwardness which must attend her sister, in seeing him for the first time after receiving his explanatory letter. She also felt a bitter stab of disappointment as she realized that he had arrived without his friend. Jane's disappointment soon turned to nervousness as she apprehended that Mr. Darcy would certainly have news of Mr. Bingley, and it would probably include some intelligence as to the state of his regard for Miss Darcy. Both sisters were uncomfortable enough. Each felt for the other, and of course for themselves, and their mother talked on, of her dislike of Mr. Darcy and her resolution to be civil to him only as Mr. Bingley's friend, without being heard by either of them.

But Elizabeth had sources of uneasiness which could not be suspected by Jane, to whom she had never yet had courage to show Mr. Darcy's letter or to relate the circumstances surrounding Mr. Bingley's departure from Hertfordshire. Elizabeth sat intently at work, striving to be composed, and without daring to lift up her eyes, till anxious curiosity carried them to the face of her sister as the servant was approaching the door. Jane looked a little paler than usual, but more sedate than Elizabeth had expected.

Mr. Darcy was announced. He was so nervous, he felt almost dizzy. He had spent the ride from Netherfield debating whether he would be able to actually carry through his vow to enter Longbourn. He had arrived in Hertfordshire the previous morning but soon realized that while he had every intention of learning Miss Bennet's state of regard for Bingley, he had no plan to accomplish the task. He once again regretted his prior reserved behavior in the neighborhood. Because he had never considered the people of the area worth knowing, he had made no acquaintances upon whom he could call to gather information about Miss Bennet. Consequently, he soon came to the realization that his only option was to go to Longbourn and see for himself. He knew how it would look to Elizabeth, but he felt he had no choice. He pledged that he would show her no more attention than anyone else, so that she would understand that he was not attempting to force himself upon her. When he saw her, he wondered whether he could muster the resolve.

Upon his entrance, Elizabeth said as little as civility would allow, and sat down again to her work with an eagerness which it did not often command. She had ventured only one glance at Darcy. He returned her look, unsure of what to say, acknowledging her with a simple bow. He soon realized that while he was contemplating Elizabeth's reaction, Mrs. Bennet had been speaking to him, expressing her surprise at his appearance in Hertfordshire. He willed himself to tear his eyes from Elizabeth so that he could offer her mother a proper response.

"I have some business in the area and wanted to pay my respects for your previous civility."

Without even attempting to make her comment believable, Mrs. Bennet told Darcy in a forced manner that he was always welcome at Longbourn, adding, "Is Mr. Bingley with you? He is quite in my debt for a dinner, and we were all surprised when he left so abruptly in the fall."

"No, I am traveling alone, although Mr. Bingley was gracious enough to give me the use of Netherfield while in the neighborhood." As Darcy was speaking, he looked at Miss Bennet to see how she reacted to his words. He thought he detected some discomfiture on her part but could not determine its cause.

Not wanting to let the opportunity go by, Mrs. Bennet ventured further, "And how is Mr. Bingley?"

"He is quite well, madam. Thank you."

"Is he still in London? Does he intend to return here for the summer?"

Darcy realized he had to tread carefully so that neither Miss Bennet nor Elizabeth misconstrued his answer. He did not want to make a promise regarding Bingley that he could not keep, so he resolved to tell the truth—as much as possible. "Yes, he is in London, but he has not indicated to me that he intends to return to Hertfordshire."

Mrs. Bennet could not hide her disappointment. "Well, I would have thought he would return. He seemed so inclined to stay. I cannot imagine why he changed his mind." Darcy instinctively looked to Elizabeth, who returned his gaze with an icy, defiant stare.

Darcy cringed and swallowed hard. He wanted to explain the reason for his return to her but knew it was hopeless. He would have to plow forward and hope for the best. Darcy turned his attention to Mrs. Bennet, who, oblivious to the pain she was causing her eldest daughter, peevishly continued, "Perhaps he finds the charms of London more pleasant. I am sure there are many entertainments there to keep him occupied."

Darcy saw Miss Bennet's back stiffen at her mother's comments. He could not determine if her reaction was from pure embarrassment at her mother's lack of tact or if it was in reaction to the implication that Bingley had abandoned her for another. Darcy realized he was losing control of the situation. If Miss Bennet still had feelings for Bingley, this was surely torture. He needed to learn the state of Miss Bennet's regard, but attempting to do so in such a public manner was neither desirable nor productive. Consequently, he desperately tried to think of something to say to change the subject. Once again, he regretted his taciturn nature and his lack of social skills.

To his relief, Elizabeth, who also wanted to change the subject for Jane's sake, entered into the conversation as her mother paused for breath. "Mr. Darcy, are Mr. Bingley's sisters well?"

Startled, but grateful, Darcy replied, "Yes, Miss Bennet, thank you. I did not have the opportunity to see them during my recent visit to London, but I am assured they are well."

Seeing that her mother would quickly turn any inquiry regarding Bingley's sisters into an invitation to return to the topic of their brother, Elizabeth attempted another subject, one she thought might convey some of her regret over her misjudgment of Wickham's character and, if she was lucky, indirectly give Jane some comfort. "Is your own sister with them? I have not had the pleasure of meeting Miss Darcy, but you have spoken of her with such high regard and affection that I am sure she is quite lovely. I hope you did not have to leave her all alone while you are attending to your business."

Feeling some of the implication of Elizabeth's words, Darcy held her eyes and smiled gratefully. "She is quite well, thank you. She is currently at study in London with her companion. She has not had the opportunity of seeing any of the Bingley family yet this year, but I hope that I will be reunited with her at Pemberley early this summer. Whenever we are apart I miss her a great deal."

An awkward silence ensued. Darcy was taken aback by Elizabeth's mention of his sister, as it seemed implicitly to acknowledge his letter. Did this mean she believed him about

Wickham? From Elizabeth's cold reception of him, it seemed clear she wanted nothing more to do with him. Maybe, though, she had accepted his information about Wickham's past dealings. He had to admit he was relieved. Mixed with his regret over her rejection was the lurking fear that she held Wickham in a special regard. Even if he could never have her, Darcy took some solace in the fact that she would never be one of Wickham's victims.

Elizabeth, in turn, was completely baffled. She could not comprehend what he was doing in Hertfordshire. Since he had not brought Bingley with him and had made it clear that Bingley had no immediate plans to return to the neighborhood, she could not believe that Darcy's return was prompted by any regret over his actions toward her sister. It seemed impossible that Darcy had come to continue their acquaintance after all that had transpired in Kent, but there seemed to be no other explanation. Luckily for them, Mrs. Bennet abhorred silence and jumped into the void. "Mr. Darcy, I did not know you had a sister. How old is she?"

Relieved to talk about a subject he felt comfortable with, Darcy explained the situation of Georgiana's guardianship and continued on to tell them of her interest in music.

Mr. Darcy had only spoken seven or eight sentences together, but it was the longest any member of the Bennet household, save Elizabeth, had heard him speak. Witnessing such apparent warmth for his sister, even Mrs. Bennet's studious dislike of him had to waver a bit. In a fit of weakness, she offered him tea and continued the discourse. "Being alone in London at such a young age must be trying for Miss Darcy. Has she much opportunity to socialize?"

"Not many opportunities, no. She is only sixteen and is not yet out."

Exasperated by such a silly notion, Mrs. Bennet exclaimed harshly, "Sixteen is not too early to be out. My youngest, Lydia, is out, and she has received much attention."

Seeing that a tactful respond was required, Mr. Darcy said, "I think in Georgiana's case, I would prefer for her to wait. Without a mother to guide her, she has lived a rather sheltered life."

Basking in the oblique compliment, Mrs. Bennet replied, "Yes, I can well imagine. In any regard, Mr. Darcy, the next time you visit, you should bring her. I am sure we would all love to meet her."

Incredulous, Elizabeth looked at her mother in disbelief. The idea of Darcy visiting again was beyond her, since she could not believe he had come in the first place. She began to feel a growing dread as she realized that she must be the reason for Darcy's visit. Worse yet, she began to worry he might do something to make his interest in her publicly known. The idea that her mother might comprehend Darcy's intentions was more than she cared to imagine.

In the meantime, Darcy thanked Mrs. Bennet for her gracious invitation. He was amazed to find himself in a situation where he appreciated Mrs. Bennet's ability to engage in meaningless small talk. The awkwardness of this visit was agony on so many levels, but he knew he could not leave without first having found some sort of opening to accomplish his avowed mission. He needed more time, and she was providing the opportunity.

Mrs. Bennet, who enjoyed both the sound of her own voice and giving advice, added, "To make amends to your sister for leaving her behind, you should be sure to bring her something from Hertfordshire as a token. Women do love such thoughtfulness."

"Actually, I try to do just that on all of my travels."

"Well, sir, I think you will find that the many fine shops in Meryton will be more than sufficient for your purposes." Unable to resist the temptation, she added, "Some people think the finer things in life can only be obtained in the city. I assure you, they are grievously mistaken."

"Yes, madam, I am sure you are correct. I typically buy my sister sheet music. Perhaps you could recommend a local establishment to me."

Elizabeth sat in amazement. Mr. Darcy had twice now answered her mother's provocation with civility. His courtesy toward her mother demonstrated a great improvement in his manners, but his visit, in itself, showed a presumption that confirmed his arrogant nature and his disregard for her feelings. Was he attempting to force her into an alliance by involving her mother, who he well knew would forward the match on mercenary grounds? Surely, only mortification could come of this. Watching him closely, she now suspected that he was simply prolonging the visit in the hopes of gaining an opportunity to speak with her privately. She took comfort in the fact that she would resist such an attempt at all costs.

"Mr. Darcy," her mother continued, "you do not always buy her music, do you?"

Finding her question inane but grateful for the diversion, Darcy replied, "No, I sometimes buy her books."

Exasperated by Mr. Darcy's lack of understanding, Mrs. Bennet decided a little motherly advice was required. "Sir, while I am sure your generosity is appreciated, there are many other things a girl of sixteen would enjoy. I speak with some authority on the subject, given that I have seen five daughters through that age."

"You may be right, but Georgiana seems to take pleasure in such things, and I could not imagine what else she would require."

"Oh, there are many things! I am sure your sister wants for nothing given your fortune, but a girl of her age would love to receive a new bonnet or a reticule, or you could even purchase for her some fabric or lace for a new dress. I am sure she has the finest dressmakers at her disposal, but a unique fabric for a new gown is always welcome. Given that money is no object for you, the possibilities are endless."

Embarrassed by Mrs. Bennet's excited mention of his fortune, Darcy attempted to drop the subject. "Yes, but Georgiana typically selects her own wardrobe."

"Well, of course, but you should not underestimate the value a little direction in that regard would produce. A girl at her age is impressionable. And with no mother to help her choose from the many styles and designs, it might be difficult for her to know what best suits her. Until you have a wife to help guide her, you should take care in this regard." Darcy colored at the mention of his future wife and could not resist a quick glance at Elizabeth to gauge her reaction to her mother's musings. Elizabeth, however, kept her gaze steadily on the floor.

Undaunted, Mrs. Bennet continued on in an authoritative tone, "Mr. Darcy, every girl needs to develop her own unique style to attract the proper attention. As you see, each of my own daughters wears a fashion that suits her. Each is a little different. A mother's hand in this regard is quite important."

Darcy hardly knew how to reply, but stammered, "Well,

madam, no one who has seen you or any of your daughters could doubt your success."

"You are too kind, sir," exclaimed Mrs. Bennet in a flirtatious manner while Elizabeth's emotions swayed from astonishment to humiliation.

Darcy sat in amazement at the turn of the conversation and Mrs. Bennet's audacity in lecturing him about how to raise Georgiana. He began to wonder how he would ever endure the remainder of the visit without proving Elizabeth's reproof regarding his ungentlemanly conduct true. On the other hand, he had to admit that while Mrs. Bennet's manner was often harsh, she and her daughters always dressed impeccably given their financial constraints. He wondered if Georgiana did, in fact, find it difficult not having a close female relative to rely upon. Given her general timidity, it was probably natural that she was somewhat unsure of herself in this regard. And while he had never thought about it before, having the funds available to buy the latest fashions was clearly not all that was required; Caroline Bingley and his aunt were prime examples of expense taking precedence over good taste. He shuddered when he thought of how many times Miss Bingley had offered to take Georgiana shopping. As he contemplated such an excursion, an idea suddenly struck him. He offered in reply, "Well, Mrs. Bennet, what would you suggest?"

"If you have previously admired your sister in a particular gown or color, buy her something to go with it. Your notice will encourage her in that direction."

"Thank you, Mrs. Bennet, that seems a wise course of action. I think I will walk into Meryton directly. But, given my inexperience in this area, I am still unsure what I should actually purchase. I think I need another perspective. Perhaps some of your daughters would be willing to help me?"

It was not under many minutes that Mrs. Bennet could comprehend what she had heard; though not in general backward to credit what was for the advantage of her family, she understood that a man of superior connections and a fortune of ten thousand pounds a year was seeking the company of one of her daughters. Mrs. Bennet smiled broadly and purred, "Of course, Mr. Darcy."

Elizabeth sat in dread. So, this was what he was after. Her anger rose as she anticipated being asked to join him. She tried quickly to think of a response. She vowed that, if necessary, she would refuse him outright. Screwing up her courage, Elizabeth waited in defiance for Darcy to request her company. To her astonishment, she heard Mr. Darcy reply, "If Miss Bennet is not otherwise engaged, perhaps she and her sisters could accompany me."

With a gleam in her eye, Mrs. Bennet answered in the affirmative for Jane, who had looked up at the unexpected mention of her name. Mrs. Bennet then added, "I am sure Kitty can also accompany you, but I am afraid my other daughters are needed at home. Kitty, did you not say you wanted to visit with Miss Lucas today? You can stop on the way."

Kitty began to say that she had not said any such thing, but was hushed by her mother into silence and directed with Jane to immediately fetch their bonnets. Mr. Darcy rose to take his leave, proposing to meet the ladies in the garden after he had seen that his horse was taken care of. As he rose, he caught Elizabeth's eye. She looked at him in astonishment. Unable to think of any other response, Darcy gave her a curt bow filled with contrition. He hoped that she understood his motivation, knowing that she most likely did not.

Elizabeth stared in disbelief, her head reeling. She was filled with determination to get to the bottom of what was happening and told her mother privately that she was going to Meryton too. Her mother exclaimed sharply that she would do no such thing. "It is clear that Mr. Darcy prefers the company of your sister Jane. They do not need any further chaperone than Kitty. The fewer people the better. Oh, Lizzy, I do not know why I did not see it before. Mr. Darcy must always have favored Jane's company. That is why he was always so sullen whenever we saw him. He resented Mr. Bingley's interference, and he must be the reason that Mr. Bingley abruptly withdrew his attentions toward her. Now that Bingley is out of the way, Mr. Darcy has returned for Jane. Oh, it all makes sense now. I was sure Jane could not be so beautiful for nothing! Oh my, think how rich and how great Jane will be! What pin-money, what jewels, what carriages. I am so pleased—so happy. Such a charming man!—so handsome! so tall!—Oh, my dear Lizzy! I must make it up to him for my having disliked him so much before."

"Mama," pleaded Elizabeth. "I think you must be misunderstanding the situation. Please, do not get carried away before you know all the facts. I will go with them to see what his intentions are."

"Oh, Lizzy, absolutely not! There is no point to it. We already know he does not find you pleasing. He has said as much. You will only be in the way. No, Jane will do fine on her own. I will hear no more on the subject."

Elizabeth was forced to watch them go. She took refuge in her room, unable to bear her mother's raptures any longer. In private reflection, she tried to sort out the tumult of emotions she was feeling. Little by little, she realized they included anger, frustration, scorn, bewilderment, embarrassment, curiosity, and, if she was honest, a touch of jealousy.

SIMILAR NATURES

AFTER ASSEMBLING IN THE garden, the three companions began their journey to Meryton. Kitty soon lagged behind, being both uncomfortable around the stern Mr. Darcy and intent on acceding to her mother's suggestion that she visit Maria Lucas. After walking for some time in silence, Darcy cleared his throat and finally addressed Jane. "Miss Bennet, I hope that I have not put you in an awkward position by requesting that you accompany me to Meryton?"

Unsure how to respond, Jane replied in her most genteel fashion that she was sure she would greatly enjoy Mr. Darcy's company and that she was more than pleased to assist him with his sister.

"My sister?" Darcy absentmindedly inquired. "Oh yes, we are to shop for her." After a pause, Darcy added, "Miss Bennet, I must be honest and tell you that I did not ask you here to talk about my sister's wardrobe. I fear that my real reason will undoubtedly give you offense, as I need to speak to you about a most personal matter. I know that decorum requires that I not assume such familiarity, but I must beg your pardon and seek leave to do exactly that. If I thought there was any other way, I assure you I would not burden you in this fashion."

With a genuine smile that put Darcy slightly more at ease, Jane replied, "Mr. Darcy, I must admit I suspected that there might be an ulterior motive for your request. But, sir, do not be uncomfortable. Please feel free to speak to me as you would to any other good friend, as that is what I hope we will soon become."

Darcy replied sincerely, "Madam, you are far too kind. Nonetheless, I will accept your invitation and, with your permission, speak frankly. I want you to know, however, that I truly appreciate your generosity of spirit. I can imagine how much it must cost you. I had feared that you would refuse to speak to me altogether."

"Sir, I would never even consider doing such a thing."

"Well, I am relieved to hear it. But, Miss Bennet, let me apologize nonetheless for asking for your company in a manner that made it very difficult for you to object. It was selfish of me, and I am afraid that in the process I may have given your mother the wrong impression."

Jane replied, "Sir, if you are to speak frankly, then so will I. You may be right that my mother misunderstood your intentions, but do not concern yourself. It will not be the first time nor, I fear, the last."

Surprised by Jane's candor, Darcy had to return her smile. He then grew quiet as he searched for the strength to broach a subject he dreaded. Jane for her part was inclined to let Mr. Darcy take his time. Suspecting that he wished to speak to her about Lizzy and understanding that it would be a painful subject for him, she wanted to let him gather his thoughts before he spoke. She had to admit this was a side of Mr. Darcy she had not expected. He now seemed so unsure of himself and at great pains to be as civil as possible. While she had never held Lizzy's poor opinion of him, she was surprised to see how amiable he could be and suspected that much of his restrained manner stemmed from shyness.

After a lengthy pause Darcy asked, "Miss Bennet, I assume Miss Elizabeth told you of the events that transpired in Kent?"

"Yes, Mr. Darcy, she did confide in me, but rest assured that I would never speak of it to anyone else."

Feeling all the embarrassment incumbent in having his rejection at Hunsford finally out in the open, Darcy was unable to meet Jane's gaze until he realized that she might think his question a rebuke. Looking at her with a self-conscious smile, he replied, "No, no, of course not, and I did not mean to imply that that was my concern."

"Thank you, sir, for trusting me, but I must tell you that if you want me to speak to Lizzy on your behalf, I am not sure that it is the wisest course of action."

"No. Miss Bennet, I think we both know that there is no point in that."

"Mr. Darcy, I did not mean to imply that I would not try on your behalf, if that is what you wish. I just thought that it might be better for you to speak to her directly given your previous misunderstandings."

Unsure of how to continue, Darcy stammered, "No, Miss Bennet, you misunderstand me. I truly understand that my... relationship with Elizabeth—Miss Elizabeth—is beyond repair, and I have come to accept that. More importantly, I would not want her to think that I came here to force my suit upon her. I think I have imposed upon her enough."

Jane felt for his obvious pain but did not know what she could say to help. She knew that he must be embarrassed, and sensed that if she tried to discuss the matter further, it would only make him more uncomfortable. The issue was decided for her when Darcy stated, "Miss Bennet, did your sister tell you about the letter that I wrote her?"

"Yes, sir, I am afraid she did, but I hope you will not hold it against her. I think she needed to talk to someone about its contents."

With a tinge of irony, Darcy replied, "Yes, Miss Bennet, I am sure she did." After a pause, he added in a more serious tone, "Knowing how close you two are and that some of the information in it concerned you, I had assumed that she would discuss it with you. I would never blame her for doing so, as I now realize you had a right to know its contents all along. That is why I have come to speak to you."

"Sir, I assume you are referring to Mr. Wickham. Rest assured that my sister and I both now comprehend the nature of his character and regret that he has been allowed to cast aspersions on your own. I believe my sister would want me to offer you an apology on her behalf as well."

"Miss Bennet, thank you. But no apology is required. While I am exceedingly grateful that you both believe me about Mr. Wickham's misdeeds and will be able to guard against any of his further contrivances, I must confess that I was not referring to him. I was hoping we could talk about the matter in the letter that concerned you directly."

Coloring slightly, Jane answered, "Sir, I am not sure what is to be said on that topic. I know that you expressed some... concerns... about some of the members of my family... but truly I have taken no offense, and you certainly do not owe me an explanation…"

"Miss Bennet," Darcy interrupted, "what did your sister tell you I wrote in my letter?"

Feeling all the more awkward, Jane replied, "She told me that you wanted to clear your name against the charges Mr. Wickham had leveled against you and that you had explained why you had reservations about proposing."

Darcy bowed his head and temporarily closed his eyes, realizing that he had once again misjudged the situation. Suddenly, his plan for coming to Hertfordshire no longer made sense. Jane knew no more than Bingley did. He was reminded once again why he abhorred deception. The complications involved were never worth the temporary gain, and pain always resulted. He resolved from now on to tell the truth whenever possible.

If the realization of his misjudgment were not bad enough, Miss Bennet had also reminded him of his poorly worded proposal and Elizabeth's reaction. After a pause, he stated, "Miss Bennet, as to your family, I want to take this opportunity to apologize for anything I may have said that gave offense. While it might be hard to believe, it was not meant to injure. Nonetheless, it was rude of me, and I heartily regret it." Pausing to collect himself, Darcy then stated, "Be that as it may, I need to speak to you about another matter entirely. I had thought that your sister would have spoken to you about it already. It now appears she did not. This will undoubtedly make my task harder, but no less necessary. I actually want to talk to you about Mr. Bingley."

Jane started at the mention of his name. While he was never far from her thoughts, especially since the arrival of his friend, she had completely turned her attention to what she thought was Mr. Darcy's attempt to broach a reconciliation with Lizzy. Trying to regain her composure, Jane replied in a shaky voice, "Mr. Darcy, I do not know what you could mean."

At that moment, Kitty called to them to let Jane know that she intended to go up the lane to see if Maria Lucas would come to Meryton. Jane gave Kitty a brave smile and told her they would wait for her in the lane. Darcy could see that Jane was struggling to regain her self-control and suggested that they wait on a bench at the edge of the Lucas property.

After Jane was comfortably seated and more composed, Darcy said, "Madam, I am afraid I must confess an offense that I have committed against you. I know that my story will give you nothing but pain, but I believe there is a purpose to be served. Please forgive me for this further transgression." After Jane nodded for him to continue, Darcy asked, "Miss Bennet, I am sure that you must have wondered about Mr. Bingley's hasty departure from Hertfordshire last fall."

"Sir, really there is no need. Mr. Bingley is free to travel whenever and wherever he chooses. He does not need to explain his reasons for leaving to me."

"Miss Bennet, I did not mean to imply anything by my statement. If you will allow me, I need to tell you what happened. It is of some importance to me, and I believe you should know the details. Will you listen?"

"All right, sir, if you think it best."

"Last fall, it quickly became apparent to me that Mr. Bingley greatly favored your company. I soon also realized that many in the neighborhood had expectations about your future together." At this Jane colored and looked at her hands. "Knowing Bingley as I do, I knew that he had given his heart freely, without thought to more material considerations. I am not offering it as an excuse, but experience has made me a little more jaded. Consequently, I began to wonder at the level of regard you held for him."

At this Jane raised her head to look at Darcy. Her wounded gaze was more eloquent than any denial. Ashamed, he instinctively looked away. He then forced himself to look back, resigned to see his task to its end. "I began to study you, to see if I could discern any affection on your part, and while your countenance was always cheerful and pleasing, I could not detect any special regard for my friend."

On the brink of tears, Jane exclaimed, "But why else would I favor his company unless I held him in high esteem?" Before he answered, Jane suddenly understood and quietly added, "Oh, I see."

"I am sorry, Miss Bennet. You must understand that Bingley has a very trusting nature, and I have watched women with mercenary motives hurt him before. I did not want that to happen again. I honestly did not see any evidence that you returned his regard, and… I was concerned that you had other influences encouraging you to accept his attentions." Understanding the reference to her mother, Jane looked away as she fought back a tear.

Seeing her distress, Darcy added, "I know now that I was wrong. But at the time, I sincerely believed it was in Bingley's interest to give him my opinion." Having regained her composure, Jane nodded for him to continue.

"While he was in London, I did exactly that, and given his great natural modesty, he easily believed me. Thinking that you did not return his regard, he decided to stay in London."

Jane impulsively asked, "But Miss Bingley told me in her letter that Mr. Bingley wanted to stay in town because he enjoyed the company of your own sister."

With a frown, Darcy said, "I did not realize Miss Bingley had written to you." Both remained silent, while he considered his options. He then continued in a resolute tone, "Miss Bennet, I came to Hertfordshire to confess my guilt only, but I now see that I must tell you a few more particulars. Before I left for London to speak to Bingley, his sisters expressed their concerns to me about the possibility of a match between you. In London, the three of us spoke to Bingley together. His sisters encouraged him to stay in town, and I told him my suspicions about your affections. I believe that Miss Bingley wrote to you to discourage any attachment you may have had for her brother. My sister was just a convenient excuse. As I recently mentioned, she is only sixteen years old and has always thought of Bingley as a brother, nothing more. Bingley, in turn, has always treated her as a sister."

"Mr. Darcy, thank you for telling me this. It has certainly enlightened me as to a great many things."

"Unfortunately, Madam, there is more, and I am afraid my conduct in this unfortunate tale becomes even more reprehensible. I knew that you called on Miss Bingley last winter in London and that she returned the visit. I also know that no one, including myself, informed Bingley of your presence. I think if he had known that you had come, he would have sought you out."

At this, Jane paled and said, "This is all too much. I do not know what to think."

"Miss Bennet, I am so sorry for having misunderstood your motives and for having deceived Bingley about your presence in

London. I have no excuse and expect no sympathy. But I did not come here just to burden you with my confession. While I was in Kent, your sister told me about the real regard you held for Bingley. It made me understand that I had committed a grave injustice against you both. I would like to try to make amends."

Before Jane could respond, Maria and Kitty joined them. After Darcy inquired after Maria's health, the party of four took their leave. Darcy and Jane waited until Kitty and Maria outstripped them. Darcy then said, "Miss Bennet, are you all right?"

"Sir, I fear this is too much to comprehend. I can barely credit what you have told me. I do not doubt all that you have said, but I cannot understand… how it came to pass."

"I cannot speak for the others, but for my part, I know I acted out of selfishness and arrogance. My selfishness is obvious, and I have recently come to learn that my judgment is far less accurate than I would like to believe. I now understand that your reserved nature made it difficult for an outsider such as myself to ascertain your true feelings. Given that our natures are very similar in that regard, my mistake is all the more unforgivable."

Seeing that Jane was deep in thought, Darcy waited until she looked up at him. "Miss Bennet, I know that I have overstepped the bounds of propriety with you throughout our discussion, but I need to ask you one more question. Do you still hold Bingley in special regard?"

"Mr. Darcy, I barely know how to respond; even if I did, what would be the point?"

"If you would consent to it, I want to tell Bingley what I have told you. I came to you first because I thought you already knew all that had happened from your sister. I wanted to discern if there was any hope for the two of you before I spoke to him."

Jane was again lost in her thoughts. Turning her attention to Darcy, she asked, "I take it that while you were in Kent, you and Lizzy discussed what you have just told me. And that you thereafter mentioned some of it in your letter?"

"Yes. Unbeknownst to me, your sister had guessed my role in the affair before I… proposed. She then led me to understand how wrong I had been. I tried to explain in my letter why I interfered in your affairs, but afterward I realized that an explanation to your sister was not enough. I came here hoping to undo the harm I have caused."

After a thoughtful pause, Jane gave Darcy a compassionate smile and stated, "It must have been very hard for you to come. I thank you for the effort. I know it cannot be easy to see Lizzy again."

Darcy colored and Jane recognized the pain in his eyes. "Miss Bennet, Mr. Bingley once told me that you were an angel. At the time, I believed it was simply the hyperbole of a man in love. I now see that he was right. That you are concerned about my feelings after the harm I have done you is more than anyone could expect."

Jane colored with embarrassment at Darcy's praise and the reference to Bingley's affections. She then replied, "Mr. Darcy, I simply believe what you have told me, as would anyone. I understand that you made an honest mistake about my regard, and I cannot fault you for attempting to protect your friend. You may have been too hasty in forming an opinion of me, but I can forgive that mistake, given that you have come all this way to correct the error, at no small cost to yourself."

"I sincerely thank you. I hope I can be worthy of your generosity. I would like to start by returning to London to speak to Bingley. May I tell him that if he were to call upon you, you would accept his visit?"

Darcy waited for Jane's response, while a contrariety of emotions crossed her face. After a pause, she said, "Mr. Darcy, I am not sure what to say. The one thing I have learned from this conversation is that things are not always what they appear. I need to think about all you have told me."

"Please, Miss Bennet, let me tell Bingley what happened and that you will consent to see him. He is innocent in this. The fault is mine alone. Please blame me."

"Sir, I have already told you that I do not blame you for what happened, and I do not intend to start. I similarly do not hold Mr. Bingley at fault. But I am not sure it would be in anyone's interest to meddle in what now seems to be the work of fate."

"But it was not fate. I wrongly interfered, and the misguided actions of others should not be rewarded."

"Yes, you are right that it was the work of humans, but that is what troubles me. I cannot discount so easily the objections of Mr. Bingley's sisters."

"But if you still care for Bingley, it should not matter what his sisters attempted to do."

Jane replied with a patient but determined smile, "Sir, you stated earlier that we had similar natures, and I think that you are right. We both have a habit of hiding our feelings, and we have both suffered for it. Like you, I also cannot simply ignore the objections that will be raised against my entering into what some will call an imprudent match. Mr. Bingley's sisters obviously have strong objections against me, and I would not want to enter into an alliance with a gentleman that would cause his family pain and strife. I know that such considerations gave you pause; please allow me the same latitude."

Darcy was struck by Jane's words and did not know immediately how to reply. He then said, "Madam, I do understand your concerns. But if I may be so presumptuous, let me entreat you not to look at the gift of love by studying only its obstacles. I have found from experience that it does not turn out well. Apparently, a leap of faith is required."

"Sir, I will take your advice to heart, but I cannot decide so quickly."

"I certainly understand, and I did not mean to rush you. I will await your decision at your leisure." Looking up, he added, "I see that we are fast approaching the town. Do not feel obliged to entertain me. I would certainly understand if you would like to be alone. Shall I summon my carriage to return all of you to Longbourn?"

With a genuine smile, Jane replied, "Thank you, sir. But I think I will not be able to return home without reporting that I have been of some use in the pursuit of your sister's gift. Do you not intend to buy her something?"

"I do." Darcy returned her smile and offered her his arm. "By all means, lead the way. I am at your disposal."

Jane called to Kitty and Maria to let them know where they would be. Despite Kitty's protests, the party agreed to head back in a half hour's time. As they walked, Jane pointed out the sights of Meryton. Darcy, who had never paid attention to it on his prior visits, noticed how similar in essentials it was to a town near Pemberley. As they chatted amiably, Jane reminded Darcy that he had to buy something for his sister to satisfy her mother's anticipated queries. He asked her for suggestions.

"Well," Jane began, "I find that my mother is often right about what sort of gift to buy. She suggested that you should get her something in a style that you previously admired to help direct her toward that fashion. Ribbons for her hair would be the simplest and quickest. Have you any preferences?"

Frowning, Darcy replied that he had honestly never given it any thought before and really could not recall anything distinctive about his sister's hairstyle or anyone else's.

With a smile Jane encouraged him to think harder. Considering her words, he finally said, "I think I do vaguely recall that I once saw a very attractive style where contrasting ribbons were used. Does that sound correct?"

"Yes, I know exactly what you mean," exclaimed Jane. "Lizzy frequently wears her hair in that fashion, and it is quite flattering."

Realizing her mistake, Jane quickly looked at Darcy, who had colored with embarrassment. "Since I know what we want, it should only take a moment," she said with a reassuring smile. Relieved by her tact, Darcy agreed to the scheme. Not long after their return, Kitty and Maria joined them.

On the walk back to Longbourn, Darcy had hoped to speak privately with Jane again. He realized he had failed to arrange how Jane would eventually convey her answer to him once she had sufficient time to reflect. An opportunity for a discreet discussion, however, did not arise. The girls monopolized Jane, excitedly telling her about the acquaintances they had seen in town. Not long after that topic was exhausted, Maria screwed up her courage and asked Mr. Darcy about news from Rosings. His brief response led Maria to a long exaltation of Lady Catherine's generosity toward her during her visit to Kent.

As Darcy approached the house to escort the ladies home,

Mrs. Bennet invited him in. Behind her he could see Elizabeth. He impetuously attempted to catch her eye, but she kept her gaze on the carpet. Darcy interpreted this as a sign of her disapproval. She was, in fact, bracing for the mortification that her mother would surely inflict.

In reply to Mrs. Bennet's request, Darcy said, "Madam, thank you for your generous invitation, but I must be going."

"Oh, certainly, sir, I understand. Was Jane helpful with your shopping? She is a very clever girl in many ways."

"Yes, madam, she was very helpful."

"Well, Mr. Darcy, I am happy to hear it. I am sure she would be willing to assist you with your sister whenever you need. Just ask. But in the meantime, I hope we will see you again soon. You know you are always welcome—dinner or tea. It does not matter. Now that… things have worked out so well, do not be a stranger. As I said, you are welcome at any time."

With a strained smile and a curt nod, Darcy simply replied, "Yes, thank you."

Unwilling to let her prey escape so easily, Mrs. Bennet continued, "Oh, Mr. Darcy, I almost forgot. Have you heard that there is to be another assembly in Meryton in just two days' time? We would all be honored by your presence. I know Jane would particularly enjoy your company. Everyone will be there. You really should not miss it. You will come, won't you?"

"Madam, my plans are yet unfixed. I am not sure…"

Interrupting him, Jane turned to Darcy and decisively said, "Sir, I do hope you can attend. I would like to continue our discussion."

Elizabeth looked up in surprise at Jane's words. Mrs. Bennet beamed with pride. Darcy gave Jane a look filled with understanding and said, "In that case, Miss Bennet, I will be sure to attend." Elizabeth watched in disbelief.

SIMILAR DISPOSITIONS

ELIZABETH'S CURIOSITY ABOUT THE events of the day had to be delayed until she could talk to Jane alone in her room. The wait was interminable. Mrs. Bennet spent the entire dinner hour speculating as to Jane's future happiness with Mr. Darcy, and the houses and jewels she would have at her disposal. Jane protested profusely, stating as adamantly as a woman of her sweet disposition could that Mr. Darcy was simply being friendly and civil. Mrs. Bennet dismissed the premise out of hand. It was clear from the way Mr. Darcy acted that he was in love with Jane, and besides, Mr. Darcy did not have a civil bone in his body.

Elizabeth knew that Jane must have been telling the truth about Mr. Darcy's intentions. She always told the truth. Nonetheless, she could not help feel that maybe Jane was too naïve to properly understand his motives toward her, whatever they were. One thing was certain: Her mother had not imagined that he had singled Jane out. But what could he mean by it? Her mind kept going over the possibilities. Only two seemed likely.

Either he had come to Hertfordshire to press his suit again and he wanted Jane to help him, or he wanted to make her jealous by actually courting Jane.

Given his actions toward Bingley, both ideas seemed preposterous. Then again, the idea of him sipping tea in their front sitting room while making small talk with her mother was even more ridiculous, and that had actually occurred. Whichever way, the underlying problem was the same. He had not accepted her rejection of his proposal. From his reaction at Hunsford, she could understand how that could come to pass. He had obviously never contemplated that anyone would reject his offer of marriage once he condescended to make it. It probably was not that he still wanted her; it was just that his intolerable pride could not allow the rebuff to stand. He wanted her to either reconsider or regret her decision. Either way, he would be sorely disappointed.

If he were trying to make her jealous, it would never work. You could not be jealous over someone you have no feelings for even if they sought comfort elsewhere. Besides, Jane would never seriously accept his intentions if she advised her against it. If anything, it was sad that he had failed to move on with his life. It was a pathetic ploy. If it were not so infuriating, she might have pitied him. But, then again, maybe Jane would accept his attentions. She had been so lonely since Mr. Bingley left, perhaps in her sadness she would latch onto Mr. Darcy as Charlotte had done with Mr. Collins. No, that was impossible. Besides, Mr. Darcy could not really want Jane; she had the same embarrassing family and lack of social connections that she did. Was he seeking to punish himself by limiting his selection of potential brides to the one family of which he could not approve? That was similarly impossible.

Since her return from Meryton, Jane had indicated several times that Mr. Darcy was not seeking her attentions. It must be true. If that was the case, then he must be trying to engage Jane as an ally. That endeavor would also prove fruitless. Jane might have agreed to speak to her on his behalf, but Elizabeth would never reconsider her refusal. The fact that he was trying to force himself on her was devastating evidence that he had not changed. To attempt a reconciliation in such a heavy-handed fashion showed that he was as self-centered as ever. It seemed like something Mr. Collins would do. Hopefully, like Mr. Collins, he would find someone else to occupy his time. It just could not be Jane.

She had to admit, though, that his continued attentions were flattering on some level. She could not imagine what she had done to inspire his continued interest, especially after the harsh words they had exchanged at Hunsford. Could he still be in love with her to such an extent? He had said that he ardently loved and admired her. But she thought him incapable of actually understanding those emotions. Elizabeth's patience was finally rewarded when she and Jane retired for bed. Unable to wait another moment, Elizabeth exclaimed, "What on earth did Mr. Darcy say to you, or did he request your company only to walk along in silence?"

"Actually, Lizzy, he talked quite a bit. I think you may have misjudged him. While I think that he has made some grave mistakes in the past, he is, in essentials, a very kind and honorable man."

"Jane, I feared that he would try to use you in this manner. You do not know him! He is neither kind nor honorable, and if he thinks he can use you to prevail on me to reconsider his offer, he is sadly mistaken."

"No, Elizabeth, he made it quite clear that he had not come to seek a reconciliation with you. He said he would not impose upon you in that fashion again. He came to speak to me. He wanted to talk to me about... Mr. Bingley."

Elizabeth sat in astonishment as Jane continued. "He has come to make amends, Lizzy. He wants to tell Mr. Bingley what happened, and he wants my permission to tell Mr. Bingley that I would see him if he returned to Hertfordshire."

Elizabeth could not be more amazed. "Jane, I am all astonishment. Did he actually say he would speak to Mr. Bingley?"

"Yes, he said he wants to return to London directly, to tell him everything. He is just waiting for my response."

Elizabeth grabbed her sister's hands in excitement and exclaimed, "Oh, Jane, this is too good to be true!" Seeing that Jane's response was somewhat restrained, Elizabeth added in a serious voice, "I hope you are not angry with me. I learned of Mr. Darcy's interference in Kent, but I did not want to tell you because I did not think anything could be done about it. I wanted to spare you any further pain."

With a generous smile, Jane replied, "Do not be concerned, Lizzy. I know that you have only the best of intentions." Overcome with love for her sister, Elizabeth gave Jane a warm hug.

Suddenly anxious, Elizabeth asked, "But, Jane, can we trust Mr. Darcy? Why did he not simply tell Mr. Bingley and bring him to Hertfordshire?"

"I am very confident of Mr. Darcy's intentions. He explained to me that he had assumed you would tell me about his letter, and because he thought I already knew what had happened, he wanted to speak to me before he approached Mr. Bingley."

"I suppose that his assumption was reasonable," Elizabeth reluctantly conceded.

"Lizzy, I think the entire affair was an honest mistake on Mr. Darcy's part. He was simply trying to protect his friend. I cannot fault him for that. Do not think ill of me for saying so, but I think our mother may have contributed to his misjudgment of my regard for Mr. Bingley."

With a wry smile Elizabeth said, "Well, I am sure that is more than possible. But, in any regard, I still cannot forgive him. I do not think you understand all that he has done."

"No, Lizzy, I do. He also told me that Caroline and Louisa never told Mr. Bingley that I called upon them in London and that he thereafter helped them conceal the fact. He truly regrets his behavior."

"And well he should," Elizabeth angrily exclaimed. "There is no excuse for his deception. It was the height of arrogance to presume that he knew what was best for his friend."

"But, Lizzy, once he realized his mistake, he attempted to correct it. Is that not worthy of our forgiveness?"

"Well, I suppose Mary could find a sermon to tell us it is, but I would still not be convinced."

"But, Lizzy, sometimes people do things that they would not normally do in order to protect the people they care about. When you returned from Kent, you did not tell me about your news of Mr. Bingley because you thought it would only bring me further pain. Mr. Darcy acted in a similar fashion because he still believed I did not have sincere affection for Mr. Bingley."

"But, Jane, I would have told you the moment I thought you needed to know."

"I know you would have, Lizzy. But that is exactly what Mr. Darcy did. As soon as you let him know that he was in the wrong, he came here to confess it to me, and he will tell Mr. Bingley as soon as I grant him leave."

Jane took Lizzy's hand in hers. She wanted to make sure Lizzy understood that her next comment was an explanation and not a rebuke. "Lizzy, if you both used a little deception in the past, it was because you both had a desire to protect someone you cared for. You both have very definite opinions, and that sometimes means you take matters into your own hands. If it is a failing, it is one I can surely overlook. Do you think you can find it in your own heart to do the same?"

"Jane, you are too good. I must confess I never considered it in that manner before. I think I am quite blind to my own shortcomings. Unfortunately, rather than making me feel more generous toward Mr. Darcy, it has made me more critical of myself. We both acted badly. I am so sorry I substituted my own judgment for yours. It was arrogant of me! Can you forgive me?"

"Lizzy, of course I can. I am not blaming you in the first place. I am just trying to make you understand why I have forgiven Mr. Darcy."

"Well, Jane, I will truly think about what you have said. But the important thing is that Mr. Bingley will soon know the truth, and I am sure that once he does, he will return on his fastest horse." Seeing Jane frown, Elizabeth entreated Jane to tell her what was bothering her.

"Lizzy, Mr. Darcy thinks… that there is still a chance… I mean, Mr. Darcy wants my permission for Mr. Bingley to further his acquaintance with me. He wants to be able to tell

Mr. Bingley as much when he sees him. I told Mr. Darcy I was not sure it was a good idea. I asked for time to think about it. At the end of our visit, I indicated I would decide by the Meryton Assembly. I am just not sure what to do."

"Jane, there is nothing to think about. Of course you will welcome his visit. I know that you still care for him. If Mr. Bingley's sisters and Mr. Darcy had not interfered, you would be well on your way to happiness. Nothing has changed in that regard."

"But, Lizzy, I cannot help but think that Mr. Bingley's regard for me could not have been as strong as I had hoped if he was so easily turned away. Perhaps it was for the best that it happened."

"Jane, he was lied to! You cannot judge his reaction by that. You have to give him an opportunity to prove himself. For once, I am in complete agreement with Mr. Darcy. You must let him speak to Mr. Bingley, and when he does, you should let him convey to Mr. Bingley that it is not too late."

"I don't know, Lizzy. Even if I thought that he still cared for me, I have other concerns. It is clear that his sisters object to the match. How can I come between Mr. Bingley and his family?"

"Jane, that is not your concern. As much as I know it pains you, you cannot please everyone. You will either disappoint Mr. Bingley or his sisters. You owe his sisters nothing. Do you really want to have Mr. Bingley hurt further by their actions? If he wants you, and you return his affections, that should be all that matters."

"Lizzy, I cannot help feeling that it would not bode well for an impending union to have one of the families involved object to the match. I think the strife would eventually damage Mr. Bingley's regard for me. I am not as independent as you, Lizzy. I am not sure I can overcome the resentment, and I do not want to disappoint Mr. Bingley in the long run."

Elizabeth gave her sister a warm hug and said, "Oh, Jane, you are so dear." Releasing her, Elizabeth added, "I wish I could make everything perfect for you because truly you deserve it. But, as it is not, I suppose we shall make do as best we can. You will have to decide, but I do not think you should throw away love simply because there are objections."

"That is exactly what Mr. Darcy said!"

Raising a skeptical eyebrow, Elizabeth asked in an incredulous tone, "Is it?"

"Oh, yes. He told me that a leap of faith was required and that I should not look at the gift of love by seeing only its obstacles… Lizzy, he said that he had learned from experience that if you do, it does not turn out well."

Jane waited for a response from Elizabeth but did not get one. After another pause, Jane said, "Lizzy, I think he truly regrets what happened between you."

Forcing a lighthearted manner, Elizabeth said, "Well, I am not so sure about that. After seeing our mother this afternoon, I am sure he is rejoicing in his near escape." Seeing Jane's frown, Elizabeth added in a serious tone, "Jane, while he may agree with me about you and Mr. Bingley, I am sure he will never recover from the injury I have inflicted to his pride. You yourself told me that he wanted to make it clear he had no further intentions toward me. I am sure laying eyes on me this afternoon was an odious task. Do remember that he still thinks very ill of our family. Hopefully, we will keep our interactions to a minimum. Maybe our mother will let me forego attendance at the assembly; that way I will spare him further discomfort."

"Lizzy, I do not think that is necessary."

"Perhaps not, but it might be in everyone's best interest. In any regard, I know for sure that Mother would never let you miss it. I am afraid she has the wrong idea about you and Mr. Darcy. She will be inconsolable if he leaves for London before he proposes to you."

"I know, Lizzy. What am I to do? I tried to tell her this evening that there is nothing between us, but she will not listen."

"Hopefully Mr. Bingley will return and set everything straight."

This time, it was Jane who did not answer. Seeing that her sister needed time to think, Elizabeth bade her good night and returned to her room. They both had fitful sleeps trying to digest the surprising events of the day.

THE SUMMER ASSEMBLY AT MERYTON

As he dressed for the assembly, Darcy tried to calm his nerves and stop squirming. He was sure his valet had already noticed his odd behavior. He had asked the man twice what he had chosen for him to wear for the evening. While not an unreasonable question in itself, it was an inquiry that Darcy hardly ever made. When he asked for the second time, having failed to listen for an answer to his first request, his man could not hide his astonishment.

To make matters worse, Darcy knew this was not the first time in the last two days that he had appeared inattentive or out of character. He had returned from Longbourn in a swirl of emotions, choosing to retire to his room after a perfunctory meal. He had failed to anticipate how much seeing Elizabeth would affect him. On reflection, he had to admit that the visit had passed in an acceptable manner. He had secured a private interview with Miss Bennet and arranged a means of speaking to her again. Her genuine kindness toward him was both unexpected and a balm to his battered soul. Despite the awkwardness of his visit with Elizabeth's family, he had escaped without causing anyone serious embarrassment. He may have unreasonably raised Mrs. Bennet's expectations regarding his interest in Miss Bennet, but that was unavoidable. Given that his goal in coming to Hertfordshire was to secure Bingley's happiness, he should have been satisfied with the progress he had made. Instead, he could only remember Elizabeth's icy stare followed by her refusal to look him in the eye.

He tried to remind himself that he had not come to Hertfordshire to persuade Elizabeth to rethink her opinion of him. But when he saw her, he knew in his heart he had nurtured the unrealistic hope that upon reading his letter she had miraculously changed her mind. It was clear from her reaction that his fantasy was as foolish as his initial proposal. He spent the night in a restless sleep, attempting to come to terms with the fact that he had to put her out of his mind, once and for all.

He awoke the next day determined to exorcise her ghost. He took a long, reckless ride through the countryside, trying to exhaust his mind by fatiguing his body. He returned in the afternoon having come to the realization that all he had accomplished was to make himself and his poor horse sore and uncomfortable.

That night he decided to try a different tack. He began drinking liberally before dinner and continued until well after midnight. He retired to his chambers, barely able to walk. He waved off his valet and fell asleep in his clothes. He awoke in the morning with a splitting headache and the faint memory of torrid dreams he had had about Elizabeth. Hot coffee and a long bath eventually repaired his ailments, and he realized that despite his efforts, he had gained no ground in his battle to purge Elizabeth from his mind.

He was brought back to the present by his valet, who had finished his task and asked, "Sir, are you satisfied, or is there something particular you require?"

"Oh, no. Well, yes. I was just concerned that I... that I... No. That will be all. Thank you for your help."

Hiding his amusement, his valet bowed curtly and bid his master good evening. Having already reviewed his own behavior and finding it lacking, Darcy turned his thoughts to his impending social obligation. He laughed as he thought that the evening ahead could not have planned to make him more uncomfortable had the devil himself orchestrated it. He would be attending a local assembly—by himself—where dancing would be required and small talk mandatory. He was only truly acquainted with one family, and his interaction with each of its members was fraught with potential danger.

It was clear that Elizabeth would want nothing to do with him, and he could not imagine what he would say to her that could improve the situation. Miss Bennet would surely have told her the reason for his visit, which might have softened her heart toward him. But the idea that she would improve her manners toward him out of gratitude—or out of fear that her sister's happiness depended upon it—held no allure. Such an encounter would be awkward at best and, in the end, a hollow victory. He would prefer her honest animosity. Avoidance was his best option.

Discussion with Miss Bennet would be necessary and most likely more than pleasant. He had to smile when he thought of her generous and forgiving nature. Bingley would be very lucky to win her. But he knew he could not spend the whole of the evening talking to her. Her mother and the local gossips would misconstrue the attention he had already shown her. He would need to ask her to dance so that he could ask her about Bingley, but any further interaction would put them both in an uncomfortable situation.

Who did that leave? The very idea of talking to Mrs. Bennet again only rekindled his headache. He could imagine her on his arm prattling away while she introduced him to her neighbors. She would most likely require him to make his introduction by listing his assets in descending order of value.

He could ask Elizabeth's sisters to dance, but in the past he had found their behavior so inappropriate that he could not imagine how he would endure the experience. He also wondered what Elizabeth would make of such a request. Would she think he was mocking her, since he had berated them in his letter, or would she imagine he was trying to curry her favor, and wonder to what end? No, there would be no point in trying to further an acquaintance in that direction.

He instinctively felt that any interaction with Mr. Bennet would be foolhardy. If Mr. Bennet knew about his previous dealings with Elizabeth, he had every right to be furious with him on several levels. If Mr. Bennet had no information as to his past interactions with Elizabeth, then he probably believed, through his wife's intelligence, that Darcy was hoping to court Miss Bennet. Knowing that his real aim was to leave Hertfordshire for good as soon as possible, any interaction with Mr. Bennet would be an insult in hindsight. Any prior explanation was impossible. The less said, the better.

Looking at his watch, Darcy realized that it was far too early to leave. He knew any occupation would be futile given his level of apprehension. So he poured himself a brandy and continued to imagine the derogation that the evening would bring. Yes, the less said, the better. He would arrive, seek out Miss Bennet, hopefully obtain her agreement as to his discussion with Bingley, and retire early with the excuse that he needed to travel in the morning. It would be the only way to minimize his discomfort.

As he reconfirmed the wisdom of his plan, he was struck with a vision of Elizabeth at Hunsford telling him it was his selfish disdain for the feelings of others that formed the groundwork of her disapprobation. But surely her criticism could not extend to his present predicament. It was natural for him to not want to mix with the inhabitants of the neighborhood. No one in his situation would be comfortable. But then again, he had to admit, this situation was of his own creation. If anyone should be uncomfortable, it was him. Given his inability to converse easily with strangers, wasn't he being considerate by not forcing his company upon others? His memory of Elizabeth again answered his query, this time by asking, "Why would a man of sense and education, and who has lived in the world, be ill qualified to recommend himself to strangers?" The words of his cousin provided the answer: "It is because he will not give himself the trouble."

Could that be true? Was he awkward at large social gatherings because, as Elizabeth once told him, he would not practice? He knew there was some truth to it. There was no question that he was naturally reserved, but he had overcome his innate shyness at certain times in his life. When he first went to Cambridge, he had been shy and uncomfortable among so many strangers. He had often relied on Wickham, who made acquaintances effortlessly, to ease his way into social circles. But Wickham had soon showed his true colors, and Darcy tried to avoid all contact with him. As a result, he had been alone more often than not. He had already been homesick, and despite his efforts to put all his energies into his studies, he had found that he needed some human contact. He had resolutely forced himself to attend social gatherings and make new acquaintances. Eventually, he had found a circle of friends he valued. Toward the end of his time at Cambridge, he had met Bingley and they became fast friends.

When he returned to Pemberley and his father's health began to fail, he hardly had time to socialize at all. When he did venture out, usually to fulfill an obligation, he came to the painful realization that much of the attention directed his way stemmed from his imminent position as the master of Pemberley and not from any sort of genuine regard. As a result, he developed an instinctual suspicion of new acquaintances. After his father's death, he maintained only his friendship with Bingley. He knew he truly valued Bingley's companionship, but on some level he also relied on him, as he had done with Wickham before, to ease his way in social gatherings. To that extent, Elizabeth was right; he was no longer practiced at the art of making friends because he counted on Bingley to do it for him. Unfortunately, Bingley would not be at the assembly tonight. Truth be told, after he advised Bingley of his meddling, he would probably never agree to share another evening with him again. He suddenly felt as alone as he had at Cambridge. Checking his watch, Darcy summoned his carriage.

At Longbourn, preparations for the assembly were progressing in a much more chaotic fashion. Elizabeth's requests to stay home were denied. Her mother explained that once Jane secured Mr. Darcy, he would be in a position to introduce

Elizabeth to other rich men. Since she was not getting any younger and she had already rejected what might be her only suitor in the person of Mr. Collins, she needed to take every opportunity to exhibit herself. Elizabeth endured her mother's lectures with fortitude. She took consolation in the fact that the evening might be worth it if, by its close, the situation between Jane and Mr. Bingley had been resolved. That outcome, however, remained uncertain. Despite Elizabeth's offers to talk, Jane kept her own counsel. Elizabeth believed that Jane was inclined to make the decision by herself since others had previously decided so much of what had happened between herself and Mr. Bingley. This time, she would at least rely on her own judgment.

While Jane sat composed in the sitting room, Elizabeth's other sisters rushed to finish dressing. Mrs. Bennet continued to instruct Elizabeth on her duties for the evening. "Now, Lizzy, do not go about giving impertinent opinions that no one is interested in. It can only hurt Jane's chances with Mr. Darcy. A man does not want to marry into a family that he does not like." Ignoring the irony of her mother's statement, Elizabeth nodded in acquiescence.

Once her mother went to see to her younger daughters' progress, Elizabeth joined Jane as she heard the carriages being brought to the front door. Reaching for Jane's hand, Elizabeth said, "Well, Jane, I suppose the time is upon us. Are you ready?"

"I suppose I am. But what about you? Are you feeling awkward about seeing Mr. Darcy again?"

"To be honest, I think it might be uncomfortable for us both. But there is no reason for us to interact. He only really wishes to speak to you."

"Yes, I suppose you are right. But if you do speak with him, I hope you can find it in your heart to be a little charitable. I feel somewhat responsible for him since he is only coming tonight on my account."

"Jane, for your sake, I will be perfectly civil."

"I never doubted you would." After a pause, Jane added, "Lizzy, I know you must be wondering what I have decided to do. I didn't mean to keep you in suspense, but even though I have given the matter a great deal of thought, I was only able to come to a decision just now. It may sound odd, but after spending so much time trying to decide, I have decided not to decide at all."

"Jane, Lizzy," interrupted Mrs. Bennet, "come at once. The carriage is ready. It would not do for us to be late. Oh, Jane, you look lovely. Mr. Darcy will not be able to resist you." Exchanging a resigned smile, Elizabeth and Jane walked with their mother to the carriage.

"Mama," Jane pleaded, "I have told you before, Mr. Darcy is simply a friend. He has no intentions toward me."

"Yes, yes, Jane. I cannot fault you for being naïve. But I must tell you, a mother has a way of knowing these things. Kitty, stop your fidgeting, or you will wrinkle your gown! Well, let us be off. I want the girls to be there early enough to secure partners for the first set." Nodding his acquiescence, Mr. Bennet signaled the carriage to depart.

Darcy entered the assembly as he had planned, after the start of the first set. He knew he could not ask Miss Bennet for that dance, as his meaning for doing so might be misconstrued. He had hoped to enter without notice, but he detected several heads turn his way as he strode into the hall and slipped into a corner. Bearing out his worst fear, he saw that Mrs. Bennet was one of his observers. He also noticed that she was disentangling herself from her conversation. He knew it would be only a matter of time before she was upon him. Retreating, Darcy maneuvered his way behind a group of women in an attempt to obscure her view.

To his astonishment, he found that he was the subject of the group's conversation. Unable to avoid them, he overheard a woman comment that Fanny Bennet had been wrong before about Jane's impending wedding. "It was more likely that she misconstrued Mr. Darcy's visit. You know Fanny's fondness for making a mountain out of a molehill." Another woman replied in an authoritative tone, "Well, I think we will be able to determine for ourselves what his intention is. Everyone knows that Mr. Darcy hardly ever dances. If he singles Jane out tonight, then there may be some truth to the suggestion."

Darcy knew he should leave before he was discovered, but he did not know where to turn. Making matters worse, he saw that Mrs. Bennet was searching for him. In distress, he surveyed the room for someone he knew. Upon noticing that Sir William Lucas was talking to a circle of people only a few steps away, he approached him.

"Sir William, it is a pleasure to see you again. I hope you and your family are well?"

Sir William was startled by Mr. Darcy's sudden and unprecedented address. After regaining his composure, he returned the inquiry. Darcy was then introduced to Sir William's son, John Lucas, who indicated that his sister, Mrs. Collins, had mentioned making his acquaintance in Kent. During the exchange, Darcy observed Sir William's other companions. They included Maria Lucas and a gentleman who was turned slightly away from him. When the man turned to make Darcy's introduction, he could now see that Elizabeth had been standing off to his side. His heart leaped in his chest as the phrase, "out of the frying pan and into the fire," unwittingly flitted across his consciousness.

After making the new acquaintance, Darcy stiffly bowed to Elizabeth and said, "Miss Bennet, good evening."

Curtseying, Elizabeth replied in a controlled voice, "Mr. Darcy."

Darcy held her gaze and said, "Miss Bennet, I hope your family is well?"

"Yes, sir, they are very well, thank you," she replied, adding, "They are all present tonight."

Unable to think of anything else to say, Darcy replied, "That must be very pleasant for you."

"Indeed it is, sir."

An awkward pause ensued. To Elizabeth's surprise, it was Darcy who spoke next. "Sir William, do you get much opportunity to travel to London?" As Darcy hoped, such an inquiry led Sir William into a long dissertation on St. James' Court, the ton, its inhabitants, and the condition of the roads leading there during the various seasons. All Darcy needed to do was periodically add a comment. The respite gave Darcy an opportunity to steal a sidelong glance at Elizabeth. He could not help but notice how lovely she looked. But he could also detect how uncomfortable his presence made her. Her hands seemed unable to stay at her side, and the bright blush of her cheeks betrayed her embarrassment at having to see him again. He resolved to put her out of her misery as soon as possible. He thought of how ironic it was that, after all he hoped they would be to each other, the only pleasure he could give her now was the gift of his absence.

He saw Jane across the room and contemplated asking her to dance immediately so that he could leave that much sooner, but he remembered the words he had overheard. If he singled her out for his first and only dance of the evening, people would misunderstand his intentions.

As he considered his options, Sir William asked, "Sir, how is your aunt, the Lady Catherine de Bourgh? I had the pleasure of meeting her when I brought my Maria and Miss Elizabeth to Kent earlier this spring to visit my daughter, Mrs. Collins."

"It is very kind of you to ask. She is quite well. I have not seen her since my recent visit to Rosings, but she has written to me several times." At the mention of Rosings, Darcy instinctively looked to Elizabeth. She caught his eye, looking grave, and then looked away.

"She must be a very loyal correspondent and a wonderful aunt."

"Yes, she writes often."

"I could well imagine. She has been very kind to both my daughters and was more than willing to help direct them on a variety of issues. Her vigilant counsel must be a comfort to you."

"Indeed."

"She seems so interested in such a wonderful variety of things."

Unable to hide the irony in his voice, Darcy replied, "Yes, I have heard it said many times that she is excessively attentive."

Elizabeth was unable to stifle a laugh before she put her hand in front of her mouth and looked away. Darcy was both shocked and delighted that she had laughed at his remark, however unintentional the humor. He cast a sideways glance, and when he caught her eye, he gave her a small smile, revealing his dimples, to express his contrition at having been caught making fun of his aunt. To his amazement, she returned his smile before recollecting herself and looking away. Darcy felt a flood of emotions. While she smiled at him, his heart swelled. They had shared a private moment, and in it he could believe that she might someday forgive him and allow him another chance. But when she looked away, he knew she had laughed in spite of herself and that his presence was a burden to her.

Darcy turned his attention back to Sir William, who was waxing eloquent about Lady Catherine's generous attention to the running of Mrs. Collins's household. As the music started for the next set, John Lucas interrupted his father. "Father, please excuse me, but I believe I must find my partner for the next set."

Sir William replied for everyone, "Oh, yes, John, so you must. Go, go. How I do love dancing. All young people should be so engaged." At that, Sir William looked from Elizabeth to Darcy and smiled broadly. Elizabeth cringed as she recalled her refusal of Mr. Darcy's invitation to dance at Lucas Lodge.

Darcy also immediately remembered Sir William's failed attempts to persuade Elizabeth to dance with him. Intent on avoiding the mortification of a repeat performance, Darcy impulsively said, "Yes, you are right. I know I have said in the past that I do not often enjoy the activity, but this evening I feel quite inclined. Miss Lucas, are you otherwise engaged?"

Now it was Maria's turn to be startled. She looked around in a bewildered fashion and finally rested her eyes on Darcy as if she could not believe the question had emanated from him. "Um, no, I mean, no, sir, I am not otherwise engaged."

Darcy extended his arm to Maria and said, "Well, then, shall we?"

As they took to the floor, Elizabeth looked on in disbelief. She was struck once again by the change in his demeanor.

While he was clearly still uncomfortable, he had interacted with her neighbors with reasonable civility. If she was fair, she also had to admit that, now that she understood the reason for his return, his behavior at her house two days prior was also above reproach. She knew on some level that the improvement in his manners must be in response to her reproof. That she could effect such a change, even if it were just for show, intrigued her. If that were not enough, however, she was now shocked to learn that Mr. Darcy had a sense of humor and that he viewed his aunt in the same light as she did. Finally, she had to grant him the thoughtfulness of his last action. While in any other situation, Elizabeth might have been insulted—or at least hurt—by someone selecting Maria Lucas as a dance partner over her, she knew that Darcy had done it to spare her the embarrassment that dancing together would cause. While she did not regret her rejection of his suit, she had to admit that he had more depth than she had previously credited him with.

She was no stranger to the issue; she had spent the last two days pondering her opinion of him. Her sister's words had given her pause. She had been wrong about his intentions. He had accepted her refusal of his proposal. He had not come for her sake, but for Mr. Bingley's and for Jane's. It was clear he had taken her words to heart and regretted his behavior toward them. If she was honest, she had to concede that she had judged him more harshly than he deserved. She also had to admit that the more she learned about him, the more she felt the compliment of his previous attentions, but that hardly meant that she could forgive him or even like him. Regardless of his present good behavior, she knew he was, in essentials, a proud and disagreeable man. If she needed evidence of this, she only had to remember his insulting proposal. More importantly, even if his conceited behavior could be overlooked, they had nothing in common on which to base a friendship, let alone a marriage.

As the music died down, Elizabeth's musings were interrupted by an acquaintance who had come to collect her for a dance she had promised. As they lined up, she was shocked to see Mr. Darcy already in position opposite one of Mrs. Philips's daughters. As the evening wore on, Elizabeth sat in amazement as Mr. Darcy found a partner for several dances. He had even asked both Kitty and Mary to stand up with him. Although she suspected his invitation to Mary was extended for an ulterior motive, as it occurred directly after she had indicated a desire to play the piano. When Elizabeth asked Kitty what they had talked about during the dance, she simply shrugged her shoulders and said, "The usual things, the size of the dance, the weather, if I walk to Meryton often." Wondering if maybe her name had come up, Elizabeth inquired if he had asked anything unusual. "Well, sort of. I thought it odd that he asked me what books I enjoy reading. I couldn't really remember, so I asked him what he liked to read, and he went on and on about some Shakespeare play. I really wasn't listening that closely."

Elizabeth found herself unable to quell her curiosity over Mr. Darcy's behavior. She often checked on his whereabouts and his interactions. She noted that he was now standing alone on the edge of the dance floor watching the participants in a manner more reminiscent of his behavior in the fall. She laughed to herself as she realized that he looked more natural when he did that than when he was dancing with relative strangers.

As Darcy stood there, John Lucas approached him. Elizabeth

was curious to see Darcy's reaction to his overture. She had known John Lucas her whole life. He was the Lucases' eldest son, slightly older than Elizabeth, and very friendly. Unlike his father, John Lucas had a quick wit and an engaging manner that made his outgoing nature a pleasure to encounter. She wondered if Darcy would find his forward behavior presumptuous. Unfortunately her position on the dance floor made it impossible for her to overhear their conversation.

Nodding his acknowledgment to Darcy, John Lucas stated, "I see, sir, we have the same thing in mind."

Darcy gave John Lucas a quizzical look. He had been engaged in the guilty pleasure of watching Elizabeth dance. He knew it was foolish of him. But he could not deny himself the indulgence since this would probably be the last time he ever saw her. Afraid that his intentions were obvious, he replied dryly, "I am not sure I understand you, Mr. Lucas."

"Well, there are very few reasons for a man to stand in this particular location. It does afford a good view of the dance floor, and if you are particularly interested in dance steps, it might prove advantageous. But I have seen you dance, and you do not appear in need of lessons. This spot also offers another advantage. Once the set ends, all of the dancers will have to pass us by. I am here for the strategic location and assumed that you were as well."

Unsure what to make of the man and his observation, Darcy cautiously smiled and asked, "And why would you make that assumption?"

"Well, if I tell you, I am sure you will think ill of me as it will require me to share something personal," Lucas said, adding with a irreverent smile, "and we both know such behavior is frowned upon."

Despite the man's presumptuous nature, Darcy could not help but be intrigued. It was the first unguarded comment he had heard all night. Darcy's suspicious side warned him of further interaction, but there was something about the man's good humor that reminded him of Bingley. The issue was decided when Darcy noticed that Elizabeth was watching them. Whatever the danger, he refused to abruptly walk off and give her the satisfaction of once again proving her reproof true. Instead, he inquired, "Then why would you dare tempt it?"

"For two reasons. First, I find these social occasions difficult, and discourse with you seems more likely to be entertaining than standing alone—although, if you prefer solitude, I would be more than happy to give you a wider berth."

"No, sir, I welcome your company. I know very few people here."

"Yes, but many people know you. As an unknown quantity, you generate great interest. I could not garner the same level of attention without doing something provocative. Be that as it may, I will take your acquiescence as leave to continue. My second reason contains the personal disclosure I mentioned. Despite my position as the eldest son, I think I am more suited for the military. I have a natural tendency to see all human interaction in tactical terms. I cannot help but view a dance such as this as a military campaign, with its various participants alternately in the offensive or defensive posture."

Darcy studied the man. His intelligence was obvious, but his demeanor a bit improper. He was tempted to retreat from the intercourse, but had to laugh to himself at his unconscious use of a military term. He recalled his earlier thoughts about his failed attempts at making friends and decided to continue.

"Despite my better judgment, I find myself inclined to ask how you interpret my movements and why it is that you think I have taken this position."

"Well met. I applaud your daring. I hope I do not disappoint. That said, I believe that you have been in a defensive position throughout the night. You have kept to the same area and appear to have selected each one of your dance partners according to their proximity to your territory, regardless of the more obvious considerations. I mean no offense; I often use the same maneuver. It allows one to get through the evening without risking much."

At this, Darcy refused to commit and simply stated, "Indeed."

"What intrigues me is your offensive movement to this unguarded position. Clearly, something has drawn you out. You must be seeking something or someone already on the dance floor." Seeing Darcy color and the set of his jaw tighten, it was John Lucas's turn to retreat. "Please, do not worry. I have only said as much because that is why I am here as well." Looking significantly from Darcy to where Jane was dancing, he added, "I am no threat. While she is very beautiful, my tastes run elsewhere."

Darcy was in a quandary. He was relieved that his real purpose was not revealed, but upset that he may have unwittingly added fuel to any gossip about himself and Miss Bennet. If he denied that Miss Bennet was the reason for his coming over, it might open up speculation as to what it was that he had been doing. John Lucas seemed too clever to let the matter drop so easily. Hoping to avoid any further comment on the subject, Darcy turned the tables and asked, "And where do your tastes run?"

"Ah, a direct question. A brilliant strategy. I see I was right in seeking you out. You also reject the confines of social rules.

We must play chess someday. I will reward your boldness with a response." Looking significantly at Elizabeth, he said, "I find her sister most appealing."

Trying to hide his intense and conflicting emotion, Darcy asked, "You must be well acquainted then."

"Oh, yes, I have known her since she was a girl. But our dispositions are too similar. I often provoke her. I doubt she will accept my invitation to dance; I recently enraged her by disagreeing with her about a passage from a play we had both read. But I have reread the entire book and am armed with evidence that my position is superior. I will attempt to dazzle her with my wit and undoubtedly will leave defeated. But a man must always make an effort. Do you not agree?"

Darcy searched for something to say, but the music ended and John Lucas bowed his exit with a smile. He then walked directly over to Elizabeth to secure his dance. Darcy watched as Elizabeth smiled and agreed. As he stood alone, he saw Jane approaching as she exited the floor. Realizing that he needed to accomplish his avowed reason for coming, Darcy attempted to put his thoughts about Elizabeth aside and deal with the subject at hand. He walked over to Jane, bowed slightly, and asked, "Madam, would you do me the honor of the next dance?"

With a small curtsey, Jane replied, "I would be delighted."

Once the dance was under way and its movement allowed some privacy, Darcy regained his composure and said, "Miss Bennet, thank you for agreeing to dance with me. I thought it might give us an opportunity to continue our discussion."

"Yes, Mr. Darcy, I agree. I am glad you asked."

"It is my pleasure."

"Mr. Darcy, I wanted to tell you how much I appreciate your

coming tonight. When we talked the other afternoon, I did not feel up to the task of responding to your question. Thank you for waiting while I took some time to reflect."

"No, madam, your request was quite understandable, and it is I who is in your debt for agreeing to speak to me in the first place. I created the situation; it is no inconvenience for me to await your decision."

"Thank you, sir; I do appreciate your thoughtfulness."

"Miss Bennet, while I do not mean to rush you, may I be so bold as to ask if you have indeed come to a decision?"

"Yes, sir, I have."

"I am glad to hear it, but before you answer, I want you to know that whatever you decide about accepting a visit from our mutual friend, I am resolved to confess my actions to him when I return to London. I feel that my honor requires it. Once I do, I would like to be able to give him some hope that the situation is not beyond repair."

"I understand that you must do what you feel is right. I also understand that doing so will not be easy for you. I sincerely hope that if you explain your actions with the sincerity that you have shown me, that our friend will understand that your intentions were good, whatever the actual outcome."

"I think, madam, that you are far too kind. But when I do speak to him, may I convey your regards?"

"Mr. Darcy, although it is very difficult for me, I have decided that I would rather you not."

"But, Miss Bennet..." interrupted Darcy.

"Mr. Darcy, please hear me out. I know I mentioned that I would be uncomfortable coming between a person and his family, and I still feel that way. But I have also decided that if I would ever be able to put those concerns aside, I would first want to be sure that I did not encourage discord or knowingly cause pain among a family. I would find it hard to live with myself if I actively sought my happiness at the expense of someone else's. As such, I think it would be best if I kept my thoughts on the subject to myself."

Darcy remained silent while he pondered Jane's words. He then said, "In the same vein, though, you would not want to discourage someone from seeking out what would truly give him happiness."

"But it is not my place to do either. Through your intelligence, I have learned the private feelings of people who otherwise did not want me to know their disinclination to form an alliance with me. I think you were right in telling me, and I am very grateful that you did. It makes it much easier to come to terms with how events have turned out. But if I used this information or tried to benefit from it, I would become part of their scheme. I simply want no part of it."

"Miss Bennet, your sense of honor and goodness is quite amazing. I do not agree with what you have decided, but I do respect it. I will not involve you any further. But from what I have heard you say, I must also assume that you would not be disposed to discount someone's attentions based on the same unfortunate intelligence. If your intent is to disregard this information, you should do it in its totality."

"Mr. Darcy, I can see that you can be very persuasive when you wish. I would not attempt to engage you in a battle of wits. I think it would be more prudent to change the subject. Consequently, I will consider this matter closed except to say again that I harbor no ill will toward you and hope that if our paths ever cross again, you will consider me a friend. That said, might I inquire about your plans for the summer? I recall that you hope to visit with your sister soon?"

"Miss Bennet, I think you should never be afraid to engage anyone in a challenge of wits or wills. Through graciousness and kindness you have effectively closed a subject that I think might benefit from further discourse, but I can see it would be imprudent for me to attempt it. I will only add that I would indeed be honored to call you a friend. Your generosity has taught me a valuable lesson as to the type of person I should strive to become. I am truly humbled by you. That said, in response to your question, yes, I am planning to return to Pemberley after my sojourn in London. My sister will be in residence there, and I am anxious to see her again."

As Darcy and Jane continued their dance, Elizabeth struggled to keep her mind on her conversation with John Lucas. Instead, she watched Mr. Darcy and Jane's interaction with studied interest. Mr. Lucas finally interrupted and asked, "You seem very concerned with your sister. Are the rumors true, then?"

"What have you heard?"

"What everyone else has, I assume. My mother and your mother recently had tea, and they could speak of nothing else but Miss Bennet's visitor. He seems nice enough and is obviously a good match. Why the look of concern?"

"Mr. Lucas, I thought you were smart enough to know better than to believe everything you hear. It is not your place— Did you say he seemed nice enough?"

"Yes, he was very engaging when we spoke, and endured my questions quite well. He seems very much a gentleman. Do you have some reason to disagree?"

"No, of course not. I just did not realize the two of you had spoken."

Detecting her lie, he decided to leave the subject alone so as not to vex her further. He attempted his explanation of his rereading of Shakespeare. Elizabeth eventually argued the point with him, but he could tell her heart was not in it. At the close of the dance, he offered to get her a refreshment. She gratefully agreed as he deposited her in a corner of the room while he fetched it.

As Darcy and Jane completed their dance, he walked her off the floor in order to bid her farewell and express his heartfelt wish for her happiness. She thanked him in return. She was then approached for the next dance. Darcy bowed to her new partner and stepped away. As he watched her go, he suddenly realized that he was standing near Elizabeth.

Elizabeth spoke first. "Mr. Darcy, I would like to take this opportunity to thank you for speaking with my sister about Mr. Bingley. It was very good of you."

"Miss Bennet, I think we both know that is not true. I am simply trying to correct my error in judgment. I deserve no praise."

Disarmed by his honesty, Elizabeth attempted another tack. "Sir, let me at least thank you for your letter and apologize for my misjudgment of you. I am ashamed that I was so easily taken in by Mr. Wickham."

"Obviously, no apology is necessary. Mr. Wickham is very adept at fooling people, and you should not blame yourself for his misdeeds."

"I fear you are too kind, sir."

"Once again, madam, I think we both know that is not true."

"Sir, let me…"

Unwilling to let Elizabeth continue, Darcy interrupted, "Miss Bennet, I know my coming to Hertfordshire must be more than awkward for you, and I apologize for it. I hope you understand why I thought it was necessary. The last thing I want to do is prolong your discomfort. I suppose there is much we could both say to each other, but I think it might be more charitable for me to simply say good evening and let you know that I truly wish you every happiness." Unable to resist the temptation, Darcy took her hand and kissed it before leaving the assembly.

Chapter 7

Visitors

THE NEXT DAY, DARCY left Netherfield at first light. He wanted to talk to Bingley as soon as possible. He needed to make his confession and put the entire incident behind him. Seeing Elizabeth had been painful, and watching her dance with another man, one whose intentions were obvious, was more than he could bear.

He had spent a sleepless night debating whether he had been too brusque in his departure from the assembly. If he had allowed their conversation to continue, they could have discussed her misjudgment of Wickham and his misunderstanding of Miss Bennet, but to what end? Maybe they would have understood each other's motives better, and in turn, that might have made their relationship more cordial. But he did not want her cordiality. When she stood near him, looking beautiful and engaging, he wanted her, and anything short of a second declaration felt hollow. Before seeing her, he had talked himself into believing that he was still angry with her for all her unjustified criticism. When he actually talked to her, however, he knew all he really wanted was for her to love him—not that he thought that it was still possible or even desirable after all that happened. He just wished that things had turned out differently. In hindsight, he probably should have handled their brief conversation better, but he had felt unequal to the task. It seemed pointless to engage in strained polite conversation when he knew he could not say what he actually felt.

While he regretted providing her another example of his incivility, he vowed not to dwell on it. His entire relationship with Elizabeth had been filled with regret. Another instance would not matter. His conversation with John Lucas was more difficult to banish from his mind. He tortured himself by trying to calculate how long it would take Lucas to win Elizabeth's hand. He had to admit that if Lucas did succeed, it would be a good match for her. He would eventually inherit Lucas Lodge, and despite his efforts to vilify him, Lucas seemed an amiable man. He obviously cared for Elizabeth—or at least cared about trying to court her. He had gone to the trouble of planning out a topic of conversation for his dance with her, and he had spoken of her in admiring terms. He would undoubtedly continue to pursue her. He would nurture an attachment between them. Eventually, he would ask her to marry him—without insulting her—and she would accept. They would be extremely happy together and most likely have several beautiful children.

His jealousy was palpable. Lucas had bested him by embarking on the radical plan of trying to win her by treating her well. Why hadn't he tried as much in Kent? He vowed that if he survived this ordeal, he would remember what was required to court a woman worth winning.

Not that it would matter in regard to Elizabeth. He would

most likely never see her again. His only real connection with her was through Bingley, and while he hoped that Bingley would eventually formalize that association through marriage to Miss Bennet, it would come at the cost of his friendship. He could not imagine that Bingley would forgive him for the pain he had caused Miss Bennet, and even if he did, his continued association with Bingley would surely make Elizabeth uncomfortable, no matter how much they both attempted to be civil. Their interaction at the assembly was proof of that. If Bingley and Miss Bennet formed an alliance, Elizabeth had every right to want to spend time with them. It was her sister after all. He truly valued Bingley's friendship, and if it could be salvaged after his confession, he would be eternally grateful, but he would not do so at the risk of imposing himself on Elizabeth. He had caused the discord between them, and if one of them needed to step back to ensure their paths did not cross again, it should be him. Besides, it would allow him the excuse of never having to witness Elizabeth as another man's wife.

He knew letting his mind drift in such a fashion was unproductive, and his musing about the future premature. Until he spoke to Bingley, nothing was certain. He intended to call on him as soon as he arrived in London. He was dreading the encounter but knew time was of the essence. Moreover, he needed to act while he still had the nerve. He would make his confession to Bingley while honoring Miss Bennet's request by omitting any reference to her present feelings. While he had hoped to be able to tell Bingley more, he felt that he could still report, without betraying Miss Bennet's confidence, that during his visit to Hertfordshire she did not appear to be engaged and that he had not heard of any imminent suitors—other than, of course, himself. That bit of gossip he would obviously omit. If possible, he would also leave out the details of his interaction with Elizabeth in Kent. It would not serve any purpose and might only complicate matters. Ultimately, what mattered was that Bingley be told that he and his sisters had been wrong about Miss Bennet.

Once he confessed to Bingley, he would encourage him to return to Hertfordshire. Even if his reception there was uncertain, he should at least try to pick up where he had left off. If he still loved Miss Bennet, it would be worth it, even if he ultimately failed, because he would know that he had done everything in his power to correct the situation. Darcy knew firsthand that there was nothing worse than regret.

Darcy thought it ironic that he was suddenly an expert on affairs of the heart; he was such a dismal failure when it involved his own life. But there was a difference between Bingley's situation and his own. Bingley was a victim of other people's unwarranted interference. Consequently, the path to correcting that mistake was clear. Darcy had sabotaged his own life, and there was no way to salvage the damage.

After a long, tedious journey, Darcy was greeted at Bingley's townhouse by his friend's steward. "Mr. Darcy, I was just leaving instructions for this letter to be delivered to you. Mr. Bingley was called away. He left just this morning and wanted you to know of his change in plans."

Taking the letter, Darcy thanked him. While Bingley's missive was difficult to read in places, the gist was clear. Miss Bingley had insisted that her brother escort her to their sister's home in a neighboring county, where she was to stay for a few weeks. Because he did not know Darcy's date of return, he thought it wiser to complete the trip now rather than later. He intended to stay at his sister's house as briefly as possible. He would leave as soon as he was sufficiently rested for the return trip. He would contact Darcy upon his arrival in town.

Darcy entrusted a reply to Bingley's steward, indicating that he would wait in town for his return, as there was an important matter that they needed to discuss. He considered also sending an express to Bingley at his sister's residence, but rejected the idea. What he needed to say could not be put in a letter, and Bingley had already indicated that he would return as soon as possible.

Darcy was thoroughly disappointed by the turn of events. He wanted to put the whole business behind him, and this was another obstacle to its completion. Bingley had only begun his journey that morning, and depending on the weather, it would be several days before his return. Moreover, he wondered how a delay would affect the inhabitants of Longbourn. He had made no promises about Bingley's return to Hertfordshire, but he had hoped to convince him to return immediately. He could not help but think that Miss Bennet might be wishing for Bingley's return and wondered if she would suffer needlessly when he did not appear within the amount of time reasonably expected. Given Miss Bennet's generous disposition and her kindness toward him, Darcy could not help but feel protective of her. Unfortunately, there was nothing to do but wait.

As the days passed, a visitor was indeed much anticipated at Longbourn. But not the one Darcy hoped. Mrs. Bennet had been anxiously awaiting his return so that he could secure Jane's hand. Jane had told her mother several times that Mr. Darcy had not indicated that he would ever be returning to Hertfordshire.

Mrs. Bennet, however, could not be convinced. Instead, she required Jane to be ever present in the drawing room so that she could receive her suitor at his earliest convenience. As the days passed, Elizabeth could not help but feel for Jane. She understood that Jane felt it would be improper to outwardly encourage Mr. Bingley, but she also wondered if Jane might be secretly hoping Mr. Bingley would visit. Their mother's constant declarations about how much time had passed since Mr. Darcy's departure could only serve to remind Jane of how many days Mr. Bingley had been aware of his friend's deception without taking action. Putting a stop to her mother's endless prattle, however, was not easily accomplished.

Elizabeth did not need her mother's constant mention of Mr. Darcy to keep him in the forefront of her mind. She was puzzled by every aspect of his recent behavior and spent an inordinate amount of time trying to resolve it. That he would come to Hertfordshire to correct the damage he had done showed a depth of character she had overlooked. His willingness to dance and converse with her neighbors was nothing short of shocking, and that people she respected, like Jane and John Lucas, thought him amiable was difficult to understand. Perhaps Jane was right, and she was continuing to hold a grudge when his improved behavior called for some charity.

But as soon as she would declare her previous opinions of him unjust, doubts would surface. She felt sure that once Mr. Bingley knew all, he would come. Yet he had not. As time passed, she began to doubt Mr. Darcy's sincerity and wondered if he had failed to tell Mr. Bingley about his interference, though she knew from Jane's earnest account of their conversation that it was not likely. She had been impressed that Mr. Darcy had told Jane that he planned to tell Bingley all that had transpired, regardless of her present feelings. She had to admit that he genuinely seemed to regret his actions, and was glad he was trying to make amends. Given all that he had already done to promote reconciliation between Mr. Bingley and Jane, the delay in Mr. Bingley's return could not, in fairness, be blamed on him.

Even giving Mr. Darcy the benefit of the doubt about Mr. Bingley, Elizabeth still could not reconcile his behavior toward her at the assembly. After Jane had told her the purpose of his visit to Hertfordshire, she realized that her earlier supposition about his continued affection for her was wrong. She felt a little embarrassed that she had so easily assumed he had come for her, and she recalled her fleeting feelings of jealousy with shame. She was grateful she had not shared her thoughts with Jane.

She attended the assembly comfortable in the fact that he had come to talk to Jane about Mr. Bingley and nothing more. But after their two chance encounters, she felt strangely unsettled, particularly when she contemplated his good-bye to her. On the one hand, his refusal to hear her out seemed typical of his overall dismissive attitude toward her. But then again, she could detect in his eyes his discomfiture and his embarrassment, and she understood his desire to end their encounter as quickly as possible. While she knew he had more than his share of pride, she had to admit that she could not imagine any man who would willingly interact with a woman after she had refused his proposal. That was what troubled her. It was not just that he seemed uncomfortable or that he despised her for her rejection. He seemed, at his essence, to have an air of sadness about him. Surely, it could not be for her. He had made it clear to both Jane and her that he did not want to impose upon her further, and it was obvious that her presence was a burden to him. Yet, her thoughts continually returned to the way he had solemnly kissed her hand and wished her every happiness.

Elizabeth was roused from her thoughts by her mother's latest round of speculation about Mr. Darcy's return. Elizabeth noticed Jane's back stiffen. She resolved to intercede on her sister's behalf. When her mother complained about the ill effects that all this waiting had on her health, Elizabeth sympathized and suggested that perhaps the apothecary could help. Mrs. Bennet basked in the attention and warmed to the idea. She then dismissed it when she realized that she could not go to town for fear of missing Mr. Darcy's visit. Elizabeth suggested that Jane go for her. At first, her mother rejected the idea out of hand because Jane had to be home to receive Mr. Darcy as well. Elizabeth, however, continued her campaign, noting that it might be good for Mr. Darcy to have to wait for Jane. It would break him of his habit of assuming that he could return whenever he chose and expect Jane to be here waiting for him. Mrs. Bennet immediately saw the wisdom of the plan and bade Jane leave to go. When Elizabeth began to depart as well, Mrs. Bennet informed her that she was needed at home. Elizabeth realized that her momentary willingness to discuss the best strategy for Jane to snare Mr. Darcy had made her appear a desirable companion, a position she did not often merit with her mother. Resigned that she had at least managed Jane's escape, Elizabeth settled down to pay the price for Jane's temporary freedom.

After a brief interlude, Elizabeth was startled by the sound of a carriage. Kitty looked out and announced that the chaise was unfamiliar but quite fine. Mrs. Bennet determined that Mr. Darcy probably owned so many fine carriages that it was no wonder she did not recognize them all. Anticipating Mr. Bingley's return, Elizabeth immediately regretted her plan to afford Jane a reprieve from their mother. She knew that nothing would salve Jane's wounds better than Mr. Bingley's return. She would have to convince him to wait. Jane had already waited for so long; Mr. Bingley could forswear a few hours more. She knew that once they were reunited, they would have much to work out. Jane's concern over his family's obvious objections would require sensitivity on his part. Despite the obstacles, she felt confident that all could be resolved if the couple were only given the opportunity. She suddenly dreaded her mother's inevitable confusion over Mr. Bingley returning, rather than Mr. Darcy, but hoped her mother's usual vice of flittering from one idea to another would actually prove a virtue in this situation.

As her mother barked commands at Kitty and recriminations at Elizabeth for having talked her into letting Jane go, the door opened and the visitor was announced. To Elizabeth's shock, it was Lady Catherine de Bourgh. To her further amazement, her mother was temporarily stunned into an unaccustomed silence.

Lady Catherine entered the room with an air that was more ungracious than usual and made no other reply to Elizabeth's salutation than a slight inclination of the head. She then sat down without saying a word. Elizabeth had mentioned her name to her mother on her ladyship's entrance, though no request of introduction had been made.

"I hope you are well, Miss Bennet. That lady, I suppose, is your mother."

Elizabeth replied very concisely that she was.

"And that, I suppose, is one of your sisters."

"Yes, madam," said Mrs. Bennet, delighted to speak to Lady

Catherine. "She is my youngest girl but one. My eldest, Jane, whose name you have probably heard mentioned, is unfortunately on an errand for me. I know she would want to meet you."

Lady Catherine stiffened at the mention of Jane's name, but Mrs. Bennet, oblivious to her reaction, continued stoutly on. "May I take the liberty of asking your ladyship whether you left Mr. and Mrs. Collins in good health?"

"Yes, very well. I saw them the night before last."

Elizabeth now hoped that she would produce a letter for her from Charlotte, as it seemed the most probable motive for her calling. But no letter appeared.

Mrs. Bennet, with great civility, begged her ladyship to take some refreshment, but Lady Catherine very resolutely, and not very politely, declined eating anything; and said, "You can be at no loss, Mrs. Bennet, to understand the reason of my journey hither. I wanted to speak to Miss Jane Bennet, but in her absence, you will do. You must know why I have come."

With a broad smile, Mrs. Bennet replied, "Well, I am a little surprised by the timing, but I understand your eagerness to meet my daughter. It reflects well on you that you are so interested in your nephew's concerns. Your visit is quite a compliment to her."

"Mrs. Bennet," replied her ladyship, in an angry tone, "a report of a most alarming nature reached me two days ago. I was told that, in all likelihood, my own nephew, Mr. Darcy, was soon to be united with your daughter, Miss Jane Bennet. Though I know it must be a scandalous falsehood, though I would not injure him so much as to suppose the truth of it possible, I instantly resolved on setting off for this place, that I might make my sentiments known to you. I insist upon having such a report universally contradicted."

Before Elizabeth could reassure Lady Catherine that no union was anticipated or desired by Jane, she heard her mother respond in a cold voice, "Lady Catherine, I am unsure how you came to hear such a thing, but it is certainly not my place to contradict such a report, nor would I want to."

"Then you do not pretend to be ignorant of it? Has it not been industriously circulated by yourselves? Do you not know that such a report is spread abroad?"

Elizabeth sat in stunned silence. Her mother must be responsible for the rumor. In the last few days, she had visited nearly every family in the countryside and talked of nothing else. She knew from John Lucas that her mother had discussed Mr. Darcy's intention with his mother five days prior. Lady Catherine had said she had visited the Collinses the previous evening, and the news must have spread to Lady Catherine from there. Unflappable, Mrs. Bennet smiled again and serenely stated, "Well, I never heard that it was, but certainly your nephew's actions must be its cause."

"This is not to be borne. Mrs. Bennet, I insist on being satisfied. I am almost the nearest relation he has in the world and am entitled to know all his dearest concerns. Has he, has my nephew, made your daughter an offer of marriage?"

With a smug smile, Mrs. Bennet sweetly replied, "I cannot say that it is a completely settled event. But if you are so close with your nephew, why don't you ask him if it is his intention?"

"Mrs. Bennet, do you know who I am? Let me be rightly understood. This match, to which your daughter has the presumption to aspire, can never take place. No, never. Mr. Darcy is engaged to my daughter. Now what have you to say?"

"Lady Catherine, are you telling me that Mr. Darcy has been

showing my daughter attentions while he is already engaged to someone else?"

Lady Catherine hesitated for a moment, and then replied, "The engagement between them is of a peculiar kind. From their infancy, they have been intended for each other. It was the favourite wish of his mother, as well as of hers. While in their cradles, we planned the union, and now, at the moment when the wishes of both sisters would be accomplished in their marriage, to be prevented by a young woman of inferior birth, of no importance in the world, and wholly unallied to the family!"

Dismissively, Mrs. Bennet interrupted her, "Oh, yes, I see now. It is something you hope will happen. Well, as a mother I can well sympathize. It is, after all, our duty to see our daughters well married. But if I may be so bold as to give you some advice: Since Mr. Darcy has obviously known your daughter since her birth, there must have been many opportunities for him to propose. Yet, he has reached his present age and has failed to do so. Perhaps your daughter should consider her other options."

"I will not be interrupted. Hear me in silence. My daughter and my nephew are formed for each other. They are descended, on the maternal side, from the same noble line, and, on the father's, from respectable, honourable, and ancient—though untitled—families. Their fortune on both sides is splendid. They are destined for each other by the voice of every member of their respective houses, and what is to divide them? The upstart pretensions of a young woman without family, connections, or fortune. Is this to be endured! But it must not, shall not be. Tell me once and for all, is your daughter engaged to him?"

As her mother paused to think how she could respond without losing ground, Elizabeth saw her chance to introduce a semblance of reason into this otherwise fantastic exchange. "No, Lady Catherine, my sister is not engaged to your nephew. I know that for a fact."

Lady Catherine seemed pleased but immediately asked, "And will she promise me never to enter into such an engagement?"

Her mother spoke before she could, stating in a defiant tone, "She will make no promise of the kind."

"But, Mama," Elizabeth pleaded, "should we not consult Jane? I think she would set the matter straight. I think she would unequivocally state…"

Ignoring Elizabeth, Lady Catherine continued to address her mother. "Does she have no regard for the wishes of his friends? Is your daughter lost to every feeling of propriety and delicacy? Have you not heard me say that from his earliest hours he was destined for his cousin?"

With a calmness and reserve that Elizabeth was shocked to discover her mother possessed, she responded, "Yes, Lady Catherine, I think we all heard you."

"Your daughter should heed my words. She should know that if she willfully acts against the inclinations of all, she will not be noticed by his family or friends. Your daughter will be censured, slighted, and despised, by everyone connected with him. Her alliance will be a disgrace; her name will never even be mentioned by any of us."

"Rest assured that I will convey your sentiments to Jane," replied Mrs. Bennet. "But I would also assume that, as the wife of Mr. Darcy, she will have other sources of happiness to make the deprivation more than bearable."

"Very well. I shall now know how to act. Do not imagine, Mrs. Bennet, that your ambition will ever be gratified. I came to try you and your daughter. I hoped to find you reasonable, but depend upon it, I will carry my point."

Lady Catherine rose to leave as Mrs. Bennet and Elizabeth followed her. Mrs. Bennet looked in the carriage at the young woman seated under a blanket and asked, "Lady Catherine, is this your daughter?"

Seething with anger, Lady Catherine simply replied, "Yes, it is."

"Oh," replied Mrs. Bennet with disdain, adding, "Does she need anything before your journey? She does not seem well."

"No, thank you! I take no leave of you, Mrs. Bennet. I send no compliments to your daughter. She deserves no such attention. I am most seriously displeased."

Mrs. Bennet simply curtseyed, saying loudly enough for the inhabitants of the carriage to hear, "Elizabeth dear, come in the house immediately. I do not want you to catch a draft; the effect on a woman's complexion can be so unappealing." In shock, Elizabeth followed her mother into the house.

❧

Darcy was sitting at his desk when he heard a visitor being escorted into the library. He was relieved to see it was Bingley, who immediately began to explain his delay. "Darcy, I got your note. I am sorry if I kept you waiting. I had intended to leave two days ago, but when I arrived at my sister's home, I found that she had invited some guests there without my knowledge. I did not want to stay, but my family apparently promised that I would make the particular acquaintance of one of the guests. As such, I could not avoid it, but I left as soon as I could."

Nodding his understanding, Darcy indicated that he

should sit. "Charles, it must have been a long journey. May I get you anything?"

Bingley was surprised by Darcy's concerned tone. He hoped that it did not indicate that he was planning on making him suffer through another heart-to-heart conversation like the one he had just endured from his sisters about his sullen behavior. "Thank you, Darcy, no."

There was an awkward pause as Darcy paced in front of Bingley. Knowing Darcy as he did, he knew this was a sign that something important was afoot. Bingley spoke first. "You said in your note there was something you needed to talk to me about. Did you lease Netherfield?"

"No, Charles, I did not. But I do want to talk to you about my visit there."

Darcy continued to pace. Bingley grew apprehensive as Darcy struggled to start. Finally, Darcy sat across from him and dragged his chair closer. "While I was in Hertfordshire, I saw Miss Bennet."

Bingley colored, looked at his hands, and said, "Oh... is she well?"

"Actually, Bingley, I was able to spend quite some time with her during my visit and got to know her much better. Yes, she is in perfect health... When I spoke with her..."

Bingley looked up at Darcy expectantly.

"Charles, there is no easy way to say this, so I will just plow ahead." But instead of doing so, Darcy hesitated as he tried to determine what he should say. He had rehearsed his speech to Bingley several times while awaiting his return. But now that he was sitting across from him, his overwhelming sense of guilt made him tongue-tied.

Bingley finally broke the tension. "Darcy, what are you trying to say? Is she all right?"

"Yes, yes, forgive me… Charles, I recently learned that I was wrong about her; last fall when we were in Hertfordshire, she did, in fact, return your affections. I was wrong in my judgment of her, and I was wrong to interfere."

Agitated, Bingley rapidly asked, "Are you sure? How do you know this? What happened when you visited? Did she actually say something to you about me?"

"A few weeks ago, I learned of it from someone else. I went to Hertfordshire, among other reasons, to confirm it. And I did determine it was true. Charles, I hope I do not presume too much, but it seems to me that you still harbor feelings for her. If that is the case, you should return to Netherfield to see her. I do not know how she will receive you after all this time, but she was not engaged or otherwise promised when I visited. Will you go?"

"Darcy, I don't know what to say. Who told you this? My sisters were very friendly with her, and they were quite sure that she held me in no special regard."

"Charles, I will tell you all that I know in a moment, and some of it does involve your sisters. But when I am finished, I am afraid that you will not want to speak to me further, so I want to say something beforehand. If you feel strongly toward Miss Bennet, then you should go see her. It does not matter what your sisters think or, for that matter, what I think. You are your own master, and you should do whatever you believe will make you happy. Your own judgment is sufficient. Remember that you were right about Miss Bennet, while I was wrong."

"Darcy, I am quite aware that I am my own master. I don't

want words of encouragement; I want to know what you know about Miss Bennet."

"Very well. As I said, I recently learned that she was receptive to your attentions last fall and was disappointed by your abrupt departure. I confirmed as much on my recent visit. I misjudged her because she did not display her emotions openly, but she clearly did have feelings for you last fall."

"You are sure about this?"

"Yes."

Bingley was silent for some time. Then his entire attitude seemed to brighten as he said, "Darcy, I must thank you—this is wonderful news."

"Charles, do not thank me yet. There is more. When we were in London in the winter, Miss Bennet called on Miss Bingley. I saw her, and I knew that your sister failed to mention it to you, but I did nothing to correct the miscommunication."

Stunned, Bingley stammered, "She was in London. She called on Caroline. Are you certain?"

"Yes. Your sister even returned the visit."

"Why didn't she tell me? Why didn't you tell me?"

"I knew you were having a difficult time getting over her. I did not think there was any point in your learning of her visit if it would only cause you more pain. I know there is no excuse for my behavior. It was presumptuous of me to make the decision for you, and I apologize for it."

"You admit, though, that you were wrong?"

"Completely."

Bingley began to pace excitedly and said, "Then I cannot hold a grudge. You were wrong not to tell me, but you are correcting your mistake now. My sisters are another matter. I suspect that their motives may have been different. I cannot think of that now, though I will deal with them later... Darcy, what must Miss Bennet think of me?"

"I think the only way to determine that is to go to her."

Before he could continue, Darcy's butler entered, attempting to keep pace with a visitor who had pushed past him as they entered the room. The butler stammered the introduction, "Lady Catherine de Bourgh."

Lady Catherine waved the butler off impatiently, stating, "Yes, yes, not now, I think my nephew can recognize me! I have no time for this. Darcy, I must speak to you immediately about a matter of grave concern. I have sent Anne to freshen up. I have just returned from Hertfordshire with the most disturbing news." Noticing Bingley's presence, she turned to him, gave him a dismissive look, and said in a commanding tone, "You will excuse us, sir."

Shocked and struggling to maintain his composure, Darcy asked in as even a tone as possible, "You were in Hertfordshire. Why?"

"Darcy, I see no reason to parade our personal business in front of this stranger. But I will tell you this: You owe me a great deal. I went there to stop a rumor of the most alarming nature from spreading. But you are not safe yet. We must act quickly before there is any further damage to your name." Bingley turned to Darcy with his mouth open, but before he could speak, Lady Catherine said, "Sir, I will ask you again, excuse us immediately."

Darcy's head began to reel. He could barely register his aunt's words, and as comprehension began to dawn, he could feel his temper rise. With her insult to Bingley, he had endured enough. "Madam, I would take care not to treat a guest in my house in such a manner. You have been introduced to Mr. Bingley many times before." In a softer tone, he turned to Bingley and said, "Charles, I am so sorry for this intrusion. I must speak to my aunt. Could you please wait for me in the next room? I promise I will not be long."

Bingley rose but hesitated. "Darcy, what is this about? Does this have something to do with Miss Bennet? I demand to know."

Lady Catherine interrupted, "Then you have heard the vile rumor too? Darcy, how could you let this happen? I know she must have used her feminine wiles on you, but have you no control?"

Lady Catherine's words struck Darcy with the force of an actual blow. He clenched his fists in response but willed himself to relax as he drew Bingley aside before he could protest. "Charles, I beg of you, it is not how it sounds. Please give me a moment to discern what has happened. I promise I will tell you everything."

Indignant, Bingley rose to his full height and looked Darcy in the eye. "Sir, you can be assured that I will insist upon it."

"Thank you, Charles. I promise this is not as it seems." Darcy then instructed his butler to escort Bingley to the parlor and make him comfortable. After Darcy walked him out, he turned to his aunt, who had seated herself behind his desk. Summoning all the control in his possession to keep from lashing out at her, he inquired in a resolute tone, "Madam, what is this about?"

"Darcy, several evenings ago I was shocked to hear that there was a rumor circulating in Hertfordshire that you had made an offer of marriage to one of Mr. Collins's cousins. I immediately knew that it must be a falsehood both because you are promised to Anne and because I know you were raised to know better than to ever consider such an unfortunate alliance. Please tell me that there is no truth to the rumor so that we can make plans to stop it from circulating any farther."

Worried about her allusion, Darcy simply replied, "Madam, I have never given idle gossip any credence, and I suggest that you do not either."

"Darcy, that is hardly the answer I am seeking. I insist you tell me at once that this rumor is groundless. I know that you would never consider connecting your name with that of the Bennets of Hertfordshire. The very idea is preposterous. But I need to know whether you did anything to compromise this Jane Bennet so that she could make a claim on you."

Staring at her in disbelief, Darcy replied with forced calm, "Madam, you have gone too far. I owe you no explanation for my behavior."

In a fit of pique, Lady Catherine spat, "How can you say such a thing? I am almost your nearest relation. Moreover, you forget that as Anne's mother I have a very real interest in knowing how her future husband conducts himself." The pair stared at each other until Lady Catherine faltered. She then added in a flustered but softer tone, "Darcy, please, at a time like this we need to work together. Do not be concerned over anything you may have done. I visited the Bennets, and I am quite sure that with the right inducement we will be able to smooth over any improprieties that may have occurred. I always thought Elizabeth Bennet's attitude was impertinent; it was nothing compared to that of her mother. She is an utterly worthless woman."

Darcy head was spinning. At least his proposal to Elizabeth was still secret. But his aunt had visited the Bennets! What had she done? It was not bad enough that she felt free to speak to him in this manner; she apparently also presumed to speak on his behalf in Hertfordshire. His mind immediately flew to what Elizabeth's reaction to all of this must have been. Mortified, he turned to his aunt, resolved to learn all that had occurred. "You visited Longbourn? What happened there?"

"I went there to put a stop to the despicable rumor that you intended to marry this Jane Bennet. She was not home, but her mother was there, and I made it clear to her that such a union would never occur. I let them know that you were engaged to Anne."

"You told them what? Who did you tell this to?"

"Darcy, I already told you. I spoke with Mrs. Bennet and two of her daughters, Miss Elizabeth and another girl. That is not important. What is important is that I told them you were engaged. I made it very clear that their scheme to trap you would never work and that it was utter folly for a girl without connections or fortune to aspire to the position of mistress of Pemberley. I appealed to their sense of honor and duty, but the mother's reaction was utterly disgraceful. There is nothing to do for it. You must publish your banns with Anne immediately so that everyone will realize it was the Bennets who started the rumor in the hope of forcing your hand. Once you are formally engaged, Jane Bennet will look like the fortune hunter she is. I would be surprised if anyone ever condescends to visit her family again."

Darcy stared at his aunt, unable to fathom what he should say, where he should start. He ultimately settled on asking, "Did Miss Elizabeth say anything to you?"

"Darcy, you are missing the point entirely. It does not matter what anyone in that family said, you must make it clear to this Jane Bennet person that she will never succeed in her plan to trap you. You and Anne have waited far too long. You must formalize your engagement."

Darcy bowed his head and momentarily closed his eyes. Things could not be worse. He could not even begin to understand what could be done to correct the damage his aunt had caused. He had hoped to take his leave of Elizabeth with a shred of dignity by graciously disappearing. But instead, his aunt had most likely reopened every wound he had inflicted on her pride by forcibly reminding her of the objections he had voiced in his proposal. In the process, his aunt had no doubt also sullied Miss Bennet's innocent character without any basis. That his aunt should attack her after she had treated him with such generosity was beyond all insult. How could he ever make amends to either of them?

There was, however, one mistake he could rectify. He needed only the courage to do so. He sat down across from his aunt and attempted to gain control of his temper. "Aunt Catherine, you said that you had a right to know about my affairs, and you are right in one regard. For too long, I have kept my feelings to myself about marriage in a misguided effort to spare you and your daughter pain. I see now that this was a mistake. I have no intention of making an offer of marriage to Miss Bennet. But by the same token, I also have no desire to propose to Anne. I love her as my cousin, but nothing more. I know that you have long hoped that such a union would be possible, but I intend to marry whom I see fit in the hope of securing my own happiness. I am sorry if this gives you pain, but I feel I must be honest with you."

"Darcy, this is not to be borne. It was the favorite wish of your mother to see you united to Anne. Will you defile her memory?"

"I hope to do no such thing, but I am resolved in this. I will not ask Anne to be my wife."

"You are not fooling me. This has something to do with that Bennet woman. She has turned your head. Do duty and family honor mean so little to you? Would you marry beneath your station and make a mockery of your name? Hear me clearly, Darcy. She will never be accepted into our family or, for that matter, into the best circles of society. Would you risk such censure? And what of your heirs? Do you feel no responsibility in that regard?"

Standing, Darcy held up his hand for her to stop. "Aunt, I will tell you for the last time that I have no intentions toward Miss Jane Bennet and never have. I insist that you stop disparaging her name immediately. She is a lovely girl who does not deserve your slander. Moreover, I want you to know that this misunderstanding concerning Miss Bennet does not have anything to do with my decision regarding Anne. When I was last at Rosings, I thought a great deal about my mother's and your desire that I marry Anne. I knew then that I could not in good conscience seek an alliance with her, and I now know that I will never change my mind. It would be unfair to Anne and to myself. I could never be a husband to her in the proper way, and our union would eventually only cause us both pain. I am sorry to disappoint you, but I owe you no further explanation. The subject is closed."

"I am appalled. That, sir, is the final straw. We will go as soon as we have rested and the chaise is ready. I am seriously displeased."

"I am sorry to hear it, but if you are resolved to go, then I must see to my other guest."

CONFESSIONS AND DECISIONS

DARCY EXITED THE LIBRARY and leaned against the wall. He took a deep breath to steady himself and then called for a servant to see to his aunt's needs. Their argument had not upset him so much as it had exhausted him. He regretted the misunderstanding that had triggered their exchange, and he was disappointed their discussion had turned so acrimonious. Despite this, he felt an overwhelming sense of relief that he had finally made himself clear about Anne. It made him realize his family's expectations had weighed more heavily on him than he had thought and that even when he had resolved to ask Elizabeth to marry him, he had not quite put their concerns behind him. There was no going back now though, and the knowledge gave him a sense of liberation. While he respected his mother's wish, he had to be his own man, and he hoped that if she were here now, she would understand.

Before entering the parlor, he paused to collect himself. He did not want his turmoil over his aunt to stop him from giving Bingley his undivided attention. He was unsure how he would fix the damage his aunt had caused, but he knew he should start by making sure that Bingley returned to Hertfordshire. As he entered the room, he saw Bingley pacing in front of the fireplace. Before Darcy could speak, Bingley asked in a hurried manner, "Darcy, what is going on? Why did your aunt go to Hertfordshire, and why did she imply that there was some sort of malicious gossip about Miss Bennet?"

"Charles, I will try to explain, but you have to calm down. There has been an unfortunate misunderstanding, but it does not change anything I said to you before about Miss Bennet. Please, will you sit down?"

Bingley reluctantly complied.

"When I was in Hertfordshire, I arranged to speak to Miss Bennet privately, and unfortunately someone must have misunderstood my intentions for doing so. My aunt somehow heard about it and got the idea that I was planning to propose to her. You know that my aunt has always held the misguided notion that I would marry my cousin Anne. In an effort to see that plan to fruition, she went to Hertfordshire to give her objections to the match."

"She did what? Darcy, are you telling me that everyone in Hertfordshire thinks you are going to propose to Miss Bennet and that your aunt spoke to her about it? How could this have happened? I must know."

"Charles, I can see you are upset. Please let me explain. While I was in Hertfordshire I wanted to talk to Miss Bennet to see if I could correct the mistake I made about her in the fall. The only way I could speak to her about it was in private, so I asked her to walk with me to Meryton. You know how her mother is. She got the wrong idea about my intentions. After that, I do not know how the rumor spread, but it did. My aunt eventually heard it and took matters into her own hands. I am very sorry, but I did nothing wrong in asking her to walk out with me."

"Darcy, this is simply too much. You invited me here to tell me that you were wrong about Miss Bennet, and you have urged me to court her. Now I find out that everyone is expecting you to propose to her. What am I supposed to think?"

"Charles, I know this must be difficult, and I am sorry for it, but you must believe me. I did nothing to compromise Miss Bennet, and I have no interest in her as a suitor."

"Darcy, I would like to believe you, but I must be blunt. Your story does not ring true. I still do not understand why you decided to go to Hertfordshire in the first place. You say you previously learned that you were mistaken about Miss Bennet's feelings for me last fall, but you give no explanation. Given what I now know, it seems more likely that you went there to court her yourself, and when she made it clear she did not prefer you, you decided that I could have her back. I suppose I should be grateful for the gesture, but forgive me if I am not!"

"Charles, that is utter nonsense. I asked you to accompany me there. You were the one who refused to go."

"That may well be. But, Darcy, I do not know what to think. On the heels of discovering that you and my sisters deceived me about Miss Bennet this winter, I hear this. My faith is shaken."

Darcy began to pace again and then abruptly stopped. He stood before Bingley and said, "Charles, you are right. By deceiving you, I violated your trust, and I can see why you would be reluctant to believe me now. But you are wrong. I have never held Miss Bennet in special regard. I did have my own reasons for not wanting you to return to Netherfield, but they are not what you believe. At the very least, I owe you a full explanation. My accursed pride has kept me from telling you this for far too long. Will you hear me out?"

Bingley indicated that Darcy should proceed. In response, Darcy paced some more and finally settled in front of Bingley. He turned his gaze to the window as he spoke. "I suppose the seeds of this misunderstanding were sown when we first went to Hertfordshire. I had not been at Netherfield long before I came to realize that I had a strong attraction for someone in the neighborhood. At first I thought it was a passing interest, but I soon found myself bewitched. I began to think of her during my every waking hour, and I often dreamed of her. She was everything that is lovely. But instead of showing my interest and courting her, I deemed her an unacceptable candidate for marriage because she lacked both social connections and a fortune. I thought that my position required me to marry someone from the highest levels of society. I had been taught that I owed as much to my family and to my name. So I foolishly fought the attraction. I tried to never let my feelings for her show, not to her or to anyone else. I forced myself to accept that I would never have her and sought to minimize my contact with her in the misguided hope that I could forget her. Unfortunately for both of us, at the same time, you had become enamored of her elder sister. At the Netherfield Ball, I could resist temptation no longer, so I asked her to dance. During the ball, I came to realize everyone in the neighborhood believed you would soon be united with Miss Bennet. At the time, I truly believed that Miss Bennet held you in no special regard, and as a result, I followed you to London with your sisters to convince you of that fact. In leaving, I resolved that I would never see Miss Elizabeth Bennet again and vowed to put her out of my mind."

The quiet was deafening until Bingley exclaimed, "Darcy, I am astonished. Miss Elizabeth Bennet. I had no idea."

"I am not surprised. I kept it a secret from everyone, including her. But, Charles, there is more. When Miss Bennet visited your sister in the winter, I wondered briefly if I had been too hasty in judging her. But I did not act. I let your sisters deceive you. I did it because I wanted to spare you any further pain, but I was also cognizant of the fact that if you were reunited with Miss Bennet, I might be thrown into the company of her sister again. At the time, I believed I was trying to protect you, but in hindsight, I understand that you have every right to question my motives."

As Bingley listened in silence, Darcy began to pace again. "I spent the following months in, I believe, the same manner as you: trying to forget our visit to Hertfordshire. In the spring I took my annual pilgrimage to visit my aunt in Kent. I hoped it would put a little more distance between Miss Elizabeth and myself. To my shock, when I arrived, she was there visiting her friend Mrs. Collins at Rosings' parsonage. As soon as I saw her, I knew that all of my vows to forget her were for naught."

"Is that how you found out about Miss Bennet: you talked to Miss Elizabeth about it?"

"Not exactly, we never really had a conversation about it. We exchanged harsh words, and afterward I wrote her a letter explaining myself."

"Darcy, you wrote her? How is it that you felt comfortable enough to take such a liberty?"

"At the time, writing to her seemed like the least offensive option. But I have skipped some of the story. I only wrote to her as I was leaving Kent." Looking steadily out the window, Darcy continued. "Before that, I visited with her on several occasions while I was at my aunt's, but I never told her how I felt. When I was not with her, however, I could not get her out of my mind. I knew I loved her. How could I not? She is charming, beautiful, intelligent, and she has the most engaging disposition. Yet despite all this, I spent my time constantly debating whether I could overlook her low connections and the improprieties that her family often exhibited. I ultimately determined that I could not live without her, so I proposed to her one night when I found her alone."

"Darcy, you're engaged to Miss Elizabeth? I cannot believe it. You should have told me sooner."

"Charles, I am not engaged. She refused me."

"She refused you!"

"Oh, yes, most vehemently. Apparently I am the last man she could ever be prevailed upon to marry. I had spent so much time absorbed in my own inner struggles that I never bothered to notice that she detests me. When she refused me, I foolishly asked her why. She gave me a long list of reasons, the particulars of which I will not trouble you with. But, apparently, Wickham had ingratiated himself with her and concocted a tale about an injustice I committed against him. More significantly, she could not forgive me for having irreparably hurt her sister by separating you from her when she returned your affections. Apparently, Miss Elizabeth had pieced together my role in all of this before I proposed to her, and it gave her yet another reason to dislike me. We quarreled over it and other matters, and I left after some very cruel words were exchanged.

"The next day, I wrote to her to explain myself in regard to her sister and also to defend myself against Wickham's slanders. I then left Kent. But I was troubled by the mistake I had made and the harm I had caused you and Miss Bennet. I tried to get you to visit Hertfordshire so that I could undo the damage I had done. But you were so adamant in your refusal to go; I thought it best for me to go there first to see for myself whether there was any hope of a reconciliation between you.

"Charles, I must tell you that I am relieved to finally speak of all of this, and I hope I have adequately explained what happened. But I am under no illusions about my behavior. I know what I have done has severely damaged our friendship. I sincerely apologize for all the harm I have caused you. I will understand if you never want to see me again, and I will importune you no further in that regard. But before I take my leave, I do want to encourage you one more time to visit Miss Bennet. I honestly do not know whether she will still receive you, but at least you should try. I know my aunt has complicated matters, but if you still care for her, you should risk it. I know that if there was still hope for me, I would not let the opportunity go by."

"Darcy, I hardly know what to say… I still cannot comprehend it all. When you talked to Miss Bennet, what did to you say to her and what was Miss Elizabeth's reaction to you coming to Longbourn?"

"Well, before I spoke to Miss Bennet I had assumed that Elizabeth—Miss Elizabeth—would have confided in her about what happened in Kent, and I was correct for the most part. She knew of my proposal and her sister's refusal, but she was not aware of my role or your sisters' role in urging you to leave Hertfordshire. So I confessed to her what happened. She was actually most gracious. She had every right to be livid with me, but she understood how I could have misconstrued her regard for you. She is truly a remarkable woman. I can understand why you thought so highly of her, and I apologize for not seeing it sooner. I think what troubled Miss Bennet most were your sisters' objections to her. She does not want to come between you and your family."

As Darcy's countenance grew more somber, he continued, "As to Miss Elizabeth's reaction to me, it was civil and appropriately cold. After the way I treated her, she has every right to dislike me. It was clear from her reaction to me that she wants nothing more to do with me, and I shall grant her that wish."

Both men were silent for a long time as Bingley tried to digest all that he had heard. Darcy watched as Bingley walked to the window and stared out it for several minutes. Bingley finally turned and said, "Darcy, I am still unable to comprehend all that has happened, but one thing is clear. We both must return to Hertfordshire."

"Charles, I am relieved to hear that you are going to go to Netherfield, and I think you should leave as soon as possible. But as to including me in your party, while it is very generous of you, there is no reason for me to go. I believe everyone involved would be happier without me."

"I beg to differ. I would not be happier without you. There are many reasons for you to go, not the least of which is that you owe it to me and Miss Bennet."

Darcy stared in disbelief. "Charles, I am not sure…"

Before he could continue, Bingley interrupted him. "Darcy, I have listened to you speak a great deal today. Given your propensity toward silence, I have heard you talk today more than a whole week's worth of visits. Now, please hear me out. First, I want to apologize to you for thinking that anything inappropriate occurred during your visit with Miss Bennet. I reacted before I knew all the particulars, and I am sorry. In fact, I am exceedingly grateful that you spoke to her. And, Darcy, I also want you to know that I appreciate all that you have just told me. I know it was not easy for you. In return I will also be honest. You are right, I still have very strong feelings for Miss Bennet, and I intend to go to Longbourn to convince her of that. I appreciate that it will be difficult, given my sisters' actions, and I expect the support of my closest friend to help me through it. You said that our friendship has been damaged by your actions, and perhaps it has, but I have never assumed it to be so fragile as not to be able to stand some strain. Have you?"

Darcy looked at his friend for a long moment, humbled by his generosity. He then answered with warmth and gratitude in his voice. "No, Charles, I suppose it is not, and I am honored to call you my friend; nonetheless, I think my presence there might be awkward."

"I grant you that it might be at first. But I am resolved to stay there until I convince Miss Bennet of my regard. I do not intend to make the same mistake twice. Hopefully, she will be able to forgive me and grant me a second chance. And if she does, as my closest friend, it will be natural for you to be in our company. Please do not follow my sisters' lead and make me choose between you and Miss Bennet. If Miss Bennet is concerned about my sisters' opinion of her, it will help to demonstrate to her that there is at least one person in my closest circle who approves the match and is comfortable in her presence."

"Charles, I am not sure. I think my presence will impede your progress, not aid it, especially since my aunt's visit."

"It is your aunt's visit that I am thinking of mostly. If everyone in the neighborhood thinks that you had intentions toward Miss Bennet but gave them up after your aunt lodged objections to the match, then your failure to reappear will confirm the truth of the rumor. Your actions will make it look as though you rejected her as unworthy. If, however, you come with me and make it clear that your previous visit was to convey your regard to the Bennets as my friend, then the rumor of your affections toward Miss Bennet will die of its own accord. As I said, you owe it to Miss Bennet and me to come to Netherfield. If you do not, it may damage Miss Bennet's reputation."

"Charles, I see what you are saying, and if that is the case, my sense of honor requires me to return with you, but the idea of staying or becoming comfortable as a visitor to you and Miss Bennet is unrealistic. After what my aunt has done, her family has every reason to dislike me, and more importantly, after all that has happened between Miss Elizabeth and myself, we will never be comfortable together. She will never forgive me for what I have done."

"Darcy, how can you be sure? You said Wickham had told her some lies about you and that you explained the truth to her in a letter. Did she believe you?"

"Yes, she did. When I visited, she let me know that she now understood Wickham's true character and no longer harbored any doubts about my actions toward him."

"Well then, there it is. Her only other real objection concerned Miss Bennet and myself. She cannot continue to hold it against you now that you are helping reunite us."

"No. But, Charles, she will never forgive me for the damage I have caused."

"But why not? Apparently, Miss Bennet and I have each forgiven you, and we were the direct victims of the events that unfolded. If we can forgive you, then surely Miss Elizabeth can do the same. Or do you not consider her to be a generous person?"

"No, of course I do. But that is not the point. Besides, she has many more objections to me than just these two things. I insulted her during my proposal, and I also insulted her family. You have no idea of the stupid things I said to her."

"You may be right, Darcy. I do not know everything that has passed between you, but it is clear from what you have said to me today that you are still in love with her. Don't you think it would be worth trying to convince her to forgive you—at least enough to let you start over? Maybe you won't win her immediately as your bride, but you could at least become friends."

"Charles, I will do whatever you want me to in order to help you secure Miss Bennet's affections, and if that includes trying to make peace with Miss Elizabeth so that we can all be in the same room together, I will do that for you. But I harbor no illusions about ever winning Miss Elizabeth's regard. The best thing for me to do is to learn to accept that fact."

"Darcy, not five minutes ago you said that if you were in my place, you would not let the opportunity go by to attempt to win Miss Bennet back. It seems to me that you are in the same place. I may go back to Hertfordshire, risk all, and fail. But it will be worth it because I care so deeply for Miss Bennet. Why is the risk not the same for you?"

"Bingley, our situations are vastly different. You—"

Before Darcy could finish, Bingley interrupted him again.

"Listen, Darcy, I do not expect you to make a decision now about events that may not occur, and you need not promise that you will stay on at Netherfield. It is enough that you have agreed to come with me in the first place. I simply ask that you think about everything else that I have said and leave the option open. Right now I think we will have our hands full getting to Longbourn, and undoing the damage my sisters have caused and erasing the effects of your aunt's visit. That said, how soon can you leave?"

"Immediately."

SECOND CHANCES

THE MORNING AFTER THEY arrived at Netherfield, Bingley and Darcy set out to visit Longbourn. They left as early as civility would allow. During the previous day's long carriage ride to Hertfordshire, they had decided it would be best if they called together. Bingley would apologize for his long absence and hope for a moment to talk to Miss Bennet alone. Darcy would attempt to dispel any rumors that his aunt's visit might have caused. It would be awkward, but there seemed no other course.

As they rode their horses to Longbourn, they were both filled with anxiety. Darcy looked over at Bingley, who was clearly lost in thought. He was somewhat surprised by his sudden silence. He had spent the previous evening listening to Bingley speak almost nonstop about the best strategy to win a second chance with Miss Bennet. Bingley vacillated between making a quick confession of his regard followed by a plea that she forgive his hasty departure last fall to resuming his attentions as if nothing had happened in the hope that she would allow him to proceed without an explanation. Bingley preferred the former option but was concerned both that his behavior would be considered improper and that the logistics of arranging the confession would prove difficult. The latter would be easy to execute, but he worried Miss Bennet might consider his attitude cavalier. As the hours passed, Darcy's tolerance for Bingley's indecision was tempered by the fact that his friend's cheerful demeanor was slowly returning. Bingley remained cautious about his chances of winning Miss Bennet's forgiveness, but his pervasive air of sadness was in retreat. As the fire in the hearth burned itself out, Bingley determined to let his actions be guided by how they were received.

Watching his friend now on his way to Miss Bennet, Darcy could not help but feel a stab of jealousy. He was truly happy that Bingley was attempting a reconciliation with Miss Bennet and wished him every degree of success. He and Miss Bennet deserved no less. Nonetheless, he could not help but lament that he was foreclosed from seeking the same absolution from Elizabeth. It seemed bitterly unfair that he should find the means of his happiness only to know that it was permanently out of his reach. He knew his quickening pulse was in anticipation of seeing her again. If only the encounter had the promise of ending well.

It would be the height of arrogance to assume that he could expect a second chance with Elizabeth, and he knew the danger of allowing his pride to rule him unchecked. The difference between his situation and Bingley's was very real, and he would be a fool to lose sight of that.

Nonetheless, there was a part of him that was spurred on by Bingley's hopefulness. When he looked objectively at Bingley's situation, it seemed reasonable that Bingley would try to win Miss Bennet's regard. His determination spoke well of his devotion. Bingley had told him he had no real alternative in the matter, since he would never be happy until he secured her hand. Was not the same true of him? He knew that his attempts at putting Elizabeth out of his mind were futile. Was not Bingley's willingness to pursue Miss Bennet without any real encouragement actually evidence of his ability to put his pride aside because he was doing so without any assurance that he would ultimately be accepted? Maybe the real difference between his and Bingley's situation was that Bingley was willing to pursue Miss Bennet even if it ended in an embarrassing rebuff. Was his resignation over losing Elizabeth simply his pride at work again?

No. Those were the daydreams of a lovesick schoolboy, not the master of Pemberley. Part of being a man of importance in the world was accepting its realities. His father had taught him as much. Didn't Elizabeth specifically say that he could not have made the offer of his hand in any possible way that would have tempted her to accept it?

But, then again, when she had said those things, she had been laboring under Wickham's deceptions and anger over her sister's loss. She clearly no longer believed Wickham, and she must have seen from his own recent behavior that he truly regretted his actions toward her sister. Why did he begrudge Elizabeth the charity to forgive him? The fact that she had tried to thank him at the assembly must have meant something. He knew she was a compassionate person. That was how Wickham was able to weave his lies, by falsely appealing to her sense of justice and fairness. Even if Elizabeth could not forgive him immediately, maybe it was not unreasonable for him to expect a pardon if Bingley eventually convinced Miss Bennet to forgive him and accept his offer. Maybe he simply needed to give her more time.

No, that was also false optimism. It was his manners that she believed demonstrated his arrogance, his conceit, and his selfish disdain of the feelings of others. It was his lack of civility that formed the groundwork of her immovable dislike of him. Given her low opinion of him, it was clearly folly to believe that he could ever convince her otherwise. As they approached the house, Darcy continued his internal debate, preoccupied by his conflicting emotions.

Inside Longbourn, the morning routine was progressing in its usual chaotic fashion. Elizabeth had woken early, dressed, and fixed her hair before her younger sisters commanded the attentions of their shared maid. As she took a quick walk in the garden before breakfast, her mind wandered to the dramatic events of the past few days. If the memory of Lady Catherine's visit had not been so humiliating, she would have found her mother's clash with her humorous. Here were two women who inevitably got their own way—one through the privilege of her position and the other by virtue of her unwillingness to heed anyone else's counsel—fighting fiercely over the propriety of a nonexistent match. If it had ended there, she might have found the absurdity of the situation amusing.

Her father certainly did. He had half-listened in a detached manner to her mother's vivid account of the exchange and then patiently heard Jane's heartfelt plea that Mr. Darcy not be blamed for the misunderstanding as he had neither pursued her nor intimated any special regard for her. Her father simply laughed and shook his head at the disparity between his wife's and daughter's descriptions. He then dismissed the entire affair as unimportant with a wave of his hand. If this young man truly wanted Jane, he would ignore his aunt's wishes, and if he did not, then Jane was better off without him. He then advised his wife to forget the episode, as Jane's honor had not been compromised and it was simply another example of human folly at its best. Their neighbors would forget the details of it as soon as someone did something more embarrassing.

Elizabeth considered her father's advice both cynical and naïve. It had barely taken a day for news of the encounter to spread, as Lady Catherine had apprised her parson of the reason for her trip before she left Kent, and Mrs. Bennet could not help but lament the details of the conversation to Mrs. Philips when she visited to inquire of the matter after being informed of it by Mrs. Lucas. Since then, there had been no indication that discussion of the visit would abate any time soon.

Try as she might, Elizabeth found it impossible to forget the encounter or its ramifications. She could not help but take offense at her neighbors' speculation that Mr. Darcy had abandoned Jane because of the inferiority of her station and connections. She knew it was idle gossip that did not deserve her consideration, but it struck too close to home. In his declarations to her at Hunsford, he had said that he had struggled against his attachment for her because he knew he would be going against the express wishes of his family. This concern suddenly seemed less condescending when juxtaposed against his aunt's aggressive and hostile attack of Jane. The manner in which he had addressed her was still unacceptable, but the fact that this concern was foremost in his mind seemed a little less arrogant. She wondered what would have happened if his aunt had lodged the same vehement opposition to her, invoking his departed mother's name in the process. Would he have abandoned her as the neighborhood now believed he had abandoned Jane? She felt an irrational sense of discomfiture as she concluded that he most likely would have.

She wondered why it mattered to her. How colossal was her own pride that she demanded his loyalty in a situation of her own conjecture? She had refused him after all. It was no longer her place to feel rejection over the possibility that his family's interference would have swayed him to reconsider. It was foolish fancy on her part to think about it. Yet, of all the thoughts Lady Catherine's visit produced, this was the one that stuck.

She did think it amusing that, in retrospect, the only pleasant thought she could salvage from the visit came from her mother's behavior. Maybe that was a little too charitable. After all, she blamed her mother for creating the situation by assuming affection where none existed and for causing the gossip that ultimately brought Lady Catherine to Hertfordshire. Moreover, her mother's motivation for standing up to Lady Catherine was a source of utter mortification for Elizabeth, as she knew it sprang solely from Mr. Darcy's generous income and not from any respect she had for him. Nonetheless, her defense of Jane—and by extension herself—was laudable. That her mother thought a man of any station would be lucky to win the hand of one of her daughters spoke well of her. If she adjusted her opinion of her mother to account for her simplistic world view, she could not help but value her loyalty. This seemed especially so when contrasted with her father's indifference. If she had accepted Mr. Darcy's proposal in Kent, apparently her mother would have been her first line of defense against his aunt, while Mr. Bennet would simply enjoy the ridiculousness of the situation it created.

Despite these somewhat charitable thoughts toward her mother, it did not change the fact that she did not want to be long in her company. Since Lady Catherine's abrupt departure, her mother could barely tolerate her frayed nerves, and her mother's discomfort always had a way of spreading to the entire family. Moreover, since her mother had unequivocally determined that only Mr. Darcy's return could placate her, Elizabeth reasoned that there was no point attempting to comfort her, as she knew he would not be returning anytime soon. By now, Mr. Darcy had undoubtedly told Bingley of his interference, and his confession would, in effect, relieve him of any further responsibility in the affair. After his aunt's visit, he certainly would want to distance himself from her family and the gossip it had created. She could not blame him for that, but it made her once again hope for Bingley's quick return. If he came and her sister accepted his belated attentions, it would go a long way to diffuse the furor over Lady Catherine's visit. She did not want to consider Jane's position if Bingley also failed to return.

It was possible they might occasionally see Mr. Darcy if Mr. Bingley eventually secured Jane's affections, but there were too many variables to predict whether it was likely. Even if he did occasionally visit, her unconventional acquaintance with him was for all other purposes at an end. She felt surprisingly unsettled by the notion. Maybe it was because he had taken his leave before she could either properly explain herself or thank him for helping her sister. Truth be told, she felt some unresolved regret for her harsh words in Kent.

Knowing him had evoked more questions than answers,

and the uncertainty bothered her. She found herself wondering what his future would bring. Would he acquiesce to his aunt's demands? His proposal to her was proof that he never intended to marry his cousin, but perhaps he would change his mind when his aunt finally caught up with him.

It suddenly struck her that they had something in common. For very different reasons, he faced the same familial pressure to marry for the benefit of his family that she had battled when she refused Mr. Collins. His need to marry for affection apparently matched her own, as he would not have chosen her, given the inevitable opposition he would face, unless it was paramount to him. In that regard, she felt sorry she could not have fulfilled his wish, as she certainly understood his need.

She also had to admit she must have underestimated the strength of his attachment, as it ultimately compelled him to undertake what she now understood was the fairly provocative step of asking for her hand. While she still could not imagine returning his affections, she did feel the compliment of his regard more acutely. The realization made her recognize that she was no longer angry at him and that, while his pride was certainly a major part of his personality, it was not the only emotion he possessed. She immediately thought again of his good-bye to her at the assembly and his sad countenance. It made her realize that, after all that had happened between them, she now also wished him every happiness in return.

Sobered by her walk, Elizabeth settled in the dining room to partake of a light breakfast. She hoped her mother would allow Jane and her to take a quick walk to Meryton so they could gain some respite from her laments about Lady Catherine's visit and Jane's chances of securing Mr. Darcy. Elizabeth's hope of an early departure was dashed when she learned that Jane had acquiesced to Lydia's demand that their maid redo her hair before starting Jane's because Lydia had decided that the original style she selected no longer pleased her. As Elizabeth waited for both her mother and Jane to finish dressing, her father and Mary joined her at breakfast. It was not many minutes later that visitors were escorted in.

As Mrs. Hill announced Mr. Bingley and Mr. Darcy, Elizabeth's face blushed scarlet. She had hoped for Mr. Bingley's return, but never expected Mr. Darcy's. She knew it was irrational, but she could not help but feel that she had somehow been caught in her ruminations about him. As a result, her eyes impulsively flew to his. Seeing her so becomingly flustered, Darcy, in his nervousness, could not help but smile at her as he bowed. She returned the acknowledgment with a nervous dip of her head.

Mr. Bennet interrupted the exchange. "Ah, good morning, gentlemen. I must say, this is a pleasant surprise. I did not expect to see you in the neighborhood, Mr. Bingley, or for that matter you, Mr. Darcy. And if I might add, I did not expect to see you both here together. We are indeed fortunate. Will you not join us for breakfast?"

An uncomfortable silence ensued. Elizabeth shuddered as she recognized the unmistakable signs that her father intended to have some sport with this awkward situation. Darcy, for his part, had instinctively paused to let Bingley answer first, as was their unspoken custom in these sorts of social exchanges. To his surprise, Bingley acted as if he had not heard Mr. Bennet and failed to respond altogether. Instead, he continuously scanned the room in a preoccupied manner, obviously searching for an absent occupant. Darcy suppressed the temptation to roll his eyes or nudge Bingley and answered for them both. "Mr. Bennet, thank you. That is very kind of you. We have eaten, but some tea would be welcome. I do apologize if we have called too early?" Darcy sat across from Elizabeth with Bingley at his right.

"No, not at all, Mr. Darcy, you are most welcome. We love visitors anytime, day or night. I must say we have had some very interesting ones lately."

At this, Elizabeth attempted to change the subject. "Mr. Bingley, when did you return to Netherfield?" Instead of answering, Bingley simply continued to fiddle with the teacup in front of him until he sensed all eyes upon him. He looked up and said, "Oh, I'm sorry."

Elizabeth quickly looked to her father, who had shot up his eyebrows at Bingley's inattentiveness. Sensing the danger, she said, "Mr. Bingley, I was just wondering when you had arrived at Netherfield."

Bingley simply replied, "Oh… um… yesterday." He then continued to absentmindedly examine the door behind Elizabeth's head.

As Elizabeth stared at him, she realized that his obvious nervousness at the prospect of seeing Jane again was making conversation with him impossible. That left only the recalcitrant Mr. Darcy and Mary, who was reading at the table, to circumvent her father from steering the conversation toward either Lady Catherine's unexpected interview or why both of Jane's supposed suitors had called together. The idea of discussing Lady Catherine's visit with Mr. Darcy in attendance sent Elizabeth into a panic. In an attempt to relieve both her own and Mr. Bingley's anxiety, Elizabeth decided to address the source obliquely. "Mr.

Bingley," Elizabeth said, with added force to garner his attention, "you must excuse us. We are all running very late this morning. My mother and sisters will be here to greet you directly. I am sure they will all be pleasantly surprised by your visit."

"Oh… oh!" Bingley brightened. "That is quite all right. I can certainly wait for… them. I hope we have not called too early. I am very much looking forward to… their joining us." Having understood her hint, Bingley returned to the study of his teacup as Elizabeth looked on with concern. After several minutes of silence, Elizabeth was startled to hear Mr. Darcy's voice.

"Miss Bennet, we actually arrived before dinner yesterday. The roads were in quite good condition, and we made very good time. Given that the trees were in bloom, it was a very pleasant trip."

His effort was rewarded by a genuine smile, which made his pulse quicken. Despite his previous reflections that his uninvited presence would be a further burden to Elizabeth, when he saw how poorly things were going, between Bingley's inattention and her father's innuendo, he could not abandon her to the awkward silence and thought even his unwelcome conversation would be better than nothing. Her obvious relief at his attempt emboldened him to try his hand further. "I noticed your garden on the way here. Has the weather in the past few days been as mild as it is today? It would be a shame if you were not able to partake in its pleasures."

"Yes, thank you for asking. On the whole, the weather has been quite good. I have been a regular visitor. As a matter of fact, I just returned from a tour of our garden earlier this morning. As you said, the trees are exquisite this time of year. It was quite lovely."

"I am glad to hear it. I know you enjoy walking out." Elizabeth sat in surprise. Mr. Darcy's alliance in this uncomfortable situation was more than unexpected. His attention to the flow of conversation was a marked improvement from his visits last fall when he was usually responsible for the lapse in discourse. That he would be a help in that regard when he had every incentive to succumb to the embarrassment of the situation made her all the more grateful for his effort. As she smiled at him in gratitude, their eyes met, and he gave her a tiny shrug and a fleeting smile to apologize for the inanity of his conversation and the awkwardness of the visit. She raised her eyebrows to indicate the same and asked, "And what of the weather in London? Has it been as pleasant?"

"Yes, it has. Thank you for asking." After a pause he added, "When I first returned to London, we had some rain. I had hoped to visit Mr. Bingley directly, but he had been called away to Scarborough, so I waited until his return three days ago. I think the wet weather made the wait seem longer than it actually was."

Understanding the implication of his statement, she replied, "Yes, we had some rain as well, and it did seem to make the time pass very slowly."

Before more could be said, Mrs. Bennet entered the room with a great deal of flourish and with Kitty in tow. Both men rose to greet her. "My dear Mr. Darcy, how very good to see you. I was just saying yesterday how welcome a visit from you would be. Jane will be down in a moment. Oh my! Mr. Bingley! I was not informed. I... What... a pleasure it is to see you, sir."

Upon hearing Jane's name, Bingley seemed to emerge from his stupor. As he bowed to Mrs. Bennet, he said, "Thank you.

The pleasure is mine. I have been meaning…" Rather than continue his thought, though, he fell silent as Jane entered the room. His obvious preoccupation effectively silenced everyone else as they watched him watch Jane demurely move behind an unoccupied chair with her eyes cast downward. Mr. Bingley then sprang to her side to pull her chair out for her. She nodded her acknowledgment without looking directly at him.

Mr. Bennet motioned for his wife to sit. Mrs. Bennet, however, stood transfixed, trying to catch Jane's eye, all the while moving her head slightly in Mr. Darcy's direction to indicate that she should acknowledge his presence. Mr. Bennet eventually tired of the spectacle and said, "Mrs. Bennet, please, let us all eat. You have not missed much yet. Mr. Darcy and Elizabeth have been discussing the comparative merits of the weather in Hertfordshire and London, but I think they have exhausted the intricacies of that topic. Am I right, Elizabeth?"

Elizabeth looked to her father in disbelief, amazed that he would choose to jest so inappropriately at a time like this. She momentarily shut her eyes and then said, "Father, we were just discussing the gentlemen's trip from London."

"Yes," interrupted Mr. Bingley, "we were. The trip itself was quite pleasant. I do regret, however, that it was so long in coming. It has made me realize that I have been remiss in our acquaintance and have been out of the neighborhood for far too long. I hope to remedy that directly. Please accept my apologies for not having visited your family sooner."

Mr. Bennet stared at Bingley over his spectacles, not quite sure what to make of him. He then added in a perfunctory fashion, "There is no need for apologies, sir."

Bingley bowed his head to Mr. Bennet and said, "Sir, you

are too kind." He then turned to address Mrs. Bennet. As he did, Jane continued to sit quietly by his side, studying her folded hands in her lap. "I was happy to hear from Mr. Darcy after his last visit that you were all well. I hope Mr. Darcy conveyed my regards to you."

Befuddled, Mrs. Bennet stammered, "Yes, he did."

"Good, I am glad. I was sorry I did not accompany him on that visit. But I was relieved to hear from him afterward that you were all in good health. It seems far too long since I had the pleasure of seeing you all." Before she could reply, he added, "It is above five months. We have not met since the twenty-sixth of November, when we were all dancing together at Netherfield."

At this, Jane glanced his way. Bingley turned and smiled at her. Jane blushed and looked down. Elizabeth felt an overwhelming sense of relief. *This*, she thought, *is a good enough beginning. Their easy natures and Jane's forgiving heart will bridge the rest.* Suddenly the awkwardness of the situation did not seem so overwhelming. Mr. Bingley's perseverance would ultimately make it obvious that his intentions were the same as last fall, and speculation about Mr. Darcy and his aunt would fade from memory without further fanfare. Elizabeth's reverie was soon interrupted by her mother's voice and the harsh realization that her calculation had neglected to include her mother's involvement.

"Yes, Mr. Bingley, it has been a very long time." Looking pointedly from Mr. Darcy to Mr. Bingley, Mrs. Bennet added in a clipped tone, "Luckily some of our friends have been more constant." Not satisfied with her efforts, she then turned to Mr. Darcy. "Sir, I am very glad you have come. We recently were introduced to your aunt, and I was somewhat concerned from something she said that your plans had changed from our last visit."

Elizabeth flushed with embarrassment and turned to look away, Jane looked up in alarm, and Bingley squirmed uncomfortably in his chair. Mr. Bennet chuckled to himself as Mary and Kitty exchanged a knowing look. Only Mr. Darcy maintained his composure. "Really, madam, I cannot understand your meaning. I do not believe I ever indicated anything of my plans at our last visit, but I am sure that in any event my aunt would have no knowledge of them. Although she is a close relation, she does not speak for me. Unfortunately, she does on occasion overreact and unintentionally give offense. I hope that was not the case, but if it was, please accept my heartfelt apologies on her behalf. I think her age sometimes allows her to forget propriety."

"Yes, yes," continued Mrs. Bennet, "she did seem to be confused about your preferences. I think she believed you were planning to call on your cousin in the near future."

Without flinching, Mr. Darcy continued to calmly look at Mrs. Bennet. "Really, I cannot imagine why; I just saw my cousin Anne when I was in Kent at Easter, and I have no plans to call there again until next year. While I do try to maintain familial connections whenever I can, the running of my estate restricts me from visiting there more than once a year. I think my aunt would wish for more, but I unfortunately cannot oblige her. In the end, I must make my own priorities with the knowledge that it is impossible to please everyone."

Beaming, Mrs. Bennet nodded and concurred. "Very true, sir."

Darcy decided to exert himself to turn the conversation to safer ground. He turned to Mr. Bennet and said, "On my last visit here I was able to conduct some interesting discussions concerning my estate with a Mr. Briggs in Meryton. Mr. Bennet, do you know him? He has some very novel ideas about planting."

Surprised to have been addressed, Mr. Bennet stammered, "Yes, I know him, but I have never had the time to talk to him about his theories."

"You should, sir. He is very interesting. When Bingley told me he intended to return to Netherfield indefinitely, I thought it a good opportunity to further my acquaintance with Mr. Briggs. I have been very interested of late in new ideas about crop rotation. Since Bingley will need to give the management of Netherfield more attention in the future, I also thought I could be of some service to him in that regard as I have more experience. Do you presently leave a field fallow?"

"Actually, I am not sure," replied Mr. Bennet.

"You should look into it, sir. I would be more than happy to ride out with you to survey your fields. You can increase your yield quite handsomely by simply employing a few management techniques."

Somewhat bewildered by the turn of the conversation, Mr. Bennet replied, "Thank you. I will discuss it with my steward."

"But, Mr. Darcy..." began Mrs. Bennet, but this time it was Elizabeth who interrupted her mother and refused to yield the floor.

"Oh, please excuse me, Mama, I was just going to suggest that if Mr. Darcy has such an interest in planting, we should at least show him our garden. He had admired it earlier."

"What a lovely idea," joined Mr. Bingley. Rising, he turned to Jane, extended his arm, and asked, "Miss Bennet, would you do me the honor of taking a turn in the garden with me?"

Taking his arm, Jane replied, "Yes, Mr. Bingley, thank you."

Darcy then inclined his head toward Elizabeth to indicate he would follow her. She nodded and led the way. Mrs. Bennet was left to stare at their retreating figures, deprived of the opportunity to arrange the couples more to her liking. At this moment, Lydia chose to enter the room, complaining loudly that she was going to faint from hunger if she did not eat immediately.

Once outside, Elizabeth and Darcy tacitly agreed to let Jane and Bingley outstrip them. After a few moments of uncomfortable silence, both spoke at once.

Elizabeth then said, "No, Mr. Darcy, please continue. I am sorry to have interrupted you."

"As you wish. I was just going to thank you for your offer to view the garden."

"Oh, you are quite welcome. I thought that we could all do with a change of scenery and that Mr. Bingley might appreciate a more informal setting."

As they both looked at Jane and Bingley, Darcy replied, "Yes, I think you were quite right in that regard." After a pause, he added, "Miss Bennet, I do want to take this opportunity to apologize for my aunt's visit. She came to see me in London, and while I am not sure exactly what she said to your family, I cannot help but assume that she must have given offense. I would have done most anything to spare you and your family from such an unpleasant encounter, but unfortunately I have no power in that regard."

In an arch manner, Elizabeth smiled and said, "I think, sir, it is now my turn to tell you that no apology is necessary. If your aunt did give offense, my mother was complicit in the turn of events that prompted it. As you know too well, I have no control over her. I think we both may have family members who give us pain from time to time. But there is nothing to be done other than simply bear it with whatever grace is possible. At this point, apologies are superfluous."

"I am not sure I can agree with you about the efficacy of an apology, but I will take to heart the insight that our families are more alike in some regards than not."

Surprised by his statement, Elizabeth quickly glanced up at him to see him staring intently at her. Embarrassed by the exchange, she then looked away.

"I should also say," continued Darcy, "that her visit is what prompted mine. I came because I was worried that my aunt might have given rise to a misunderstanding about my intentions toward Miss Bennet. After talking to Bingley about it, I thought the most honorable course was to come here with him to make plain that there was no substance to any rumor of the kind. I apologize if, in the process, my presence has made you uncomfortable."

Elizabeth looked away, slowly formulating her answer. She then looked him in the eye and said, "Since you have been honest, I will take the liberty of being so too, even at the risk of giving offense. While I might have thought a visit from you would have made us both very uncomfortable, your help inside just now made me feel quite the opposite. I truly appreciate the effort you have shown in coming here under these circumstances." Looking significantly at Jane and Bingley, Elizabeth added, "I think we are both united toward the same goal."

"Yes, I quite agree."

He was rewarded with a smile. Elizabeth then added, "I must say, I was quite impressed at the way you handled my mother's inquiries. I think she does not know what to make of you."

Unsure how to respond to such a statement, Darcy simply

smiled in return. After a pause, Elizabeth asked, "Your aunt, though, must have been relieved to hear that the rumor about my sister was not true?"

"Actually, I do not think my aunt was at all pleased with our visit. It was a conversation long overdue, and I think she is unaccustomed to not getting her way."

With a quizzical look, Elizabeth asked, "But you must have let her know that she need not fear an alliance between you and Jane?"

"Yes, I did make that abundantly clear. But my aunt will never be satisfied until she is able to arrange every detail to her liking, and I had to disappoint her in that regard. I think our relationship will be in disrepair until she can accept that I am my only master."

Blushing at having elicited such a personal response, Elizabeth hastily added, "I am sorry, sir; I did not mean to pry. You owe me no explanation."

"No, I… it is I who have overburdened you with the workings of my family. I would suggest that we return to the house, but I think Mr. Bingley would think it too soon."

Relieved to have lightened the air, Elizabeth smiled broadly and said, "Yes, I think you are quite perceptive in that regard."

"If I do not ask too much, maybe you could give me that tour of the garden that you mentioned?"

Elizabeth blushed, tentatively took his offered arm, and agreed. As she pointed out the various trees and plants, Darcy listened with rapt attention, reveling in the feel of her hand on his arm. He asked a few questions, which she answered cheerfully, and they then fell into a companionable silence.

As they walked on, Darcy thought about all that had

transpired this morning. It seemed evident, even from a distance, that Jane and Bingley were deep in conversation. He hoped that this interlude would provide them with the opportunity to resolve their differences. Watching them now, he understood the wisdom of Jane's decision. She had not granted Bingley permission to attempt a second chance because a true second chance should be earned, not bestowed. Bingley needed to show her his continued affections in order to begin to overcome her reservation about his family's disapproval. If she had taken the lead, as he had urged, then she would never have been certain about the strength of Bingley's resolve. Instead, she left it up to the natural flow of events. While her approach was far more risky in securing her own happiness, in the end it would be a much more satisfying basis upon which to build a future.

In a different way, the same logic applied to his situation. He could not lie to himself when Elizabeth was on his arm. He still wanted her, now more than ever. But he had been debating whether she would ever grant him a second chance. He now understood that the question was meaningless. He needed to earn a second chance, not be given one. He felt fairly certain that despite her slightly improved estimation of him, she still objected to his manners and thought him uncivil and inconsiderate. He could not expect her to forgive his past misdeeds, because they were indefensible. What he needed was for her to see that he had changed because of her and that he could strive to be worthy of her regard in the future. The only way to demonstrate civility was to practice it. He resolved, then and there, that he would do exactly that. He certainly had nothing to lose. In his last two encounters with her, he had kept her remonstrations at the forefront of his mind and attempted to act accordingly. As a result, she had endured his presence more graciously than she ever had during the previous fall or during all their time together in Kent. Dizzy with the feel of her so close, the course ahead suddenly seemed clear. He would prove to her that he had changed.

As they rejoined Jane and Bingley, Darcy spoke first: "Charles, I think we should not overstay our welcome."

"Yes, Darcy, of course." Bingley then solemnly turned to Jane and asked, "Miss Bennet, may I have the privilege of calling tomorrow?"

Keeping her head bowed, Jane quietly said, "Yes, thank you."

Darcy then turned to Jane. "Miss Bennet, it is a pleasure to see you again."

"Thank you, Mr. Darcy; I do hope we will have an opportunity to talk again soon. I did so value our last discussion. Will you be staying long in the neighborhood?"

"Yes, as a matter of fact, I believe I will here for a while. I look forward to seeing you again." Jane returned his compliment with a gracious smile. Darcy waited until Bingley had made his adieu to Elizabeth, and then stood before her and said, "Miss Bennet, thank you for such an enjoyable visit." He then smiled at her as he bowed and took his leave.

ENLIGHTENMENT

ON SUNDAY, THE GENTLEMEN attended church. Bingley and Darcy tarried by the door, each hoping to see a certain lady. Bingley's hopes were soon answered as Jane arrived with her mother and her three youngest sisters. Bingley greeted them warmly. Mrs. Bennet was still torn as to whom she should bestow with the greater part of her attentions. Mr. Darcy had more to offer, but Mr. Bingley had visited three times already since his arrival in Hertfordshire. Mr. Bingley took the lead, exchanging pleasantries with both Jane and Mrs. Bennet. Darcy, who was disappointed that Elizabeth was not with them and afraid to inquire after her, spoke barely a few words. The women eventually bid them a good day and took their seats in one of the front pews.

Darcy scanned the churchyard one more time before entering the church. He told himself that he was searching for Elizabeth because he was concerned that she might be ill. But if he was honest with himself, his concern and disappointment went deeper. During his last visit to Longbourn, he had vowed to do everything in his power to show Elizabeth that he could change, but he knew there would be few opportunities to see her, let alone engage her in conversation. He knew visiting Longbourn was not an option, and with none of Bingley's sisters in attendance at Netherfield, his friend would not be entertaining guests. Church seemed an ideal neutral territory, but as the final bell chimed, he resigned himself to the fact that she was not coming.

As the men took their seats at the back of the church, Darcy could not help but smile at Bingley's improved countenance. After he and Bingley had returned from their visit to Longbourn, Bingley's emotions had swung to dramatic extremes. Bingley thought that Jane had received him well enough on their first encounter, but worried that she was only being polite. While they were alone in the garden, Bingley had apologized for his abrupt departure in the fall. He decided not to mention his sisters' misdeeds, as he worried that it might only serve to put Jane on her guard and it did not fully explain his failure to ardently court her. She graciously accepted his apology, but he detected hesitation. He then changed the subject in an attempt to bring them back to their prior familiarity. On their walk, they spoke of many things and nothing in particular. When he took his leave, she granted him permission to call the next day. On the ride back to Netherfield, he viewed the exchange positively. But by nightfall, the events of the day had taken on a different tenor, and he began to find fault with the bulk of his behavior and ominous significance in all of Jane's reactions.

He left the next morning for Longbourn, sure of his disappointment. Darcy watched him go with mixed emotions. He once again wished Bingley every success, but felt irrationally dejected that he could not accompany him. Darcy knew that his visit might be misinterpreted, but the knowledge did not stop him from wanting to see Elizabeth again. Bingley came home buoyed by his reception. Throughout the visit, Jane had listened to him with interest, and while she did not do anything overt, he could sense that she was happy to see him. At the end of his visit, as he again walked with her in the garden, Bingley decided to speak directly. He told her that he knew that his sisters had caused her discomfiture in the past and that it was his fault for not seeing it. He vowed that it would never happen again. He paused and gathered his courage, and then told her that her happiness was his foremost concern. Jane blushingly looked away as she thanked him for his apology. As she turned back to look at him, their eyes locked in unspoken intensity. After several minutes, Bingley finally broke into a wide grin that infectiously spread to Jane. At that moment, as she smiled back at him, he knew the distance had been bridged.

The next day, Bingley again visited Longbourn, and Jane received him with ease. No new ground was gained, but the couple fell into a comfortable pattern that Bingley thought boded well for their future. That night, after he had fully recounted his tale to Darcy, Bingley was finally able to put his own mind sufficiently at ease to start to think of someone else's concerns. With the help of a little brandy, Bingley set about his task and slowly broached the subject of how Darcy's time alone with Elizabeth in the garden had gone. After some initial evasiveness, Darcy told him that it was not as uncomfortable as it could have been. He knew, however, that it would be foolish to read too much into her reaction, as he still had a long way to go to gain her forgiveness. As the conversation turned more serious,

Bingley urged Darcy to stay on at Netherfield indefinitely. Darcy thanked Bingley but was noncommittal about a departure date. In the end, he would only confirm that he intended to stay for church on Sunday and determine his plans after that. He had hoped that seeing Elizabeth today would help him fashion those plans. As the service began, he now knew that his wish would not be granted.

Darcy's sullen mood was somewhat improved by the words of the elderly clergyman. He was surprised at how engaging the man's message was and soon became focused on it. The minister spoke of the relative burden each human is consigned to carry and that happiness in life requires each person to be continually cognizant of the size of his own tribulations in comparison to those less fortunate. Darcy took the minister's words to heart. While his life was incomplete without Elizabeth, he knew he had many more blessings than most and that he would be a wretched creature if he did not appreciate them. As the minister preached the importance of setting aside one's own desires to help those in need, Darcy contemplated his own actions in that regard. The Darcys, as a family, had always been generous. His father had taught him at a very young age that their wealth carried with it the responsibility to help others whenever possible. Determining, however, what was possible and what was enough was an ongoing battle for Darcy.

If his attention had not been caught by the cleric's words, he might have noticed the lady who had slipped into the pew behind him. Elizabeth had awoken earlier than usual that Sunday morning and had gone for an amble through the countryside in order to avoid her mother's constant fluttering about Jane's marriage prospects. She left word that she would walk to church and meet them there. But once she was out in the fresh morning air, she lost sight of the time. Seeing that the service had already begun, she opted to grab a seat quickly in the back rather than disturb the congregation by marching to the front to claim her usual place with her family. After sliding in as quietly as she could, she looked around to acknowledge her immediate neighbors. She was startled to see that she had taken a seat directly behind Mr. Darcy. While initially mortified that she might appear to be seeking out his company, she soon accepted her fate. It seemed totally natural that his physical presence would be unavoidable, since the intricacies of his character had been at the forefront of her mind for some time.

Despite her good intentions to ignore his presence, she could not help but watch him as he listened to the sermon. Her old defensiveness immediately sprang to life as she studied Darcy's posture to detect any sign that he found her minister, an old and dear family friend, insufficient to the task of preaching to a man of his station. She watched to see if he found Reverend Fischer's expressive style too colloquial and his mannerisms too reminiscent of the archetypical country preacher. She thought that, if Mr. Darcy did discount the good reverend on those grounds, the loss would be his, since she knew that the reverend's simple and direct manner masked a keen intellect and that his oratorical style was by design meant to challenge without confrontation. To her surprise, Mr. Darcy appeared to be listening with rapt attention. Unwilling at first to give Mr. Darcy credit, she thought to herself that it was actually impossible for anyone to tell if someone else was paying attention based solely on outside appearances. She looked around to confirm this, but was surprised to see that all of the people she examined were obviously less interested in the service than Mr. Darcy. Bingley was clearly disengaged, as he spent an inordinate amount of time glancing in Jane's direction. Her mother's actions obviously betrayed her boredom, as she seemed fascinated by the lace cuff of her gown. As she looked at John Lucas, she was surprised to see that he was already looking in her direction and was trying to catch her eye. She ignored him and then glanced around the room. To her chagrin, she saw that most of her neighbors looked less than interested, while Mr. Darcy continued to pay close attention.

The exercise was sobering. It made her realize that she still habitually thought the worst of Mr. Darcy without any evidence to support her rash judgments. Had she learned nothing from her unquestioning acceptance of Mr. Wickham's falsehood? She thought her behavior particularly unchristian, especially within the walls of her childhood parish, and vowed to try to see Mr. Darcy for what he was, and not based on old, inaccurate prejudices. In retrospect, she thought it quite odd that she had made such a snap judgment of him, as he now seemed to be one of the most complex men she had ever met.

His behavior since returning to Hertfordshire seemed at every turn to contradict all her prior knowledge of him. On occasion, he still exhibited a decisive and somewhat proud manner that brooked no opposition. But she now recognized that his pride was not his only personality trait and that, on occasions, his unyielding demeanor was an asset. He had used it with her mother to great advantage, and she thought it must have been all the more necessary when he spoke to his aunt. She admired that he had the strength of character to stand up to both women. She wished her father exhibited some of the same resolve when dealing with her mother and her younger sisters, even if it was considered high-handed. Interactions with some individuals required as much.

But it was not just her sudden understanding of Mr. Darcy's harder side that required her to reassess her judgment of him. It was the discovery that a softer side existed. His letter to her, which was kinder than could be expected, stood out, as did his treatment of Jane. His return to Hertfordshire to squelch any rumors about his rejection of her showed a sense of honor and thoughtfulness that she could not help but value. His willingness to suffer various humiliations at her mother's hands in order to aid Jane and Mr. Bingley's reconciliation was also unexpected and appreciated. As a matter of fact, his dutifulness in that regard was almost beyond the pale, and it made her wonder why he continued to stay in the neighborhood. Clearly Mr. Bingley was well on the way to courting Jane without his friend's further help. Was his sense of duty so strong that he intended to remain until the task was completed? That seemed more than was required. Or did he have some other motive?

Elizabeth continued to watch Mr. Darcy furtively as he diligently followed along in his Book of Prayers. As Reverend Fischer began to discuss the importance of Saint Paul's first letter to the Corinthians, she watched Mr. Darcy for a reaction. The familiar passage was a guidepost for true Christian charity. It declared that the love that God commanded each of us to practice was patient and kind, and not proud, resentful, or rude. She colored at the words. She thought that the verse would surely remind Mr. Darcy of their disastrous meeting at Hunsford and her critique of his character. Seeing his clenched jaw, she wished she had held her tongue or at least tempered her criticism. Warranted or not, she had no right to hurt someone intentionally. At the time, she thought her words would hardly touch him, but seeing him here in Hertfordshire attending to her reproof regarding his conduct toward Jane, she knew better. As Reverend Fischer continued on to opine that the more important part of the passage was the admonition that Christians should never be easily moved to anger and should never keep a record of wrongs, she realized that the passage might be a more appropriate critique of her own behavior.

Darcy, for his part, was indeed moved by Saint Paul's words, as they seemed to speak directly to him. He took the passage as one more sign that he needed to change his behavior. But, rather than simply be reminded of his shortcomings, the verse gave him hope. The passage ended with a declaration of the power of love, with the intonation, "Love always hopes, always trusts, always perseveres. Love never fails." Whatever his other flaws, he knew he truly loved Elizabeth, and if that was the case, it was not unreasonable for him to hope.

As the parishioners were asked to pray on the generosity of their own spirit, she watched as Mr. Darcy knelt, deep in thought. She wondered what he was thinking about so intently. As she examined his kneeling form, she realized she had never really looked at him closely before. She noticed how broad his back and shoulders appeared in his finely tailored coat. While she always knew he was wealthy and could afford the most flattering cut for his garments, she had never noticed before that his physique required no such enhancement. Nor had she noticed how curly his black hair was. She chastised herself for having such thoughts while she was supposed to be at prayer, but her vantage point made concentration on anything else impossible. She watched as Mr. Darcy bent his head and shoulders farther forward. She thought how different he looked than she would have expected, as he continued to kneel, oblivious to his surroundings.

As most of the members of the congregation, including Mr. Bingley, took their seats to indicate they had finished their prayers, Mr. Darcy continued to kneel. She wondered once again what so preoccupied him, and thought that he looked anything but proud at that moment. Finally, before Mr. Darcy's inattention became embarrassing, she noticed Mr. Bingley gently nudge Mr. Darcy's elbow with his leg. Mr. Darcy looked up, startled, and then sank back in his seat. As he moved, Elizabeth instinctively bowed her head toward his back to keep out of his peripheral view. By doing so, she found herself very close to the backs of the two gentlemen's heads as they exchanged whispers.

With his eyes staring straight ahead, Bingley leaned ever so slightly toward Darcy and quietly said, "Sorry, but I thought you might have fallen asleep on your knees. Or were you having an epiphany?"

From the side of his face, she saw Darcy suppress a smile, as he replied, "No, I was simply lost in thought. I can see why it confused you, though, since I know you never contemplate an idea for longer than a minute."

"My ideas are obviously more well formed than yours. As such, they don't require labored contemplation."

"It shows."

The two men then gave each other a discreet smile and turned their attention back to the altar. As Elizabeth attempted to do the same, she had to smile at their easy camaraderie. She could not help but imagine what they were like as boys, and pictured them being caught by the schoolmaster for speaking out of turn.

As the minister directed the congregation to the page for the final hymn, she noticed that it was one of her favorites. She watched as Darcy found the page and then closed his book. He apparently knew the song well. As the tenor and bass parts began the song, she had the guilty pleasure of listening to the men in front of her sing. She was surprised by the resonance and strength of Mr. Darcy's voice. As she listened, she had to admit to herself that he had many appealing attributes. She wondered, if she had not been so blinded by Mr. Wickham's lies, whether she would have found it more difficult to refuse Darcy. She laughed at herself for even considering it and tried to concentrate on the song lest she miss her part. As her own strong voice chimed in at the chorus, she saw Mr. Darcy flinch and then heard him falter as he began to turn around and then stopped himself midstream. She thought it unlikely, but she almost believed that he had recognized her voice. Unwilling to be caught watching him, she decided to leave immediately at the close of service.

As soon as the music stopped, Darcy turned around. He knew Elizabeth must have been standing behind him. Her singing voice, like everything else about her, was deeply committed to his memory, as it was a familiar part of his nightly dreams. But when he turned, there was only an empty space at the end of the aisle. As he exited the church, he could see that she was not in the courtyard, so he stationed himself at the door to watch the parishioners leave the church. As the Bennet party exited, he was surprised to see Elizabeth in line behind Jane. He knew she had not been at the front of the church during the service but could not explain her appearance there now.

Bingley was more than happy to stand at the door with Darcy, as it meant he would have another opportunity to talk to Jane. As Mrs. Bennet approached, Mr. Bingley told her how much he had enjoyed Reverend Fischer's sermon. She readily agreed that it was one of the best she had heard and began explaining the history of his service to their parish. As their other sisters began to converse with the Lucases, Darcy took the opportunity to say good morning to Jane and then Elizabeth. Darcy then looked directly at Elizabeth and asked if she had enjoyed the service.

With a slight smile upon her lips, she replied, "Yes, indeed I did, sir. I found it very enlightening."

"I am glad to hear it." He then impulsively added, "I did not see you come in though."

Smiling all the more sweetly, she said, "You did not? Are you certain?"

Looking at her intently, he replied, "Yes, I am quite sure."

"Oh, that is odd." By way of clarification, she raised one eyebrow and finally added, "There is a side door by the front of the church."

He continued to stare at her, hoping to gain further intelligence. She simply smiled back, unwilling to say more. They were clearly at a standstill. Neither was willing to ask what the other was trying to say or not say, and neither would look away. Despite his lack of progress at unraveling this mystery, Darcy felt it a pleasant sensation. He wondered why she would have moved if she were, in fact, sitting behind him, and wondered, all the more, why she would now be reluctant to reveal it. His pessimistic side worried that it was an attempt to avoid him at all costs, but her present playful demeanor seemed to suggest otherwise. No, this was clearly a game of sorts, and he was thrilled that she was willing to let him play.

The stalemate, however, ended too quickly as Mrs. Bennet's loud voice was heard inviting Mr. Bingley to dinner and then nervously adding, "Mr. Darcy, you are also welcome."

Darcy slowly tore his eyes from Elizabeth. "Thank you, madam, I would be honored."

As Darcy entered the library, he saw that Bingley, who was also already dressed for dinner, was deep in thought while drafting a letter. "Charles, you look busy; do not let me disturb you. Call me whenever you are ready to leave. I am at your service."

Tearing himself from the page he had just written, Bingley replied absentmindedly, "Um, yes... Thank you." Then looking up he said, "Actually, Darcy, perhaps I could impose upon you for some advice. I should discuss this with you in any event, as it concerns you."

"By all means, what can I do?"

"The invitation to the Bennets' tonight has made me realize that I will soon need to return the courtesy. Obviously, I will need someone to act as a hostess for me. I have been putting off dealing with Caroline or Louisa until I had settled matters with Miss Bennet, but I now think that was a mistake. Whenever I visit with Miss Bennet, I feel that she is on the verge of forgiving me for leaving last fall. I think she hesitates, however, because she cannot forget my sisters' objections to the match. The only way for her to overcome her reservations is for my sisters to return and show her that they will accept her into my family. I have been attempting to draft a letter to Caroline to invite her here, but I am having trouble wording it. I have tried to explain how I feel about Miss Bennet, and everything that has happened since I returned from Scarborough, but it is already four pages long, both sides, and a hopeless muddle. I think I should start over, but I simply do not know where to begin."

"Charles, I am not sure what help I can be. They are your sisters. You should tell them how you feel and let them know what you want. If I may be frank, I think, at times, they take advantage of your good nature by tending not to accede to your wishes. It is important to maintain a cordial relationship with them, but you should also be clear about what you expect of them in regard to Miss Bennet."

"I suppose you are right," Bingley conceded. "I have always avoided conflict with them because it is easier to keep the peace than engage in a battle of wills. But their reception of Miss Bennet and her family is too important to leave up to chance. I think I will start the letter over and be more direct."

"Charles, just do what you think is right. If it is only legible, it will be a vast improvement over your typical correspondence."

"Yes, very well," Bingley drawled. "I see that you are in a humor to make sport of me and to be of no further use, so I will drop that subject and move on to a more important one." After a pause, he sheepishly added, "Once my sisters return, I have decided to ask Miss Bennet to marry me. I am not sure if she will agree, but I do not want to waste any more time."

Patting Bingley on the back while warmly shaking his hand, Darcy said, "Charles, I think that is wonderful. I wish you every success."

"Thank you, Darcy. I appreciate the encouragement. That, however, brings to mind another issue that I want to discuss with you. Earlier, you said you would make some decisions about your plans after you attended church. You certainly did enough soul searching during the service to be familiar with your own mind. Have you made a decision?"

"To be honest, no—not completely."

"You should seriously think about staying on here. But when you decide, be aware of my invitation to Caroline. I know she sometimes makes you ill at ease. More importantly, once she is here, it is my wish to invite the Bennets on a regular basis. I worry that some of their party might also make you uncomfortable."

"Charles, thank you for being so considerate of my feelings. I am not sure what I want to do, but I appreciate your invitation more than you know. Would you mind if I slept on the decision?"

Smiling broadly, Bingley replied, "Not at all. But I have a suspicion that you are actually looking for your answer tonight at Longbourn and that sleeping on it has nothing to do with it."

Darcy looked away and then could not help but smile at his friend in return as he said, "It is a good thing that you are so friendly and good-natured. It fools most people into thinking that you are simpleminded. It allows you to observe the world unencumbered. Very little gets by you, though, and most people never recognize it."

Bingley replied with a small laugh, "If that was a compliment, thank you. But, Darcy, knowing what I know, I would be a fool not to have noticed your improved disposition after church today and connected it to Miss Elizabeth. I have not seen you in such a good mood in months. Will you tell me what has happened to cause such a transformation?"

"Actually, absolutely nothing has happened. That is why I want to see how things go tonight. I suppose I am in an optimistic mood because it seemed she was not so uncomfortable in my presence this morning. In saying it out loud, I realize how pathetic that sounds, but that meager morsel has allowed me to nurture the unrealistic hope that I might be able to befriend her. If I do, perhaps in time she can forgive me."

"Darcy, I think that is wonderful. My only desire is to see you happy. I think the advice you gave me about pursuing Miss Bennet applies equally well in your case. Let us face the evening with high hopes. I will be ready in just a few moments, and I will meet you in the foyer."

After his friend left, Bingley scribbled the following missive without a single inkblot:

Dear Caroline,

I recently learned that Miss Bennet visited you last winter and that you returned the call without telling me of either event. I have been courting Miss Bennet since my return to Netherfield. I request that you immediately join me here so that you can host Miss Bennet and her family. We can discuss the continuation of your allowance at that time. You should bring Louisa, as I expect both of my sisters to extend every courtesy to my intended fiancée and her family.

Your loving brother,
Charles

RIVALS

As the gentlemen rode to Longbourn in Bingley's carriage, each contemplated the evening before him with a mixture of hope and trepidation. Darcy was buoyed by Elizabeth's reception of him after church, but he knew full well that he had misjudged her moods in the past with disastrous results. He knew that he would have to learn how to navigate social occasions if he wanted to win her regard. He was just unsure of his skill in such situations. Whatever his ability, the first step toward obtaining his goal was refraining from imagining every pitfall. He needed to try to act naturally in Elizabeth's presence, without being on guard and without giving offense. He thought it a daunting prospect and searched for a distraction. Speaking more abruptly than he wished, Darcy turned to Bingley and asked, "Did you finish your letter?"

Bingley, who was deep in thought, turned to Darcy with a vacant gaze, obviously trying to comprehend his meaning. "Oh... um, yes, I sent it off by express before we left. I asked Caroline, in a direct fashion, to come to Netherfield to receive Miss Bennet. I told her to bring the Hursts as well."

"That seems a wise course of action."

"Yes, but the difficulty will begin once they arrive."

With a sympathetic smile, Darcy replied, "That may be."

"I have been trying to decide what I should say to Miss Bennet. Tonight, if I have an opportunity to speak with her alone, I thought I would tell her about my invitation to Caroline and Louisa, and then ask her if she will agree to let them call on her. I am not sure my sisters deserve a second chance, but I think the only way for Miss Bennet to accept my regard is for her to see that my sisters will receive her with the civility she deserves."

"I think you are right in that regard. But I would not worry. Miss Bennet has a very forgiving temperament. I think if your sisters apply themselves, she will receive them with her usual grace. How will you know, however…? How can you be sure…?"

"That my sisters will behave in her presence? I am not, but I intend to make it crystal clear to them that I expect no less."

Smiling at his friend's sudden assertiveness, Darcy offered, "If I can be of service to you in any way, please tell me."

"Thank you. I will keep that in mind. And what of you? What do you hope to accomplish this evening?"

"Charles, you have a plan of action to win Miss Bennet and a concrete goal that you wish to obtain. I am simply appraising the situation. I have no realistic chance of achieving what I desire. At this point, I simply hope to dine without giving offense."

With a broad grin, Bingley replied, "Do not be so pessimistic, Darcy. With a little effort that sounds like an obtainable goal."

Darcy simply chuckled and stared out the window as the carriage pulled up to the entrance of Longbourn.

As the gentlemen entered, Mrs. Bennet greeted them with every courtesy. Her usual brash manner, however, was somewhat in retreat. She had invited Mr. Bingley to dinner on the spur of the moment, after he had been so pleasant to her at church. She included Mr. Darcy in the invitation when she realized that neglecting him might unintentionally give offense. The fact that the gentlemen were now calling together posed a particularly complex problem for her to solve. She knew that one of them should marry Jane and that it was her job to see that it happened, but she was unsure which man she should instruct Jane to encourage. Mr. Bingley seemed both more willing and more pleasant, but his wealth was nothing in comparison to Mr. Darcy's. She suspected that Mr. Darcy's aunt had discouraged his interest in Jane more than he would admit. As such, she worried that he might never come around. If that were the case, she could not have Jane wasting her attentions on him at the risk of offending Mr. Bingley. But then again, the chance of securing Mr. Darcy, with all of his wealth, could not be ignored. It was a difficult problem indeed.

As they entered the parlor, Mr. Bingley noticed that a seat near Jane was unoccupied. Leaving Darcy to fend for himself, Bingley quickly resumed his place by Jane's side. Darcy smiled good-naturedly at his friend. He could not blame Bingley for deserting him; he would do the same if the situation were reversed. Darcy scanned the room for Elizabeth and attempted to hide his disappointment when he realized she was not present. Darcy set about paying his respects to Mr. Bennet, who received him with an air of indifference. Darcy then acknowledged Sir William, who received the compliment of his attention with far more fanfare. As Darcy moved away to stand slightly apart from Sir William and his wife, Jane called to him.

"Mr. Darcy, how good it is to see you. Would you join us?"

Darcy smiled appreciatively to her. "Thank you, madam. Are you sure I am not intruding?"

Mr. Bingley responded for both of them, "Not at all, Darcy, please sit. We were just discussing Miss Bennet's tastes in literature. Like yourself, she is quite fond of poetry."

"Are you?" Darcy exclaimed with genuine interest. "And who is your favorite poet?" While Mr. Darcy and Miss Bennet spoke at length about their favorite authors and passages, Mr. Bingley remained mostly silent. His animated personality did not often lend itself to the type of quiet reflection that the study of poetry required.

Mrs. Bennet watched the exchange with some alarm. While she hoped both men found Jane attractive, there was no use in having them pursue her simultaneously. One's presence would surely impede the other from proposing, and their rivalry could drag on without a tangible result. Determining that it was time to settle the matter, she followed Darcy as he rose to get Miss Bennet a refreshment.

Darcy had offered to fetch some wine as an excuse to make his exit. While he truly appreciated both Miss Bennet and Bingley's kindness by inviting him to join them, he knew that Bingley was hoping to speak to Miss Bennet alone, and he did not wish to put his own needs before those of his friend. He also hoped his walk would afford him the opportunity once again to scan the room for signs of Elizabeth. As he began to pour some wine, Mrs. Bennet greeted him enthusiastically and exclaimed, "My dear Mr. Darcy, it is so good to see you again. I had been worried that you were not well. I was surprised when you did not call. I think Jane was also concerned."

Darcy was amazed at Mrs. Bennet's audacity. That she would make such a pointed inquiry, with Bingley sitting beside Miss Bennet, just a few feet away, was incomprehensible. He thought that if he had one obtainable goal for the evening, it should be to put the matter of his interest in Miss Bennet to rest. "Thank you, madam, for your concern. I have been very well. I apologize for not being able to call, but I do hope that Mr. Bingley expressed my regard on his visits."

Clearly disappointed, Mrs. Bennet replied in a perfunctory tone, "Yes, yes, he has."

"I am glad. I knew that while I might not be able to visit as often as I would like, Mr. Bingley would surely come whenever possible."

Unwilling to take the hint, she replied, "Yes, he has been quite attentive, but I hope you will call on your own accord soon. You should not let your business concerns keep you from your friends."

"I am afraid, madam, that it is more than likely that they will do exactly that."

"Mr. Darcy, I know that the responsibilities related to as large an estate as yours must be daunting, but you must make an exception in your schedule for us. I think Jane would be quite disappointed if you did not."

Darcy replied in a tone meant to put the subject to rest, "Madam, I will try my best, but at this point, I am afraid I cannot make such a promise. But if the opportunity does arise, I will be sure to accompany Mr. Bingley on one of his visits. In the meantime, I will have to satisfy myself with news of your family through him. I hope you will forgive me, in advance, if I am unable to be as attentive as I should." Moving his head toward

Bingley and Miss Bennet, he then added, "Will you excuse me? I promised Miss Bennet that I would bring her some wine."

For a moment, Mrs. Bennet studied Darcy's face while she attempted to comprehend his meaning. She barely knew how to react. He clearly did not intend to court Jane. She was, at least, consoled that Mr. Darcy appeared to be encouraging Mr. Bingley toward Jane in his stead. Nonetheless, she could not imagine why he did not want her for himself. What a vexatious man! If he was too timid to defy his aunt, then he would be of no use to her family. Jane had already wasted enough time on him. Her impatience with him began to take tangible form as her face began to color. If he was destined for his cousin, then there was no need for him to continue to distract Jane. At length, she finally replied in as polite a voice as she could muster, "Really, Mr. Darcy, there is no need. I can take the wine to her myself. I need to inquire of Mr. Bingley's comfort in any regard."

Darcy stood affixed, somewhat surprised by her brusque manner, but nonetheless happy with the result. Seeing that Mrs. Bennet had thereafter left his friend and Miss Bennet to their own devices, he decided to do the same. As he took a tour of the room, he briefly attempted to converse with Mr. Bennet, curious about Elizabeth's close relationship with a man who, from the outside, seemed so disengaged from his family. He soon realized, however, that Mr. Bennet was a man of even fewer words than he was when in social situations not to his liking.

As he began to walk about the room again, he saw Elizabeth enter with a book in her hand. His relief at seeing her was short-lived, as John Lucas immediately followed her into the room. He suspected that they had been off talking together, and his chest immediately tightened. He had vowed before he came that he would not overwhelm Elizabeth with his attentions. Instead, he would simply make himself available for conversation if she chose it. But watching her converse with Lucas was too much. His desire to go slowly was overtaken by his fear that Lucas would secure her affections before he had the opportunity to show her that he could change. His fear won out, as he purposefully walked over to them. Bowing, Darcy greeted them each in a solemn voice. "Mr. Lucas, Miss Bennet."

Lucas was the first to speak. "Ah, Mr. Darcy, it is a pleasure to see you again. I hope you are in good health."

Looking more at Elizabeth than Lucas, Darcy answered in a perfunctory tone, "Yes, thank you. And yourself?"

Lucas good-naturedly replied, "Quite well, thank you. I noticed you in church this morning. My mother had said that you had arrived with Mr. Bingley, but I did not realize that you planned to stay."

Responding in a tone that implied more of a challenge than he had intended, Darcy said, "Yes, as a matter of fact, I do intend to stay for a while." He then looked to Elizabeth for her reaction. She continued to stare toward a window. As an awkward pause ensued, Darcy wondered at his lack of control. Why would he declare that he would be staying, when he had not even determined if such a course of action would suit his purpose? Did he expect Elizabeth to voice her approval? Or was he trying to give Lucas a warning? Either motive seemed unlikely to impress Elizabeth. He resisted the urge to close his eyes in despair, as he realized that Elizabeth's proximity apparently divested him of all reason, and the presence of a competitor for her affections doubled his impulsive behavior. He felt he could barely trust himself to speak in such a situation. Recalling his vow to show Elizabeth his civility, he fought the desire to excuse himself. Instead, he squared his shoulders and said, "Yes, I enjoyed church service this morning a great deal. Your reverend seems an interesting man. Has he been in service here long?"

Darcy had asked the question in the hope that Elizabeth would understand his reference to their encounter at the church door. He would have been surprised to learn, however, that it was the mention of her minister that sparked her interest. Rewarding him with a smile, she replied, "Yes, Mr. Darcy, he has been with our parish for over fifteen years. I always find him an engaging speaker."

"Yes," interrupted Lucas, "he is a very good man, but he is constantly threatening to move to the seaside. While I would miss him, I must say that there is something to be said of change for change's sake. I sometimes think that it is hard to listen to the same passages of the Bible, given over and over again by someone who, by human nature, possesses the same perspective."

Elizabeth eagerly interjected, "But I disagree, Mr. Lucas. The passages of the Bible are, hopefully, quite familiar to all of us. It is a minister's ability to help us to relate them to new situations that makes the sermon worthwhile. It should not matter whether the message or the messenger is familiar, as long as the underlying meaning is new."

"I suppose," Mr. Lucas replied, "but take today, for example. Reverend Fischer read a passage from Acts."

"Corinthians," corrected Darcy, as Elizabeth nodded her acknowledgment.

Lucas smiled easily at Darcy's correction and Elizabeth's assent. "Yes, I obviously misspoke. He read a passage from

Corinthians that I have heard many times before, but I cannot say I felt any new insight was offered."

To Elizabeth's surprise, it was Darcy who responded. "I think perhaps you are looking at it from the wrong perspective. It is not whether the passage was offered in a different fashion; it is whether you were willing to hear it in a manner you had never allowed before. It is only in such a state that new meaning is evident. The job of the minister is to present the chosen passages freshly, each time, in the eternal hope that they may indeed reach someone in a new way. If the minister can do that, time and time again, then the mark of his ministry is ensured."

Caught up in his words, Elizabeth impulsively added, "Yes, that is it exactly. It is the promise of new understanding that makes the difference. It is the point of the service." At her words, Darcy looked intently at her, hoping she understood some of his recently acquired vision. Caught off guard by his intense gaze, she smiled weakly in response.

Lucas, however, soon interrupted the moment by asking in a jovial air, "But, Mr. Darcy, having had the benefit of hearing my brother-in-law's sermons during your visit to your aunt, you cannot argue that sometimes a fresh voice might be a good thing? I would imagine that is what drove you from Kent."

Darcy looked down quickly in embarrassment. Being reminded of what drove him from Kent, in front of Elizabeth, was the last thing he wanted at that moment. Struggling for a reply, he stated, "I suppose there is always some benefit from change."

As both fell silent, Lucas studied their reactions. He assumed their silence was due to their unwillingness to openly chide Mr. Collins's ability. He had thought both of them less fainthearted, but apparently Mr. Darcy's aunt held more sway over him than he would have imagined, and Miss Elizabeth was holding her tongue for his sake. Taking the hint, Lucas replied, "I suspect, Mr. Darcy, that you are more accustomed to the oratory style presently *en vogue* in London."

Darcy could see from Elizabeth's heightened color and her sudden unwillingness to return his gaze that the reference to Kent had also embarrassed her. It made him feel how tenuous his position was. No matter how much progress he made with her, his past missteps were always lurking in the shadows, waiting to intrude. It seemed an impossible task for him to start any conversation without invoking their prior interactions. In a vain attempt to change the subject, Darcy offered, "Actually, I am more at home in the smaller setting of the parish at Pemberley, in Derbyshire."

Unwilling to let pass an invitation to discuss an issue that he had wondered about, Lucas smiled politely and slowly said, "Yes, I think I had heard that you were very particular about who is installed in the clerical positions you bestow."

Before Darcy could answer this oblique reference to the slander that Wickham had circulated, Elizabeth came to his defense. She spoke in a lighthearted manner, but Lucas could see that it masked a serious message. "I am not sure, Mr. Lucas, that it is our place to opine on the methodology that Mr. Darcy employs to make his appointments, but I have every confidence that he accomplishes the task in a fair and thoughtful manner. Nonetheless, the process must produce disappointment in those who feel themselves worthy of a position when they are, in fact, undeserving. I suppose enduring their bitterness is an unfortunate by-product that cannot be avoided."

Darcy stared at her for an extra beat before turning to Lucas and adding, "Actually, the criteria I use when I am charged with the responsibility of bestowing a living in the church is quite simple, and I am more than willing to share it with anyone who is interested. I have no qualms discussing any of the details of any of my appointments. Though I am aware that not everyone would agree with all of the actions I have taken, I am more than willing to defend them."

Somewhat surprised by his earnest reply, Lucas regretted having brought up the rumors he had heard about Darcy, and vowed to give them no further credence. "Yes, Mr. Darcy, I can see that. I apologize if I seemed to imply otherwise. It must be a difficult responsibility that inevitably creates critics of your actions. I think most people would understand, though, that the perspective of such a critic is necessarily biased."

Darcy responded with a slight bow. "Thank you, sir. I appreciate the sentiment. I hope you are right." More than encouraged by Elizabeth's defense of his character, Darcy decided to press his luck. "But, Miss Bennet, let us talk of more pleasant things. I know you are fond of reading, but I recall that you once told me you would not discuss books in a ballroom. I see that you are now holding a volume. Do you adhere to the same prohibition during small, informal gatherings?"

Surprised by his playful tone, Elizabeth met his challenge. "Sir, lately, I have had an opportunity to reevaluate many of the rules of conduct that I live by. Not only am I willing to discuss books at small gatherings, but I might even be prepared to revise my ban regarding the dance floor. I have found that in the past, I have been too rigid in the application of some of my more decided opinions."

As his pulse began to race at her response, Darcy gave her a wide smile that revealed his dimples. "I am very glad to hear it. I can only hope that there is an opportunity to test your resolve. I do so love books."

She was saved from responding to that provocative comment by the call for dinner. She was half relieved and half disappointed to see that Mr. Darcy was seated as far away from her as possible. She could not help but feel some discomfort on his account, as she realized that the only people he probably wished to speak with during dinner, his friend and her sister Jane, were seated with her. She smiled to herself at the thought of him enduring Mrs. Long and Mary's dinner conversation, but knew there was nothing to be done about it.

She wondered why she cared. She thought it odd that her estimation of him had changed so radically. She understood that her previous opinion of him was in serious need of revision, as it was based on misinformation and bruised feelings. Mr. Lucas's reference to Mr. Wickham was proof of that. But she questioned the degree of his transformation in her own mind. She now thought him a good man and appreciated his help with her sister. But there was more.

To her surprise, she sometimes enjoyed his company. She thought it strange that she would get the opportunity to see this side of him now, when it was really too late. She knew that her presence in company must on some level embarrass him; as a spurned suitor, how could it not? But she was amazed to see that he still tried to interact with her. Was this part of his effort to make amends for any affront she suffered during his proposal? It seemed more than was called for, given that she had insulted him just as much. Perhaps he was just trying to set matters straight between them, and the most convenient method to do so was to show her his friendship. But even that explanation did not really account for their oddly evolving relationship. She resolved, however, to put him out of her mind, as she realized that her dinner partner to her left, John Lucas, was asking her a question.

Darcy took his seat, somewhat disappointed with its location. He consoled himself with the thought that his recent conversation with Elizabeth more than made up the difference. While he was troubled by Lucas's reference to Wickham, he was heartened by Elizabeth's quick defense of his character. He now knew he would need to pay more attention to the damage Wickham had done to his reputation in the neighborhood, but for the time being he could only think of the challenge Elizabeth's proximity posed. He would have preferred their discourse to involve more neutral topics, but on the whole, he was satisfied with the smile she had given him and the loose promise that she might dance with him again.

As dinner progressed, Darcy engaged in polite conversation with those around him. Mrs. Long was willing to speak about almost anything as long as Darcy periodically made a feeble response to her statements. Mary was also willing to talk at length. Unfortunately, the only topic that interested her was morality, and he had neither the inclination nor the time to puzzle over that subject. Instead, he felt moved to spend most of the meal glancing at Elizabeth as she talked to John Lucas.

After dinner, Darcy roamed about the room, looking for an opportunity to approach Elizabeth again. Unfortunately, as coffee was served, she was surrounded by several women who refused to give way to his attempts to move toward her. Realizing that he could not fall into his old behavior and simply stare out the window until she was available, Darcy turned to Elizabeth's neighbor, Mr. Robinson. Darcy's efforts were soon rewarded as they shared a common view on the troubles in France and what England might do to stop Napoleon. Elizabeth, from her vantage point behind them, could not help but overhear their discourse. She was struck by the wisdom supporting Mr. Darcy's beliefs and his knowledge of the world. She had seldom heard such an interesting exchange in her mother's parlor and had a sudden impulse to join them but was distracted by her mother, and the moment passed.

Later, after the coffee things were put away, Darcy was pleased to see Elizabeth standing alone behind the piano. He walked over to her immediately and asked, "Miss Bennet, can I prevail upon you to play?"

"I…"

"I hope you will say yes. There are few things that give me greater pleasure than hearing you sing and play."

Surprised by his words, she meekly said, "Yes, I did intend to play. I am afraid, though, with such high praise, I am bound to disappoint."

With complete earnestness, he solemnly replied, "Madam, that is simply not possible." As she looked at him from across the piano, she was once again surprised by his intense gaze and began to wonder if it was friendship he felt.

As she took her seat, however, John Lucas once again joined them. "Ah, Darcy, you are in for a treat! Miss Elizabeth has agreed to play for me. She is quite good, I am sure that she cannot compare to what you have heard in London, but she always gives it quite an effort." Easily taking the seat beside her on the bench, Lucas added in a low, playful voice that was still audible to Darcy, "I will turn the pages for you, but I want you to play this for me. It is my favorite."

Darcy stood trapped at the piano. His head reeled at the impossibility of the situation. He had hoped for time alone with her, but he now understood that he was intruding upon her time alone with Lucas. He would have walked away, if he could, but he knew it would be utterly rude at this point. Instead, he braced himself to listen to Elizabeth sing to Lucas. He wondered how he would manage to keep standing, watching her sing, while disappointment and jealousy fought for the greater share of his heart.

Elizabeth, for her part, was seized with embarrassment. She suddenly realized that John Lucas's familiar behavior would imply that there was some sort of understanding between them. She wondered where this had come from. John Lucas had always showed an interest in her, but she never took it for more than a passing fancy. There was a time when she thought him well matched to her, but she soon realized that, while their temperaments seemed well suited, their basic characters were not. She had long understood that his devotion to her was easily interrupted by brief infatuations with other girls. While she always found him interesting, intelligent, and witty, she could not think of him seriously because she did not believe him capable of serious feelings. She knew she required something more constant. Safe in the knowledge that he could not really touch her heart, their friendship developed naturally, as they fell into an easy camaraderie. He would often accompany her at social gatherings when no one else was available, and she thought it a pleasant and wise arrangement. But his behavior now, in front of Mr. Darcy, no less, seemed to go much further. It was the fact that it was in front of Mr. Darcy that made it so unacceptable.

As she began to play, she resolved to simply sing and ignore the implications. But when she looked up and saw Mr. Darcy's stiff expression, she knew it was impossible. She quickly returned her eyes to the keyboard. Whatever she felt for him, it was too cruel to have him stand there and watch her sing at John Lucas's request when he had so eloquently asked her to sing as well. Even if Mr. Darcy had nothing but regret for his proposal to her, this was clearly a slap in the face. He would think that she had jumped from his interest in her at Kent to an alliance with John Lucas within a matter of days and then had not even bothered to indicate it to him when she had the opportunity. Or worse, he would believe that she had always had an understanding with Lucas and chose to refuse his proposal, not on those grounds, but because she felt the need to point out his character flaws. Either situation would give him an impression she did not want to leave him with.

As the song came to a close, everyone applauded. Mr. Darcy gave a slight bow and said in a formal tone, "That was quite lovely. Thank you."

As he started to walk away, Elizabeth impulsively asked, "Mr. Darcy, I think I remember from Kent that you prefer German composers. Do you have a favorite? I would be more than happy to play it."

As he stepped back to the piano, Darcy studied her for a moment before a small smile began to grace his lips. He then said, "Actually, if you are indeed taking requests, while I do enjoy the German composers, after I heard you perform Mozart, I became enamored of the Austrians. Do you think you could play one of his pieces?"

Keeping her head slightly bowed to mask her smile, she replied, "Yes, I have something right here." She then looked up at Darcy and returned his intense stare. Without turning her head, she casually asked Mr. Lucas if he was willing to continue to turn the pages for her. Lucas nodded in assent but sensed the deeper ramifications. Throughout the song, Darcy stared at Elizabeth, and she often returned his gaze with a smile. Lucas had realized before dinner that while he had a tendency to look at most things from a military perspective, his skill had clearly failed him while assessing Darcy's character. He had somehow missed the obvious, and in doing so, he had violated the first rule of combat: Know your opponent.

At the close of the song, Darcy smiled broadly and said, "Miss Bennet, that was… beautiful. Thank you very much." She nodded her acceptance as Mary approached to announce that she intended to play next.

Darcy walked to the refreshment table to get a glass of wine to calm his nerves. As he drank it, he leaned against the wall trying to sort out the mix of his emotions. As he did, he could hear Mrs. Bennet mention Elizabeth's name. It was not long before he realized what was being said. "Oh yes, she does play well, but I wonder if it is all a waste. With her high standards, I doubt she will ever find a husband. When I think that she has already rejected a perfectly acceptable proposal, I can barely calm my nerves. Even if she did not like his manner or find his person attractive, accepting him would have saved Longbourn. She obviously thinks she owes nothing to me or to her family."

Sympathizing with her plight, Mrs. Philips consoled her. "Yes, Fanny, I quite agree. I have told you, time and time again, it will do her no good in the end. I am curious, though, as to how he received her when she saw him again. It must have been uncomfortable for both of them."

Unable to listen any further, Darcy sought out Bingley in order to request their immediate removal. Seeing him deep in conversation with Miss Bennet, he thought better of the idea. No matter how urgently he wanted to leave, he would not impede Bingley's progress with Miss Bennet. Instead, he strode from the room.

As Elizabeth passed the front door on the way to the parlor, she saw Mr. Darcy put on his great coat as he turned to leave. Surprised by his actions, she quickly inquired, "Mr. Darcy, you are not leaving, are you?"

In an icy voice, he replied, "Yes, madam, I am afraid I must."

As she smiled and curtseyed in a somewhat shy manner, she said, "Oh, good evening, then." Darcy breezed by her with barely an acknowledgment and began to walk down the steps. Elizabeth called after him. "But, Mr. Darcy, Mr. Bingley's carriage is not yet ready."

He came to a stop, turned, and said, "Mr. Bingley is not ready to go. When he is, he will take his carriage home." Darcy then began walking again.

Confused by his odd behavior, she impulsively followed him out the door and down the stairs. "Are you planning to walk then? Sir, I must caution you, it is too dark. The path is not clearly marked and would be very difficult to follow at night. Shouldn't you wait until Mr. Bingley leaves? Or I can call my father's carriage for you, if need be?"

Stopping in his tracks once again, Darcy spoke without turning, "Madam, I wish to leave now. I do not mean to be rude, but I cannot stay here a moment longer. Please excuse me."

Elizabeth moved toward him and asked in a concerned tone, "Mr. Darcy, what has happened?"

Turning to look at her, he said in a terse manner, "I really think there is no point in discussing this. Good evening."

Elizabeth followed him a few more steps and asked, "Sir, did I say something to offend you? If I did, I certainly did not intend to. Will you not tell me what this is about?"

"Madam, as I have said, I see no point in discussing this."

Feeling her temper rise, she asked, "Did a member of my family or one of our guests say something to upset you?"

"Madam, I must insist. Good evening."

Exasperated, she replied, "Very well then, sir. I certainly cannot explain what I do not understand." As Darcy nodded and began to walk on, she added in a low voice, "I suppose, though, it was simply a matter of time before you found fault with your surroundings. As we know, your standards are quite exacting."

With his eyes flashing, he turned and answered in a voice barely under control, "Madam, that is hardly fair. Pardon me if I do not apologize for my behavior, but I think I am the injured party in this matter."

"I can hardly see how that is possible. But if you will not explain what has happened, I certainly cannot judge."

Staring at her with clenched fists, he sputtered, "Madam, in coming here, I thought… I did not know that everyone knew… I never would have…" Stopping to gain control, he took a deep breath and said in an even tone, "I simply cannot stay here any longer. I will not subject myself to ridicule. I know you believe that I am more intolerant than most, but I truly believe no man would be comfortable in such an untenable position. I suppose I had no reason to believe otherwise. You were under no obligation to keep my dealings with you private, but I simply assumed that your sense of honor would require as much, or that you would at least have warned me. Your sister led me to believe that events between us had remained private. The mistake is mine, and I will clearly take responsibility for my behavior, but pardon me, madam, if I refuse to prolong your neighbors' entertainment at my expense."

Seething with equal parts anger and frustration, she replied in a forced calm, "Sir, I do not have the pleasure of understanding you."

"Madam, can you deny that your indiscretion has placed me in a most uncomfortable position?"

Raising her voice, she replied, "My indiscretion? Sir, if anyone has the right to be uncomfortable, I do."

Raising his voice to match hers, he retorted, "Yes, but the decision to let everyone know the details of what would have been better left private was yours alone."

In utter exasperation, Elizabeth looked away in an attempt to calm herself. She then asked, "Mr. Darcy, I am at a loss. What are you referring to?"

"Madam, I can hardly believe that your confusion in this matter is genuine. But I will be explicit, if you insist. Inside, I heard your mother commenting about the proposal you rejected that would have secured the financial stability of your family. As I said, I am responsible for my own actions in that regard, and if you saw fit to share the details of what I assumed was a private matter, then that was the risk I took. But I will not remain here and allow the whole of the neighborhood to speculate about such a personal matter."

Elizabeth blinked at him several times in disbelief and then said, "Sir, if you will calm down, I can explain."

Crossing his arms in defiance, he spat, "Truly? I find that hard to believe."

"Sir, I can understand your confusion, but your tone and manner are making it very difficult for me to proceed. You seem quite willing to think the worst."

"That, madam, may be a trait we share." With that remark, they stared at each other in defiance and anger for several minutes, each unwilling to look away.

At length, Elizabeth began to calm down as she recognized the absurdity of the situation. She then said, in an even tone, "Sir, the proposal my mother was referring to occurred last November."

"Last November? I… I do not understand."

"Yes, that much is evident. Despite your earlier statements, I am not in the habit of sharing personal information with someone so unconnected with the underlying events, but since you overheard my mother, I will make an exception. My mother was referring to the proposal that I turned down from my cousin, Mr. Collins."

Mr. Darcy looked at her uncomprehendingly, then colored and impulsively exclaimed, "Mr. Collins! I can scarcely believe… But how… He asked you… Surely he could not have believed you would accept him?"

"Mr. Darcy, I have no idea what he thought. I suppose he felt that the improvement to my family's situation made the match appealing. Otherwise, I really cannot say. You must remember, sir, that a woman has no control over who proposes to her."

With a conciliatory tone and a contrite smile, Darcy replied, "Yes, madam, I believe I have learned that lesson."

Startled by his statement, Elizabeth looked up at him and found him staring at her intently. Embarrassed by the magnitude of the error he had just committed, he could find no words for several minutes. He then said with great emotion, "Miss Bennet, please accept my most profound apology. I let my anger rule me, and the results were unpardonable. I regret everything I said, and the manner in which I said it. I beg your forgiveness."

Pausing to search his face, Elizabeth replied with sincerity, "Mr. Darcy, I thank you for your apology, and I accept it. Under the circumstances, the misunderstanding was quite reasonable. The lion's share of the blame must go to my mother. She should never have discussed such a private matter in public. I am afraid my mother so regrets the loss of the opportunity that she cannot accept the result."

Looking at her with apprehension, Darcy could not help but ask, "If I may be so bold, then, I take it that it is the only proposal she is aware of?"

Elizabeth colored, looked away, and stared into the darkness of the path. As she continued to avoid his gaze, she replied, "You are quite correct, sir. If she knew otherwise, I do not believe either of us would be able to escape her attention on the subject." She then added in a barely audible voice, "I have told only Jane."

"I thank you for your prudence in that regard, and I apologize again for what I implied. It was unfair of me, in many ways. I had no right."

Turning to look at him, she replied, "Let me also apologize for my intemperate words. Perhaps it would be best if we put this misunderstanding behind us."

As Darcy contemplated her words, he resolved to do more than that. "Miss Bennet, I realize that this conversation may make you uncomfortable, but I think I would be remiss if I did not take this opportunity to clear the air. I want to apologize for my rash actions this evening, and I also want to apologize for my behavior in Kent."

Interrupting him, Elizabeth said, "Please, sir, we have already discussed this. You need say no more. Let us put that episode behind us also."

"I would very much like to do exactly that, but I do not think it will be possible until I let you know how much I regret my offensive conduct toward you."

Staring at the ground, she replied, "Truly, sir, there is no need. I also said many harsh things that I regret."

"No, it is not the same. I owe you the apology…" Pausing to gain his courage, he then began to speak in an urgent manner, "Madam, since I have come into your company again, I have attempted to show you that I harbor no ill will toward you for the things that you said to me in Kent. They were justified. By hearing your reproofs, I have been able to see myself more clearly. As circumstances have recently required us to be in society together, I had hoped that we could simply ignore our past dealings and attempt to forge a friendship. I wanted to do so both for Miss Bennet and Mr. Bingley's sake, and for my own. After tonight, and not just because of my foolish misunderstanding, I have come to realize that I have set an impossible goal. We cannot ignore what has passed between us; it seems to haunt me at every turn. I know it is presumptuous of me to believe that we can be friends, but if you are willing, I would like to try. I now know, however, that we cannot become friends by ignoring the past. Instead, we would need to become friends in spite of the past. I am not sure if you would wish to have me as a friend, but I would very much appreciate it, if you could see your way to considering me as such. Miss Bennet, I know my manner of address had been improper, and I hope you can forgive me for speaking plainly. I do not expect you to answer now; I just ask that you consider it."

Elizabeth continued to stare at Darcy as she tried to understand all that he had said to her. While she was surprised by his request, she was no less moved by it. As she puzzled over all that he had meant by his words, she suddenly realized that she had failed to respond to him for several moments. His furrowed brow and the anxious set of his jaw showed his concern for her reply. She finally offered, "Mr. Darcy, I am sorry. I must admit that the eloquence of your offer has somewhat taken me by surprise. I do not need to think about your request any further. I would very much like to call you a friend. If you feel you can forgive my misjudgment of you, then I am more than willing."

Darcy expressed his thanks with a genuine smile. After taking the indulgent pleasure of studying her face for a moment, he forced himself to speak. "Miss Bennet, I suppose you should return to the house. I have kept you in the night air far too long. I think you are wrong, though, about the path. The moon seems to be quite bright tonight, and I believe the walk will do me good. Please give my apologies to your family."

As he bowed and she curtseyed her adieu, he impulsively added, "Miss Bennet, at the risk of losing the generous pardon that you have bestowed upon me, I must beg leave to ask one more question."

Arching her brow, she replied, "I am at your disposal, sir."

As he exposed his dimples to her again, he said, "I must admit that I am quite surprised to find I have something in common with Mr. Collins. I never would have thought we would be members of the same club, so to speak. It naturally leads me to wonder if there are other members."

"Excuse me."

"I was just wondering how many other proposals you have refused?"

Staring at him with her head cocked to one side, she replied, "Sir, while you are free to ask any question you wish, I am, of course, free to refuse to answer."

"Yes, Miss Bennet, you are quite right. It is none of my business how many proposals you have rejected. I suppose, now that I have given it some thought, I would only really be interested if you were to accept one."

As she stood pondering his words, he said, "Good evening, Miss Bennet," and began his journey to Netherfield.

Chapter 12

BILLIARDS AND OTHER GAMES

AS MORNING BLOOMED BRIGHTLY at Netherfield, two of its occupants sat in the breakfast room anticipating the day with very little joy. Bingley's usually cheerful disposition was darkened with anxiety. His sisters had returned the day before, while he was calling at Longbourn. When he returned home, he found that they had retired to their rooms, with word that they would receive him the following morning. Bingley had been concerned about his sisters' reaction to his letter, especially Caroline's, ever since he had sent it four days before. Putting off their inevitable first encounter, even if by only one more night, seemed designed to ensure that he lost more sleep.

Darcy, on the other hand, had slept quite well. After his encounter with Elizabeth at Longbourn three nights before, the tenor of his dreams had changed. Elizabeth had been the primary focus of his nightly visions since he had met her in the fall. It was then that he began to memorize her every detail. To his surprise, after Hunsford, the frequency and intensity of his dreams increased. Their vividness, however, was not always welcome. While her presence always evoked an erotic response, they seldom ended well. Often he would spend the entire dream pursuing her through a forest or through shrouded mist, only to finally catch her hand as she transformed into Caroline Bingley or his cousin Anne. Or he would dream that Elizabeth had accepted his proposal and they were in their bedchamber. She would be dressed in a translucent gown, with her hair flowing freely down her back. She would accept his invitation to join him in his bed. He would watch her as she lay down surrounded by dim candlelight, but when he attempted to join her, he would find his path inexplicably blocked or she would disappear once he neared the bed. Sometimes, he would reach the bed and find that she had already begun to accept the advances of another version of himself. He would watch as his alter ego would slowly slide the strap of her gown off her shoulder. His initial interest in seeing her in so intimate a pose would slowly turn to panic, as he realized something was amiss. He would suddenly understand that it was impossible for there to be two versions of himself, one in the bed and one watching. The man in the bed would then reveal himself to be Wickham or sometimes his cousin Fitzwilliam, and he would attempt to warn her, but his voice would fail him.

Worst of all, every now and then, his dreams would not be dreamlike at all. They would start out well enough. His mind would envision a previous encounter with Elizabeth that he had enjoyed—her playing the piano in Kent, teasing him at Netherfield, or walking with him at Rosings. His pleas-ant memory would then inevitably turn into his proposal at Hunsford and her rejection. The scene would then become a tedious replay of their conversation. The order of events would get jumbled. He and Elizabeth would repeat certain things that they had said out of sequence so that the conversation would loop back upon itself and never reach resolution.

For the last few nights, though, things had been far more pleasant. He had returned from his dinner at Longbourn in a mix of emotions. He was mortified that he had jumped to so stupid a conclusion about what he had overheard, but he felt relieved that he had spoken plainly to her about his desire to stay in the neighborhood and court her friendship. He found himself in the unfamiliar position of wanting to talk to someone about what had transpired. Unfortunately, he had left Bingley at Longbourn before the night was even half over. He determined to wait for him in order to gain some intelligence as to Elizabeth's behavior after he left, and to seek his friend's advice. He had not counted on Bingley's unending willingness to stay in Miss Bennet's presence or the effect the several brandies he drank while waiting would have on him. In the end, he stumbled to bed before Bingley returned. He slept in a deep, uninterrupted slumber, the likes of which he had not experienced in months.

The next day, he went hunting with Bingley and several gentlemen from the neighborhood, including John Lucas. Bingley had planned the outing after he learned that the Bennets were to be away from home visiting at their Aunt Philips for the whole of the day. While Lucas was amiable during the outing, Darcy could not help but feel challenged by his presence. He retired for the evening feeling less confident and dreamed, once again, he and Elizabeth were in his bedchamber. But this time, to his astonishment, his progress to the bed was not impeded, and she did not disappear. Instead, she willingly accepted him and no imposter emerged to ruin the encounter.

He spent the next day alone, while Bingley visited Longbourn, distracted by the vivid details of his dream. In an attempt to think of something else, he went to Bingley's study, with orders that he not be disturbed, and began the arduous task of reviewing his correspondence. As he examined the many letters that required his personal care, he realized how much his obsession with Elizabeth had diverted his attention from his responsibilities. He decided that he should leave for London the next morning to meet with his steward in order to prepare him for his continuing absence from Pemberley. He would also need to speak to his cousin about visiting with Georgiana. It made sense for him to go now, since it was unlikely he would see Elizabeth until after Bingley's sisters returned and resolved their differences with Miss Bennet. Nonetheless, the idea of leaving filled him with anxiety. His relationship with her was still tenuous, and he had not even seen her since their last misunderstanding and his confession.

He went to bed exhausted, heavy with the weight of his unresolved concerns. When he finally obtained sleep, he had an altogether new dream. He dreamed that he was at Pemberley and that he was walking with Elizabeth in the garden. When she stopped to pick a flower, a thorn cut her finger. He took her glove off to stop the emerging blood from spreading. He supported her bare hand in his, as his other hand firmly held the tip of her finger to stop it from bleeding. They talked of many things as he continued to hold her hand and administer pressure. He then carefully surveyed the damage and kissed her fingertip. Instead of reproaching him for his forward behavior, she smiled her thanks and they walked on. He awoke surprised that it was already morning, and while he regretted that this dream was so chaste, its pervasive pleasantness enveloped him in a sense of well-being. It was only after he recalled his travel plans that his mood blackened.

Caroline Bingley entered the breakfast room, and both men were drawn from their thoughts as they stood to receive her.

Kissing her brother with an exaggerated show of affection, she said, "Charles, it is so good to see you. I missed you exceedingly." She then moved to the other side of the table so that she could sit beside Darcy. Holding out her hand to greet him, she purred, "Ah, Mr. Darcy, what a pleasure. It is always a joy to see you," adding in a conspiratorial tone, "even if the location leaves much to be desired."

With a perfunctory bow, Darcy replied, "Miss Bingley."

"Caroline, please join us. I trust that you had a pleasant journey?"

"Actually, Charles, the roads were in terrible condition, and the timing of your summons could not have been more inconvenient. I cannot imagine what would have moved you to write such an incomprehensible letter. We came only because we were so worried about you."

"Miss Bingley, excuse me. You and your brother obviously have matters to discuss. Charles, I will take my leave now. Thank you for all of your hospitality and your friendship. Please give my regards to the Hursts."

Rising to shake his hand, Bingley replied, "Darcy, thank you. Have a safe journey."

Sounding more desperate than she hoped, Miss Bingley exclaimed, "Mr. Darcy, you are not leaving? We have just arrived. You are my only hope for civilized conversation in this neighborhood."

"Yes, I am sorry, but I have some business in town that can no longer be delayed. I will be leaving immediately."

Exasperated, she let her temper flare, exclaiming, "You see, Charles, no one would willingly stay here." Tempering her voice somewhat, she added, "We must follow Mr. Darcy's lead and also go to town. There is so much going on there now. It would be a crime to miss it for the likes of what the society here has to offer."

With a rarely displayed stern countenance, Bingley replied in an even but firm manner, "Caroline. That will be enough. I will brook no more criticism of the neighborhood. Netherfield is my home; you will not disrespect my neighbors."

Shocked by his words and his manner, she colored and exclaimed, "Charles, what has gotten into you? Mr. Darcy, you must help me speak sense to him. He is acting most strangely..."

Interrupting her mid-sentence, Darcy answered, "Miss Bingley, I suggest you give the area another chance. I believe it will grow on you. Despite my previous misconceptions, I have found that the society here has much to offer."

After Darcy left, Caroline added in a shrill tone, "Charles, see what you have done; you have driven him away. I will be surprised if he returns at all. You must go after him."

Exasperated, Bingley replied, "Caroline, that is enough. I can assure you, Darcy will return as soon as he is able. But that is beside the point; I want to speak to you about Netherfield. You and I need to talk about your future."

Losing her composure, she replied, "My future, Charles? I think you need to think about your own future, about what you are doing here. You are making a fool of yourself. Louisa and I both agree. It was all we could talk about on the journey here.

For you to come back here, to pursue Jane Bennet, the thought of it is mortifying. You know she does not return your affections. She is simply obliging her mother by paying you any heed. You simply must forget her. In Scarborough, you were introduced to several lovely women. You must admit that Miss McClennen was particularly charming and her connections are impeccable. I believe she has quite a fortune of her own. After your departure, she inquired of you twice. If we return immediately, I believe you could call on her before she leaves."

"Caroline. I am staying here, and for the moment, so are you."

"Charles, I am only thinking about you. I do not want to see you hurt."

Bingley bowed his head, trying to gather his thoughts. He then stood and crossed the table to sit beside his sister. Taking her hand, he began speaking in a very tender tone. "Caroline, I want you to listen to me now. It is very important to me. I love you, and I respect your opinion, but I am not leaving Hertfordshire. I have spent a great deal of time of late with Miss Bennet, and I intend to spend even more time in her company in the future. I know full well what I am about, and I believe I, alone, am the best judge of Miss Bennet's motivations. My only concern is that your relationship with her has not been all that it should be. I want you to rectify that. I want you to call on her with me this afternoon, and when you do, I want you to welcome her as you would a sister. In doing so, I also expect you to treat her family with respect. I know this will pain you, but I must tell you that I was very angry with you when I discovered that you had concealed Miss Bennet's visit this winter. But I do not want to dwell on that. What I want is for you to accept Miss Bennet and make her feel welcome at Netherfield."

Dropping his hand in contempt, Caroline replied defensively, "Charles, I can only imagine the nonsense that she must be telling you. The misunderstanding regarding her visit has been exaggerated out of proportion, no doubt to suit her mother's devious intent. I do not think..."

Raising his hand to indicate he had heard enough, Charles stood and continued in a firmer tone, "Caroline, I will not argue over who was at fault this winter because I know that, in the end, the lion's share of the responsibility belongs to me. I let other people make my decisions for me, and if I am now unsatisfied with the result, I have no one to blame but myself. It has taught me a valuable lesson, though. My plans are no longer open for debate. I am staying here and courting Miss Bennet. The question is whether you will be staying here too. If you do not believe you can receive Miss Bennet in the manner that I expect, then I will not allow you to stay on here or in the townhouse in London. I am not sure how you will be able to make your way on your income, but I will try to help you get started. I want to see you happy, and I hope it can be at my side, but if it cannot, I will understand."

Caroline looked at him aghast, formulating her next move. While she had never had the interest or patience to learn chess, she analyzed her options in a manner befitting the game. Determining that the connection to her brother and, by association, Darcy, was her utmost concern, she calculated that her best move was to stay at Netherfield. If in the process, an opportunity to help minimize Charles's chances of winning Miss Bennet presented itself, all the better.

"Charles, you have misunderstood me. If you believe that Miss Bennet returns your affection, then I am nothing but happy for you both. But in any case, I am more than happy to further the acquaintance. I would rather call tomorrow, though; I have so many things to do today. The household is in utter disarray. It appears I must oversee every detail personally or nothing will be done properly."

"Caroline, I must insist that you come with me today. I think after the misunderstandings that have passed between you, your calling so soon after your arrival will demonstrate your eagerness to improve your relationship. While you are there, you can invite Miss Bennet's family to dine with us tomorrow night."

"That is impossible, Charles! I could not possibly get this household in shape on such short notice."

"Very well, Caroline. Come with me today, and invite just Miss Bennet and Miss Elizabeth to tea tomorrow. You can put off hosting her entire family for a few days longer. I must say, I think it is wonderful that you are so concerned about making a good impression. But even if the dinner cannot occur immediately, let us extend the invitation today. I will leave you now; you obviously have much to do. We leave for Longbourn in two hours. I will see if Louisa wishes to accompany us."

As Caroline watched him go, she made a mental note not to underestimate Charles's tactical ability again.

~

Elizabeth approached Netherfield with a sense of apprehension that she could barely comprehend. She knew it was not on account of seeing either Caroline Bingley or Louisa Hurst again. When they had called the previous afternoon at Longbourn, they greeted Jane and, by extension, herself, with all that was civil and insincere. Jane accepted their attention with a graciousness that Elizabeth knew she could never have mustered. Nonetheless, the visit passed pleasantly and without incident. At its close, Mr. Bingley's sisters insisted that Jane and Elizabeth come to tea at Netherfield the following afternoon. For Jane's sake, Elizabeth willingly accepted the invitation.

As the time for the visit approached, however, she was surprised to find that her stomach felt as if it contained butterflies. She knew that her anxiety stemmed from the fact that she would be seeing Mr. Darcy for the first time since their misunderstanding outside Longbourn. She chastised herself for getting into such a state. She usually left the art of useless worry to her mother. While her opinion of Mr. Darcy had taken a decided turn for the better, she thought they had little in common. In the past, on the few occasions when her prejudice against him had not colored her judgment completely, she had felt that it was either impossible to read him well enough to determine what he was thinking or she had not bothered to even try. Maybe their further acquaintance was a good idea. If nothing else, it might allow her an opportunity to ascertain who he really was.

As they entered the drawing room, Mr. Bingley excitedly welcomed them both. Caroline and Louisa parroted his greeting without any of his enthusiasm. They briefly talked of Netherfield and the renovation that Miss Bingley believed it required. Mr. Bingley's earnest attempts to garner Jane's opinion on the subject made it manifest that her thoughts carried more weight than Caroline's. Elizabeth was heartened by the turn of the discussion. It not only showed that Caroline was resolved to the fact that Mr. Bingley would be keeping Netherfield for the distant future, but it also revealed Mr. Bingley's belief that he could not envision his home without Jane's imprimatur. Despite her interest in the topic, Elizabeth found herself distracted. She wondered if Mr. Bingley's friend would be joining them. She had to admit that even though she was nervous about seeing him again, she was more disappointed that he had not yet paid his respects. Maybe he regretted what he had said about their friendship. He may have thought better of it in the cold light of day. She was surprised that the thought was sufficient to unnerve her.

As the visit began to come to a close, Elizabeth realized that she had been far too silent. In an attempt to mask her inattentiveness she addressed Miss Bingley. "Do you intend then to stay on here for the summer?"

It was clear from Caroline's reaction that Elizabeth had hit on a sore subject. Caroline coldly responded, "Our plans, as of yet, are unfixed."

"Well, Caroline, that is not exactly accurate," interrupted Bingley. "I intend to stay on indefinitely. Darcy had invited us to Pemberley for the end of the summer, but that is not certain, as I am not sure that he has fixed his own plans yet."

At this Jane spoke up, "Mr. Bingley, how is Mr. Darcy? I had hoped to see him today so that we could finish our discussion about poetry."

Nodding in a knowing manner, Bingley took Jane's hint. "He had to leave on business yesterday, but I know he will very much regret missing your visit."

Seeing her moment to shine, Caroline said, "Oh, Jane, I did not know you were interested in poetry. I so love a good verse. Mr. Darcy and I have talked many times about poetry. He is such a proficient reader and his tastes are so varied. I always look forward to our literary discussions. I was inconsolable when he had to go to town, but he specifically promised to return to us at his earliest convenience."

"Yes, well…" sputtered Bingley, looking uncomprehendingly at his sister, "I do expect him to return when he is able."

Jane replied, "I am sure we all look forward to his arrival. But I am afraid we must take our leave. Caroline, thank you so much for your lovely hospitality. I am in your debt. Louisa, it so good to see you again."

With a perfunctory nod, Caroline replied, "Oh, you are quite welcome. You must come again soon."

Standing to kiss Jane's hand, Bingley addressed his sister, "Caroline, did you not have another invitation to offer? I remember yesterday when we left Longbourn, you were lamenting that you had forgotten to broach the subject."

With false cheerfulness, Caroline thanked her brother for the reminder and turned to Jane. "My brother is quite right. I do not know what has come over me. I was hoping your entire family could dine here in five days' time for a small family dinner, if that is convenient. If not, we can choose a later date."

"Oh, Caroline, how lovely of you. I believe that would be fine, and I know my mother would want me to accept on her behalf."

Clapping his hands, Bingley responded with an infectious smile, "Then it is all settled. Miss Bennet, Miss Elizabeth, let me escort you to your carriage."

As they walked out, Elizabeth heard Bingley request permission to call on Jane the following morning. As Jane acceded to his request, he helped her into the carriage and kissed her hand. Elizabeth could not help but see how he lingered a little longer than necessary. While Elizabeth celebrated the obvious progress her sister and he had clearly made in their relationship, she felt a pang of sadness at her own lack of comfort in that regard. Her mind immediately flew to Mr. Darcy's smiling face, as he left her several evenings ago for his nighttime stroll to Netherfield. The thought discombobulated her, as she attempted to formulate a coherent reply to Mr. Bingley's adieu.

As they drove along, Elizabeth wondered again at the disappointment she felt over Mr. Darcy's departure from Netherfield. It made her realize how much she had anticipated seeing him today. During their acquaintance, he had always appeared unexpectedly in her company, and therefore, on some level, she took his presence for granted. Her recent vow to try to get to know him better was based on her belief that she had all the time in the world to do exactly that whenever she chose to do it. Now that she could imagine commencing a friendship with him, he was gone, and his absence made her oddly unsettled. She felt frustrated that she did not know why he had left and had no idea when he would return.

Before the carriage arrived at Longbourn, Jane broke the silence. "Lizzy, do you think I should have accepted Caroline's invitation on our mother's behalf?"

Squeezing her hand in reassurance, Elizabeth replied, "Of course you should have, Jane. You know Mama would most definitely want to attend. If you had not, she would probably have sent us both back on Nellie to accept for her."

After laughing briefly at the thought, Jane again turned serious. "I thought it was very nice of Caroline to invite us all for dinner."

"Well, I think the invitation best pleased her brother, and that is what matters. I think you are in danger of him falling very much in love with you. I hope you will not leave him in suspense for too long."

"Oh, Lizzy, I think you are imagining things. But do be serious, do you think his sisters are sincere about wanting to continue a friendship with me?"

"Jane, I think what is important is what Mr. Bingley wants. I think his sisters now understand that he intends to call on you quite frequently and that their acquaintance with you will be a long one. Given that, I think they want you to be easy in their company and develop a friendship from there."

Thinking for a moment, Jane asked, "And do you think that is a sufficient basis from which to form a friendship?"

"Yes, I do. What you have in common is that you all love Mr. Bingley. Do not try to deny it. I can see it in your eyes, and I know Mr. Bingley's sisters can too. In the end, that is what will bind all of you together, and I do not think it matters whether his sisters came to it willingly or not. Ultimately, if Mr. Bingley chooses you and you accept him, then everything else will fall into place of its own accord. You need only worry about your feelings for him. You need not worry over how he feels about you. It is quite obvious."

Upon their return to Longbourn, Elizabeth was proven correct about her mother's reaction to their invitation to dine at Netherfield. Her excitement was only surpassed by her anticipation of what Mr. Bingley's visit on the morrow might bring. By the time he did call, Mrs. Bennet had everyone in a state of confusion, as she attempted to orchestrate an opportunity for Jane and Mr. Bingley to be alone in the drawing room. In the end, her machinations proved worthwhile, as Mr. Bingley soon withdrew to Mr. Bennet's library for a private conference.

As Elizabeth approached Jane, the joy was evident on her sister's face. "Oh, Lizzy, I am so happy. I do not deserve it. I wish everyone could be this happy."

Laughing, Elizabeth replied, "I take it, then, that you have something to tell me?"

"Yes, you know I do!" With tears of joy springing to her eyes, she continued, "Lizzy, he asked me to marry him. He told me that he loved me and that he has always loved me. He told me that I had to accept his proposal because he would never be happy without me and that, even if I were not ready to accept him now, he intended to wait for me forever. He promised to make me the happiest of women."

"And what did you say?"

"I told him that he had already succeeded in that regard and that I want nothing more than to be his wife. I told him that I loved him dearly."

"Oh, dear, sweet Jane, I am so happy for you."

"Lizzy, you will be shocked, but after I accepted his proposal, I let him kiss me, and it was exquisite! I was completely lost in his arms. He is so strong and sweet. I felt dizzy at his touch, and when he took me in his arms, I thought my heart would leap from my chest. I cannot tell you how wonderful it feels to love someone who loves me in return. It is almost too much. I feel I shall burst with excitement."

"Well, we cannot have that! You will just have to survive and be the happiest of women."

"Oh, Lizzy, my joy will only be complete when you are as happy too."

"Jane, I can never be as happy as you. Till I have your disposition, your goodness, I never can have your happiness. No, no, let me shift for myself, and, perhaps, if I have very good luck, I may meet with another Mr. Collins in time."

Mr. Bennet's assent to the match was quickly given, and the day was filled with joy for everyone at Longbourn. That evening, Bingley told his sisters of his proposal, and to his satisfaction, only well wishes were heard. Thereafter, Bingley was, of course, a daily visitor at Longbourn, coming frequently before breakfast and always remaining till after supper. His friend remained in London, attending to his many responsibilities.

The day that the Bennets were to dine at Netherfield, Jane and Elizabeth called late in the morning to visit by themselves. All of the Bennet women had come the previous afternoon, at Caroline's request, to view Jane's future chambers and the whole of the residence. The offer to view the estate was mandatory for Caroline, but Elizabeth was glad to see that it came without delay or any hint of reluctance. Elizabeth thought Caroline bore the visit well, despite her perfunctory responses and her obvious exasperation at their mother's comments regarding the worth of each piece of furniture. Her mother clearly would have tried anyone's patience as she waxed on about Jane's sudden wealth and gave her unsolicited advice about every aspect of the household. While Elizabeth was once again disappointed that there was no news or mention of Mr. Darcy, she was actually relieved that he was not present to see her mother's tactless inventory of Netherfield. That night, Jane confided to Elizabeth that, through Charles, she had secured an opportunity the next morning to see the house again, without her mother's meddling, and that she wished Elizabeth to join her. Elizabeth gladly accepted the invitation, both as a means to help her sister and to escape their mother's endless conversations about the wedding.

As they began the tour, Elizabeth found Caroline's comments almost as aggravating as her mother's had been the day before. Today, Caroline's tone was clearly instructional. She obviously welcomed this second visit, as it was an opportunity to school Jane on what she had determined needed to be done at Netherfield and exactly how it should be accomplished. In the process, Jane's opinions were brushed aside. As Elizabeth lagged behind, she contemplated challenging Caroline, but thought that ultimately it would not matter, as Jane would have the final say and Mr. Bingley would support her in whatever fashion was required. She would let Caroline have a few final moments to rule the roost before advising Jane to voice her own opinions more forcefully. Listening to Caroline, however, was easier said than done. Deciding that the only way she could hold her tongue was to separate herself from Caroline, she wandered off into the next open door to take in its decor alone. To her shock, she stood face to face with a coatless Mr. Darcy, who apparently had been playing pool in the billiard room.

Quickly putting his cue stick on the table, he bowed and exclaimed, "Miss Bennet."

"Mr. Darcy… I did not mean to intrude. I did not realize you had returned. I will leave you to your game. I am sorry for interrupting…"

Walking with long strides, he quickly stood in front of her as he said in a rushed manner, "No, you are not intruding at all. I had just arrived from town. The servants told me that Mr. Bingley was out. I thought I would just pass some time in here until he returned. I did not want to bother Miss Bingley. I was not aware that she had company."

Looking away in embarrassment and, thereafter, often at the

ground, she said, "Yes, Jane is visiting, and I accompanied her. I thought I would just take a moment to myself. But I would not dream of intruding on your privacy."

"As I said, you are not intruding. But if you wanted privacy, I am in your way."

"No, you were here first. Let me leave you to your game."

Stepping toward her, he said in an earnest tone, "Miss Bennet, I would like you to stay." At his words, she looked up to see him staring intensely at her. He then said, "I believe you walked in on me once before, in this very room, and at the time I failed to invite you to remain. I have long regretted that decision. Please give me the opportunity to correct my prior mistake. Let me just retrieve my coat."

Shocked at how nervous she felt, she simply said, "Very well, sir," as she continued to stare at the pattern in the carpet.

After turning around to put on his coat, he stood before her, smiling broadly. After a pause, he asked. "How have you been?"

"Quite well, thank you. And you?"

"Very well, thank you for asking... I just returned from town... I had some business with my steward that could not be delayed, but I wanted to return as soon as I could."

Somewhat startled by the implication of his statement, she could not help but respond, "Is that so?"

"Yes, Mr. Bingley wrote to tell me of his proposal and Miss Bennet's acceptance. I wanted to congratulate them as soon as possible."

"Oh, yes, of course. It is very joyous news. They seem quite happy."

Smiling, he said, "I am sure they are."

After a somewhat lengthy pause, she added, "My sister has

come to view the house. Caroline is conducting the tour, and I thought they might progress further without my interference."

"Oh, that seems wise." After another awkward pause, he asked, "Miss Bennet, can I ring for some tea or refreshments?"

"No, thank you, I am fine."

"Yes, very well…" Trying to think of something to say, other than declaring how much he had missed her and inquiring if she had even noted his absence, he impulsively said, "Well, I was just passing the time by playing billiards. Do you play? Maybe you would consent to a match?"

Incredulous, Elizabeth repeated, "Do I play? Mr. Darcy, I am taken aback by your question. I would be reluctant to respond, even if I did. It is not typically seen as a woman's game." Unable to resist, she added, "I am afraid there must be some mischief afoot in your inquiry."

Smiling broadly, he replied, "Not at all. I was simply trying to ascertain if you were interested in a game. I assure you, I would never dream of attempting any mischief in your company. It would clearly be folly on my part."

Suppressing a laugh, she asked, "Do you think so?"

"Oh, yes, that I know for certain." As they smiled at each other, he added, "I suppose my question could be considered somewhat unorthodox, but it does not necessarily seem so to me. I am probably divulging a family secret that my sister will regret, but, as I am sure you know, the winters at Pemberley are very harsh, and without the superior guidance of my mother, I must admit, I let my sister talk me into teaching her to play. She is quite good. We often pass the time in such a manner. I suppose I assumed there were other women who played, and I thought that if you did, you would not be averse to a game of competition."

With her eyes alive with laughter, she challenged, "Are you insinuating that I have a competitive nature? I am not sure that is flattering."

"I was simply noting that you always seem to enjoy a challenge. Clearly that is a praiseworthy trait."

"Even in a woman?"

"When an attribute is scarce, it should be appreciated all the more."

"That may be so, but would you not be embarrassed to compete against a woman? What if I were to win?"

Raising his eyebrow to accept the challenge, he replied, "Miss Bennet, as I have told you before, I am not afraid of you."

His response made her catch her breath. As he held her gaze, Elizabeth was surprised at how flushed she felt and hoped her cheeks did not reveal it. As she tried to determine what response she could give, she heard the unwelcome high-pitched voice of Miss Bingley. "Mr. Darcy, I was not informed that you had returned! Please forgive me; I should have waited on you immediately. Has Thomas placed your belongings in your room? You must be tired from your journey. Do you wish to retire? Can I get you some refreshments? I am so pleased you have returned."

Despite the interruption, Darcy continued to gaze at Elizabeth for her response. He then slowly turned to Miss Bingley. "I just arrived and did not want to impose on you. My bags have been delivered, and I am quite comfortable, thank you." Turning to Jane, he walked forward and took her hand as he said, "Miss Bennet, Mr. Bingley wrote me of your engagement. I am so pleased. He is a very fortunate man, and I wish you both every happiness."

Smiling, Jane replied, "Mr. Darcy, it is so good to see you.

Thank you for your gracious sentiments. I know Mr. Bingley was eager to tell you of our engagement, and he will be quite pleased to learn that you have returned."

As Darcy thanked Jane, Caroline came forward to claim his arm. "Mr. Darcy, you must join us in the sitting room; we were just discussing what changes must be made to Netherfield, and your opinion would be most welcome. Pemberley is the standard by which all gracious homes must be measured, and I think Jane would benefit from your wisdom as to how one goes about decorating a fine estate. I am afraid that with her limited background, the task may be daunting."

Darcy colored and looked down. He knew the obvious slight to Jane might remind Elizabeth of the unkind things he had once said about her family's station in life. Resolved to make his position clear, he extricated his arm as he said, "Thank you, but no. I am sure such issues would best be left to the ladies. I am confident Miss Bennet is more than capable of handling all of the details related to the running of Netherfield. She only needs the time and freedom to become comfortable making her own decisions."

Missing his message completely, Caroline continued. "Yes, but until she has that confidence, I want to make sure she has all the help she needs. I was just telling her that she should, at least, consult a master furniture maker or a fabric designer, someone who is abreast of the latest fashions here and abroad, to help guide her. I am sure that each room of Pemberley has been carefully crafted with the help of countless craftsmen so that they reflect what the highest levels of society have to offer."

"Actually, in the past, only major renovations have been completed with the consultation of an architect, and the furnishings have been mostly selected by the people who use them. I know my mother decorated all of the main family rooms herself, based on sketches she made. Georgiana also recently redid her suite. She was able to obtain the effect she wanted by a simple meeting with a few local tradesmen. In the end, it came out quite well."

In a cooing voice, Caroline added, "I am sure Georgiana did a beautiful job, but she has been raised in such elegance, it was probably second nature to her. I think our dear Jane might need a little more direction."

Trying to extricate himself from the conversation, but seeing that Caroline had no intention of leaving until she felt she had said all that she wanted, he flatly added, "I was unaware that Netherfield required renovations."

"Oh, yes, it is in dire need of updating. I am sure that if it were your home, you would require many alterations."

"Actually, no, I cannot think of anything, other than allowing Miss Bennet, as the new mistress of the house, the opportunity to change anything she desired."

Clearly disappointed with his responses, Caroline began to usher the party from the room, until Darcy added, "I can think of one thing, although it is a very small point." Looking directly at Elizabeth, he continued, "I believe this billiard room might benefit from a less austere design so that it did not appear an exclusively masculine domain. I must say, I have never had a more enjoyable time within it than today, when the company was mixed."

Although she kept her head down, Elizabeth could not repress her smile as she left the room. Noting her reaction, Darcy watched her go, feeling more optimistic than he had in a very long while.

TABLE TALK

ELIZABETH LEFT THE BILLIARD room in a state of confusion and excitement. She wondered at Mr. Darcy's ability to incite such turmoil. She knew part of her response was due to the fact that his comments had a double meaning intended solely for her benefit. As such, they seemed more intimate. She also understood that because her reaction obviously had to be internalized, it seemed more intense. The truth of the matter was that he had been flirting with her, and to her own astonishment, she had been flirting back. While she was not the most beautiful woman in Hertfordshire, this was not the first time she had received the attentions of a man, or even returned them. But she had never felt such exhilaration before. Maybe it was their tumultuous history, but his overt attention, even if it were only obvious to her, made her heart race and made her long for a more intimate setting. She wondered what she would have said had they not been interrupted. There were a million reasons for her to deny that she knew how to play billiards, but the one idea that kept flittering across her consciousness was that her denial might prompt him to offer her a lesson on the subject. She was shocked at the impropriety of her thoughts, but could not help laughing silently at her foolishness.

As Elizabeth and Jane took the short carriage ride back to Longbourn to dress for dinner, Elizabeth tried to sift through her feelings for Mr. Darcy. She had not expected to see him at Netherfield. Now, though, she anticipated their next meeting with a fair amount of impatience. She had to admit that her opinion of him had undergone a dramatic transformation. When he went away, without explanation, she regretted his absence; as she got to know him better, she began to develop an affinity for his quick wit, superior intellect, and determined style. And if she was truly honest with herself, whenever he was close to her, she found him most attractive.

But the more uncertain side of her personality wondered at what her emotions actually amounted to. Was this just vanity, enjoying the attentions of a man she had rejected? His steadfastness was certainly flattering. Or did it stem from a simple desire to find her own happiness as she watched her beloved Jane find her partner in life? No, that seemed unlikely. There were other men who had expressed their interest; John Lucas, for example. But it was not the general need for a husband or attention that was spurring her on; it was a specific interest in Mr. Darcy himself.

Despite all this, she wondered if she really knew him well enough to be developing these feelings. Understanding that all her prior opinions of him were wrong was not the same as knowing him. In some ways, she knew his character far more intimately than she did that of any other man. The intensity of their fights had allowed them to speak more frankly than was otherwise permitted in society, and his initial declaration and his subsequent actions toward her told her more about his temperament than would be obvious if their acquaintance had followed a traditional path. But she did not know much about his interests or tastes. They both seemed to have a similar affinity for literature, and each had a close bond with a sister, but she did not know about his childhood or what his everyday life was like. This, she thought, was not really a stumbling block, since it simply required that she try to get to know him better. He had requested as much, and she now thought the idea not just pleasant but essential.

As the Bennets entered Netherfield, Elizabeth tried to remain subdued and resist the temptation to seek out Mr. Darcy's countenance. Their eyes, however, soon met and they exchanged a smile as they performed their formal acknowledgments. As Mrs. Bennet began to speak at length about the beauty of the decor, Elizabeth sought a chair at the far end of the room, next to an empty seat. While her actions stemmed from a desire to separate herself from her mother, she soon realized that it had the added benefit of providing an opportunity for Mr. Darcy to seek her out. As she watched him in conversation with Miss Bingley, she noticed that he often looked her way. The realization made her look down at her hands in embarrassment, as he excused himself and began to walk toward her in an unhurried manner.

Before he reached her side, however, she heard her father's voice as he took the seat beside her. "Ah, Lizzy, I see that you have anticipated me. You have found a most secluded spot from which to monitor the forms of human folly that will most likely exhibit themselves here tonight. Well done. We will look on together and compare notes later." Elizabeth smiled at him, as she noticed Mr. Darcy move past her and take up a place by the window behind her.

As the group was called to the dining room, Elizabeth was surprised to find Mr. Bingley at her side, extending his arm and saying, "If you would not mind my company, I thought this might be a good opportunity to better acquaint myself with my new sister."

Caroline was upon them in a moment. Her only consolation in having to host this tiresome dinner was her knowledge that she would be seated at the head of the table with Charles and Jane, which, in turn, would allow her to ignore the rest of the Bennets as much as her role as mistress of the house would allow. She had already arranged for Mr. Darcy to be her escort, and she intended to spend the night impressing him with her skills as a hostess and her attention to his comfort. They did not need Eliza Bennet ruining the ambiance. "Charles, whatever are you doing? As her fiancé, you should be escorting Jane."

"I thought we might try something new this evening. I want our two families to get to know each other better. We will, after all, soon be one family. Hurst, would you do me the honor of escorting Jane to dinner? Perhaps Mr. Bennet would be so kind as to escort Louisa with Mrs. Bennet?"

Jane, seemingly unfazed by the turn of events, smiled graciously at Mr. Hurst and said, "Sir, I hope you are not too disappointed. I am afraid you will have to make do with me."

Looking confused, and anxious that dinner not be further delayed, Mr. Hurst simply grunted and offered Jane his arm.

Somewhat baffled by what was transpiring, Elizabeth nodded her acquiescence to Mr. Bingley as she approached what should have been Jane's seat. She began to suspect something was afoot when she saw Mr. Darcy standing behind his chair, attempting to suppress a smile. As she reached the table, she saw that Mr. Darcy was directly on her other side. Elizabeth immediately sought out Jane's face, but it was now Jane's turn to stare steadfastly at her hands folded in her lap. As Mr. Bingley pulled out her chair, Mr. Darcy cocked an eyebrow and bowed to her.

Seeing that she had been outmaneuvered, Caroline indignantly took her place, throwing Elizabeth a venomous stare in the process. As Mr. Darcy's name began to form on Caroline's lips, Mr. Bingley turned to her and impatiently indicated that the first course should begin. After Caroline saw that it was accomplished, Mr. Bingley began to question her thoroughly as to the minute details of the meal. By the time he finished, she looked up to see Elizabeth and Mr. Darcy deep in conversation.

Once Elizabeth sat down, Darcy addressed her. "Miss Bennet, this is a lovely surprise. I had hoped to speak to you earlier but was unable. I was beginning to feel that Fate was not on my side. Your presence here may mean that the tide has turned."

She replied in an embarrassed manner, "I am not sure that Fate would ever be bothered by such a trivial matter as our seating arrangements. It seems more likely my soon-to-be brother and my sister are to thank." Elizabeth caught her sister's eye. Jane looked a little contrite but then smiled back broadly at them both.

Noting Elizabeth's exasperated expression toward her sister, Darcy added in a sincere manner, "I believe that the debate over the degree to which Fate intervenes in our everyday lives has raged for centuries. Without attempting to solve that conundrum, I would nevertheless want you to know how sincerely grateful I am for the results." Softening his tone even more, he added, "I am sure Charles and your sister simply want to share their joy by having their families become better acquainted. I do not think anyone should take anything by it." Taking his meaning, she nodded her response. He then continued in a lighter manner, "But in any regard, I have long thought that the entire system of prearranged seating is oppressive. I know its purpose is to ensure that conversation is well rounded about the dinner table, but I inevitably find that I am somewhere other than where I would wish to be. If there is a benefit to be had, I do not recall it ever being bestowed upon me. If this is the result of anarchy, I would opt for it every time."

"You sound quite the radical, Mr. Darcy. Am I to believe you? Do you really hold social conventions in such disdain?"

"I would think, Miss Bennet, that by now you would have noticed that I am often unable to follow social conventions. That being the case, it should come as no surprise that I do not hold many of them in high regard."

His response made her laugh involuntarily, and the release of tension put her at ease. It seemed clear that he did not think her responsible for her change in location, and she had to admit that she had often also felt victimized by the order of precedence. Why could she not accept that this unexpected change was not only for the best, but being placed beside Mr. Darcy for the evening was something she had secretly been hoping for? In an attempt to remain focused on their conversation, she asked, "You must, however, think there is some efficacy in there being rules for social interactions?"

After pausing to think for a moment, he replied in a serious tone, "I suppose my answer would be both yes and no. I understand the usefulness of such rules in establishing order and to show respect where respect is due, but their effect is often to elevate form over substance. For instance, the rules of social discourse often seem designed to mask one's comments with a sense of sameness. Certain statements are required, and certain responses expected. When such a conversation is complete, I know no more about the speaker than when we began. I am not sure if the person's intention in seeking my companionship stemmed from an urge for friendly intercourse or whether the conversation was preordained to fulfill a social obligation."

"You sound quite cynical."

Smiling, he replied, "I do not mean to be."

Smiling back, she retorted, "Then, sir, I believe you must explain yourself."

"I simply intended to convey that the rules regarding social interaction are so formalized that they are sometimes beyond me. I am often unsure where the rules of discourse end and where more personal remarks are appropriate. I am afraid I often find it easier to remain silent than to attempt to navigate unfathomable waters. Otherwise, I fear all of my conversations would involve only the weather."

"I see what you mean, but there is a happy medium."

"That may well be, but I have a hard time locating it. I know you have told me, in the past, that the solution to my problem lies in practice, but I fear it is not that easy. Perhaps now is a golden opportunity to test your premise. Knowing Miss Bingley's love for elaborate meals, I am sure we will have some uninterrupted time to talk at length. We can, if you wish, attempt a prolonged conversation, and you can teach me what I am lacking."

Once again, she had to laugh at the charm of his response.

Seeing his behavior now, she thought it amazing that she ever thought him cold or in need of improvement. He was certainly doing quite well. That he would honestly discuss the subject of one of her previous reproofs made her respect him all the more. And the wit with which he approached the subject made her see him in a new light. Trying to hide her amusement, she replied, "While it is true that I might once have suggested that practice would improve both one's skills at conversation and musical accomplishment, I do not believe I ever went so far, either in the past or the present, as to infer that you needed formal instruction in that regard. I believe it would be foolhardy for me to take on such a task."

"Perhaps, then, I spoke too strongly. I am not sure I need a teacher, so much as a friendly guide. Could I not entreat you to take on that role? My motives are not all selfish, after all. Otherwise, I fear that I will bore you the whole of the evening: The weather has not really been interesting enough of late to sustain much prolonged analysis."

As he smiled disarmingly, she knew she could hardly refuse him the request. As a matter of fact, at that moment, she wondered if she could refuse him any request and found herself involuntarily leaning closer to him as she retorted, "Perhaps we can come to a compromise. You will agree that I need not hold school on the subject, and in return, we shall dispense with any concern as to each other's verbal performance. We will simply talk to each other about whatever subject interests us, without judging whether it falls strictly within the borders of polite dinner conversation or whether our utterances contain the degree of whimsy and fawning required of fashionable social exchanges."

Happy to agree to any idea where Elizabeth would talk to

him exclusively, he eagerly replied, "I think that a fine idea, and I thank you in advance for your kindness. But I am still somewhat unsure of the ground rules. Is any topic of conversation fair game? That certainly seems interesting, but I wonder if that is what you truly mean."

Catching the mischievousness in his eye, Elizabeth replied, "I may have spoken too quickly. I simply meant to imply that we need not wait for an opening to broach a topic. That is what I consider to be the hardest part of polite banter. I can often think of what I might wish to ask someone or what I might want to relate about myself, but the difficult task is fitting that information into a preexisting conversation. Because we are, as you put it, inclined to do away with the rules of social discourse, we may simply discuss whatever subject interests us without fear of the order in which we approach a topic."

As Darcy leaned toward her in the same manner, he said, "I appreciate the fine points of your response, but unless I misunderstand you, you have answered my question in the affirmative: I can ask whatever I wish?"

As Elizabeth laughed, she also sensed the danger and replied impertinently, "Perhaps it would be best if I went first." After a pause, she asked, "I suppose I have been wondering whether, given the length of your stay here in Hertfordshire, you miss your home at Pemberley?"

Darcy understood, though maybe Elizabeth did not, the fuller implications of her question, but decided it was yet too early to discuss the real reason for his extended stay in the neighborhood. Instead, he decided to answer her more direct inquiry. "I would have to say both yes and no. Pemberley is my home in every sense of the word. I only feel totally comfortable there. But I have learned of late that a house is only a home to the extent it contains the people whom you care about. At present, my sister is not residing there and… my closest friend, Mr. Bingley, is here. I would not want to miss his engagement, so while I do miss the comforts of my home, I would rather remain here to share in his and your sister's joy."

"Are there comforts there, then, that are not available here?"

"Not anything in the material sense. Just the familiarity of my surroundings, my memories, my sense of family, and, I suppose, the land itself."

"Yes, I have heard from Miss Bingley that your landholdings are quite extensive. Do you find Netherfield too confining, then?"

"I was not referring to the extent of the surrounding lands, as much as to their character. The countryside around Pemberley is quite wild, and I spend a good deal of my time outdoors. The land here is lovely, but I am afraid I have become so partial to the more rugged beauty of Derbyshire, that other terrains pale in comparison."

"Then Pemberley's surrounding park is materially different from Netherfield's, or say, Rosings'? I have always had an interest in nature in all its forms and the different manners in which the countryside is utilized."

Smiling, he retorted, "Miss Bennet, your question is quite astute. I think the best way to describe Pemberley is by reference to Rosings."

Trying to mask her true opinion of Rosings, she simply added, "Oh, is that so?"

"Yes, I think it is useful because we are both familiar with that estate, and sometimes comparison is the best manner of description. Pemberley is much older than Rosings, and as such, its gardens and park were designed long before the formal French fashion that so characterizes Rosings. The Darcys, as a lot, are a stubborn breed and, consequently, never deviated from the early style of the English rustic garden. The park therefore can barely be considered a garden at all. The natural landscaping that has developed over hundreds of years has, for the most part, remained intact. It is more accurate to say that the house is surrounded by a forest and a lake, rather than by a park, as that term is now used. I find the variety of its natural beauty quite breathtaking, but some, such as my aunt for instance, find it an untamed wilderness. In some ways, the beauty of Pemberley is truly in the eye of the beholder. Most people either love it or find it wanting—although few people actually say so to me directly."

"Then how do you know it is true?"

"From the comments of certain guests who are always suggesting that I obtain the services of a French master gardener or ask if I have ever visited some nearby garden that employs a more formalized design. I think they believe I am unaware of what could be done and hope to direct me toward what they believe to be a more civilized approach."

"Am I wrong to wonder, sir, if many of these guests are women?"

Laughing, he replied, "It seems, Miss Bennet, that all of your questions tonight are quite astute. But I do not want you to get the wrong idea. While some aspects of Pemberley might only appeal to a select type of woman, there are also more formalized gardens that I believe have universal appeal. My mother cultivated a very fine rose garden that produces a dazzling array of species in great abundance. I think it one of the finer examples of a formal garden. My mother's tastes, however, on the whole tended to a more naturalistic approach. She executed a very exacting planting design around the lake that employs a wide variety of local and rare wildflowers. Her success in that regard cannot be understated. The lake is an integral part of the house, visible from most vantage points within it, and her plantings surrounding the lake enhance its natural beauty in a most dramatic way. I think one would be surprised to find that the flowers were planted by design, as they blend into the natural order of the landscape so wonderfully, but, at the same time, the variety of color, height, and texture is glorious." Suddenly, Darcy stopped, cleared his throat in embarrassment, and added in a subdued tone, "I fear I have gone on too long."

"Not at all, Mr. Darcy. Your passion has made your descriptions so clear that I can almost imagine the views. I have found it most interesting."

Darcy, however, hardly heard her words. He had felt so comfortable talking to her about Pemberley, and he thought her interested. But, as he realized he had been speaking at length, he sudden wondered how his glowing descriptions of Pemberley sounded to someone else. In trying to judge her reaction, he suddenly recalled all of the times that he had misread her mood and was drained of his former assurance. He quietly replied, "If you are sure. I know I have released you from any obligation as my instructor, but I do hope you will stop me if I am trying your patience."

Elizabeth was struck by his sudden tentative demeanor and his lack of confidence. When she had disliked him, she imagined him haughty, cold, recalcitrant, and demanding. Since getting to know him better, she had found him witty, honest, and sincere. She had never before understood that he was also somewhat shy and, at moments, oddly uncertain of himself. Desiring to put him at ease once again, she asked, "And how would you describe the house?"

To her surprise, in attempting to formulate an answer, his cheeks blushed scarlet. After a pause, he simply replied, "I would like to think it is comfortable and inviting."

She immediately sensed her mistake. After having previously accused him of vanity and excessive pride, he hardly felt comfortable extolling the virtues of his furnishings. She tried another tack. "The lake near your home sounds delightful. Do you utilize it much in the summer?"

"Yes, we do. It is large enough to swim in, and there is also fishing, although the stream that flows into it is better suited for that endeavor. We actually use the lake more in the winter. It almost always freezes over, and we skate upon the ice." In the hope of taking the focus off himself, Darcy then added in a hurried manner, "Do you skate, Miss Bennet?"

"Actually, no, I have never tried. There is not much opportunity in this area for it."

'Well, you must learn; you cannot be at Pemberley in the winter without partaking in the exercise... I mean, that is to say, anyone who visits the area would find that it is a much-favored winter pastime."

With her brow raised in challenge, she replied, "That and, apparently, billiards."

Heartened by her response, he smiled back. "That reminds me; you never did tell me if you play."

As their eyes locked, she detected movement at her elbow. Leaning in even closer, she whispered in a conspiratorial tone, "I am afraid, Mr. Darcy... that the main course is being served."

At that, she leaned back in a fluid motion to give the server room to exchange her plate. She did so while smiling broadly at Mr. Darcy and without breaking eye contact. After a moment, she turned her attention to Caroline Bingley. "Miss Bingley, the meal looks superb. I must extend my compliments."

Darcy continued to stare at her with a faint smile on his lips as the server attended to his needs and the others began to eat. It was only after a few more minutes that he looked down at his food. He then addressed Charles and, by unwanted extension, Miss Bingley about the wedding plans. It was only after the main course was coming to a close that he saw the opportunity to again engage Elizabeth in intimate conversation.

"Miss Bennet, I have told you a great deal about my preferences for the outdoors, but you have not told me yours. Do you prefer Hertfordshire to the exclusion of other locations, or are you more at home in town?"

"I have not traveled extensively, but I would say that I prefer the country to the city. And while Hertfordshire is quite beautiful, I have a general desire to see as much of the rest of the country as possible. Until I do, I cannot say that I have a decided preference."

"By your response, should I gather that you do not enjoy London?"

"I think my answer might mirror one you recently gave. I do enjoy London, but mostly because it contains within it people whom I love. My aunt and uncle reside there, and my time with them has always been pleasurable. As a result, town has a special appeal for me."

"Are they your maternal or paternal relations?"

"I am afraid only Mr. Collins bears the distinction of

a relationship on my father's side of the family. My uncle Gardiner is my mother's brother, although he is several years her junior and bears no other striking resemblance, either physically or by disposition. My aunt is closer to my age than not, and as a result, she is both a friend and a role model for my sister Jane and me."

"Then she must be quite an extraordinary woman. Do you have the opportunity to visit them often?"

"Only on occasion. When I do, there is the added benefit that my uncle enjoys the theater and always takes us. The lure of that, added to the felicity of seeing my dearest family members, makes London a destination I would never willingly forgo. But my heart mostly resides in the countryside. Later this summer, I hope to have the best of both worlds. My aunt and uncle are planning to travel to the Lakes region and have invited me to join them. I am greatly anticipating that area's beauty."

"I have visited the Lakes on several occasions, and I think you will be justifiably impressed. But in the meantime, hopefully the beauty of Hertfordshire will be sufficient to entertain you. I remember from Kent that you enjoyed daily walks. Is that your custom at home?"

"Yes, I do try to walk out whenever I am able."

"And where do you find the most pleasant vistas?"

"The walk to Oakham Mount is quite nice."

Hoping he was not being too obvious, he then asked, "And when is it best to view?"

"I would say it is lovely at any time of the day, but as with the majority of elevations, it is most dramatic either early in the morning or before sunset."

After an awkward silence befell them, Elizabeth was the first to speak. "Mr. Darcy, you said your sister is not at Pemberley. Is she in London?"

"No, actually, she is visiting Bath, but I expect her in London soon. She has expressed an interest in attending the wedding here. I am presently considering whether she should come."

"And what have you decided?"

"Nothing at present. I need to give it more consideration."

Puzzled by his behavior, she stated, "I would think the request is a simple one. What other factors need be considered?"

"In the past, I have learned that my responsibility to my sister is great. As a result, I endeavor to mediate with great seriousness any action that concerns her."

Elizabeth's reply was interrupted by the sound of Caroline clearing her throat. She stated that the ladies should retire, but before that occurred, she would be remiss in letting the announcement of her brother's betrothals go by without acknowledgment. Caroline then said, "In honor of the occasion, I would ask Mr. Hurst to speak for our family."

That gentleman's surprise could not have been greater. He had barely been listening, and even the most disinterested observer could see his obvious confusion. It was clear to Elizabeth that Caroline had not notified Mr. Hurst of the honor she had assigned him. After several uncomfortable minutes, Mr. Hurst stated, "Yes, er, Charles, now that your engagement has been announced, may you be happy, and Miss... Bennet too."

Elizabeth thought she heard an audible sigh of relief from Louisa Hurst when her husband correctly remembered Jane's name. Seeing Caroline's smug expression, Elizabeth knew that this had been accomplished by design and wondered at the other surprises she had in store for Jane during their long engagement.

To their added embarrassment, Elizabeth then heard her mother whispering to her father, in a voice clearly discernible in the foyer, that he should say something for their family as well. Her father's voice was then clearly heard to say, "Fanny, that is enough. I will, but only if you promise to be quiet for the rest of the evening." Elizabeth could feel the hot color rising to her face. Her father then said, "I believe that someone once said, that 'Marriage is an evil that most men welcome.' Given Mr. Bingley's obvious enthusiasm for the affair, let us wish the couple every happiness."

As everyone murmured their agreement, Elizabeth could not help but be mortified by her parents' performance. But more than that, she was deeply grieved that the joy surrounding her sister's impending wedding had not been recognized with the respect or reverence it warranted. Jane deserved better. To her surprise, she was roused from her sad reverie by Mr. Darcy's voice. "Miss Bingley, I would hope that you would forgive my forwardness, but with your leave, I would like to add my wishes for Miss Bennet and Mr. Bingley's happiness. I know that I am not actually a part of either of the two families represented here tonight, but I feel moved to add my own sentiments to what has been said."

With a shocked expression upon her face, Caroline managed a perfunctory, "By all means."

Darcy looked to Jane at one end of the table, and then to Charles. "I wish you both the joy you deserve. Charles, while I have not always warranted your friendship, I have always required its steadfast support. I count myself lucky to call you my friend, and nothing could give me greater pleasure than to see you happy. I know that with Miss Bennet as your wife, your contentment is guaranteed. While Petrarch warned that 'rarely do beauty and great virtue dwell together,' Charles, you have found the exception that proves the rule. I have seldom seen a couple more suited to each other. Your even temperaments and genial dispositions make you ideal partners, and your obvious affection and regard seem destined to secure your happiness. I am doubly blessed to know you both, because through Charles's great fortune, I have undeservingly acquired a most gracious friend as well. My wishes for a long and happy life together."

As the women abandoned their chairs and began to move toward the drawing room, Darcy took Jane's hand and bestowed a warm kiss upon it. He then bowed to Elizabeth, who gave him a dazzling smile. But before he could speak to her, Caroline Bingley interceded. Having been thwarted at dinner, she was not to be deterred now. She moved between them and exclaimed, "Mr. Darcy, that was so lovely. It was very thoughtful of you to speak. Your kindness to my brother is exemplary. It was also nice of you to mention our dear Jane. But enough of this! We will leave you to enjoy yourselves."

Another opportunity to speak to Elizabeth did not arise, but as he watched her carriage drive away at the end of the evening, his heart was full. He knew that whether sleep came easily or not, his dreams would be pleasant.

Chapter 14

BOUNDARY LINES

THE DAY AFTER THE Bennets dined at Netherfield, Darcy woke early and went to the stables. As his horse was saddled, he asked the groomsman for directions to Oakham Mount. He was not sure if Elizabeth would have understood his intentions in asking about her favorite walks, but he planned to wait there in case she did. He was buoyed by their easy interaction at dinner the night before and hoped to continue in that vein.

As he waited for her, he reviewed their troubled history and tried to make out her present state of regard for him. He knew that she no longer held him in contempt and had, in fact, forgiven him his prior mistakes. He also thought that as their relationship had slowly progressed, she had noticed the changes he had attempted in response to her reproof. As a result, he felt that she now thought of him as a friend and did not find his company a burden. During dinner, he had felt, at times, that she had enjoyed herself and that she looked at him with some affection, but he was not sure if that was her overriding opinion of him, or if she were just displaying the warm regard of friendship that she might bestow on any companion. He knew he should be grateful for her friendship; a few weeks ago he would have thought it unimaginable. But no matter how much he appreciated the progress they had made, it was not enough, and he longed to have her for his own. He just needed to remind himself that the path to that goal needed to be tread with caution and patience. As he waited for her, and she failed to appear, he attempted to keep that thought in the forefront of his mind. Despite the beauty of the sunrise, he returned in a sullen mood. As he reentered Netherfield, he was immediately accosted by Caroline Bingley, who had apparently just risen.

"Mr. Darcy, I see you are returning from a ride about the grounds. How industrious. As always, your timing is impeccable. You can join me for breakfast. You must be famished from the exercise."

"Actually, Miss Bingley, I ate before I left and am quite content. May I inquire, though, is your brother about? I wanted to speak to him about his visit today to Longbourn."

"I saw him talking with his steward just now. But there is no rush, sir. His solicitor is visiting this morning, so he will not be scurrying off to Longbourn today. I am sure you would agree that his constant visits there are rather unsightly. While his engagement is now public knowledge, there is still no reason to act the lovesick puppy over it. There are appearances to consider."

Trying to mask his disappointment that his second plan to see Elizabeth was also unworkable, Darcy simply replied, "Oh, I see."

"Yes, I, for one, am quite relieved that we will all be together for a change, without the burden of entertaining the entire neighborhood in the process. I am certainly exhausted from the spectacle of last night's socializing, if you can call it that. I am

determined that today we will have a more genteel environ-
ment. It will just be our party, with perhaps the addition of
Charles's solicitor. I am planning a special menu for us." Batting
her eyelash, she added, "Do you have any preferences, sir, that
I could satisfy?"

Thinking quickly, he replied, "Actually, Miss Bingley, I see
that your brother and I have the same idea. I desperately need
to catch up on my estate business as well. I plan to lock myself
in the library and give myself over to it completely. As a result,
I am sorry to say that I will be unable to lunch with you. Please
accept my apologies."

"But, Mr. Darcy, you cannot work all day. I will not hear of
it. You will make yourself sick."

"Thank you for your concern, but I will be fine. But if you
insist, I will not work the whole of the day. Before sunset, I will
take another ride to clear my head."

Flattered that he had taken her advice, she nonetheless
added, "But, sir, in the meantime, you must eat."

"If I require anything, with your leave, I will order a tray
brought to me."

"Why, of course. I will instruct Chef myself to await your
orders. But could you not join us for just a small visit?"

"I am afraid that if I do not attend to the mountain of
correspondence awaiting me, I will eventually have to cut my
visit short."

Torn between the hope of immediate gratification and long-
term success, Miss Bingley finally relented. "I will instruct the
staff to be at your disposal. But would you not be more comfortable in the parlor?"

"Thank you, no. If Charles is meeting with his steward and

then his solicitor, I would be in his way. If I may use the library, it would be more than sufficient."

With sickly sweet solicitude, she replied, "By all means, it is yours."

❧

Elizabeth awoke from her dreams a little startled over their content. Mr. Darcy had figured prominently in all of them, and their vivid nature made her blush. Her mind immediately traveled back to the events of the previous evening. She had to admit he had been a most charming dinner partner, and she had enjoyed his company exceedingly. While she had clearly enjoyed herself, she wondered how he had perceived the evening. As she began to dwell on the various things he had said and the manner in which he had said them, she chastised herself for her foolishness. She then vowed to put such thoughts aside and concentrate on dressing. For once her mother's meddling had turned to her advantage. As a result, she would more than likely see him again today, and when she did, she could judge for herself.

On the previous night's carriage ride home from Netherfield, her mother had waxed on about the courtesies that the Bingleys had shown them at dinner. She insisted that she needed to return the favor by hosting the Netherfield party at Longbourn as soon as possible, to show her own good breeding. She settled upon the idea that she would extend the invitation to Mr. Bingley herself when he visited in the morning. When Jane let her mother know that the gentleman's business concerns would keep him at Netherfield for the whole of the day, she determined that Jane would have to call on Miss Bingley to personally extend the invitation. Despite Jane's pleas, her mother would not relent.

"Jane, it is not as if I am sending you there alone. Lizzy or Mary can go with you. I am sure neither of them have plans of their own. If you do not see Mr. Bingley, then you can invite him through Miss Bingley. You will simply have tea and come home. If you see him, all the better."

"But, Mama," Jane begged, "we will surely see him on the following morning. Can we not wait and invite him then?"

"No, it will be too late; I want them to dine with us the day after tomorrow. No, you and one of your sisters can take the carriage tomorrow as early as it is appropriate."

With a panicked look on her face, Mary said, "But, Mama, I am far too busy with my studies to ignore them again tomorrow. I have already wasted the whole of last night."

Exasperated, Mrs. Bennet spat, "Fine, Mary, stay at home. It is unimportant which of you goes. Lizzy can do it. But, Lizzy, do not go walking all over the countryside beforehand. I don't want you looking like some wild creature. You would be wise to take a lesson from Miss Bingley. Her appearance is always impeccable." Elizabeth nodded her assent. While she had planned to walk to Oakham Mount in the morning, she had to admit that her mother's idea to accompany Jane was not without merit.

When Jane and Elizabeth were announced, Caroline Bingley could barely control her temper. The day was definitely not turning out as she had planned. After venting her frustration to her sister, Louisa, she prepared to greet her visitors with cold civility. She would entertain them for as little time as possible and then ship them off before Charles learned of their presence and prolonged her agony. After pleasantries were exchanged and tea served, Jane once again thanked them for the kindness that they had shown them the previous evening and extended the dinner invitation that her mother had requested.

Elizabeth tried to hold her tongue as she watched Caroline formulate an answer. Her superior attitude was truly difficult to accept. That Caroline had the audacity to treat Jane with contempt, when she should be grateful that Jane did not hold a grudge toward her for all of her previous scheming, made her smugness unforgivable. For Jane's sake, however, Elizabeth attempted to stay quiet.

Looking bored, Caroline replied, "Thank you for the compliment. I will have to check our social calendar to see if we can fit it in. But I do not mean to keep you; I will just send a note."

To everyone's surprise, Jane did not answer but simply continued to smile broadly. After a moment, Elizabeth realized that Jane was looking past Caroline to the door where Mr. Bingley had just entered. After standing there for a moment, smiling at Jane, he recollected himself. "Miss Bennet, Miss Elizabeth, what a pleasant surprise. I hope you are both well?" After receiving a satisfactory answer, he turned to his sister and said, "Caroline, I did not mean to interrupt. To whom are you sending a note? Is someone ill?"

With a level voice, Caroline replied, "Oh, no, Charles, not at all. It is nothing to concern yourself with. We were just trying to organize some social engagements."

"Well, Caroline, you know I love social engagements. What do you have planned?"

Trying to keep up her mask of indifference, she casually replied, "The Bennets have invited us all to dinner tomorrow night, but I was just saying that they should not go to the trouble just for us."

Smiling demurely, Jane volunteered, "It is no bother at all, and my mother is most anxious to return the favor."

Clapping his hands in delight, Mr. Bingley responded, "Well, then, it is settled. We would not want to disappoint her. We have no prior engagements that I know of, unless, of course, Caroline, there is something of which you have not informed me."

Creasing her brow in thought, Caroline took her time and then responded, "No, now that I think about it, we are free tomorrow evening. Jane, please, thank your mother for me for her kindness. We would be happy to attend."

Nodding to Caroline, Jane replied, "She will be so pleased."

Mr. Bingley then added, with a jovial air, "And speaking of invitations, could I convince you to dine with us? My work with my solicitor has gone far more quickly than I would have anticipated. I should be finished in one half hour."

Interrupting, Caroline said, "Oh, Charles, you cannot monopolize all of dear Jane's time. I am sure she and Eliza have other social commitments."

"Caroline, I am sure that is true, but I was hoping to take advantage of Miss Bennet's generous nature and have her make a special exception for us." After he exchanged a demure smile with the object of his affections, he added, "Not only would that be a delightful manner in which to spend the afternoon, it might prove practical as well. There are some issues my solicitor thinks I should familiarize Jane with, and it might be easier to do it today while they are fresh in my mind."

Smiling first at Elizabeth to get her consent, Jane shyly replied, "If you think that is best, we would be happy to stay."

"That is wonderful. I will just wrap up some details and join you as soon as possible. Caroline, perhaps you could show them the private chambers again. I want Jane to redecorate them, and it might help her organize her thoughts. My solicitor needs to return to town today, so he will be unable to join us, but I am sure Darcy will want to attend."

Attempting to respond in a disinterested air, Caroline said, "Charles, I saw him as he was taking a ride this morning, and he said he would be unavailable all day."

Looking to Jane and then Elizabeth, Mr. Bingley added, "Oh, I am sure that he will regret having missed your visit."

Elizabeth and Jane endured Caroline's tour as well as could be expected. Elizabeth was secretly disappointed that Mr. Darcy was unavailable. She was nonetheless glad for the opportunity to help Jane. Despite Caroline's interference, Jane was able to come to some decisions about the master suites, and the tour actually proved quite productive. The meal also turned out to be a pleasant affair. The Hursts excused themselves, wanting to eat in their room. That left Caroline in the minority, and Mr. Bingley's infectious good mood proved too powerful for Caroline's barbed comments and stiff demeanor. After lunch, Mr. Bingley suggested a walk in the garden. Caroline saw that her hostess duties were at an end and excused herself from their company, saying that she needed to review some menus with the chef.

The three companions then set out to tour the flower gardens and paths surrounding the house. They had not traveled far before Elizabeth felt that she was somewhat in the way. Mr. Bingley had said he wanted to discuss some matters with Jane that surely concerned their upcoming marriage, and her presence would impede that discussion. Moreover, Elizabeth got the distinct impression that Mr. Bingley wanted a few stolen moments alone with Jane for other reasons.

As they turned to leave the garden, Elizabeth stopped and said, "This is a particularly lovely spot. I think, if the two of you do not mind, I would like to sit here and rest. It is a beautiful view."

"Oh, Miss Elizabeth, I hope I have not overtaxed you. If you like, we could all rest here."

"No, I would not hear of it. It is too lovely a day to miss. Maybe I will borrow a volume from your library and bring it here to read for a time."

Hoping for such an opening, Mr. Bingley replied excitedly, "Oh, yes, by all means, be my guest. Feel free to borrow anything that interests you." He then pointed to the side of the house and added, "You can access the library from those glass doors."

Smiling at them both, she replied, "Then it is settled. I will get a book and either read it here, or if it gets too cold, sit just inside the library with the doors open to the garden. That way if you need me, I will be available."

Pleased with what an agreeable chaperone she was, Mr. Bingley insisted that she call him if she required anything. Elizabeth entered the library through the garden door. The difference between the bright sunlight she had just left and the darker room she entered made it difficult for her to adjust her eyes as she absentmindedly looked about the shelves. At the far end of the room, the gentleman at the desk had no such problem with his vision, although he did wonder for a few seconds if his eyes were playing tricks on him. He immediately realized that she had not seen him, and remained still, simply watching her. She slowly traveled down the stack of books, unconsciously dancing her fingers across the back of a leather sofa as she walked. As she came to its end, she turned to the desk. Her eyes opened wide in shock. "Mr. Darcy!"

Smiling at her in a relaxed manner, he asked, "Miss Bennet, to what do I owe this honor?"

"Sir, I... I did not know you were at home... here... I thought you were away."

Clearly enjoying that he had unnerved her for a change, he continued to stare at her unabashedly. "No, as you can see, I am right here. Unintentional or not, I am most grateful for the visit."

"I... I..." Blushing, Elizabeth resolved to calm herself and speak intelligently. She took a deep breath and said, "Mr. Bingley offered to lend me a book. I did not realize you or, for that matter, anyone else, occupied the library. Miss Bingley mentioned that you were gone for the day, and I just assumed that no one else was in this part of the house."

"Yes, I see. I told Miss Bingley that I had duties to attend to for the bulk of the day, but I never meant to infer that I would be from the house."

Looking down, she quietly replied, "I must have misunderstood."

Hoping to put her at ease, he attempted to change the subject. "Are you visiting with your sister? Have you once again deviated from Miss Bingley's tour?"

She gave a light laugh and said, "Yes and no. Jane came to extend an invitation to dine tomorrow at Longbourn, and I accompanied her here. Mr. Bingley pressed her to stay, and they have now taken a walk. I felt my constant presence was a little stifling for them and thought that I would get a book to better occupy my time."

With a smile playing upon his lips, he said, "That was very thoughtful of you."

Unsure of what she should say or do, she replied, "Thank you. But, Mr. Darcy, you mentioned that you had duties to attend to, and I am clearly keeping you from them."

"No, not at all. I would welcome a diversion." He then added in a more subdued tone, "I would be most pleased if you would join me."

She shyly replied, "Just for a moment then."

"Well, at least until you find a book."

"Yes."

After a slight pause, he asked, "Did you have any specific volume in mind?"

"No, not really. Being more familiar with Mr. Bingley's library, perhaps you could suggest something?"

"I'd be honored. But let me think for a moment. I do not want to disappoint."

As he looked at the shelf behind the desk, Elizabeth looked at the piles of papers stacked upon it and asked, "May I enquire what it is I am keeping you from?"

Turning, he smiled as he replied, "Certainly, although I am afraid it is quite dull."

"Whatever it is, there appears to be a great deal of it."

"Yes, unfortunately, there is. I am attempting, rather poorly, to attend to my correspondence from Pemberley."

"Is this the usual volume, or have you been neglecting it for several months?"

Laughing, he replied, "You would think it had accumulated over a great deal of time, but it is actually a week's worth of papers and letters that need my attention. I think it looks a little more daunting because it is not arranged in a coherent manner."

"I am surprised to hear that. You strike me as very fastidious."

"I am not sure if that is a compliment, but I will take it as one. You are right, I am usually quite organized but not through any talent of my own. I have a most valued steward, Mr. Edmund Lynch, who is exceedingly skilled at organizing my papers—and me in the process."

"I find it hard to believe that you do not possess some skill in that area. But in any case, I take it your steward is back at Pemberley and therefore unable to help."

"So to speak, but I would be doing him a disservice if I did not explain further. He is quite adept at organizing my life from a great distance. His physical absence is not the problem. Usually, he sorts through my papers, and when I am away from my estate, he sends them to me in a thoroughly organized fashion. Over time, we have developed a finely tuned system. For the past eight days, though, he has been unavailable, so I have had my correspondence sent directly to me unsorted, and I miss his help exceedingly."

"Is he ill?"

"Not at all. It is actually a joyous occasion. Mrs. Lynch gave birth to a son two days ago. As her date approached, he became so nervous that I thought it best that he stay home with her for the duration of her confinement. I met him in London last week to dispose of some of the more pressing matters and then sent him home to his wife. Despite my good intentions, I am afraid Mrs. Lynch may never speak to me again. In his high state of anxiety, I am sure he was more of a burden than a help. Nevertheless, since the child's arrival, I have received word that they are all healthy and happy. Mr. Lynch will come back to work in a fortnight."

"And in the meantime, you are fending for yourself? I

would have thought that there would be someone else who could help you?"

"Mr. Bingley has offered the services of his steward, but he was engaged with Mr. Bingley and his solicitor today, so I did not want to bother them with my concerns. I might have waited until he was free, but this morning, the timing seemed most opportune for me to begin. I have since regretted my decision, but my stubbornness has stopped me from quitting."

"Have you been working on your papers from Pemberley all morning then?"

Eyeing her intently, he said, "No, early this morning I went for a ride to see the local scenery. Did you get a chance to walk out?"

Awkwardly, she replied, "Actually, no. I had to call here. So I was prevented from doing so."

"Yes, of course... In any regard, when I returned, I went through my letters from my townhouse in London, but that was a much smaller contingent of documents. I have just finished with them. I was now going to face the papers from Pemberley." Smiling at her, he added, "But inasmuch as Mr. Bingley has company, I will see to them another day."

Concerned, she asked, "But will it not make the task even more difficult if you put it off?"

"It might, but I am willing to take that risk."

"But does not some of the correspondence require your immediate attention?"

Looking at her intently, he said, "Miss Bennet, you are making me feel quite guilty. Yes, you are right. Some of it might require my immediate attention, and it might be best if I stayed here to work, but I am actually finding it quite difficult to do so."

She stared back at him for what seemed an eternity, as

she understood the full meaning of his words. Apparently, he wanted to be in her company as much as she wanted to remain in his, but she knew selecting a book would not serve as an excuse to tarry in the library for very long, and she genuinely did not want to disrupt his work. She had recently vowed to try to get to know him better; maybe this was a golden opportunity. With a decisive air, she moved a chair closer to the desk, sat down, and replied, "Ah, yes, Mr. Darcy, I see it clearly. You intend to blame my sister and me for your own lack of industry. I will not have it on my conscience. I will help you organize the papers. You can then read them, decide what needs immediate attention, and leave the rest for when Mr. Lynch returns or seek the help of Mr. Bingley's steward tomorrow."

Looking incredulously at her, he asked, "Miss Bennet, are you suggesting that you act as my steward?"

Smiling at him impishly, she retorted, "I am simply offering my help. I have some free time while Jane is occupied. I was only going to start a new book; it can wait. I know that some of the papers might be quite complex, but I should be able to help you with some of the more repetitive tasks."

Frowning, he replied, "It is not that the work is too difficult. It is just that it is most… irregular."

Suddenly feeling far too presumptuous, she rose and said in a formal voice, "You are quite right, sir. I have overstepped my place. Your private letters are not my concern. Please forgive me. I will leave you to your work."

As she turned to go, he stepped to the side of the desk and remarked with some urgency, "Please, Miss Bennet, you misunderstand me. There is nothing in my correspondence that I would feel uncomfortable letting you see. I just did not think you would want to spend your time in such a pursuit. I am no expert, but I never imagined that a lady would want to undertake such a task."

Sensing that she had started something that it would be unfair to blame him for, she attempted to regulate her embarrassment and replied in an even tone, "You are right; it is not an activity a lady would typically engage in. But we have agreed to dispense with some of the more cumbersome social conventions. I have helped my father with his correspondence before, and I think I could follow your instructions and be of some limited use. But if you think it is unworkable, I quite understand."

Glad to see her at ease again, he smiled in relief. His primary goal was to stay in her company, and if she was willing to spend time with him in such a manner, then the endeavor had great merit. "Miss Bennet, your offer is quite kind. I could use your help. Thank you."

As they both sat back down, she looked at him expectantly. He, however, seemed content simply to stare at her. She cleared her throat and said, "What do you suggest, sir?"

"Oh, yes, well… Mr. Lynch usually opens all of the correspondence and sorts them into three piles initially. Perhaps you could do that. My personal letters have been sent to me as they are received, so you need not worry about them." Pointing to the desk, he said, "The mix of letters on the desk concern estate business, social invitations, tenant matters, charitable requests, patronage requests, and other types of solicitations. Once they are sorted, I attend them in order of priority."

"That seems manageable. Three piles, in order of their date: social invitations, estate business, including tenant matters, and requests."

Smiling at her, he enthusiastically said, "Yes, exactly. In the meantime, I will pull these maps out of the pile to review; they concern a dispute over a property boundary between tenants. Unfortunately, the situation has degenerated to a point where I need to step in."

She smiled at him and began her work. The task proved quite interesting. As she opened each letter, she became more amazed at the volume of correspondence and the breadth of subject matter covered. She began to understand the extent of his responsibilities. It struck her that he was a very young man to carry such a heavy weight. As she worked, she could not help but sneak furtive glances at him, while he gazed with great concentration at the maps. With his brow furrowed, he unexpectedly looked up and caught her looking at him. He raised his eyebrows to inquire what she required, but she shyly looked back to the papers in front of her. It was then his turn to study her as she read the correspondence in her hand. He wondered at how they had come to this point in their relationship. He knew that she did not realize how her closeness affected him. More than that, her interest in his affairs was a balm to him. When he had first begun to fall in love with her, he had imagined her as his lover; as time progressed, he began to see her as the mistress of his estate, and when he asked her to marry him, the mother of his children. But since then, he had thought of her more as a partner, someone who could share his bed and his life, someone to share his sorrows, his concerns, his joys, and, in the process, end his loneliness. Sitting across from him, he could not help but imagine that she had already accepted the arrangement, and he reveled in it.

As she worked silently, she was amazed at how comfortable

she was in his presence. After a long, companionable silence, she sighed and announced, "I have only a few letters that I need to ask you about. Otherwise, I believe the bulk of the papers have been sorted. You said you would look at the three categories of documents in order of importance. I assume you will look at the social correspondence first as there are several invitations where a reply is almost overdue."

Studying her with his brow once again furrowed, he said, "Actually, I usually look at the invitations and social correspondence last. I rarely find anything of interest in that pile. I usually review the estate business first and then turn to the requests. I then quickly review the invitations and mark any I will accept. My steward can otherwise decline the rest on my behalf when he returns." As he saw the height of the pile, he frowned and added, "I would ignore them completely if I was not mindful of the fact that my sister will one day be out in society. I would not want my behavior to injure her reception."

"With that in mind, sir, I would point out that there are several requests for your attendance at various events that contain postscripts from people I assume are friends. Will you not give insult if you ignore them?"

"I am sure that very few of them are from close friends, as I tend to maintain regular correspondences with them. Their names would be recognizable to my housekeeper and their letters would be forwarded with my personal papers. I find that members of the *ton* often write personal notes on invitations when the extent of our acquaintance is, in fact, quite limited. I do not believe my absence from any of the events will create a hardship."

Nodding her acquiescence, she then added, "There is one

letter that I was unsure how to classify. It is an invitation to a wedding, but I believe it is from someone connected to your estate." Given their history, she was not sure that she wanted to bring up the subject, but it was the one piece of correspondence that had piqued her curiosity. "There is a very odd notation on it too. Apparently, the groom thought you would wed before him."

She handed him the invitation, which was written out in a simple but tasteful fashion on plain paper. He chuckled at the contents as he read. "Yes, this is an invitation from the cooper on my estate. He is my age, and we grew up together, until his duties as his father's apprentice eventually occupied his time. When we were boys, we could not imagine ever wanting to wed. We vowed to remain single for as long as possible so we could spend all our time fishing. Whoever stayed single longest was to provide the other with fresh fish. His is referring to that pledge in the note. He would like me to attend, but apparently, I need not bring any fish as there will be sufficient food at the wedding breakfast."

She had to smile at this genial picture of him as a boy and his own amusement at the recollection. After staring at the letter for a few more moments, he added, "Unfortunately, I will not be able to attend as it will be at the same time as your sister's wedding. Maybe as a gesture, I should send them fishing rods and tackle to celebrate their marriage."

She had to laugh at his suggestion. She was surprised that he would think of such an odd gift, but was intrigued at his willingness to be perceived in such a lively light. "Do you truly think the gesture would be received by both of them in the manner you intend? His bride might prefer something more useful or traditional."

Thoughtfully, he replied, "Yes, you might be right. I am not acquainted with his bride, but if they are well matched in disposition, she should see the humor in it." Seeing her skepticism, he added by way of clarification, "My housekeeper will, of course, send something from both Georgiana and myself. The Darcys have always sent a complete set of linens to each new bride on the estate. I would be sending the fishing equipment from myself, as a personal gift." Seeing that she was now laughing openly at him, he put the invitation aside and said, "I see I am not to receive any support from you on this. Maybe I should consider the issue at a later date. Are these the remaining documents?"

Trying to suppress her laughter, she handed him the papers that concerned the operation of the estate and then familiarized him with the location and organization of the requests. As she gained control of her countenance, she asked, "Mr. Darcy, as I sorted through the documents, I was struck by the number and the variety of issues you are called upon to settle. May I inquire how you go about resolving all of this?"

"I simply try to be thorough and attentive."

Genuinely interested, she asked, "But there must be more to it than that?"

Thoughtfully, he replied, "I suppose. I try to look at each request or issue dispassionately and render as quick and fair a decision as possible. I am mindful that many of the decisions a landowner is required to make have a great impact on the lives of the people who work the estate. But, while decisiveness is required, it sometimes comes at a cost. In the end I have to take responsibility for any mistakes, but I can take some consolation from the fact that I did my best and acted as promptly as possible."

As she listened to him, she was struck by how different he was from her father, who seemed to try to avoid resolving disputes at all costs. It was his usual philosophy to ignore a problem in the hope that it would go away. He practiced this philosophy both at home and in the running of his estate, and in both cases, the results were seldom impressive. By comparison, Mr. Darcy's decisiveness, as he called it, was obviously the better approach. It also went a long way toward explaining that gentleman's periodic impulsiveness. Once he came to a decision, he apparently acted on it.

Suddenly embarrassed that he had said so much, he added, "Miss Bennet, you have surely let me talk on about matters of little interest to anyone else. I apologize for trying your patience."

Smiling, she replied, "Not at all, I found the entire exercise most interesting. But, Mr. Darcy, surely you will not decide all of these matters in one sitting?"

"I will attempt to. Although there are some issues that, because of either their complexity or seriousness, I put aside for further consideration. I usually like to discuss those with Mr. Lynch or a friend before I make a final decision. That is what I was doing with this boundary dispute."

"Will you discuss it then with Mr. Bingley?"

"Yes, unless… would you like to hear about it?"

"I am flattered, sir, but I am not sure what help I could be."

Smiling at her intently, he said, "It simply requires a sense of fairness, and I believe you would be more than capable in that regard." He then indicated that she should join him on his side of the desk in order to look over the maps.

He gave a brief description of the parties involved, and then indicated where the first boundary line was located. In order to see what he was describing, he beckoned her closer. She complied until she was standing beside him. As she leaned over the map to look for herself, she felt him by her side, his breath brushing her ear as he continued to explain the boundary dispute. His rich voice seemed to have a hypnotic effect on her as she struggled to listen. As he leaned ever closer to trace the line for her on the map, she felt her pulse quicken and hoped that it was not obvious to him. Equally caught up by her proximity to him, his narration temporarily faltered. As they both stood there looking down at his hand on the map and hers inches away, he swallowed hard and then unconsciously leaned even closer toward her. As if frozen, she watched as he moved his hand toward hers and then ever so slowly began tracing his finger along the line of her thumb and then her wrist. The sensation was small but exquisite. Her senses combined to overpower her. She closed her eyes and let herself lean completely into him. The contact made him dizzy with excitement, and he knew his breath was coming far too fast to mask his emotions. They remained there for a moment, until he craned his neck toward her ear and whispered, "Elizabeth," as he gently let his lips touch her neck. The trance was broken by the sound of Mr. Bingley's voice in the hall. Darcy immediately stood up straight and stepped back. Elizabeth did the same and attempted to regain her composure.

Mr. Bingley stepped into the room with his sister following closely behind. He then said, "Yes, Caroline, you are correct; Mr. Darcy is in the library." Jane followed them into the room, and Mr. Bingley added, "Miss Elizabeth, I hope Mr. Darcy was able to help you find that book."

Eyeing Elizabeth with suspicion, Caroline snapped, "Miss

Eliza, I thought you were with your sister and my brother. If you needed attention, I would have been more than willing to help."

Before she could respond, Mr. Bingley added, "She was with us for a walk outside. I just sent her into the library to look for something to read."

Placated by the thought that Elizabeth's contact with Mr. Darcy had been brief, Caroline went to his side and asked, "Sir, I hope you have been keeping your strength up while working so diligently? I know I promised that you would be uninterrupted, but I was unaware that Miss Eliza was roaming the halls. Hopefully, the interruption was brief, and you have been able to attend to your work."

Finding his voice, Darcy replied, "Yes, Miss Bingley. As a matter of fact, I have had a most productive afternoon."

An awkward silence ensued until Jane ventured forth. "Lizzy, I am afraid we should be going. Mama will be expecting us."

"Yes, Jane. I think we must."

After they had escorted the women to their carriage, Mr. Bingley and Darcy stood alone in the library. After a prolonged silence, Mr. Bingley said, "Darcy, I did not know it was your intention to work in here today. If I had known, I would have let you know that we were entertaining company."

"I apologize for not telling you directly. I did not want to disturb you since you were clearly busy with your solicitor."

"I quite understand. It is of no real consequence. I just thought that you might have wanted to know that Jane and her sister were here. I only learned of it myself through Mr. Gaines. He is a most trusted butler."

Wondering what he was getting at, Darcy simply replied, "Oh really?"

"Oh, yes. After this winter, I no longer leave such matters to my sister. Mr. Gaines is under strict instructions to notify me whenever Miss Bennet visits. He is the epitome of discretion. It might be wise for you to leave a similar instruction." Smiling at Darcy in his typical good-natured manner, he then added, "And, Darcy, whenever you wish to remain undisturbed from my sister, either because your work demands it or because you are helping Miss Elizabeth select a book, you might also want to ask him to help you with that."

Embarrassed by the implication, but unwilling to concede the point, Darcy replied, "Thank you, Charles, but I hardly think such precautions are necessary."

With a light laugh, he replied, "Darcy, I would not be so sure. You know, Jane and I will not always be available to stand guard for you in the manner we did today."

BETWEEN COURSES

As the day wore on, Darcy continued to attend to his correspondence in the library, taking his dinner on a tray. The daunting volume of his workload was tempered by his pleasant memories of Elizabeth's presence there that afternoon. He could close his eyes and imagine her working silently across from him, teasing him, and listening with interest as they discussed the business of his estate. But more than that, he could recall the wonderful sensation of her standing next to him by his desk. If he closed his eyes, he could recall the scent of her hair and the silkiness of her skin as he traced his finger on her wrist. He could relive the exhilaration he felt as she leaned against him and as he kissed her neck. While these pleasant memories left him breathless, the seeds of doubt and reproach inevitably intruded.

He wondered if his momentary lack of control had destroyed the hard-earned equanimity he had obtained with her. Her reaction to the liberties that he had taken with her was difficult to gauge. He thought she had felt the attraction between them and had been as overwhelmed as he had been in the excitement of the moment. But it all happened so quickly, he could not be sure whether she felt as he did or if she had been on the verge of upbraiding him for his presumptuousness. In hindsight, he wished that he had chosen a more opportune moment or had been better able to temper his reaction to her closeness, but he knew that if the opportunity arose again, he would behave in exactly the same manner. And that knowledge led him to a decision. Through his recklessness, he had declared himself, and regardless of whether he would wish to go back in time to do so in a more appropriate manner, the deed was done. Having clearly shown her, through his actions, what he desired, he now needed to make his intentions explicit. He knew he risked rejection, but he had come too far to turn back. While he had enjoyed the interlude of their friendship, it eventually had to lead to more or end of its own accord. He would never be happy simply as her valued acquaintance, and if she could never be more than that, he needed to know it. He could not live a fantasy forever.

But the thought of seeking her out on the subject brought him equal parts hope and dread. He had long ago perfected his fantasy of her accepting his renewed offer. But when he tried to imagine how they would remain on pleasant terms if he placed her in the situation of having to reject him again, he could not envision it. They would obviously have to remain civil for the sake of Miss Bennet and Mr. Bingley's match, but he knew she would never trust his friendship again. He would be risking so much, but deep within himself, he knew he had no other option. His unspoken, unwavering desire for her permeated his entire being, and the risk of obtaining that goal was worth everything else. He knew it was selfish, but he could not resist his nature. He had been patient for far longer than he thought possible.

He placated himself with the thought that propriety required that he declare himself to make amends for the liberties he had taken, but he knew that they were far beyond such concerns, and that the rules of social discourse held very little guidance for the terms of their tumultuous relationship. Ultimately, the deciding factor for him was that, on some level, he had felt that she had responded to his touch, and he could not let the opportunity pass to find out if it were true. Once his intent was decided, he then began to work out a plan to maximize his opportunities to see Elizabeth alone. With a decisive nod, he rose to seek out Bingley in his study.

"Am I disturbing you?"

With a welcoming grin, Bingley indicated he should sit. "Not at all; please join me."

"Thank you, no. I would only take a minute of your time." After an uncomfortable pause, he fixed his gaze on the window and said, "I need to… I intend to take an early morning ride tomorrow, but I also wanted to accompany you to Longbourn thereafter. I was wondering if you could wait for me, if I have not returned by the time you are ready to leave? I do not anticipate that I will be too late."

"Darcy, normally that would be a simple request to fulfill, and I would welcome your company on any other occasion, but I was not planning to visit Longbourn until tomorrow evening. I believe that the ladies of the house have an early morning dress-fitting in Meryton, and then Miss Bennet and her sisters will be shopping for wedding clothes." Bingley then added with significance, "I think I specifically recall that Mrs. Bennet was insistent that all of Jane's sisters join her."

Unsuccessfully trying to mask his disappointment, Darcy frowned and said, "Oh, I see."

"I think they will be back by mid-afternoon, but I told Jane… Miss Bennet, that since we were dining there, I would wait to come with my sisters. Caroline made it quite clear that she did not want to arrive too early or unescorted. Given her tentative state, I did not want to incite her displeasure unnecessarily."

Resuming his formal air, Darcy replied crisply, "Oh, thank you. Do not concern yourself. It is not important."

With a generous smile, Bingley replied, "Darcy, I have a suspicion it is very important, but if you are reluctant to confide in me, I quite understand."

Surprised by Bingley's direct approach, he was momentarily speechless as he tried to formulate a response. "Charles, it is not that I do not want to confide in you. At this point, there is simply nothing to say."

"Are you sure? You seem even more pensive than normal, which is quite an accomplishment."

Darcy had to smile at his friend's words. "No, I just… I want to… speak to Miss Elizabeth, but it can wait until dinner."

"I notice that the two of you have become friends. Jane and I are so glad that you have been able to put the past behind you. Darcy, I do not mean to pry, but is there anything you would like to talk about?"

Touched by his friend's concern, Darcy gave Bingley a genuine smile. "Thank you, Charles, but no, I am fine."

"Are you certain?"

"I have some things I need to tell her, but until I speak with her, nothing has really changed."

Nodding his understanding, Charles replied, "If there is

anything I can do, or if you would like to discuss this further, you know I am at your service?"

"Thank you, Charles, I do. But I think I will just return to my work."

"Certainly, but if you do not get the opportunity you seek tomorrow night, then maybe you can accompany me the following morning for a call to Longbourn."

"Thank you; I may take you up on that offer."

Darcy returned to the library filled with restless unresolve. While he would go to Oakham Mount in the morning just in case she came there, he thought it highly improbable given the timing of her dress appointment. He had planned to go to Longbourn with Charles, in case he had been unsuccessful earlier in the day, but he now knew that was unworkable. He could wait until he saw her at dinner, but the chance of speaking to her alone, in the manner he wished, seemed unlikely. He could go to Oakham Mount before sunset, but it might make him late for dinner. More importantly, the timing of dinner meant that Elizabeth would be late for it as well if she attempted to walk such a distance, and since her mother would never allow it, the chances of her going were very slim. He could ride to Oakham Mount early and simply wait there until he needed to leave for dinner. He did not mind wasting his time in such a fashion, but he wanted a plan of action that might actually ensure their meeting. If only he had asked exactly what time in the afternoon she would be likely to walk out, he could catch her outside Longbourn and then they could take a shorter walk.

As he stared blankly at the walls of the library, a plan struck him. He spent the rest of the evening leisurely perusing the stacks and then went to bed filled with nervous anticipation.

Darcy and Elizabeth were the first to rise in their respec-tive households. As Darcy prepared to ride out, Elizabeth continued to dress. She wondered if Darcy's comments about his ride the previous morning were designed to let her know that he had expected to see her at Oakham Mount. She would like nothing better than to walk there now, to see for herself, but she knew it would make her sisters late for their appoint-ment, and her mother would never forgive her. Unwilling to bend totally to her mother's demands, she decided to take a short walk, just in case Mr. Darcy happened to have wandered in her direction. It was an unlikely plan, but it was better than nothing. As she left her room, however, she heard her mother call.

"Lizzy, is that you? Wake your sisters. We need to get started."

Her mother was never an early riser, but the excitement in her voice betrayed her purpose. It was not often that she had free rein to shop without providing justification. Even her father's usual disdain for his wife's spending habits had to give way to the clear need they all had to purchase new things for Jane's wedding. Apparently, her mother intended to extend the day for as long as possible, and the excitement of getting started held more allure than sleep. Elizabeth went to her mother's door and said, "Mama, I will wake the others, but I am already fully dressed. I shall take a light breakfast and stroll in the garden while the rest of you finish preparing."

"Lizzy, you will do no such thing. You will wander off and make us all late. Do not test my nerves. I have so much to think about as it is. I cannot be worrying about you in addition. I need to think carefully about which fabrics we need to buy. I have settled on a color for you and Kitty, but I am not sure what I should get for Lydia. I think peach for Jane. It will highlight her beautiful complexion."

Trying to get away before he mother became engrossed, Elizabeth quietly said, "I am sure you will pick out something lovely. I will just get some breakfast."

Frantic, her mother squealed, "There is barely time for breakfast. I want to leave early enough so that the new dresses can be finished this afternoon. I want us to wear them tonight. We cannot be seen in the same gowns over and over again. Mr. Bingley's sisters will surely have something new on. Once the final fittings are complete, we can shop for fabric for the wedding." Holding a wet cloth from her basin to her head, she continued in a rushed manner. "But we need all of the details of dinner finished before we leave so we can shop uninterrupted. Since you are already dressed, you will have to finish the preparations for me. Here is the menu. I want you to go over it with Cook. There are notes on it. Be very specific with her. You need to oversee everything with her, or she will do it all wrong. Before you do that, tell Hill to come up and help me. I need her immediately. I will instruct Hill on the service that I want laid out, but I do not have time to see to every detail."

Elizabeth gave a resigned nod and saw to her tasks. After she finished with Cook, she entered the dining room. She had to laugh secretly to herself. While she was disappointed that her mother had foiled her plans for a walk, she could not fault her for wanting their dresses finished today. She would not mind having a new dress ready for dinner tonight. While she did not think that Caroline Bingley's gowns were very attractive, by comparison, she did feel slightly embarrassed to see Mr. Darcy again while wearing a gown he had surely seen many times in

Kent and several times in Hertfordshire as well. She was not usually so vain, but she felt an irrational desire to look better than Miss Bingley. Was this jealousy? No, whatever the state of Mr. Darcy's regard for her, she knew he did not hold Miss Bingley in any special esteem. Elizabeth realized that it was simpler than that. She wanted to look her best for Mr. Darcy. She wanted him to admire her and hopefully look at her in the same manner that she had caught him doing in an unguarded moment in the library. The revelation made her blush. She was acting like a schoolgirl. After unsuccessfully attempting to regain some composure, she laughed at herself for trying. There was no denying it. She was thoroughly attracted to him and wanted nothing more than to spend some uninterrupted time with him. She hoped dinner would provide the opportunity.

The morning in Meryton passed much as she had expected. Her mother's constant flittering about was difficult to bear, but her new dress did look good. Jane had even encouraged her to buy contrasting hair ribbons that matched the emerald and ivory of her gown. Unfortunately, her mother's insistence that they look at every fabric in town before ordering even one new dress caused them to return home later than Elizabeth would have liked. Nevertheless, there were still more than two hours before dinner and she intended to attempt a walk in the direction of Oakham Mount.

Toward that end, she began a conversation with her mother, hoping that she could produce the desired result through flattery, by seeking her advice. She first mentioned how much she liked her new gown, knowing that it was a subject her mother never tired of. After some time she asked, "Mama, do you think the dark emerald makes me look a bit too pale? I am worried that my complexion looks slightly sallow. Perhaps if I walked out, my cheeks might appear rosier. What do you think is best?"

"Yes, Lizzy, now that I look at you, you are pale. That might do the trick. But also remember to pinch your cheeks whenever you can."

As the carriage returned home, Elizabeth was surprised to see a gentleman's horse tied out. Her hopes that it might be Mr. Darcy were dashed as she approached the front door, and observed the mount more closely. As they entered the house, Hill announced that Mr. John Lucas was awaiting them in the front room.

After the formalities of their greeting were accomplished, their guest spoke first. "Mrs. Bennet, I hope I have not come at a bad time. I have recently been thinking that I have not visited you and your lovely daughters as often as I should. I want to remedy my oversight, but if this is an inopportune time, let me extend my apologies."

"Oh, not at all," beamed Mrs. Bennet. "'Tis very gracious of you. Please stay for tea."

"Thank you; that would be lovely."

"Mrs. Bennet, I hear you were shopping today. I hope you were able to find what you needed?"

As Mrs. Bennet talked merrily on about the difficulties of finding quality lace in Meryton, Elizabeth eyed John Lucas. It was not completely out of character for him to call, but she could not believe he wanted to discuss fashion with her mother. At any other time, she might have found his feigned interest in her mother's conversation worthy of examination, especially as they delved into the finer minutiae of judging the quality of a fabric, but she was anxious to set out for a walk. Even if she did not see Mr. Darcy on her way, the exercise would settle her anxiety.

She was jarred into the present by her name being spoken by John Lucas.

"Oh, yes, Mrs. Bennet, Miss Elizabeth had relayed that story to me. It was quite amusing." He then smiled toward Elizabeth in a most ingratiating manner. "But as you well know, her wit is unsurpassed."

Unaware of the subject being discussed and somewhat muddled by his praise, Elizabeth replied, "Sir, you are too kind."

Bowing his head in response, he cooed, "Not at all," then added, "Miss Elizabeth, I recently received a missive from my sister in Kent. She inquired as to your state of well-being. May I respond on your behalf?"

"Certainly, tell her I am quite well and that I know I am a letter in her debt. I will endeavor to write to her tomorrow. And is she in good health?"

"Quite so," he replied, adding in a conspiratorial tone, "although she tells me her husband suffers from some indigestion, but she believes that it can be remedied by moderation."

Attempting to hide her amusement, Elizabeth asked in a dry manner, "He is otherwise well, then?"

Nodding at her knowingly, he said, "Oh, yes, I believe so. Marriage seems to suit them both. From the outside, some would wonder at their match, but I think their felicity is a testament to the state of matrimony itself. It transcends and transforms those who enter it. I envy my sister the stability, and I think Mr. Collins values the companionship."

Mrs. Bennet's ears perked up at this statement, as she found nothing so pleasing as a marriageable-age man lauding the state of matrimony while admiring one of her daughters. "You are quite right, Mr. Lucas. A man is incomplete without a wife, and at a certain age, every man must consider its advantages and act accordingly."

Smiling easily at Mrs. Bennet, he replied, "I think you are correct, madam, although most men might shy away from the idea being stated so succinctly. It is, of course, the inevitable conclusion to one's boyhood."

"Yes," beamed Mrs. Bennet, "and the sooner it is realized the better."

Laughing, Mr. Lucas replied good-naturedly, "Yes, Mum, I have already crossed that threshold and reached that conclusion."

Having witnessed her mother's brashness on this subject before, Elizabeth sought to flee before she was made any more uncomfortable. Seizing her prearranged excuse, she said, "Mama, may I be excused? I should take my walk before it gets any later."

Before Mrs. Bennet could answer, John Lucas stood and turned his gaze significantly to Elizabeth, "What a lovely idea, Miss Elizabeth. It is a beautiful day for a walk. May I accompany you? I think the fresh air would do me wonders."

"What a splendid idea!" exclaimed Mrs. Bennet, "I know Lizzy would love the company, and then perhaps you could stay for dinner?"

Keeping his gaze on Elizabeth, he replied, "Unfortunately, I have an obligation already this evening, but maybe I could call again tomorrow? Miss Elizabeth, will you be available in the morning?"

Stunned by his response and his desire to walk out with her, Elizabeth could only respond, "Yes, I do not believe we have any prior engagements tomorrow."

With another ingratiating smile at Elizabeth, he replied, "Then I will make a point of it." Turning to Mrs. Bennet, he bowed to her as he added, "Thank you again for the invitation to dine this evening. If I had known, I never would have dreamed of accepting another request."

"Oh, Mr. Lucas, you are too kind, but I have your promise that you will stay another day. I will keep you to it. Now, you young people should go before the weather changes."

At this, Elizabeth spoke up, "Mr. Lucas, I hope I have not excited your anticipation unduly. I only intended to take a short stroll in the garden."

"No, that will be fine. I know I will enjoy the company more than the scenery."

As Elizabeth put on her bonnet and awaited her escort in the front hall, she wondered at his forward behavior. She hoped it was her imagination. She could hardly fathom what he was up to, but she knew her mother would misinterpret his interest, and as a result, she would have no peace.

They had not traveled long down the path before she saw a rider approaching. Her heart both soared and sank as she recognized his broad shoulders. From his position on his horse, she saw Mr. Darcy slow his pace as he searched out her face. As she smiled to welcome him, he smiled broadly in return. She then saw him turn ever so slightly to examine her companion. As he eyed Mr. Lucas, he took on a stern countenance.

Once Mr. Darcy was directly before them, he greeted them in a formal tone, "Miss Bennet, Mr. Lucas, good day."

Lucas responded first. "Mr. Darcy, how nice to see you again. I hope you are well."

Darcy replied stiffly, "Thank you, I am quite well."

"I am glad to hear it. I did not realize you intended to stay on in the neighborhood for so long."

"Yes, I... Mr. Bingley has been kind enough to extend the invitation."

"It must be quite pleasant for him to have your company as he prepares for his wedding."

Frowning, Darcy replied more briskly than he had hoped. "Yes, I am sure." He then looked to Elizabeth, who had been silent since his arrival. "Miss Bennet, Mr. Bingley wanted to extend his compliments to your sister."

Trying to convey some of her own happiness at seeing him, she replied, "Thank you, sir, I will relay the message. I know she is eager to see him this evening at dinner."

As they looked at each other, each unsure of the other's reaction, Mr. Lucas interrupted, "Well, Mr. Darcy, unless we can be of some other service, it was a pleasure to see you again. Miss Bennet has agreed to talk a stroll with me, and I would be remiss if we did not begin." He then smiled at Elizabeth as he offered her his arm. She had no other option but to take it as Mr. Lucas turned to continue their walk.

Before they had taken a second step, Darcy impulsively spoke up. "Actually, Miss Bennet, I came to return your book."

Turning in relief, she asked, "My book, Mr. Darcy?"

Looking at her intently, he replied, "Yes, the one Mr. Bingley suggested you borrow from his library. I saw you did not have the opportunity to take it with you the other day, and I thought you might like to have it sooner rather than later."

Masking her surprise, she replied demurely, "Thank you, sir, it is very kind of you."

"Not at all... May I leave it for you at your house? I would not want you to have to carry it with you on your walk. Do you intend to go far?"

At this, Lucas replied in a jovial manner, "No, unfortunately not. I had hoped to talk her into a longer stroll but she would not hear of it. We will remain in the garden." He then extended his arm again and said to her in a playful tone that Darcy could not miss, "I think we have agreed that we are not so much interested in the exercise as the company."

Seeing his position was untenable, Darcy crisply replied, "I am sorry to have delayed you. I will leave the book with your housekeeper." He then directed his horse toward Longbourn. As he approached the front door, the absurdity of the situation suddenly struck him. He had been hoping to court a woman who had already rejected him. He had misread her willingness to forgive his prior mistakes as a warming of her regard, when the only evidence he had of it was his own wishful thinking. All of his self-doubt returned. He had once again misjudged her feelings for him. While it was true that she had been easy in his company, it was because she was comfortable and vivacious with everyone. It was one of the things he admired about her. He had mistaken her friendship for something more and then made the unpardonable mistake of forcing himself on her. She had been unable to react because they were interrupted. She was probably mortified in his presence and had been spending all of her time since then contemplating how to let him know that he had once again presumed too much. Throughout his time in Hertfordshire, John Lucas had been ever present in her company, yet he had never understood the relationship until now. He felt so very foolish. He had been hoping that she might have been seeking an opportunity to meet him at Oakham Mount, when she was more than content to stroll the garden with John Lucas.

He briefly contemplated trying to excuse himself from dinner to avoid the torture of seeing her again, but he knew he could not. If nothing else, he needed to apologize to her for his unacceptable behavior before he could say good-bye. After watching Lucas lead her around to the side of the house, he spurred his horse to leave as a wave of jealousy overwhelmed him.

After enduring John Lucas's small talk for almost an hour, Elizabeth anxiously returned to the house. She immediately asked Hill whether a book had been left for her, but was told that there had been no deliveries or visitors in her absence. Seeing she would be late for dinner if she did not begin to prepare, she put the issue aside for the moment. Despite the fact that she dressed very quickly, her progress was nonetheless delayed. Her younger sisters usually dressed at the last minute and monopolized their only maid during the process. Her late entrance into the schedule meant that she had to wait until they were finished. To her embarrassment, she arrived downstairs after the Bingley party had arrived.

As she surveyed the parlor, she saw Mr. Darcy standing apart from the other inhabitants of the room, staring out the window. He had arrived hoping to speak with her alone, in order to apologize for his inappropriate behavior. As more time passed, he had begun to suspect that her absence was by design and that it was evidence that she was uncomfortable in his company. He once again vowed to seek her pardon for his unwanted forwardness and then leave her in peace. As she began to walk toward him, Mr. Bingley approached her and said, "Miss Elizabeth, you are looking lovely tonight. I was worried you were not going to join us."

Smiling at his easy manner, she replied, "You are too kind, sir. I apologize for my tardiness. I was unfortunately delayed."

Upon hearing this, Mrs. Bennet chimed in, "Yes, Mr. Lucas was visiting. He is such a charming man. Mr. Bingley, have you had much opportunity to get to know him? You should. I am sure you would like him very well, and it would be good for you to have a close friend in the area. Your dispositions seem so very similar: easy in company and always eager to join in. You are both my ideal of the perfect gentlemen."

Elizabeth momentarily closed her eyes in embarrassment at her mother's slight of Mr. Darcy. Unsure how to respond, Mr. Bingley simply said, "Thank you. I have met him before. He seems very friendly."

Darcy turned back to the window as his countenance grew darker. Elizabeth was relieved to see her mother's next sentence interrupted by Hill as she informed her that dinner was ready.

As the party took their seats, Darcy cautiously smiled as he held out the chair beside him for Elizabeth. "Miss Bennet, I have not had the opportunity to greet you earlier. I hope you are well?"

She smiled generously as she took her seat and said, "Thank you, sir. I am."

Moved by her welcoming countenance, he could not help but say, "It is quite a pleasant to be seated beside you again at dinner. It seems that I was utterly wrong about seating arrangements. I now find the system quite worthwhile."

She gave him an impish look and replied, "It seems, sir, that you are not the only one who likes to profess opinions that are not your own."

He looked at her, unsure how to continue. She seemed so open to him, and he longed to resume their familiarity. As he debated what he should do, Elizabeth spoke first. "Mr. Darcy, I was a little concerned earlier this evening. I was unable to find the volume that you brought me. Did its delivery go astray?"

He found the topic unnerving. He felt foolish telling her that he had left her house in a jealous rage when he realized that John Lucas was courting her. He had no actual claim on her, and he would betray the extent of his arrogance if he let her know that he had assumed that she had no other callers, when he had never called himself. Should he simply tell her that the book was designed to convey a personal message and it now seemed inappropriate? That seemed just as presumptuous, given that he was, in essence, seeking to take another liberty without ever having apologized for his first transgression or having ascertained her reaction to it. In the end, he simply replied, "Actually, I did not want to trouble your housekeeper. I still have it."

"But you came all this way. It would have been no trouble at all to leave it."

"Yes, well… perhaps I acted too rashly. I thought there would be another opportunity. I am sorry for any inconvenience that I may have caused."

Sincerely puzzled by his behavior, she replied in a distracted tone, "No, there is no inconvenience. I hope I have not unnecessarily troubled you."

"Not at all." As a prolonged silence overtook them, Darcy cursed himself for his inability to express his feelings. He felt too exposed to explain further.

Before they could continue any further, Caroline Bingley spoke in a voice clearly meant for the whole of the table. "Mrs. Bennet, earlier tonight you and I were discussing one of our neighbors, Sir William's son, Mr. Lucas. I want to thank you for your kindly suggestion that my brother call on him. We do so want to become more at home in the area. I believe you mentioned that he is the oldest son and therefore destined to inherit Lucas Lodge. Is that correct?" As she finished speaking, she gave Elizabeth a self-satisfied smile before resuming her attention to Mrs. Bennet. In that moment, Elizabeth suddenly realized what her mother's previous talk about John Lucas entailed and Miss Bingley's delight in having it exposed to the whole of the table.

"Oh, yes. You are quite right. One day he will be the master of Lucas Lodge, and while its income is nothing in comparison to Netherfield, it will be quite sufficient. When he was younger, he was inclined to let his mind wander from one thing to another, but as of late, he has become quite interested in the running of the estate. When he called today, we discussed that very subject. I think, like most men, he longs to settle down. I would not be surprised if another wedding is not soon announced. He has always paid particular attention to our Lizzy."

As her mother finished speaking, Elizabeth momentarily closed her eyes in shame. She knew it had the potential of esca-lating her mother's impropriety, but could not hold her tongue. "Mama, this is hardly the place to discuss such a thing. You have completely misinterpreted the situation."

"Nonsense, Lizzy, we are all practically family now. Well, of course not Mr. Darcy. But in as much as he is in charge of his sister's happiness, he must understand the importance of a woman securing a good match. Lizzy, you cannot wait forever, and you would do quite well to be the mistress of Lucas Lodge."

Smiling condescendingly, Caroline Bingley added, "Yes, Lucas Lodge does seem a lovely little estate. Did you say he called here today?"

"Yes, he was quite disappointed that he could not stay for dinner, but he promised to call again tomorrow. He took special care to ensure that Lizzy would be home to receive him."

In a desperate voice, Elizabeth whispered, "Mother, please."

"Oh, Lizzy," interrupted Lydia, "You know you have always liked him. I never understood why the two of you have waited so long. I know that I will marry as soon as I have the opportunity."

At this, Mr. Bingley asked in a tone slightly too loud, "Darcy, speaking of your sister. How is she?"

Looking down at his plate, he replied in a grave voice, "She is quite well, Charles, thank you."

Ignorant to all that had transpired, Mrs. Bennet added, "Mr. Darcy, I remember you saying that your sister is not yet out. You should not wait forever. I know that you apparently have no need of a wife just yet, but it would not do for you to put it off for too long. Matters of the heart change very quickly, and all of the good prospects may be gone by the time you decide to act. The early bird does get the worm."

Keeping his eyes on the plate in front of him, he simply replied, "Thank you, madam, I will consider it." Mercifully, Mr. Bingley was able to turn the conversation to a discussion of when Maria Lucas came out and then a lengthy discourse on which of Mrs. Philips's daughters were out. As the discussion raged about them, Darcy and Elizabeth sat in silence.

After finally recovering from her embarrassment, Elizabeth raised her head to look tentatively at Mr. Darcy from her position at his side. From her vantage point, she could see his embarrassment and mortification. But she could also detect something else; she thought it akin to despair. She suddenly understood his position. Impulsively she brought her hand to her lap and then slowly moved it toward Mr. Darcy's chair where his hand sat by his side. With a surge of determination, she reached over, took his hand, laced her fingers in his, and squeezed his hand to express her reassurance. Keeping her head down, she moved her eyes to the side of his face. His eyes flew open. He then darted a glance at her and then back down again. He then swept a look about the table to see if anyone had noticed anything. No one had. As he tried to understand what had happened, he began to feel a warming in his chest and a giddy feeling in his stomach that was spreading, but before he could react further or get used to the comfort of her hand in his, she began slowly to pull her hand away. It took him a moment before he reacted. He then tightened his grip on her hand and brought it back to rest by his leg. He then broke into a wide grin. It was now her turn to look over at him in surprise. Flustered, she attempted to pull her hand back again. To the extent she was able to pull it a few inches toward her, he swiftly moved it back to its original resting place. She attempted to pull her hand away again, but he would not relent. He locked his arm and continued to apply pressure so that both their hands remained resting on his chair. Seeing that she would gain no ground in a physical struggle with him, she turned her head to him and asked, "Mr. Darcy, are you quite well? You look a little flushed."

Turning to look at her, he was unable to repress a smile so broad it made his eyes twinkle as he said, "Thank you, Miss Bennet, I am fine," adding with emphasis, "I truly appreciate your concern, though. I was feeling slightly uncomfortable before, but I suddenly feel remarkably well." She flashed him an impish look and attempted to extract her hand again. He simply smiled, exposing both of his dimples, and pulled her hand back.

He then asked, "Miss Bennet, if I may be so bold, you look a little flushed yourself. Are you comfortable?"

"Actually, sir, I am not. I believe it is too hot in here."

With a smug smile, he leaned toward her and said, "I am sorry to hear that, but maybe if you tried to relax you might be more comfortable. Just a few moments ago, I was feeling quite overwhelmed, as if the confines of the room were too close, but now my entire outlook has changed. I am enjoying myself exceedingly well. I can honestly say that I hope this dinner never ends."

"Mr. Darcy, the evening will eventually end. It will follow the same course of every other dinner, and as such, when the main course is served, I believe both of us will be expected to cut our own meat."

"You are probably right. But in the meantime, I will simply enjoy this course."

QUESTIONS AND ANSWERS

UNFORTUNATELY FOR DARCY, THE soup course was served swiftly. As the dishes were placed in front of them, Elizabeth gave him a quick look of expectancy. He responded with a resigned smile. But he did not intend to relinquish her hand as easily as his expression implied. Before he let it go, he brought his other hand to where their joined hands were resting. He then cradled her hand in his own as he traced his thumb in small circles on her palm. Elizabeth felt a shiver go down her spine. She knew her cheeks must be bright pink from the sensation. He then gently squeezed her hand before letting go, hoping that she had felt the poignancy of their connection.

Elizabeth initially retrieved her hand with a sense of relief. She dared not imagine how the inhabitants of the dining room would have reacted had they been caught in such a wanton display. Her relief was soon replaced with a series of other emotions: a sense of loss from the absence of his touch, giddiness at her daring, humor at the ridiculousness of the circumstances that propelled her to act, mortification at her lack of propriety, and, ultimately, doubt as to the manner in which her gesture was received. As she stole a look at Mr. Darcy, she realized that once again, she could not quite fathom his frame of mind.

As they both sat there looking at their plates, Darcy wondered what he could say to her in this setting. His joy and relief at her taking his hand could not be understated, but he knew there was still much between them that was unsettled. He remembered his vow from the previous evening to tell her how he felt, even at the risk of losing all that he had gained with her, and determined to stick to his original course of action. He would disregard John Lucas's presence completely. At the very least, her overture toward him was clearly meant to reassure him in that regard. Whatever her mother thought, Lucas was not a competitor for her affections, and she would never accept the offer of a gentleman against her will. She had already proven that proposition true twice.

As he thought it through, he realized he still needed to declare himself to her and hope that she could be convinced to accept him. She had risked so much in holding his hand; now was not the time to be shy in response.

Squaring his shoulders, he said, "Miss Bennet, when I was first here in Hertfordshire, I had the impression that you enjoyed the outdoors. As a matter of fact, I think I even recall you being described as 'a very good walker.' In Kent, I also noted your affection for long ambles through the countryside, but since I have returned to the area, I must say, I am beginning to doubt the accuracy of my opinion of you in that regard."

Surprised and relieved by his teasing manner, she turned to him with her eyebrows arched and simply answered, "Is that so?"

With mock sincerity, he replied, "Yes, I regret to say it is. Since my return, I have witnessed you take two strolls in your own garden, but nothing more. Do you only enjoy walks in other counties, or have you lost interest in the endeavor altogether?"

Smiling, she replied, "Sir, really, I cannot account for your misperception. I walk often and always enjoy the exercise."

"Yes, that is clearly what you profess, and you have even been gracious enough to tell me of the paths you prefer, but I have yet to see any verification of your actually walking out."

As she looked at him with a mixture of curiosity and mirth, she replied in a tone unable to mask her amusement, "I was not aware that you needed proof. Are you inferring that my word is insufficient?"

"I just thought that there might be a way to satisfy my curiosity and put the matter to rest once and for all. Maybe you could tell me when you plan to walk out again, and I will endeavor to take my daily ride at the same time. If we meet, then I would be resolved to the fact that you do indeed enjoy the exercise and my faith would be restored."

In a playful tone, she responded, "But, Mr. Darcy, if I were to accept such a plan, I would risk everything and you nothing. If I walked out, but our paths did not cross, I would be branded a liar through no fault of my own."

"Yes, but the lanes in the neighborhood are clearly marked. I think it highly unlikely that our paths would not cross."

"That may be so. But I still have reservations as to the soundness of your premise. If you truly doubt my word, then I'm not sure that the proof of a single stroll would suffice."

Fearing that Elizabeth might not cooperate, he suddenly turned very serious. He stared down at his plate for a moment and then turned his gaze intently toward her. After a pause, he leaned imperceptibly closer to her and admitted in a hurried and hushed tone, "Truly, Miss Bennet, I know I do not deserve such consideration, but I would be forever grateful if you saw fit to share such information with me."

The clear intent of his words and the earnestness with which he made his last statement temporarily took her breath away. As she looked out the window to regain her composure, she meekly replied, "I believe I will try to walk tomorrow at first light."

Breathing out in relief, he leaned slightly closer to her still and quietly said, "Thank you so very much." Having abandoned his more playful tone in fear that he would not be able to accomplish his goal, he now found it impossible to regain their easy discourse. He sat in silence, contemplating what to do next.

Their momentary discomfort was relieved by the appearance of the next course. As they ate in a prolonged silence, she reviewed their previous discourse and resolved to gain something from him. She impulsively asked, "Mr. Darcy, what book did you bring me today?"

Caught off guard, he swallowed ungracefully. Regaining his composure, he put his fork down and turned his attention to her. "The other day, you asked me to select a book for you, and I must say it took me a great deal of time to settle on one. In the end, I brought you a copy of Christopher Marlowe's *Hero and Leander*."

As she contemplated his words, he became uneasy in the silence and asked, "Does your father's library already contain that volume?"

Smiling enigmatically, she replied, "No, it does not."

Nervously he continued to explain. "I know it is not typically the type of book that is recommended for a woman to read, but I thought you might appreciate the honesty conveyed in the writing, even if it might be considered provocative by some."

"I see."

"I was also hesitant to select it because I know your general dislike of poetry, but it has long been a favorite of mine. The story, of course, is taken from Greek mythology, but Marlowe's treatment of the emotions between the ill-fated couple has always moved me. I find his portrayal of Hero intriguing, as her femininity incorporates both loyalty and a strong, spirited independence." As he locked his gaze upon her, he added with hushed intensity, "I was hesitant to choose it because the story does not have a happy ending, but at its essence, it is a tale of a man who will brave any obstacle to win happiness with his beloved."

She gasped ever so slightly, unable to look away from him, as he continued to stare at her intently. The moment seemed to go on indefinitely, until she realized that Mary had requested that she pass her a dish. Once the task was accomplished, Elizabeth could not help but stare at her plate as she attempted to take in all that had transpired between them. Darcy's subtle clearing of his throat interrupted her reverie. Leaning slightly toward her, he quietly asked, "Perhaps I could bring you the book tomorrow? I would be curious to see if you enjoy it. When you are finished reading it, we could discuss it."

Smiling at him, she replied, "I would like that very much. But I have, in fact, already read it. I would, however, enjoy looking at it again, as your vivid description seems to give the tale a new perspective."

"You are already familiar with it? But I thought you said that your father's library does not contain that volume..." Giving her a broad smile, he added, "Oh, I see; I did not ask you the right question. I always seem to forget that I should never assume anything with you."

She smiled in response and then attempted to lighten the air by asking about his sister. They talked easily throughout dinner and were surprised when the ladies were called to retire to the drawing room.

When the party was reunited, Darcy kept by Elizabeth's side, but was soon forced to retreat from his position when she was assigned the duty of pouring the coffee. As he stood alone, trying discreetly to watch Elizabeth's every move, Bingley called him over to talk. As the men stood slightly apart from the rest of the guests, Bingley asked, "Darcy, how are you? I was a little concerned for you at dinner."

"Charles, I am fine. Do not worry on my account."

Skeptical, he replied, "I know that it is in your manner to keep things to yourself. But in this regard, I think that would be a mistake. Miss Bennet and I had an opportunity during dinner to speak privately, and she tells me that you should not put any stock in what Mrs. Bennet has to say about impending nuptials. You should not forget that she once believed that you intended to marry Miss Bennet."

"I know, Charles. I have disregarded it."

"Darcy, Miss Bennet also told me that Lydia is the last person that Miss Elizabeth would confide in, and that her comments were spoken without thinking."

"Yes, Charles, I know."

"I do not want you to feel that there is no hope. I think it is simply a misunderstanding."

Chuckling, Darcy put his hand on his friend's shoulder.

"Charles, I said I agree with you. In your zeal to speak with Miss Bennet in private during the dinner, all other matters escaped your attention. If you had looked around, you might have noticed that Miss Elizabeth and I are on cordial terms. I am not concerned about John Lucas's attentions. Well, that is not exactly accurate. I am concerned about his intentions, but I am not overly concerned with Miss Elizabeth's reception of them."

"Oh, well, that is good." Smiling broadly, he added, "I am glad." Before he could ask any more questions, Lydia ran excitedly up to him and began speaking without even acknowledging Darcy's presence.

"Mr. Bingley, you absolutely must help me. You are the only one who can."

"Well, I suppose I can try. What is the problem?"

"You must promise to postpone your wedding. My father says we will not be able to go to Brighton when the regiment removes there, because we will be preparing for your wedding breakfast. Would it not be more fun if we could all go to Brighton instead? You could come with us, and then you and Jane could get married afterward. We would have such a grand time. All you need to do is tell Jane and my mother that you do not mind putting off your wedding date for a few weeks. Once they see that you have agreed to it, they will have nothing to say on the subject. You simply must say yes."

Keeping an affable countenance, he replied evenly, "I am sorry to disappoint you, Miss Lydia, but I am afraid that the wedding date must stand as it is. Many of my relations have already made plans to attend on the date selected. Hopefully, you will be able to enjoy yourself just as much at the wedding festivities."

Clearly exasperated, she cried, "Oh, bother. Why does

nothing good ever happen to me? Now that Lizzy is to be engaged, the regiment will have more time for me. I think there is one among them who prefers me, but Lizzy was always monopolizing his time. I think I shall cry for a week. Maybe my mother will let me go with Colonel and Mrs. Forster by myself. I could be back in time for the wedding." With that said, she was off, leaving Bingley amazed and Darcy deep in contemplation.

The rest of the evening was, on some level, measured torture for Darcy. Mrs. Bennet mentioned John Lucas's name whenever possible, and Caroline Bingley sought his attentions even more aggressively than usual. He was able to smile through these assaults by recalling the memory of Elizabeth seeking his hand. It was a sensation he would treasure, and the thought that she had initiated the contact made it all the more significant. He also had the pleasure of watching Elizabeth from across the room, when she agreed to play a song at Mr. Bingley's insistence. But the opportunity for conversation with her did not occur many more times that evening, and when it did, it was brief and there was little opportunity to say anything of substance. When he made his adieus, he did think she looked at him with some feeling, but the moment passed far too quickly. He returned to Netherfield deep in thought, and after making one request of Mr. Bingley, he retired to his bedroom, anxious for the morning to arrive quickly.

Despite Elizabeth's intention to retire early in order to be well rested for her morning walk, she found that the opportunity for sleep eluded her. Once their guests had departed, Mrs. Bennet spent an inordinate amount of time alternately praising the manner in which the dinner was received and anticipating tomorrow's call from John Lucas. Being the focus of the latter, Elizabeth was not allowed to retire until she had been thoroughly instructed on the art of how to comport oneself in order to elicit a wedding proposal. Despite the foolishness of her mother's advice, Elizabeth had to laugh, that for once, their minds were contemplating the same subject—although envisioning different men as the protagonist. When she finally was able to escape to her bedroom, she soon heard a knock that she knew would be from Jane.

"Lizzy, am I bothering you?"

"Jane, you know you could never bother me. In fact, I was expecting you. You, no doubt, want to offer your congratulations on my impending betrothal to Mr. Lucas."

"Oh, Lizzy! I know Mama means well, but I was so sorry when she jumped to such a conclusion. I hope it did not embarrass you too much?"

"It did, but there is nothing to be done about it. I think Mama had some help from Caroline Bingley, but it still does not excuse her behavior. I will just have to hope that when I fail to become engaged to Mr. Lucas, the rumor that our mother started tonight will be put to rest."

"I am sure it will. But I wonder if she is wrong about Mr. Lucas's intentions. What will you do when he calls tomorrow?"

"Hopefully, it will not be an issue, but if it is, I will simply make it clear to him that while I have always valued him as a friend, I have no other feelings for him. I think he will understand that. It is our mother's reaction I fear."

"Lizzy, I'm sure our mother will understand. She just needs some time. Despite the results, her intentions are good." Eyeing her sister carefully, Jane added, "But I was also a little concerned for Mr. Darcy when our mother mentioned that you might become engaged. He did not seem to take the news very well."

With an air of indifference, she replied, "Oh, I would not worry too much for him. I am not sure if he had the most pleasant evening, but I think our mother's incivility will soon be forgotten."

"That may be so, but I was nonetheless concerned for him during the meal. When I saw him say good-bye to you, I was less troubled. You both seemed very comfortable in each other's presence."

"Oh, did you think so?"

Exasperated, Jane exclaimed, "Lizzy, stop being coy. Will you not tell me what happened?"

Smiling, she took her sister's hand and said, "Jane, nothing in particular has occurred, but I did let him know that I did not hold Mr. Lucas in any specific regard, and I think he was happy to hear it."

"Lizzy! I am so glad. I know that things are not settled between you and Mr. Darcy, but I did not want him to become unduly discouraged. But what did you say to him? How did you even broach the subject?"

"I just made it clear to him."

"But how?"

"Oh, Jane. I am afraid to even tell you. You will think me most scandalous. It was an impulsive act on my part. I didn't know what to do… Mother would not stop talking about it, and he looked particularly stunned by her declaration, so I… I grabbed his hand under the table."

"Lizzy! You didn't!"

"I am afraid I did."

"What did he do?"

"Well, at first he looked shocked, and then he wouldn't let go of my hand."

"He wouldn't let go of your hand? What did you do?"

"Well, obviously, I eventually convinced him to release it. But now I am not sure what he thinks of me."

"Lizzy, I am quite sure he thinks very well of you indeed. I think you know you have no concerns in that regard."

"Oh, Jane. I hardly know what to think. I acted very foolishly, but I could not see him so hurt. I acted without thinking."

"Lizzy, I think you were acting from your heart, and that is never a bad thing to do. It is clear that he has always been in love with you. I think you just needed to realize how you felt about him. But it is getting very late. I will not keep you when you obviously have much to think about. Have a good night."

Elizabeth prepared for bed, musing quietly over how everything had changed.

Darcy was always an early riser, but this morning he had awoken even before his usual custom. When he had returned from Longbourn the evening before, Darcy had told his valet about his need to leave before sunrise. His valet was accustomed to serving his master whenever the need arose and had often attended him very early in the morning to accommodate travel plans. He was not, however, used to the level of instruction the master had given concerning which coat and vest he wished to wear. That, and the master's other recent odd behavior since entering Hertfordshire, made it clear to him that something was afoot.

As Darcy reviewed the results of his valet's handiwork in the mirror for the third time, his valet approached Darcy's private traveling case to retrieve his watch fob. Before he reached the case, Darcy's commanding voice stopped him in his tracks. "Walbridge, that is enough. I will get my watch myself."

"Sir?"

Embarrassed by the tone he had used, he attempted to soften his rebuke. "I am sorry for being so abrupt, but I need not trouble you any further. You may be excused."

"Very well, sir."

"Thank you again for your help."

Once he was alone, Darcy sighed at the ridiculousness of his own behavior. The contents of his traveling case seemed to have been mocking him all morning, and his servant's attempt to open it, before he had decided what to do about it, temporarily unnerved him. The genesis of his problem began as a spur-of-the-moment decision in London, when he was recently at his townhouse reviewing matters with his steward. As he took stock of the contents of his safe, in order to make various household payments, he spotted his mother's jewel cases. He opened them because he was feeling particularly lonely, having left Elizabeth in Hertfordshire without any resolution of their relationship in sight. His mother's belongings had always brought him comfort, and when he noticed the posy ring that his father had given his mother upon their betrothal, he impulsively determined to take the ring back with him to Hertfordshire. He thought it unlikely that he would have occasion to use it, but if the opportunity with Elizabeth presented itself, he thought his preparedness would communicate something of his constancy to her. He knew that in Kent, aside from her distaste of his character, the manner in which he had asked her to marry him had contributed to the disastrous reception of his proposal. The fact that he had not even thought far enough ahead to have an engagement gift with him was emblematic of how little he had thought about Elizabeth's reaction to his request. He would not make that mistake twice.

When he returned from London with the ring, he had asked Bingley for leave to use his safe. Last night he had retrieved the ring before he went to bed as a gesture of hope. It now sat in his traveling case as a symbol of his indecision. He knew he wanted to use the ring to help declare his love and constancy, but he was unsure if today was the opportunity he was seeking. Once they were alone, he had determined to tell her of his continuing affection, but he did not want to frighten her off again. Despite his overwhelming impatience to have the issue decided, he knew that he had achieved far better results with Elizabeth when he had taken his time with her. John Lucas's presence had made this leisurely approach unworkable, but it did not mean that their relationship was ready for such a milestone.

Seeing that his indecision was delaying his departure, he made up his mind. He resolved to take the more cautious route by declaring his intention and then asking permission to court her. He would ask for her hand when he was surer of her feelings for him. His ability to wait for her would be a sign of his devotion and the consideration that he had for her feelings. He strode from the room with purpose. He returned several minutes later, opened the case, retrieved his watch, and impulsively stored the ring in his coat.

⁂

As Elizabeth left Longbourn, she started down the path to Oakham Mount. She was relieved that the path would not join up with the approach from Netherfield for quite a distance. She would use the time to compose herself. She needed to both calm her racing heart and put her thoughts in order regarding her feelings toward Mr. Darcy. She knew that she cared for his well-being, that she was attracted to him, and that she was flattered and relieved that he seemed to return the interest. Moreover, she had to admit that she found his touch an exquisite exhilaration and that she could not presently be persuaded to miss the opportunity to speak to him in private today for any reason. Was this in fact love? As her heart soared, she felt the answer deep within herself. She laughed, knowing that such thoughts would hardly help calm her beating heart. As she turned the first corner of the path, she was startled to see Mr. Darcy standing before her, with his horse tied off the path.

"Mr. Darcy!"

"Miss Bennet. I am sorry to have startled you." As she looked away in embarrassment, he felt his heart begin to sink. In a grave voice, he stuttered, "I… I thought you understood that I hoped to join you on your walk this morning. I am sorry if I am disturbing you."

"No, I did. I mean—you are not disturbing me. I did think that I might meet you, but I thought… I just assumed, that I would not see you until farther down the path, where it joins the walk to Netherfield."

Heartened by her words, he smiled and explained in a halting manner, "I thought I might see you as you walked by that point in the path as well, but I grew nervous that you might take another route or that I did not correctly understand your destination. As I had arrived there quite early, I ventured this way and found myself at your door before I knew it. I thought it made more sense to wait here, at the edge of your property. That way, if you walked out in any direction, I would see you. I am sorry to have come upon you unawares. I should have made my presence more obvious."

"No, no, it is quite all right." Adding with an impish smile, "May I say, Mr. Darcy, you seem a very thorough strategist. Do you have any formal military training?"

Somewhat chagrined, he told her, "No, nothing formal, although my cousin, Colonel Fitzwilliam, has explained some of the rudimentary points to me."

Stifling a laugh, she added, "You must be a quick study then."

As she smiled at him in anticipation, he found all rational thought beyond him. He had rehearsed what he wanted to say to her so many different ways that he hardly knew where to begin. Moreover, he had hoped to set the tone of their discussion by beginning the conversation with an apology for his forward behavior in the Netherfield library. Now that the course of the conversation had inexplicably veered to his cousin, he did not know how to broach the matter at hand. Elizabeth finally broke the silence.

"Mr. Darcy, would you like to join me on my walk?"

"Of course, of course. Yes, I am so sorry." Untying his horse and letting the reins drop so that the animal could follow him at a distance, he offered his arm to her and asked, "Please, may I escort you?"

As she took his arm, it was her turn to feel unsteady. She had teased him about his obvious eagerness to meet her this morning, but in reality his accidental information startled her. From it, his interest in her was clear. She could hardly continue to pretend that this was a simple stroll between friends. This was more in the nature of a rendezvous, and she was not sure if she was really ready for the consequences. Moreover, she hardly knew how to act, what she should say, and who should speak first. She was surprised to find her palms damp. As they continued to walk along in silence for several minutes, she finally ventured a thought.

"Mr. Darcy, do you wish to walk to Oakham Mount? There is a more direct path up ahead. We could take that route if you desire."

"Yes, that would be fine. Actually, no. I mean... could we perhaps stop and rest for a moment?"

She was about to tell him that she could hardly be tired from a walk they had not yet begun, but his serious countenance made her think better of it. "If you wish."

After securing his mount, he brought Elizabeth slightly off the path to a felled tree and placed his handkerchief on it, indicating that she should sit. As she did, he smiled at her. His expression, however, soon turned to a frown as his apparent nervousness took physical form in both his expression and in his sudden pacing in front of her. He stopped pacing as abruptly as he had started, looked at her, and then looked all about the area. He then appeared to be about to say something, but aborted the idea at the last minute. He finally blurted out, "Miss Bennet, I want to apologize for my inexcusable behavior in the library the other day. I should never have taken such a liberty, and I can offer no excuse. I have heartily regretted my actions ever since. I only hope that you can forgive me for my lack of propriety."

Embarrassed by the recollection of her own lack of propriety that day and somewhat astounded that this was the subject that he most wanted to speak to her about, she gazed at the ground and mustered a barely audible response. "Sir, I was just as much to blame as you were. I certainly accept your apology."

Overwhelmed at how awkward the conversation felt, he attempted an explanation. "I would not want you to have the wrong impression of my intentions. I truly regret my behavior."

Feeling the unintended sting of his words, she gave him a defiant look and replied, "It is quite all right, sir. As I said, I was just as much at fault as you. I have no intentions of demanding anything from you, other than your word that we shall both forget the incident in its entirety."

Suddenly stunned by the slight anger he heard in her voice, he attempted to understand what he had done to upset her. "Miss Bennet, I think you misunderstand me."

"Really, sir, in what way?"

As he tried to think of a response that might convey his true intentions, he decided that a longer explanation was required. "I think you misunderstand my intentions in broaching this subject. Although I should not be surprised that you do. I have come to realize that you are both the easiest person in the world to speak to and the hardest. When I am with you, and we have the opportunity to talk privately, as we did at dinner at Longbourn and Netherfield, and in the library, I feel totally comfortable telling you my innermost thoughts—nothing seems more natural—but when I attempt to tell you of my feelings for you, I inevitably find myself tongue-tied. It may be simple nervousness, but I suspect it is something deeper too. Whatever the cause, I apparently fail to comprehend how my words sound before I utter them. Despite the risk of infuriating you further, I find I can no longer be silent on this subject. May I ask your indulgence in hearing me out and your forgiveness for my inarticulateness in the process?"

She felt frozen to the spot where she sat. He was gazing at her with such intensity that she felt he was silently communicating his need for her to trust him and for him to be able to trust her in return. She nodded, hoping to convey both her wish that he continue and an affirmative response to his implicit request.

"I did not mean to imply that I regretted kissing you. I could never lament something that gave me such joy. I regret taking that liberty without first having ascertained whether I was forcing myself upon you. I request your forgiveness in that regard only. It would be disingenuous of me to seek your pardon for the act itself, because I know I would welcome the opportunity to repeat that endeavor at the slightest provocation. I knew after I kissed you in the library the other day that I needed to declare myself in order to determine if you could ever receive me as a suitor. Obviously, given our past, I was more than a little hesitant to do so, but it was various circumstances beyond my control, and not my apprehension, that kept me from attempting this conversation before now. I want you to know that while I truly value the friendship we have forged since my return to Hertfordshire, I would be lying to you if I continued the pretense that your friendship is what I seek." Stepping closer, he took her hands in his and told her what he had waited so long to say. "The plain truth of it is, I love you. I have never stopped loving you, and I would do anything to have you as my own. My need for you is overwhelming. It is all I think about, and it is my deepest wish that you could one day return my regard, in even the smallest way. I know you once told me that you could never love me, but I am unable to let you relinquish your hold on me. I will love you, no matter what your response, but if your feelings are still what they were last April, tell me so at once. As you can see, my affections and wishes are unchanged, but one word from you will silence me on this subject forever."

As he waited for a response, she looked at him clearly, in some ways for the first time. Before her stood a vulnerable man who had exposed his emotions to her, knowing full well, from experience, that he risked her rejection a second time. She felt the intensity of his regard as a physical presence. That he could care for her in such a way, after all that had passed between them, made her feel valued in a manner she had only imagined. But it was not just the fact that he valued her that made her love him in return. It was more than that. He had mentioned the primary reason himself. When she was with him, like this, she felt she could bare her soul to him. Nothing felt more natural. His intellect, wit, and the way he viewed the world coincided with her own, and the differences between them, which she had once thought were so great, now seemed merely a dissimilarity of style and not substance. She knew she respected him, admired him, treasured her time with him, and longed for him in a manner she had never felt for another person before. As she finally replied to him, she broke into a dazzling smile. "Yes, Mr. Darcy, I think it is safe to assume that my feelings for you are nothing like what they were in Kent."

He could not help but return her smile in full force. "I am very glad to hear it… but I am not sure that you have answered my question."

Giddy with excitement and overwhelmed by their conversation, she could not help but reply in a teasing manner, "Mr.

Darcy, I may be wrong, but I do not think that you actually asked me a question."

"I think I did, but the more material point is that I have told you of my continuing regard for you and my hopes that you could consider me as a suitor. You have allayed my fear that you no longer despise me, but you have not told me what your feelings for me are."

Feeling suddenly shy, she looked at him with a slightly pained expression and then decided to take the leap. Smiling at him bravely, she told him, "You once said something to me that, at the time, I callously disregarded. I have often thought about it since. It seems appropriate now. In response to your request, you must allow me to tell you how ardently I admire and love you."

At hearing her words, his breathing became rapid, and as a wave of joy washed over him, he involuntarily grasped her hands tighter. He stared at her in disbelief for what seemed a long time and then found his voice. "Then I take it you would consent to me courting you?"

His words awoke her from her somewhat trance-like state. Confused by his request, she repeated, "To court me?... Oh. Oh, yes, I suppose so. Yes, certainly. Do you wish to speak to my father then?"

"Yes, I would. May I return with you now?"

Letting go of his hands, she replied, "Actually, no. I think it would be better if you waited until tomorrow morning. I feel awkward mentioning this after all... that has passed between us, but Mr. Lucas intends to call this morning. It would be easier if you were not there."

"It seems to me that his presence is the best reason for me to go to your father directly."

"No, I would ask that you do not. I will speak to Mr. Lucas, and I will make my intentions clear to him. He will understand, but I think there would be very little served by making your request before he visits." Seeing his dark countenance, she asked, "You do not think it a wise plan?"

"No, I must be honest. It is not. I do not feel comfortable knowing he will be seeking your attentions when we have already come to an understanding."

Replying more formally than she intended, she said, "We have not actually come to an understanding, but that is beside the point. I am not sure that Mr. Lucas has any specific design in mind by his visit. It is my mother who is convinced of it, not me. But if he does, I will make it clear to him that I do not welcome his attentions. I want to do that, regardless of the state of our understanding. It is not as though he has lost me and you have won me. I simply do not hold him in any special regard, and he deserves to know that. He has long been a friend of mine, and I owe him as much."

He studied her for several moments, attempting to under-stand all that she had said. While he disagreed with her estima-tion of Lucas's regard for her and the manner in which it affected him, he was more troubled by something else she had said. "Why did you say that we have not come to an understanding? I thought we had. Do you think your father will not approve?"

Trying to respond in a casual tone, she replied, "Well, no… actually, yes, my father may be slightly difficult to convince, but that was not what I was referring to. I simply meant that we have not yet come to an understanding as to our future. You have simply requested to court me."

He began to protest but thought better of it as he noted

that the look in her eyes, which he had seen when she had told him that she cared for him—that he had hoped to see in her eyes for so long—was no longer there. Instead, he simply asked, "Have I offended you in some manner? I told you before that I seem to stumble when attempting to discuss my feelings for you. If you are to accept me, if we are to be together, then I would imagine that we will need to do something about this, or we will be destined to misunderstand each other far more frequently than necessary. I have been trying to improve in this regard, but I think I will need some assistance from you. If I have offended you, even slightly, would it not make more sense for you to just tell me, rather than hope I will realize my misstep of my own accord?"

She had to laugh at his logic and the endearing manner in which he had sought her guidance. "You are absolutely correct. In our last few encounters, we dispensed with the usual strictures of polite conversation. Maybe we should adopt that approach overall. We will attempt to be honest with each other, even at the risk of hurting each other's feelings directly, in order to avoid the injuries we inflict without recognizing them."

He thoughtfully replied, "That seems quite wise. But will you tell me now what injury I have unintentionally inflicted?"

"I did not mean to imply you have injured me at all. It is nothing really. In attempting to say it out loud, I can see how silly I am being. I... I was just surprised that after what you said to me—what I said to you—that you felt a courtship was necessary."

"I just thought that given our history, it was the wisest choice."

"If your decision was based on our history, I am even more confused. When you were unsure of my regard, you asked me to marry you. Now that you are sure of it, you wish only to court me. Under your plan, if our mutual regard continues to grow, we shall be only slight acquaintances by the close of the year."

Amazed that she had so totally misunderstood his intention and disturbed by her teasing tone about something so important, he blurted out, "That is simply unfair."

"I may have overstated it, but if you need more time to make a more formal commitment to me, or if you need time to convince your own family of the suitability of our match, I will understand. You should just say so."

Looking at her in utter frustration, he attempted to formulate how he would tell her that their courtship was for her benefit, not his. Instead of speaking, he quickly stepped in front of her. Startled, she moved slightly back, but he quickly closed the gap between them and cupped his hand to the back of her neck. He then slowly drew her face to him, giving her a fiery look. As their lips were inches apart, he whispered, "I know exactly what I want. I have no doubts. No reservations. I will marry you today if you will let me. Never doubt my resolve in that regard." He then kissed her. She was, at first, shocked by his conduct and, in her confusion, resisted as he drew her face to his, but once their lips met, the overwhelming flow of her emotions washed over her and she relaxed into his touch. As their kiss deepened, she felt in danger of losing herself completely in the moment. As he reached one arm around her waist and placed the other behind her, resting his hand between her shoulder blades to support her, she relished in the feeling of him enveloping her. As they continued their kiss, she felt an overpowering surge of emotion. She felt both hot and cold at the same time, and she was drawn inexorably to him by the intimacy of this simple act and the tenderness that she felt for him.

He finally broke away and rested his forehead on hers. He then whispered to her, "I have just learned a valuable lesson. It seems I can put my mouth to far more effective use with you than arguing a point." He then kissed her again and was rewarded for his effort by the feel of her arms entwined behind his back, pulling him closer. He eventually stopped to look at her in order to confirm that this was, in fact, real.

As he looked down at her in his arms, he saw that her beautiful face was flushed in a most becoming manner. She returned his gaze, and they both eventually broke into infectious smiles. As he leaned toward her to kiss her again, he said, "By the way, our courtship is officially over. Will you marry me?" As he started to kiss her, he could feel her beginning to laugh, but she soon turned serious as he continued to explore her mouth in the most tantalizing manner.

He eventually pulled himself away from her, aware that his control was precarious and that they were on an open path where people might soon pass now that the morning was in full swing. "Elizabeth, I would gladly stay here all day, but I think we might be seen. Should we continue our walk?"

She looked at him for a moment, lost in her emotions, unable to comprehend his words. She had often laughed to herself to see Jane in such a dreamy state after her visits with Mr. Bingley. She now understood it completely and knew she must look far worse. She eventually felt capable of a coherent reply. "Yes, I think we must leave, but I am afraid to say that I should return home. The events of the morning may test my mother's nerves, and it will be far worse if I am missing when she arises."

As he nodded his agreement, he nonetheless took her back in his arms. After a breathless exchange, they separated as he heard the distinct sound of someone approaching. He strode quickly from her and saw that a young woman was walking up the path. He quickly indicated her approach to Elizabeth, who nervously straightened her hair and clothes. Elizabeth then stepped forward and greeted Maria Lucas, hoping that she looked more in control than she felt. After exchanging awkward pleasantries, Maria informed them that she was coming to visit Kitty and was delighted to have Elizabeth to walk with. Casting a quick glance at Darcy, Elizabeth smiled her acquiescence to Maria. She then smiled at him and said, "Mr. Darcy, it was such a pleasant surprise to run into you this morning. Extend my regards to Mr. Bingley and his sisters."

"Yes, Miss Bennet, I certainly will. And please extend my regards to your entire family, particularly your father. Of late, I have not had the pleasure of his company, but I hope to rectify that as soon as possible."

As they exchanged a knowing smile laced with some mischief, he bowed his adieu and walked to his mount. He watched her leave before he continued up the path back to Netherfield. Before he arrived at his destination, he met Bingley traveling in the other direction to Longbourn.

"Darcy, I wondered where you had gotten to. I tried to wait for you, but I despaired of you ever returning in time. The other night you said that you would accompany me this morning when I called on Miss Bennet, but you left before I awoke without leaving word. I am so glad I found you. It is not too late, turn around and join me."

Darcy smiled at his friend and then sat in contemplation for several moments. "Charles, I probably should return to Netherfield, but I cannot resist your offer. Lead the way."

Answers and Questions

As Darcy approached Longbourn, he began to question his decision to arrive at Elizabeth's doorstep uninvited. She had already told him that he should call on her father tomorrow. But, he reasoned, she had told him that before he had asked her to marry him, when she was vexed at him for seeking a courtship rather than offering a proposal. It was his unfinished proposal that was drawing him here, when he knew he should probably wait. In his desire to seal their union with the intimacy that he had waited so long to savor, he had forgotten to elicit a response to his question. At the time, her kisses seemed more important, but now he knew he needed more. On some level, his need to hear her say "yes" seemed self-indulgent. Her answer to the question seemed somewhat obvious given that she had brought up the idea of the proposal in the first place. But his possessive side wanted her pledge to him to be clearly understood, at least between them, before she entertained the likes of John Lucas. He hated to think it was pure jealousy that motivated him; it was actually something subtler. He simply wanted to have their commitment to each other formalized so that everyone, friend and foe alike, would understand exactly what she was to him and who he hoped to be to her. He had waited so long for their union to become a reality that he felt he could not wait any longer to secure it. Besides, he had not given her his ring. Ultimately, though, what drove him forward was a sort of irrepressible excitement. He was so elated by her acceptance of him that he had to see her again, to bask in it, to verify that it was real, and to show her how much it meant to him. It all combined to make the temptation to see her again irresistible.

As he entered the gate, he saw a mount already tied to the post. He knew it probably belonged to Lucas, and a wave of irrational animosity washed over him. As they were announced, he entered the parlor behind Bingley.

His eyes immediately went to Elizabeth, who was sitting in a chair at the end of the room, with John Lucas seated to her left. Jane sat on a sofa to Elizabeth's right, sewing. He immediately noted that Jane had chosen to sit at the end of the sofa, farthest from Lucas and Elizabeth. It was clear that she was acting as a chaperone, and that Lucas was visiting with Elizabeth specifically and not the sisters together. While he already knew as much on an intellectual level before he arrived, the visible evidence of it made his jaw taut with irrational anger. When his eyes once again rested on Elizabeth, he could not resist the temptation to make his connection to her evident to everyone in the room.

As Elizabeth noticed his arrival, her countenance registered a succession of emotions. At first, she was surprised and excited to see him, and her face could not hide her impulsive joy. As he returned her smile with an impudent grin meant to communicate their secret understanding, she felt embarrassed and flustered at the awkwardness of receiving him, in this manner, with Lucas present. As she realized that the situation need not have occurred at all, and that she and Mr. Darcy had only an hour before discussed avoiding it, she felt the pique of annoyance. Despite her misgivings, however, her tender regard for him made her resolve to give him the benefit of the doubt. As she quickly surveyed the situation, she determined that there was no real cause for concern. Whatever motivated his visit, the situation was salvageable, as long as she and Mr. Darcy did nothing to betray their mutual regard. If they both behaved as if nothing was afoot, she could dispatch Mr. Lucas speedily, as she had planned, and then enjoy Mr. Darcy's company. It would be a slightly more awkward visit but not beyond successful accomplishment, as long as she acted with a little finesse.

Setting her mind to the task, Elizabeth greeted Mr. Bingley and Mr. Darcy with the utmost formality and indicated they should join them. Mr. Bingley immediately took his place beside Jane on the sofa. That left Darcy to sit in the vacant chair next to Lucas, across from Jane. She watched in mortification as Mr. Darcy looked from her, to the open chair, and then to back to Mr. Lucas. He then walked purposefully to the sofa and sat on the end closest to her. The problem with his plan was that Jane and Mr. Bingley already occupied the sofa and the amount of space left next to Mr. Bingley was hardly sufficient to house Mr. Darcy's frame. Mr. Bingley, who was busy with an intimate communication with his fiancée, was somewhat taken aback by Darcy's decision to join him. Executing several particularly ungraceful movements, the two men struggled unsuccessfully to reposition themselves on the limited space of the sofa. Elizabeth momentarily closed her eyes in embarrassment, unwilling to watch. She eventually looked to Lucas, whose demeanor made clear that he saw both the import of the gesture and the humor in its execution.

As the room fell silent, Lucas eventually began the conversation. With a voice full of sarcasm, he stated, "Mr. Darcy, how good to see you again. Two times in two days. I must say you are becoming quite a permanent fixture in the neighborhood."

Darcy returned Lucas's gaze with cold stiffness. He was mortified at his own conduct in making such an inelegant show of choosing his seat, but he also felt the challenge in Lucas's words and the mockery of his smile. While a part of his brain alerted him to the folly entailed in the course of action he was about to take, the rest of him was spurred on by pure instinct to claim what was his and warn off his competitor. Forcing an amiable tone, Darcy replied, "Thank you, Mr. Lucas, it is also a pleasure to see you again. You are quite right. I do feel very at home in the neighborhood. I had the pleasure of dining here yesterday as well, and I wanted to make my gratitude for such hospitality explicit." Darcy then turned significantly to Elizabeth and bowed his head.

In response, Elizabeth turned her face away from Lucas, and toward Darcy, and gave him an imploring look, indicating her exasperation. Darcy ignored her gesture and smiled warmly in return.

Darcy then turned to Lucas and said, "But I do not mean to direct the topic of conversation toward me. I am interrupting after all. I have had the pleasure of your company several times, but never a chance to further our acquaintance. Perhaps you would indulge me?"

Lucas easily replied, "By all means, sir."

"I understand you are the heir to Lucas Lodge."

"Yes, sir, that is correct."

"From my rides through the countryside I have had the opportunity to travel some of its borders. It seems an admirable estate."

Surprised to find himself on the receiving end of a compliment, Lucas genially replied, "Thank you. I am quite proud of it."

"The holdings seem extensive for the area; do you find it difficult to manage?"

"Yes... I mean no." Seeing that Darcy's compliment was actually aimed at a different sentiment, he regained his composure and attempted to reply in an affable tone. "My father is much more involved in how the estate is managed than I have been, so I could not tell you how much trouble is involved in its administration." He then smiled at Elizabeth and added lightheartedly, "As you well know, it has been my philosophy for quite some time to dwell only on the more enjoyable aspects of life, and I am afraid that the running of an estate will not qualify in that regard."

Unwilling to relent, Darcy continued, "But you must play some part in overseeing it. I would assume that your father, at his age, would welcome your input and that you would have long ago sought to lessen his burden."

Surprised at such a rebuke, Lucas replied in a more serious tone, "Actually, no. He has been content to hold the reins himself. But of late, I have come to realize that it is time for me to make some inroads in that direction."

Acting as if he were discussing the weather or another innocuous topic, Darcy calmly continued on. "Well, I would highly recommend it. My own dear father insisted that I take an active role in our estate at a very young age. I think you will find that while the responsibilities are great, the rewards are proportional. It is only through the experience of learning how to rely on one's own judgment and decision-making skills that one is truly able to develop a sense of oneself. It is, of course, an acquired taste. Once you become comfortable taking responsibility for all of the aspects of your life, then you can no longer imagine a time when you ceded such authority to another, even a parent. But I have gone on too long about my philosophy. I am sure you have put your time to better use. Did you study at university?"

"Yes, I did."

"When did you complete your education?"

"A little less than two years ago."

"And how have you been occupying your time since then?"

Before he could answer, Mrs. Bennet entered and began chattering. While Elizabeth typically dreaded her mother's interaction with Mr. Darcy, she presently welcomed the diversion, thinking that the situation could hardly get any worse. Her sense of embarrassment and anger at Mr. Darcy's interrogation of Mr. Lucas had become intolerable, but she was unable to think of a way to divert the conversation to more neutral ground. While her mother began speaking, she attempted to catch Mr. Darcy's eye, but he was apparently content to avoid her gaze and pay attention to her mother.

"Oh, Mr. Bingley! I was just informed that you had arrived. How wonderful to see you again. I see you have found Jane. Very good." As her eye moved further up the sofa, her smile faded. "Oh, Mr. Darcy, you are here too. Yes, well. I see." Looking significantly at Elizabeth and then to Mr. Lucas, she frowned and turned to Jane. "Jane, dear, it is such a beautiful day. I was just saying that I have not seen such fine weather in above a fort-night. I know Lizzy and Mr. Lucas walked in the garden when he arrived, but maybe you would like to take your company there for a stroll now too?"

Seeing the opportunity to gain a little more privacy, Bingley quickly responded for them both. "Mrs. Bennet, what a lovely idea." Extending his arm to Jane, he added, "Shall we?"

Smiling gracefully, Jane joined him. Mrs. Bennet then turned her full attention to Mr. Darcy. "Sir, would you not be more comfortable in the fresh air? I am sure Jane and Mr. Bingley would welcome your company."

"Actually, Mrs. Bennet, I am quite satisfied where I am. You are quite right about the weather, though. I took a walk early this morning, and I cannot remember ever enjoying myself more. But, nonetheless, I am quite content where I am." Turning to Mr. Bingley, he added, "Charles, would you mind terribly if I remained indoors?"

"No, Darcy, of course not."

Unable to hide her disapproval, Mrs. Bennet eyed Mr. Darcy intently and curtly replied, "Very well, then. I will order tea."

After Mrs. Bennet's departure, the three remaining occu-pants sat quietly, each attempting to determine what he or she could do to reduce the number of people in the parlor to two. Elizabeth decided on a course of action first. Turning to Mr. Darcy, so that Mr. Lucas could not see her expression, she raised her brow to signify her disapproval and indicated the door with her eyes. "Sir, I know how busy you are. Did you not tell me last night that you had an appointment this morning? I would not want to keep you."

Ignoring her gestures, Darcy simply smiled back and answered, "No, Miss Bennet, I think you are mistaken. I believe I mentioned that I had an early morning appointment, but I have already attended to it. There are some issues that still need to be addressed in that regard, but at the moment, I am otherwise at leisure."

After another awkward pause, Mr. Lucas determined to ignore Darcy's presence. He turned to address Elizabeth, asking, "Miss Bennet, have you heard that Mr. Smythe has become betrothed?"

Relieved to have the subject changed to a seemingly neutral topic, Elizabeth replied easily, "No, I have not. When did that happen, and how is it that our mothers have not been apprised?"

Smiling genially, Lucas leaned toward Elizabeth and said in a conspiratorial tone, "It is actually quite an amusing tale. I will tell it, if you promise to keep the secret." Looking at Mr. Darcy, he added, "Sir, please forgive us. It is local gossip that I am sure would not interest you as you know none of the participants, but Miss Bennet and I have a long history of speculation in this regard, and I would be remiss if I did not enlighten her about the particulars."

As Darcy watched Lucas tell Elizabeth about their neighbor, their familiarity with each other became more obvious and his exclusion complete. Each word that Lucas uttered felt like sand grating on the thin thread of his tenuous self-control.

When Lucas finally finished his tale, Elizabeth could not help but laugh at the clever way Lucas had concluded the story. As she did, Darcy cleared his throat. When she turned to him, she saw his brooding expression and withdrawn posture. She could not help but regret her actions. She was angry with him for his presumptuousness in coming and for his high-handed comments to Lucas, but her heart still belonged to him, and she did not want her momentary disappointment in his behavior to make him doubt her regard. Her laughter died in her throat, and her expression softened for the first time since his arrival in the parlor. Smiling at him, she asked, "Mr. Darcy, are there comparably ridiculous characters in Derbyshire, or does Hertfordshire hold a special monopoly on foolishness?"

He looked at her for a long moment, relieved that she had seen fit to include him purposefully in the conversation. He once again realized how much he appreciated her grace in continually forgiving him his impetuous conduct. He then gave her a knowing smile and replied, "I think each county has its own supply of such characters. While I do not know the people involved, I take it the gist of the story simply proves a long-held truth, one to which I heartily subscribe: Love makes people do foolish things. Your neighbors' actions may seem ridiculous from the outside, but I am sure that the sentiment that underlies their behavior is more in the way of sublime."

Touched by the force of his emotion, Elizabeth warmly returned his gaze and said, "That is quite a lovely way of looking at it. I think we would all do well to emulate your perspective."

"Thank you. I cannot claim always to have had such empathy, but of late, I have had some personal experience with both the ridiculous and the sublime."

As he smiled at her, Lucas took note of her response. Before more could be said, however, Hill entered and informed Elizabeth that her mother needed to see her immediately.

Once Elizabeth quitted the room, her mother beset her in the hall. "Lizzy, you must get that man to leave, right away! He will spoil everything."

Unable to resist the temptation, she asked, "Which man is that?"

"Lizzy, there is no time for your foolishness. I am talking about Mr. Darcy, of course. I have no idea why he continues to lurk about, interfering with everything, but it must be stopped. He will put John Lucas off."

"Maybe, Mother, that is for the best. It may be that Mr. Darcy has come specifically to see me."

"Lizzy, do not be silly, and even if he was, I will not be fooled again. To think that I almost encouraged him over Mr. Bingley for Jane's attention. If I did not eventually see through Mr. Darcy's purpose, it could all have ended in ruin. No, he is simply here to be in the way and nothing more. I think he enjoys vexing us. You must get him to leave so that Mr. Lucas can speak to you alone."

"Mother, even if I agreed with you, I do not know what I could do to accomplish such a task. I have already tried to no avail."

"Well, you must simply try harder. Now, go back in there and make sure Mr. Lucas understands where your allegiances lie."

"As to that, Mother, I think I can promise more success."

After Elizabeth had left the parlor, Lucas studied Darcy for a moment and then spoke. "Well, Mr. Darcy, we appear to have dwindled from five to just two, and while I believe both of us would prefer that number, I think we each had a different pairing in mind."

In response, Darcy simply raised his eyebrow, indicating that Lucas should continue.

"I once told you that I often see social exchanges in military terms. Would you like to hear my assessment of this morning's interactions?"

With his expression blank, Darcy replied, "Very much so."

"I think I came here this morning expecting to annex a neighboring territory through peaceful negotiation. I assumed that our long-standing mutual interests would bode in favor of an alliance. To my surprise, I now see that I have stumbled, ill prepared, into heavily guarded territory and that my chances of success here are very slim. Would you be willing to confirm my appraisal of how the land lies?"

Darcy looked at Lucas for several minutes and then replied in a thoughtful tone, "I think you are right. You are much more suited to the military than to the role of the elder son."

As both men continued to warily regard each other, Elizabeth reentered the room. The men stood, and Lucas spoke first. "Miss Bennet, I am afraid I have overstayed my visit. Thank you for your hospitality. As always, I have enjoyed my time with you exceedingly. But I believe we both have other matters that need our attention."

Elizabeth bowed her adieu. After Lucas's departure, she turned to face Mr. Darcy in exasperation. "May I ask, sir, what caused his sudden departure? And while we are on the subject, maybe you could also explain your decision to come here, after we had decided against it, and the meaning of your conduct after you arrived."

"I do not believe we ever decided that I would not come."

"We specifically discussed it."

"No, you said that there was no point in my coming because we had not really come to an understanding. Because I then offered for you, the reason for me not coming was removed, and there was no impediment to my visit."

"Sir, even if I could follow your logic, it is hardly an accurate view of what transpired."

"Are you saying that I have misinterpreted the facts or that I have misstated them?"

"Does it matter?"

He looked back at her in defiance, but soon thought better of it. She looked so appealing with her eyes animated with emotion. In the end, all he really wanted to do was kiss her again. Couldn't he somehow get to that point without so much resistance? He could see some of the justice in her criticisms. Why did his pride require him to defend his actions, even when he doubted his own motives for taking them? He thought it ironic how much she had already changed him. After his father's death, he had never allowed anyone to question his actions. He was now anticipating her reproofs and questioning himself on her behalf.

As she waited for a reply, she watched his face take on a softer expression as he said, "I suppose there are many reasons why I came here this morning, and I am more than willing to explain them all to you, but ultimately, I simply needed to see you again. Given the newness of our understanding, would you deny me the pleasure?"

Elizabeth had braced herself for his response, but she had not counted on such uninhibited honesty. Disarmed, she replied in a more amiable tone, "I suppose, under normal circumstances, I would not. But you must admit that the timing of your visit was quite awkward, and even if I could understand your need to come, I cannot fathom your hostile posture toward Mr. Lucas. You have already secured my regard. Would not the more generous thing have been simply to exhibit a level of civility?"

Her references to his lack of civility awoke in him his old fears, and those doubts translated into a fear of losing her. He gravely replied, "Yes, I suppose you are right. But you must understand… I have truly attempted to take your previous words about my… lack of civility to heart and… I hope you have seen that I have endeavored to gauge my actions accordingly… But I am afraid there are some things that I do not believe are in my control."

Seeing him struggle with his emotions, she took a step toward him and laid her hand on his arm in support. Surprised by her actions, he looked down at her hand on his arm and felt the kindness of her gesture wash over him. As he looked to her face, he saw her concern for him, and it was a balm to his soul. Without warning, he pulled her to his chest. With his head bowed to the top of hers, he whispered in her hair, "I cannot bear the thought of losing you. I still can hardly grasp that you have accepted me. I know I have many failings, and I want you to understand how seriously I took to heart your reproofs, but I cannot promise something I cannot keep. When another man is seeking your affections, I will never be able to respond with civility."

As he solemnly searched her face for her reaction, he was surprised to see a mischievous smile come to her lips. "I suppose that is a fault I can live with. Are there others?"

As relief spread over his features, his own smile spread to his eyes. "Oh, yes, far too many to catalogue. But I think it will be wisest for me simply to let you encounter them as they arise. I do not want to scare you away." As they stood inches apart, staring at each other, both relieved that the tension between them had abated, their smiles suddenly turned serious as they both could feel the heat of their closeness. As he gazed intently at her, he could not resist the temptation of her lips. Their kiss was tenuous at first, but soon intensified as they began to explore each other's mouths. Just as she was beginning to lose herself in the embrace, she felt him pull away. Resting his forehead on hers while he slowed his breathing, he eventually whispered, "My love, you are so tempting, but I will not make the same mistake I did this morning. Your kisses make me forget all else. One of the reasons I returned is that I realized you never answered my request."

Smiling and somewhat dazed, she asked, "And what request might that be, sir?"

"I think there was only one that stood out. Have you forgotten it so quickly?" As he waited for his answer, he began to lightly kiss the exposed skin below her ear down to the nape of her neck.

As she attempted to maintain her composure and he continued his exploration of her skin, she replied, "No, I do recall something about marriage being discussed, but you are right, I am not sure how it was resolved. Maybe you should ask again."

Stopping his ministrations, ever so briefly, he inquired, "Why would I ask again when there is already one proposal outstanding?"

As she grazed her lips over his, he closed his eyes momentarily at the sensation and then attempted to capture her lips. But before he could succeed, she pulled back and said, "Your last proposal was such an improvement over the first, I can only imagine how well you might do now."

"Madam, I think you overestimate me. At the moment, I can barely maintain a coherent thought, let alone formulate several sentences."

As he continued to caress her neck, she absentmindedly replied, "Are several sentences required?"

Laughing, he stopped what he was doing and tipped her face toward his so that he could look into her eyes. "Maybe not so many, but I want to hear you say that you will be my wife. If that requires me asking again, I will. Elizabeth, I love you, and I cannot live without you. I want you to be mine in every way. Will you marry me?"

"Fitzwilliam, I am already yours. All I wish is to be your wife and for you to be my husband."

A look of heartfelt joy spread across his face as he pulled a small box from inside his coat. "I also came back this morning because I wanted to give this to you. It is a ring that my father gave to my mother. The sentiment it expresses mirrors my own heart. I would be honored if you would take it as a sign of my love and devotion."

The ring was intricately crafted with the finest metals and the words, "Many are the starrs I see but in my eye no starr like thee," were delicately inscribed within it. As she read them, she exclaimed, "It is lovely. I can hardly comprehend that something so beautiful should be mine."

"That is exactly how you make me feel, so it is apparently a fitting choice. I know you cannot wear it until I speak with your father, but please keep it with you. Knowing you have it makes me feel connected to you."

"As you wish. But you had this with you? I thought you were only planning on asking to court me. Why did you bring the ring?"

Looking sheepish, he responded, "I had not decided between the two, and I wanted you to have the ring in either regard."

Laughing at his response, she added, "You continue to surprise me."

"As long as it continues to be in a good way, I am content. Elizabeth, I think I should speak to your father now. I may have made it clear to Mr. Lucas where my intentions lie, and I should seek your father's consent before he hears of it through other channels."

"Certainly, but what exactly did you say to Mr. Lucas?"

"Nothing in particular, but I think it was apparent."

"That it was. May I ask what you hoped to accomplish by your inquisition of him?"

Laughing, he thought for a moment and said, "I suppose I wanted to point out to you the differences between us."

"And in your estimation, what might they be?"

"Only that he is a boy and I am a man."

Laughing, she asked, "And what might that prove?"

"While other women might be content to fool themselves as to the difference, I believe you know better and that you also know yourself well enough to know which you require."

Blushing, she replied, "Mr. Darcy, I believe there is no proper answer to that statement. Perhaps now would be an opportune time to seek out my father."

With an impudent grin, he bowed and replied, "By all means."

❧

As Darcy prepared to knock on the door to Mr. Bennet's study, the elation he had felt from his time with Elizabeth began to be replaced by a sense of anxiety. He knew a certain amount of nervousness was natural, but felt he was suddenly experiencing more than was to be expected. He knew part of it stemmed from his natural shyness and the fact that he really did not know Mr. Bennet, but he also knew he was particularly inexperienced at requesting anything of anyone that he could not obtain himself. In business matters, his steward often carried out his negotiations for him, but when the task did require his involvement, it was with the knowledge that if he did not like the terms, he would simply walk away from the transaction. This was something entirely different. Nothing was more important to him than acquiring Mr. Bennet's consent to marry Elizabeth, and he could not rest until he succeeded. Adding to his worry was Elizabeth's admission to him during their walk that her father probably would not look upon his request with favor. The final weight on his shoulders was the knowledge that he also needed to broach another subject with Mr. Bennet that neither would enjoy.

Knowing that there was no alternative, he knocked on the door, and after being granted leave, he entered. Mr. Bennet's surprise and his annoyance at seeing him were momentarily clear on his face. After composing himself, Mr. Bennet offered in a perfunctory manner, "Mr. Darcy, please come in. To what do I owe this honor?"

"Um, yes… Mr. Bennet, I was hoping to speak to you about a matter of some importance. Actually, I need to speak to you about two matters of some importance."

Mr. Bennet stopped to survey the younger man's demeanor before answering in a measured tone. He immediately noticed how ill at ease his visitor was, but attributed it to his obvious distaste for his surroundings. Now that he thought about it, he had hardly ever seen the man comfortable, except perhaps during dinner once, but he could not immediately bring the occasion to mind. Deciding that it might be amusing to see what would motivate such a man to enter his study with, of all things, a request, he indicated that Darcy should sit. "Well, you have certainly piqued my interest, but I must tell you at the outset that I have no control over or, for that matter, interest in any of the finer details of my daughter and your friend's wedding. If you are here on Mr. Bingley's behalf in that regard, I must direct you back to Mrs. Bennet. I learned long ago that it is far easier to let her determine the contours of such issues than attempt to get involved in any dispute that, in the end, will hardly matter in the great scheme of things."

"Sir, while I do wish to speak to you about marriage in general, I am not here on Mr. Bingley's behalf. I have come on my own."

Somewhat shocked by what Mr. Darcy was implying, Mr. Bennet looked over the edge of his glasses at Darcy and replied, "Oh… well… then, I am not sure I can be of much help. You do understand that Jane is already betrothed."

Unsuccessfully attempting to hide his exasperation, Darcy replied, "Yes, I am well aware of the fact, and I wish them nothing but happiness." He then looked at Mr. Bennet for what seemed to the older gentleman an inordinately long time. As it became clear that Mr. Bennet was not going to make any sort of reply, Darcy suddenly rose and paced back and forth several times; he then tentatively sat back down on the edge of his chair. He fixed his gaze on the window beyond Mr. Bennet's head and stated, "Mr. Bennet, I have come to ask permission to marry your daughter; your daughter, Miss Elizabeth." Having finally blurted it out, he looked to Mr. Bennet for his reaction, and seeing the alarm on his face, he began to speak very rapidly. "On my behalf, may I say that I believe I will be a good husband to her and I will do anything in my power to make her happy. I am not sure if you are aware, but I have more than sufficient holdings to support her quite comfortably. She will want for nothing. She will always have at her disposal whatever funds she sees fit. My younger sister is under my care, and I believe Elizabeth will be a wonderful companion and sister to her. I realize that I will be taking her from Hertfordshire, but I think she will find my estate, Pemberley, in Derbyshire, quite to her liking. While Pemberley is at quite a distance from here, we have several carriages, and I am sure she will be able to visit Hertfordshire twice or perhaps even three times a year. I realize this may seem sudden on my part, but it is actually the product of much thought and devotion. I know that you have Miss Bennet's wedding to consider and that this is a complication to those proceedings, but it cannot be helped. I would not bother you if I felt I could wait any longer. But… I cannot. Therefore… I would like your permission to marry Elizabeth as soon as possible."

Mr. Bennet looked at Mr. Darcy in utter disbelief. That this arrogant young man felt he could come in and simply select Lizzy as his bride and then attempt to convince him of the suitability of their obviously ill-conceived match by listing his assets was beyond belief and bordering on an insult. Stunned by the sheer ridiculousness of the situation, he responded, "Mr. Darcy, this is quite extraordinary."

Darcy was feeling both relief at having publicly declared his intentions and rising concern at Mr. Bennet's reaction. "Do you mean to say that the manner in which I made my request is extraordinary or that my request itself is extraordinary? If it is the former, I beg your leave. I have obviously never asked for permission of this kind before, and if there are questions that you wish to ask me, please feel free to do so. I will obviously have my solicitor send you whatever information you require as to my financial standing. May I say at this point, that I understand that Miss Elizabeth does not have much by way of a dowry. Obviously, given my financial holdings, I am not in need of any sort of contribution to my assets, and as a result, we need not even consider it as part of our discussions."

Taking off his reading glasses with much deliberation, Mr. Bennet gave Darcy a level stare and then said facetiously, "Well, thank you. That is quite a relief off my mind." He then added in a grave tone, "Mr. Darcy, I think there is very little for us to discuss. I do not mean to speak on Elizabeth's behalf, but I think I can say, with quite some certainty, that she would not accept your offer, and I will not force the matter. Except maybe to say that I find your interest in her to be quite unusual. I understand that you were disappointed by Jane's selection of Mr. Bingley, but I hardly think substituting her next sister in her place makes any sense. In that regard, perhaps for your sake, I should take this opportunity to make myself clear on the subject. I do not believe any of Elizabeth's other sisters will accept your offer either."

Darcy stared at Mr. Bennet in disbelief as his cheeks flushed red with both embarrassment and anger. He attempted to calm his rising frustration by remembering how Elizabeth had felt in his arms that morning and the way she had looked at him just before she had welcomed his kisses. Steeling himself with the knowledge that only the two of them understood the depth of their affection and all they had endured to reach this point, he willed himself to respond to Elizabeth's father with patience. Darcy cleared his throat and said, "Mr. Bennet, I have already asked Elizabeth to marry me, and she accepted my proposal this morning. She is aware that I am making this request to you now. I understand that this might seem sudden to you, but it is not. I have every confidence that Elizabeth, Miss Elizabeth, returns my affections. Other than your concern that she would not accept my offer, do you have any other objections?"

"Mr. Darcy, I find this quite difficult to comprehend. Do you mean to say that Lizzy has accepted you?"

"Yes, sir, she has."

Mr. Bennet looked at him for several moments before he added in a voice full of concern, "Mr. Darcy, I am not sure what has prompted Lizzy to accept you, but I would ask that you think twice about it. Obviously, I cannot complain about your ability to support her, but I think it would be a grave mistake for you to attempt it in the first place. I do not mean to be blunt or, for that matter, cruel, but this is a matter of such gravity that I find I have no alternative. Mr. Darcy, it is my understanding that Lizzy has always disliked you. If she has accepted you, it must be for the material considerations you can provide, and while some women might be able to live a life built on such a basis, I know Lizzy would never be able to, even if the allure of all you can offer has momentarily blinded her. I cannot claim to comprehend the basis of your interest in her, but I think I am safe in assuming from your aunt's recent visit that your family will no more welcome Lizzy than they would have Jane. But, whatever your motivation, I must advise you to put it aside. Mr. Darcy, please believe me when I say I speak from experience. In the long run, it will only make you both unhappy. I know you have said that your interest in her is not sudden, but you have only returned to Hertfordshire a few weeks ago. You must look at it in the long run and understand that you will soon find something or someone else to divert your attention. In the end, you will see it is for the best."

Darcy knew his interview with Mr. Bennet would not be easy, but he had never counted on a refusal. With the panic evident in his voice, Darcy exclaimed more forcefully than he intended, "Mr. Bennet, you do not understand the situation. You must speak to your daughter; she will confirm our mutual regard, and I can assure you that it is not based on material considerations on her part. Nor is my interest in her a transitory indulgence. I have been in love with Elizabeth since I met her last November."

"Mr. Darcy, I would caution you. You have twice referred to my daughter in a most familiar manner, one which you have no right to claim. She may have caught your fancy last fall, but you have not seen her for months, and I know she did not return your affection at that time."

Trying to calm himself, Darcy replied with as much civility as he could muster. "Mr. Bennet, you are correct. Please excuse my impropriety. It was most unintentionally done, and it will not happen again. With all due respect, though, I still believe you do not understand the situation. My acquaintance with Miss Elizabeth is more extensive than you may be aware. I saw her also in Kent while she was visiting Mrs. Collins. My aunt is Mr. Collins's benefactor, and I was visiting there at the time your daughter was at Hunsford."

"Are you trying to tell me then, sir, that Lizzy formed an attachment to you while you were in Kent?"

Closing his eyes momentarily in exasperation, he replied, "No, I did not mean to imply that she returned my affections while we were together in Kent. She did not. I only meant to point out that our acquaintance is more extensive than you might have previously understood."

"But you had affections for her while you were in Kent?"

"Yes, sir, that is correct. Even before then, when I was here in the fall."

"But you never sought permission to court her?"

Feeling the sting of his words, Darcy simply replied, "No. I did not."

"Mr. Darcy I am having a great deal of difficulty following you, but are you trying to tell me that you first liked her in the fall, but the attraction deepened in Kent?"

"Yes."

"You then returned here this spring to continue to pursue her—and not Jane?"

"Yes, well, there is more to the story than that, but it is accurate in its essence. So you can see my interest in your daughter is more than a passing phase."

"Mr. Darcy, even if I could overlook the fact that you came here to pursue my daughter and failed to seek my permission to court her, all this shows is that it may be more difficult than I first comprehended for you to move past your interest in her. But my underlying concern remains the same. You, yourself, have admitted that Lizzy had no special regard for you in Kent, but only accepted you after your very brief reunion here this spring. Despite being in your company for several weeks, she never developed even a friendship with you, before you suddenly began to pursue her with an offer of matrimony. I know my Lizzy, and I know that she would not accept your attention for your wealth alone, but perhaps she is feeling the pressure to marry now that her sister is spoken for. She may be willing to accept you for the wrong reasons, but I am under no such obligations."

"But she is not accepting me for the wrong reasons. I know that for a fact."

"Mr. Darcy, the masculine mind is an amazing thing, but being able to discern the basis of a woman's attraction to it is not one of its skills. I am afraid you are particularly unqualified to clearly see Lizzy's motivations, and while I am surprised by her behavior, there is no other rational explanation."

Darcy boldly replied, "I know for a fact that Miss Elizabeth has accepted my proposal out of her regard for me, without any thought to my financial or social standing."

Amazed at Mr. Darcy's singular behavior, Mr. Bennet replied, "Mr. Darcy, I will ask my daughter, but after making such a declaration, I must say, I would be remiss not to hear you out. What makes you so sure?"

As Mr. Bennet awaited his reply, Darcy realized the position he had placed himself in. He loathed being forced to expose his innermost struggles to this man—to any man. It was something he was particularly unaccustomed to enduring. Especially as he was being forced to do so, in order to defend himself. But what was his other option? He tried to imagine himself in Mr. Bennet's position. He knew that if it were someone seeking Georgiana's hand, he would feel entitled to ask such questions. If he was honest with himself, if he put himself in Mr. Bennet's shoes, he probably would have thrown himself out after he had admitted to having pursued Elizabeth for an extended period of time, without first making his intentions clear to her father. No, he owed this man an explanation, even if some of it would not sit well. It was only his pride that was stopping him, and he had long ago vowed that he would not let that get in his way when it came to Elizabeth.

But in telling his tale, he knew he would have to divulge information about other people who might not wish it. Certainly, he could not discuss all of the details of what had transpired between Miss Bennet and Mr. Bingley without their permission. Moreover, his story would not reflect well on Mr. Bingley's sisters, and given that they were soon to be related to Mr. Bennet, he felt it would cause more harm than good. The same, however, was not true about Wickham or, for that matter, even Georgiana. From what Miss Lydia had said the other night about her wish to follow the regiment, he had vowed to discuss Wickham, in general terms, with Mr. Bennet today, in any regard. It was a risk, but he could hardly allow Wickham to continue to insinuate his presence in Elizabeth's family.

Squaring his shoulders and giving Mr. Bennet a grim smile, he said, "Mr. Bennet, I would be happy to tell you, although there are parts of this story that will not please you. I apologize in advance."

Mr. Bennet indicated that he should continue. "As you know, I first met your daughter last fall. Suffice it to say, I did not make a good impression. Despite what you may have heard about my estimation of her, though, I was indeed very quickly taken with her, with everything about her. I found her spirit, her wit, her natural goodness, and her beauty unequaled by any other woman I had ever met. But concerns that I have long since realized have no consequence intruded, and I attempted to ignore my attachment toward her. I left with Mr. Bingley, thinking that I could put Miss Elizabeth out of my mind. When I saw her again in Kent, I realized the extent of my love for her, and that whatever my family's objections, I wanted her as my wife or I would never marry... So I asked her to marry me in Kent. She refused my proposal outright. So you see, I know that Miss Elizabeth is not presently accepting me for my position or for my wealth. If she were interested in either of those things, she could simply have accepted my first proposal. If she wanted, she could have been my wife months ago, but she refused simply because she did not like me. I also do not believe her sister's impending marriage has motivated her to accept me now. I know I am the second suitor she has rejected in a year. It seems clear she would rather remain unmarried than enter into an alliance that did not please her."

For once, Mr. Bennet let his detached demeanor slip and exclaimed, "This is most extraordinary. I had no idea. I am not sure if I am more vexed that you and Lizzy never saw fit to let me know any of this or amazed that you have now secured her acceptance. How did this come to pass? Why has she accepted you now?"

"When I asked Miss Elizabeth to marry me—for the first time in Kent—I was stunned by her rejection." Darcy bowed his head as he added, "Your previous comments about the male mind were quite apt. In my confusion, I asked her why she had refused me. She was good enough to list her reasons in a very forthright manner."

Despite a repressed chuckle from Mr. Bennet, Darcy continued to explain. "She let me know she found my personality lacking in several respects and that she felt that Mr. Bingley's failure to return to Hertfordshire was my fault. But more than that, she explained she could never accept someone who had treated another human being so poorly. Apparently, she had credited a story Mr. Wickham had told her about me dishonoring my father's dying request that he receive a living in the church. May I ask, sir, have you also heard Mr. Wickham's complaints against me in this regard?"

"Mr. Darcy, since you have been forthright with me, I will be so in return. Yes, I have heard the rumors. While I felt Mr. Wickham a little too eager to tell his tale of injustice to anyone who would listen, there was nothing in your previous behavior in Hertfordshire to discredit his accounting of your personality."

"Yes, I realize that now, and I have attempted to slowly rectify that. In Kent, with Miss Elizabeth, I was a little more direct. I attempted to explain to her all of my interactions with Mr. Wickham. I did so, both in my own defense and because I did not want Mr. Wickham to be able to continue to deceive her as to his true nature. I would like to tell you as well. I would request, however, that after you hear some of what I have to say that you not share it with anyone else unless you deem it absolutely necessary."

"Certainly, sir."

"Mr. Wickham is the son of my father's most valued steward. Being the same age, we grew up together, almost as brothers. My father saw to it that he received the best education possible, and we attended university together. From his exploits there and from other incidents in our childhood, I soon learned that Mr. Wickham's true character was as dissolute as he was skilled at hiding it. We grew apart, but when my father died, he was indeed provided for in his bequests. Mr. Wickham, however, mercifully chose to forgo a profession in the church given that his nature was so ill-fitted for such an endeavor. Instead, he requested and received a generous settlement in cash. He soon ran through that money and came back to me requesting the original living provided in the bequest. Looking back at it, maybe I should have given it to him, knowing now how much it almost cost me. But I did not. Having been rejected, and finally forced to fend for himself, Mr. Wickham's resentment of me apparently grew. In my absence, he set upon a scheme to make me suffer for my supposed injustices toward him and cure his financial woes at the same time. He attempted to seduce my sister, who was at the time but fifteen years old. Luckily, chance allowed me to intervene. He has since made it his business to soil my reputation wherever he goes, counting on the fact that I will not retaliate for the benefit of my sister's reputation.

"Mr. Bennet, I told you when I first sought this audience that I had two matters of importance to speak to you about. Whatever the outcome of the first, I need to discuss the second issue with you now, as it concerns Mr. Wickham. I could not help noticing that your youngest daughter, Miss Lydia, has expressed some desire to visit Mr. Wickham's regiment in Brighton. He cannot be trusted, under any circumstances. I know that you only have my word against his, but if you seek confirmation as to my financial dealings with Mr. Wickham, my solicitor can provide you with whatever proof you request. If you need further substantiation as to the other details that I have related here today, you have my permission to contact my cousin, Colonel Fitzwilliam, who is joined with me in the guardianship of my sister."

Mr. Bennet sat in stunned silence, trying to comprehend all that he had been told. At length, he finally responded, "No, Mr. Darcy, that will hardly be necessary. I appreciate your candor. I know this must have been difficult for you to share with me. I will take your warning to heart."

"Thank you."

"Sir, I am still besieged with questions as to how your experiences in Kent with Lizzy led you to my library now. Obviously, her opinion of you was swayed by your revelation about Mr. Wickham."

"Yes, in part. I found out later that she did believe me in that regard, but she still had other complaints against my character. We did not depart Kent on good terms." Looking out the window to avoid the embarrassment of his next few statements, Darcy continued, "I did, however, take her criticisms to heart as to my demeanor, manners, and the way in which I have treated people. I determined to return to Hertfordshire with Mr. Bingley, now understanding that his reception here would mostly likely be received with favor. Unfortunately, that required that I first visit here alone, and when I did, and then sought out Miss Bennet to discuss Mr. Bingley, some... people involved got the wrong impression as to my intentions. I apologize for that and for my aunt's visit based on that misinformation."

"Ah, yes, we are very adept at acting on misinformation in this house. It is almost a skill, but our folly in that regard does not diminish my concern about your aunt's visit. But before we get to that, you should continue your story. Obviously, the details are of great interest to me, but it is also one of the more interesting tales I have heard in a long time."

Unaccustomed to being made sport of to his face, Darcy endeavored to remember his goal in suffering through this ordeal. "There is very little more to be said. When I returned with Mr. Bingley, I attempted to take your daughter's reproaches to heart. With our previous misunderstanding behind us, she was willing to give me a second chance. I have been lucky enough to win her affection, and she has now agreed to be my wife. As I said before, I believe she will confirm that she has accepted my proposal because she returns my regard and not for any other reason."

"So, you asked her to marry you twice?"

Darcy was tempted to tell him that it actually took three times to obtain an affirmative response, but decided the better of it. Instead, he replied, "Yes, that is correct. As to your question about my motivations, they are simple. I have loved your daughter for a very long time. I realized, after Kent, that I was not worthy of her, but I have endeavored to learn how to make her happy, and I believe I can."

Mr. Bennet eyed Darcy for what felt an extended period and then finally smiled. "Well, Mr. Darcy, you have surprised me, and that does not happen often. In retrospect, I can see that my previous doubts about you were all based on—what did you call it?—misinformation. My only complaint of your character, which I have gleaned from my own observations of you, is that you might be excessively proud, but given that you have had to undergo two proposals to get my Lizzy to accept you, I cannot imagine that is still an issue between you."

With a stony expression, Darcy replied, "No, sir, I would imagine not."

Seeing that he had pushed the young man to his breaking point, Mr. Bennet added, "Sir, I appreciate all that you have told me here today. I would like to confirm with Lizzy some of the particulars of her present feelings for you, but I otherwise rescind my previous misgivings about your match."

Interrupting him, Darcy said, "Thank you, sir. You will not regret this."

Bemused, Mr. Bennet replied, "I suppose only time will tell on that score. But I was not finished. While I no longer have concerns about yours or Lizzy's intentions, I do have some misgivings about the reception Lizzy will receive from your family if I were to consent to this match."

Darcy quickly replied in a decisive tone, "Sir, you should have no concerns in that regard at all. While my aunt has expressed some disapproval over an alliance between our families, she does not speak for me or, for that matter, the whole of my family. In any regard, I am master of my own estate, and I do not need anyone's permission to marry. My wife will be accorded the respect she deserves, and if my aunt cannot do that, then I will sever ties with her. I can promise you, sir, that no one will ever give Miss Elizabeth reason to regret her acceptance of my hand."

Stunned by the energy and fervor of Mr. Darcy's response, Mr. Bennet looked at him once again, attempting to take stock of a man he had clearly underestimated. "Thank you. That is good to hear. I will just ask Lizzy to join us."

Darcy listened as Hill was instructed to bring Elizabeth to them. As Darcy watched Mr. Bennet watching him, a wave of anticipation washed over him as he waited for Elizabeth's arrival. All he could contemplate was that another hurdle was soon to be removed from the path to his heart's desire.

As she entered the room, Mr. Bennet watched Lizzy immediately look to Mr. Darcy, who returned her gaze with a heartfelt smile that seemed to animate his whole countenance. Lizzy looked back at him with a dazzling smile of her own, as their eyes met for a brief moment. She then cast her eyes downward and took a seat in front of her father. Through these simple actions, Mr. Bennet's most fundamental question was answered.

"Well, Lizzy, it seems this young man wants to marry you. What have you to say?"

"Papa?"

"What have you to say about it?"

She immediately looked to Darcy, who raised his eyebrows to express his puzzlement. She clearly did not know what to think. Before she had been summoned to the library, she had been exceedingly concerned about the amount of time Mr. Darcy's request was taking. She thought it did not bode well for their cause. She knew her father had only spent a few minutes with Mr. Bingley before he consented to his offer for Jane. She thought her father would be pained by her choice, given all of the unkind things she had previously said about Mr. Darcy, but this seemed worse than she had expected. If her father was looking to her for her reaction, she decided to make her feelings on the subject crystal clear, so that her father could have no reservations based on her behavior. Coming to a decision, she boldly replied, "Father, I have accepted Mr. Darcy's proposal. I know I will be very happy. I can only hope that I can make him happy in return. While I did not always know it, he is the very best of men. I know we both want your blessing, but if you are not willing to give it, you should know that it will not matter in the long run, as I intend to marry Mr. Darcy in any regard."

Mr. Bennet looked at Elizabeth, surprised by her response. He thought she would defend her choice, but had not counted on her allying herself with him over her family. He felt the sting of her rejection of his authority but soon tempered it with the realization that her response was what it should be. The reality of the situation was that she was, in fact, choosing Mr. Darcy over her family, over her father; her definitive commitment at the outset was a sign of her resolve. Attempting to stem his rising sadness over his impending loss, he turned to Mr. Darcy and said in as lighthearted a manner as he could muster, "It seems, sir, that your attempts to convince me of your suitability were unnecessary. My permission was never needed in the first place. Apparently, you are to wed my daughter."

Darcy was ecstatic at Elizabeth's steadfast declaration. It was more than he had imagined. To hear her choose him without equivocation made his pulse race and his heart swell. But as the import of her gesture became evident, Darcy suddenly recognized Mr. Bennet's position. Turning to him, he stated, "I think your daughter has spoken too quickly, sir. Your blessing is both required and requested."

Standing and extending his hand, Mr. Bennet humbly replied, "Thank you, Mr. Darcy, for that. You may be assured that you have my blessing. We must now simply determine how to tell the others."

"Father, perhaps it would be best if I spoke to my mother by myself, unless, of course, you wish to speak with her."

"Oh, no, there is no need of that. With two daughters to be married, I will soon hear of nothing else but wedding plans. Let me have a reprieve for as long as possible."

"Very well, Papa." Turning to Mr. Darcy, Elizabeth added, "Perhaps, sir, if I do not ask too much, you could retrieve Mr. Bingley and Jane from their walk. It would be best if I spoke to my mother alone. Afterward, I could join you in telling them."

Smiling broadly at her, Darcy replied, "It would be my

pleasure." He then formally bowed his adieu to Mr. Bennet. As Elizabeth moved to follow him, Mr. Bennet asked, "Lizzy, do you think I could have a word with you privately?"

"Certainly, Papa." Before turning to her father, Elizabeth gave Darcy a secret smile as he closed the door behind them.

"Well, Lizzy, it seems you are to leave us."

Smiling, she replied, "I hope it was not too much of a shock."

"I must own that, at first, it was. I am now more reconciled to it, but regardless of your choice, I am still wrestling with the fact that you will be leaving Longbourn. Derbyshire seems so very far away. I just wanted you to know that if you have any reservations, you should speak them."

"Truly, Father, I have none. I am so very happy. I think I am happier even than Jane. She only smiles; I laugh."

Mr. Bennet held out his hand to her and said, "Very well, child. I can see that this is what you want, and I believe you have enough sense about you to understand what it entails." Hugging her, he then kissed her head. He closed his eyes as the reality of her impending departure settled over him. He then quickly moved away, attempting to hide the emotions he knew were visible on his face. Elizabeth watched him for a moment as he turned to stare out the window, feeling all the tenderness he could not express. She then left, silently closing the door behind her.

As she turned to go to her mother, she was startled to find Mr. Darcy standing in the hall, his eyes alight with joy. Even in her momentary confusion, she was able to note how very handsome he looked. As she started to speak, he gave her a devastating smile and put his index finger to her lips to indicate that she should remain silent. He then took her hand and pulled her to follow him into the dark corner of the adjoining empty hallway. He looked both ways, drew her to him, and leaned down to kiss her. Before his mouth met hers, however, she leaned her head slightly back from him and asked, "I thought you were going to find Mr. Bingley?"

"He is found. They are in the garden. We can go there at any time." He then leaned in to kiss her neck. While doing so, he slowly said, "Once my errand was complete, I had an over-whelming desire to see you."

"I may not be particularly experienced with such matters, but it seems to me, sir, that 'seeing' me is not what you have in mind."

It took a moment for him to hear her words. When he did, he immediately stopped his attentions to her neck, stood straight, and then released her completely. His face took on a grave countenance. He then stammered, "I am sorry... if I... I did not mean to offend. I simply... I needed... I have no excuse. I do not know what I was thinking... I am very sorry. Please believe me that I meant you no disrespect. Forgive me."

Seeing him in such discomfort, she regretted her playful jest. She had forgotten that he was not used to being teased. As she tried to find a way to alleviate the distress she had caused between them, she lamented her words all the more as she real-ized how awkward it would be to tell him now that she wished him to resume exactly what he had been doing. "I did not mean to reprimand. I... I was jesting, a very poor attempt indeed."

With his head bowed, he tersely replied, "Perhaps we should join the others."

As he began to stiffly walk away, she impulsively caught his wrist and pulled him back into the corner in the same manner he had previously done. She then put her finger to his lips and said, "Shhhhh." As he stared at her in shock, she slowly traced her finger down the middle of his lips to his chin. She then took his chin and gently moved his face toward her. Looking deeply into his eyes, she kissed him in a lingering fashion and then began to feather kisses on his chin and jawline. When she reached his ear, she whispered, "It is I who should apologize for incorrectly leading you to believe that I do not welcome your attentions. I have never felt such pleasure than I have in your arms, and I did not mean for you to stop." Moved beyond imagination, he clutched her to him as he began to kiss her fervently.

When they broke apart, he rested his forehead on hers and sighed, "Oh, Elizabeth." After catching his breath, he added, "My... need for you sometimes colors my judgment. You will tell me if I make you uncomfortable."

Smiling broadly at him, she replied, "I believe that our actions just now were my responsibility, not yours."

"Yes, but I started it. The responsibility is mine alone."

Seeing that he was serious, she earnestly replied, "I would beg to differ, but be not concerned, I will tell you if I feel otherwise," adding with a mischievous smile, "But then, sir, you must promise to do the same if I make you uncomfortable."

"Madam, that is simply not possible."

Laughing at him, she asked, "Perhaps we should move to a safer topic. You said you needed to see me. Was the interview with my father so terrible?"

"Not terrible, no. But there was a point when I worried that he would not give his blessings. His opinion of me was not very impressive. I needed to tell him somewhat of our tumultuous history. I hope you do not mind, but I feared that there was no other way to convey how it was that you had come to accept me."

"No, I am relieved you did. I suppose if I had shared some of my newfound appreciation for you with my family beforehand, your interview might not have been so difficult."

"That may be so, but in explaining it to your father, I realized that anything short of a full accounting does not quite do it justice. In light of that, may I ask how will you explain it to your mother?"

"With as little detail as possible. I think in the end, the result will matter more to her than the journey." As an awkward silence followed, Elizabeth colored. She wished her mother would not embarrass her.

Seeing her blush, Darcy immediately thought of the harsh words he had once said to her about her family. Attempting to ease her concern, he pulled her to him and said, "All that matters is that you marry me. Unfortunately, there will be some who will not understand how we came to care for each other or our motivations for doing so. That is simply not our concern."

Searching for the right words, he continued, "During our discussion, your father indicated his reservations about my aunt's reception of you. I told him, and I want you also to know, that she will show you the respect you deserve or I shall not receive her. I will not knowingly allow anyone to give you pain."

"I appreciate the sentiment. But I think that is too much for even you to ensure. We will simply have to bear it with grace."

Holding her to him, he said, "I am eager, though, to have you meet the rest of my family, my sister, Georgiana, in particular. With your leave, I will write to her today, and to Colonel

Fitzwilliam, as well. They are in London; perhaps they could come to Hertfordshire to call upon you."

Smiling at his thoughtfulness, she said, "I would like that very much."

"May I ask, now that your father has given us his blessing, will you wear my ring?"

Smiling at how shyly he had asked, she replied, "If you would like. Once my mother knows, there is no reason not to."

"I would very much like to see it on you. I can remember my mother wearing that ring, and it will help to make this all seem real. It is hard to believe that you are finally to be my wife."

"I suppose, though, we should start to make it a reality by informing my mother. Perhaps we should join the others now."

"I imagine you are right, but may I confess to you that I have no desire at this moment to do so. I would much rather hold you like this while I am able."

"I am not quite sure how long this opportunity will last. My sisters may be home at any time, and the servants will have their duties to carry out as well."

"Yes, but no one is in sight at the moment, and it seems too lovely an interlude to waste. At least, let me use the opportunity to ask you something that I will be unable to in company."

"By all means, but I must say, I am somewhat apprehensive as to what it is you wish to know, if it must be accomplished in such secrecy."

"It is just that my asking such a question will expose both my vanity and my impropriety at the same time. If I were wise, I would forgo the question altogether, but my curiosity has the upper hand."

Laughing, she replied, "I think your answer should give me more anxiety than solace, but I am still willing."

"It occurred to me, when I was attempting to explain to your father what made you change your mind about me, that I do not actually know how it came to pass. I know I risk losing the good graces you have generously bestowed upon me, but I must admit to more than a passing curiosity."

"Ah, you want to understand the working of a woman's heart. I am not sure such a disclosure would be in my best interest. If I let you know how easily you can gain my good graces, then I will be giving you a power over me that I do not think would be wise to bestow before we are even married."

"I hardly think it is accurate to describe my quest to receive your good graces as an easy one. It certainly was not a direct path, and there were times when I despaired of ever being able to hold you in my arms as I do now. Given my poor performance in the past, it would seem only sporting of you to help me in whatever way you can. You have had complete power over me for so very long; may I not know even some of the secret of my success?"

"Very well, but then you must do the same. While your affection for me is apparently older than mine for you, it seems no less difficult for me to comprehend, especially when you consider how much trouble I have given you in the process."

"My affection for you is a straightforward story. I fell in love with you long ago, and while I did not always understand how to value it or express it, it never wavered. It became such an integral part of my makeup that it did not diminish even after there seemed to be no hope of it ever being returned. I am simply the fortunate recipient of your change of heart. But, madam, I believe you are trying to change the subject in an attempt to misdirect my purpose. I thought you had agreed to answer my question, not pose new ones of your own."

"Sir, you have very exacting rules of discourse. If this love you profess for me is so great, can you not indulge me?"

At this he laughed and, with a broad smile, replied, "Now you are trying to trick me. I hope you do not want me to be so besotted that rational thought should escape me altogether."

Laughing in return, she replied, "I suppose I would tire of it soon enough. But indulgence is always welcome, and I think it may well be required at times."

"That you shall have in abundance, as I am sure I will require far more of the same from you. But on this point I will not relent."

"Very well," she said, "I will tell you to the extent that I can. I suppose there was some point after you returned to Hertfordshire that I realized how unfair I had been to you. I began to see you for who you are, not clouded by prior prejudices, and your kindness to my sister helped greatly in that regard."

"But that only explains why you forgave me, not how you changed your mind about me."

"That is true. I suppose after your aunt came to call on Jane, I began to see you in a new light. I think it was when I first saw you in Longbourn parish that I began to regret having lost your regard."

"But you never had."

"But at the time, I did not know that. I could hardly predict that you would still be civil to me after all the injustices I had unfairly heaped at your door, let alone still hold me in favor. I suppose it was your very behavior in that regard that made me realize your generous spirit. That you could pay me every courtesy, when I hardly deserved your attention, made me begin to understand how much I had undervalued you. When I saw you at church, you seemed so different from my previous perception of you, and I realized that I had never allowed myself to really study you. I began to that day and thereafter. Upon closer inspection, you seemed to improve quite rapidly."

Laughing at her characterization of him, he asked with a smile, "And where, may I ask, did your closer inspection of me in church on that first Sunday begin? I have always suspected that you were not quite forthcoming with me when we spoke after church. I suspect now that I was being spied upon."

Raising her brow in mock defiance, she replied, "Sir, I do not have the pleasure of understanding you."

"Very well, if you insist on keeping your secrets, I shall relent for now." He pulled her to him and rested his head upon hers as he contemplated all she had said. He then looked intently into her eyes and added, "Thank you for telling me that. I am very lucky to have you. I must say that, when the time comes, it will make it all the more special to take our vows in that church, knowing that your first pleasant thoughts of me originated there."

"It was not my first pleasant thought of you, but I think you are quite right that it will indeed be most fitting."

"May I have the honor of escorting you to church tomorrow? That way, I will have the pleasure of your company and full knowledge of your whereabouts throughout the service."

"I suppose that might be less interesting, but far more enjoyable. I will look forward to it." Hearing the arrival of her sisters, Elizabeth smiled apologetically to him. "I believe we must face the others."

PERCEPTIONS

DARCY AND ELIZABETH'S REUNION with Mr. Bingley and Jane was most joyous, and it was settled very quickly that they were both to be the happiest of couples. Mr. Bingley felt free, as hardly anyone else did, to tease Darcy liberally as to the amount of time it took him to get to the point.

Before the couples retired indoors, Elizabeth excused herself in order to speak to her mother, who took the news as one might expect, exclaiming simultaneously at the shock of it while attesting to her earliest information as to Mr. Darcy's partiality toward her second daughter. When Elizabeth returned, she was happy to see that Jane had kept the gentlemen outside, as it saved her the embarrassment of having Mr. Darcy overhear her mother's cries of joy and exclamations over the fortuitous match she had made. She wondered briefly whether it might have done him good to hear her mother's sudden low opinion of Mr. Lucas, after all the previous praise she had bestowed on him at Mr. Darcy's expense.

She was surprised, however, to see how restrained he was when they returned indoors and told her sisters. His formality and reticence seemed to reemerge as if he had never before been relaxed and engaged in her presence. She was puzzled at his reaction and was somewhat displeased that it allowed her younger sisters to retain their less-than-enthusiastic opinion of him. They were each pleased for her and said so directly, but she could see from their expressions that none of them understood her feelings for him. Lydia, in her typical impulsive manner, said as much, as she marveled over how rich Elizabeth would one day be and could understand wanting that above all else.

After securing Mr. Darcy's and Mr. Bingley's promises to dine with them, her mother urged her and her sisters to dress for dinner. The gentlemen awaited them in the sitting room, where Mr. Darcy requested pen and paper to write his sister and cousin. As her maid put the finishing touches on her hair, Elizabeth gazed at her reflection, attempting to understand Mr. Darcy's reaction to her sisters. She wondered if it was simply because he was ill at ease in company or whether his behavior reflected that he still held her younger sisters in the low opinion he had previously professed in his letter. She was roused from her thoughts by the beauty of her ring, and as she looked at it, all her tender feelings for him returned. She remembered his intimate words and his intense look as he kissed her, and she vowed that whatever the cause, she would help him reform his opinion of her sisters and, by extension, his behavior toward them.

As she entered the parlor, the unrestrained smile Mr. Darcy bestowed upon her made her blush. It soon vanished as her mother followed her into the room and began prattling away about wedding plans. While his face took on a polite but disengaged expression, she could tell from his eyes that he was not listening to her mother at all, but rather, watching her take her seat beside him. As he continued to observe her, she became both diverted and alarmed as he failed to answer her mother's inquiry. As an awkward pause ensued, Elizabeth eventually hid her smile and responded, "Mama, I am sure there is more than enough time to determine such things. Do you not agree, Mr. Darcy?"

"Yes... er, in what regard... do I agree?"

Smiling at him, she replied, "My mother, sir, was saying that we need to set a wedding date right away as she needs to be able to make various wedding preparations and she wants to plan a short trip to London to shop. I was saying that we need not decide tonight as we have only become engaged today."

Looking somewhat contrite for his inattentiveness, he responded, "Yes, I agree." He then added, "Actually, let me rephrase that. I do concur with your mother that we should set a date soon, as I think a trip to London would be quite useful. I am sure that you would want to shop there, and I would very much like to show you my townhouse. I also need to meet with my solicitor, and we could coordinate that as well. In that manner, we would not need to be separated." Turning to Elizabeth, he asked, "Would that suit you?"

Understanding the quiet emphasis he had given the word "separated," Elizabeth gave him a shy smile and demurely answered, "Yes, I would like that very much."

Gazing at her intently, he replied, "I am very glad."

As they continued to stare at each other, Mrs. Bennet beamed, "Well then, Mr. Darcy, it is all settled. I have already thought of several wedding dates that might do quite nicely. I can pick one and take care of all the arrangements. I am sure you will agree that it should be a wedding to rival no other."

As he began to comprehend Mrs. Bennet's words, his countenance took on a look of concern. In a tone that clearly brooked no opposition, he turned to Mrs. Bennet and said, "Madam, I will need to consult with my steward as to my calendar before any final decisions can be made, and when I do, I will let you know what dates would be advantageous."

Mrs. Bennet, surprised at having a topic she held so close to her heart foreclosed, sat in stunned silence. Elizabeth was a little taken aback too, but it was her younger sisters' reaction that gave her greatest pause. Lydia rolled her eyes knowingly at Kitty, who nodded her understanding. Clearly Mr. Darcy seemed controlling and intimidating. Before more could be said, Jane arrived with Mr. Bingley. Seeing a much more sympathetic partner with whom to discuss wedding preparations, Mrs. Bennet quickly recovered and began debating the value of one milliner over the other while Mr. Bingley listened with his usual good nature. Mr. Darcy seemed content to feign interest and periodically gaze at Elizabeth.

As they were called to dinner, Darcy immediately took Elizabeth's arm. It was an act he had longed to do, and he reveled in the freedom to do it without apology. As he pushed in her chair for her, he leaned close to her ear and whispered, "You look so very beautiful tonight."

As a blush crossed her face, she leaned toward him as he sat and said, "Sir, I believe you enjoy teasing me."

"I am not teasing you. I have never been more serious. Anyone who looked at you would agree. You are beautiful."

"I think there are those who would disagree, but I was referring to the timing of the compliment. I think it was designed to surprise."

"I would hope that receiving a compliment from me at any time would not surprise you. You can be in no doubt of my regard for you."

As she returned his gracious smile, she said, "I am not, but you seemed so serious in the parlor. I was surprised by your change of mood."

"I think I am in the same mood with which I began the evening, but I am always most pleased when I will be able to speak to you with some modicum of privacy. I am simply glad to have you as my dining partner. I have been anxious to ask you how your interview with your mother went. I see she has accepted the arrangement, but I was wondering if it was what you had hoped."

"Well, it was what I expected. Actually, I think she was quite stunned. She could barely respond for several moments, which is quite a feat as far as my mother is concerned. In the end, she simply wanted to know what your favorite dishes were so that you would be pleased at dinner."

"Then she does not lament the loss of Mr. Lucas's attentions?"

"No. I think she is well pleased with my choice."

"I am glad to hear it. So, may I ask, what did you reply?"

"Reply?"

Smiling easily, he said, "As to my favorite foods. I am actually quite hungry this evening. What do I have to look forward to?"

"I am embarrassed to say that I did not know how to respond. It made me realize that, in many ways, I know very little about you."

"I hope you feel you know me well enough to have made an informed choice this morning."

"Yes, in that I am quite assured. I only meant I have much

to learn about you. Would you not confess to feeling the same about me?"

"Yes, I suppose, although I believe we have dined together on enough occasions, both in Kent and at Hertfordshire, for me to feel confident in saying that you do not seem to prefer fish, that you are partial to fruit in general and to all forms of berries in particular, that you always finish your vegetables but seldom your meat or poultry course, and that you always welcome dessert enthusiastically."

Deeply surprised by his attention to her preferences, she stammered, "I see. I am not sure if I should feel flattered or spied upon. Is that the breadth of your knowledge on the subject, or is there more?"

"Yes, there is more. I believe I have never seen you take eggs at breakfast. I believe you prefer bread and jam instead. I have watched you spread it with fascination on several occasions, and I am always entertained by it."

"Mr. Darcy, I am shocked."

Leaning in close to her, he replied in a hushed voice, "Well, I cannot imagine why. There is nothing improper about being observant, and did you really believe I could love you for these many months without having paid you some attention? I would suggest that you become accustomed to it, as I believe I will be paying even closer attention to you in the future." Before she could answer, he added, "But on a separate note, if you still profess to return my affections, do you not think it is time to forgo calling me Mr. Darcy? Would not something more informal be in order?"

"Yes, I suppose you are right, Fitzwilliam, and I will endeavor to remember that. But before we leave this topic, may

I say in my defense that I am absolutely certain that you take your coffee black?"

Laughing, he replied, "In that, you are absolutely correct."

"Thank you, I feel exonerated. I suppose, though, it is not a laughing matter. If I am to be a proper mistress for your home, I should know your tastes."

"Yes, but there is ample time for us to learn about each other. It is one of the things I am looking forward to. But in any regard, I have a trusted housekeeper, both in London and at Pemberley, who is familiar with such things and will be more than helpful. And if you must know, roasted duck is my favorite meal."

"Thank you. I will not forget."

"Speaking of my townhouse, I was very pleased to hear that you will consent to a trip to London. I am hoping things can be timed in such a way to ensure you have an opportunity before our wedding to make any changes you deem necessary."

"Thank you. That is very generous, but I am certain everything will be very much to my liking and more than sufficient to fit my needs." Turning more serious, she carefully added, "As to the timing of the trip, I am sure that whatever plans you make, we will endeavor to accommodate your schedule."

Taking in her odd behavior, he replied, "But I have nothing planned yet. I am asking you now so that we can decide together."

"But you seemed to indicate to my mother that your schedule would dictate such matters."

Furrowing his brow, he replied, "Oh, then I suppose I gave the wrong impression. I did not want to commit to your mother as to the timing of our wedding or a trip to London without us having discussed it first. You said you did not see the need to set a date yet, so I was agreeing. I do need to check with my steward, but it is really just a formality. I simply wanted us to be in agreement before we discussed it with your mother."

"Oh."

"I hope this does not sound too odd, or maybe even blunt, but I suppose I have been used to deciding things for myself for a very long time now. I am not foolish enough to believe that I can continue in this manner. I understand I must now consult you first about such matters, but the idea of having to get your mother's approval is somewhat foreign to me."

"Well, she will need to make plans, and she has Jane's wedding to consider too."

"I appreciate that, and I do understand that we will have to accommodate her wishes. But the idea of the three of us discussing our wedding date in front of everyone else is not appealing to me."

"I see."

"In some ways it is a very private decision. I would not feel comfortable saying what I want to say to you about the subject in front of her, or anyone else for that matter."

"Well, now you must tell me directly, because you have not only confused me, you have piqued my curiosity."

After looking to see if anyone was paying attention to them, he leaned near her ear and whispered, "I have waited for you for what seems a very long time. And after this afternoon in the hallway, I am not sure how much longer I can wait. I think for both our sakes, we should marry sooner rather than later."

In response, her eyes widened, and she blushed. Looking down at her plate, she quietly replied, "Oh."

"I see that I have made you uncomfortable. I am sorry. Perhaps we should discuss this another time."

Gaining her composure, she looked him in the eye in an impertinent manner and said, "No, that is not necessary. Since you have succeeded in gaining my undivided attention, I think I should hear you out."

It was now his turn to blush. Undaunted, however, he replied, "Very well, I think a short engagement would be preferable. I know that it might conflict with Bingley and Miss Bennet's wedding, but I was discussing the very matter with him while waiting for you to join us for dinner, and he suggested a novel proposal that might suit everyone's needs."

"Pray tell me, what could accomplish all of that?"

"It would require Miss Bennet's approval and, of course, yours, but we considered a double ceremony." As he waited for a response, he impetuously added, "I know your mother may not like it, but we could be married in less than five weeks. I had hoped that Georgiana and Colonel Fitzwilliam would come to Hertfordshire by the end of this coming week, and after they had visited for a few days, we could all return to London. I believe there would be ample time to accomplish everything that needs to be done. Your mother has already finalized most of the wedding details. She would simply need to enlarge the arrangements to accommodate my family, who are not so many in number."

Elizabeth watched him in fascination; she did not believe she had ever heard him speak so quickly. That he was nervous touched her heart tenderly. She replied definitively, "I think it a splendid idea."

"Do you really? If you would rather not, I will understand. We can think of some other arrangement. I want you to have exactly what you want, nothing less."

"I can think of nothing that would make me happier than sharing such a special day with Jane. I love her so very dearly too. My only concern is whether Jane would approve."

"If you are sure that you approve of the idea, then we need only to see your sister's reaction. Bingley said he would ask her about it at his first opportunity. If she agrees, do you think your mother would be averse to the idea?"

"I do, but she will have to relent if we are all in agreement. I think it would also suit my father as well, as he would not have to suffer through the preparations for two weddings."

As they laughed, Elizabeth looked to the other end of the table at her father, who, to her surprise, was watching her and Darcy closely.

As Mr. Bennet studied their easy interactions, he suddenly remembered when it was that he had previously seen Mr. Darcy so relaxed. It was at this very table, at a previous dinner. He and Lizzy had had their heads together all evening in what looked to be animated conversation. At the time, he thought Elizabeth was valiantly carrying out her duties as a hostess—eliciting dialogue from a man who rarely ever spoke. He had thought it a testament to her ease in social situations that she could initiate a discussion with a man who held her in so little regard. Now, as he watched the way Mr. Darcy looked at her, he saw his obvious admiration and understood that it had always been part of his countenance. Here was a drama that had occurred before his very nose, involving his best-beloved daughter, and he had never seen the signs.

As he thought about it, he looked around the room and espied Jane looking adoringly at Mr. Bingley. It abruptly struck him that he did not know how that relationship had come to fruition either. Jane seemed so placid and agreeable, but the course of her engagement to Mr. Bingley was not without event. He had never wondered how Jane fared, as he always thought of her as so serene that her heart could not be easily touched. It clearly was, but he had never noticed it.

As he looked around at all of the members of his family, he realized that he had long since stopped paying any real attention to them. Instead, he let his opinion of them stand unchallenged by the passage of time. It was an apt way to look at his wife. He had long ago surmised her strengths and weaknesses, and he could judge her reaction to almost any situation before she actually responded. He had come to assume that the same was true of his daughters. In his mind, Elizabeth was a keen judge of character who felt comfortable speaking her mind to him about any topic. Jane was good and sweet, and while many men paid her attention, she took it all in stride. But apparently, through his inattention he had misapprehended both daughters. Elizabeth had never bothered to inform him about any of her dealings with Mr. Darcy, and Jane had apparently struggled over Mr. Bingley for many months.

As he looked at his other daughters, he wondered what he had missed about them. As he observed Mary, he had to admit he found very little there of interest. She meant well and was, in fact, well read. But in his mind, her interpretation of what she read always missed the mark. Maybe, however, that had more to do with her age and limited experience. Kitty seemed to follow whoever would lead her, but at times he had detected a sense of humor there. Maybe both girls had hidden depths. But then there was Lydia. She was clearly her mother's daughter in every respect and, like her mother, closer examination seemed redundant.

Before he could dismiss her altogether, however, he thought of Mr. Darcy's warning and wondered if her foolishness meant that she needed more observation rather than less. If she was indeed like her mother in every respect, the fact that she was becoming a young woman who would attract men of every stripe boded very ill indeed. If Lydia's discernment of the company she kept was as poor as Mr. Darcy intimated, then Lydia might soon find herself in a predicament without an honorable ending. He had always deferred the issue of the suitability of the men who called on his daughters to his wife, as she made the endeavor her life's work, but seeing that she never even had the smallest hint that Mr. Darcy was pursuing Lizzy, he wondered how he could trust her to know what Lydia was doing with her time when so much more was at stake.

His meditations were interrupted by the ladies withdrawing. Later, when he returned to his family after a quick brandy with the gentlemen, Mr. Bennet approached Lydia and Kitty and extended each an arm. That they were surprised by his actions was obvious, but no more so when he asked, "So, girls, how can you account for your time today? Have you done anything to recommend yourselves?"

Despite Lydia and Kitty's discomfort over their father's sudden interest, the inhabitants of Longbourn passed the evening pleasantly. Mary enjoyed the brief discussion she had with her father about the book she was reading, and Mrs. Bennet spent the night envisioning the jealous reactions she would elicit when she told her neighbors at church about Elizabeth's engagement. Jane and Mr. Bingley spent most of the evening in deep discussion, oblivious to anyone around them.

Elizabeth and Mr. Darcy were not allowed the same luxury,

as the novelty of their engagement had not yet worn off. Elizabeth noted Mr. Darcy's reserve when they were in general discussion with her entire family, but when they were afforded an opportunity for private discourse, she found him attentive, thoughtful, and thoroughly charming. He spoke tenderly of Georgiana, his parents, and the colonel's family, and he listened with great interest while she described her aunt and uncle, who resided in Cheapside. They both agreed that they looked forward to meeting the members of each other's family and hoped it could be accomplished during their visit to London. No word was spoken of his aunt in Kent, as the evening was too pleasant to entertain such a disagreeable subject. Darcy was disappointed that their farewell was accomplished so publicly, as he had observed Mr. Bingley bidding Miss Bennet adieu alone on several occasions, but Mr. Bennet seemed insistent on accompanying him to the door. Consequently, he had to console himself with only a kiss on her hand and her promise that she would see him at church in the morning.

The morning dawned brightly at Longbourn, and even her mother's attempts to throw the household into chaos, by insisting that several of her daughters wear something different from what they had selected, could not dampen Elizabeth's spirits. By her mother's design, they arrived at church early, as she wanted to tell as many people as possible her news before services began. Despite her mother's pleas, Elizabeth stood fast to her intention to wait for Mr. Darcy outdoors, leaving her mother to spread the word without the benefit of embarrassing her in person in the process. As the time for the service drew nearer, Elizabeth grew impatient. While she knew it was irrational, she did not want to enter the church without him.

As she waited by the walkway to the steps of the church, she saw the Bingley carriage arrive. She watched in disappointment as Mr. and Mrs. Hurst exited the coach followed only by Caroline Bingley, who gave her the barest of nods before she entered the church. Elizabeth was tempted to ask her where Mr. Bingley and Mr. Darcy were, but she would not give her the satisfaction. She thought it petty that Caroline would not acknowledge her engagement, as she must have learned of it either last night or at breakfast this morning.

Caroline entered the church and quickly scanned for Mr. Darcy. He had come home after she had retired for the night, and to her dismay, Charles and he had eaten very early and left for a ride before she had made it downstairs for breakfast. Caroline resolved to seek out Mr. Darcy to sit with her before the service started. To her surprise, she did not see him or her brother in the church. Instead, she watched as Mrs. Bennet animatedly explained that her daughter had received a ring as a token of esteem that had been in the owner's family for generations. Fearing that Charles might have given Jane a gift that should belong to her, she leaned closer. She heard Elizabeth's name mentioned with the word engagement, but before she could move forward to better hear what was being said, a woman to her right asked the man she was with if John Lucas had arrived yet. He replied he had not and gave the woman a knowing nod. As Caroline suddenly realized the import of what was being said, she indulged in a self-satisfied smile. Maybe today would turn out better than she had anticipated. As she thought of Elizabeth standing outside awaiting John Lucas's arrival, she decided to investigate the matter, as it would give her a similar opportunity to wait for Mr. Darcy.

As Caroline walked to Elizabeth, she said, "I see you are waiting patiently for the rest of your party to arrive. May I join you?"

"By all means."

As Caroline saw Elizabeth's ring, she gasped. She had clearly underestimated the Lucases' resources, but then, on the other hand, maybe it was the only piece of jewelry in the family's collection. Whatever it was, she was still certain that Lucas Lodge was far beneath her notice, and Eliza Bennet was more than welcome to it. She had disliked Mr. Darcy's habit of talking with her at dinner. That her time would now be consumed by her new fiancé more than suited Caroline. "Let me congratulate you on your engagement. I had not heard formally, but I just now surmised as much from your mother. You must be very happy."

Surprised at her generous words, she replied, "Yes, I am. Thank you very much."

As an awkward pause ensued, Elizabeth eventually asked, "Your brother and Mr. Darcy did not accompany you this morning?"

Taking Elizabeth's question as a tacit understanding that she was rightfully waiting for Mr. Darcy to escort her to church, Caroline bestowed one of her rare sincere smiles. "No, they left for an early morning ride. When they had not returned by the time we were to leave, we assumed that they had gone straight to church, and we came along directly."

"Oh. I see."

They stood for a moment or two in uncomfortable silence, before they saw Mr. Darcy and Mr. Bingley arrive on horseback. Mr. Bingley dismounted and, after a quick greeting, indicated that he was going to go in to find Jane. He offered his sister his arm, but she impatiently waved him off, stating that it was not necessary. Darcy walked briskly over to them and quickly explained, "I am sorry to be late. Charles and I both arose very early this morning, and with too much time on our hands, he suggested a ride. Unfortunately, we strayed farther than we planned. We would still have been on time, but it takes Charles an inordinately long time to get ready. I am sorry to have kept you waiting; please accept my apology."

Both Elizabeth and Caroline responded in unison: "It is quite all right."

Suppressing a smile at Caroline's misstep, Elizabeth added, "I have not been waiting long. Do you often lose your way riding? Maybe it is too dangerous a hobby for you to partake in."

Enjoying her teasing tone, he replied, "Not at all. I consider an early morning ride to be one of life's greatest pleasures."

Caroline stood in stunned silence. She could hardly believe the impertinence of Elizabeth Bennet. The familiar tone she had used to address Mr. Darcy was totally inappropriate, and what had she meant by saying that she had not been waiting long?

In the interim, Elizabeth smiled and replied, "Unfortunately, I have never had much inclination beyond attaining a destination. I think it is an art I am not meant to conquer."

"Nonsense," Darcy responded. "There are only two things you need to learn how to ride well: a good horse and a good teacher. If you wish, I could help you in that regard. I taught Georgiana to ride. She was quite nervous at first, but she is now very accomplished."

Unable to let this travesty continue, Caroline moved to stand by Darcy's side and interrupted, "Mr. Darcy, I am sure Eliza could find someone much more suitable to teach her. Did you know that our congratulations are in order, to both her and to Mr. Lucas?"

Darcy looked quizzically at Caroline and then to Elizabeth, whose brow was also furrowed in confusion, before he inquired, "Mr. Lucas?"

"Yes," Caroline purred, "our own Eliza has become betrothed to him. Her mother is announcing as much in church."

Elizabeth began to stammer, "Miss Bingley, I think you misunderstand..." but was interrupted by Mr. Darcy, who asked in an imperative tone, "She specifically told you that Elizabeth was engaged to Mr. Lucas?"

"Yes, she is in the church... well, actually, no, I overheard as much, and in any regard, Eliza is wearing his ring."

Darcy stared at her for several seconds, attempting to comprehend what she was saying. After a moment, he responded in a firm but patient tone, "Miss Bingley, I think you are confused. That is my ring on Elizabeth's finger. I asked her to marry me yesterday morning, and I am exceedingly pleased to state that she has accepted me. We had no opportunity to speak to you this morning, and I assumed you already knew our news since you were here with Elizabeth. You must have misunderstood Mrs. Bennet."

Caroline's head spun. Each time Mr. Darcy uttered the name "Elizabeth" she felt as if it were a slap to her face. To add to this dreadfully unimaginable news was the fact that she had made such a stupid assumption and then blindly acted on it. She was heartsick, mortified, and slightly ill to her stomach. She gathered all her courage and smiled insincerely. "Oh, what a silly mistake on my part. How foolish of me. Of course, it is you two who are engaged. What a striking pair. I, of course, wish you the best of luck. Congratulations. Well, I should take my place inside."

As Caroline departed, Elizabeth and Darcy looked at each

other, sharing both their shock and confusion and, if they were honest, a little amusement.

Offering his arm, Darcy said, "Elizabeth, I suppose we should go in."

"Yes, I think that would be best."

As they headed up the stairs, Elizabeth felt Darcy falter ever so slightly. With an impertinent tone she leaned toward him and asked, "Are you changing your mind, sir?"

"No, of course not, but I just realized that now we are so late and your mother has had ample opportunity to discuss our betrothal, everyone's eyes will be upon us as we enter. I have never felt very comfortable with such scrutiny."

"Yes, I am afraid you are correct. But if Miss Bingley's reaction is any indication, I would rather have everyone know now at once."

Laughing, he replied, "Yes, you are right and, ultimately, I will feel comfortable wherever I am, as long as you are by my side."

Chapter 19

LESSONS LEARNT

As ELIZABETH ENTERED THE dining room, she was relieved to find that she was apparently the first to arrive for breakfast. The swirl of excitement over her engagement meant that she rarely had time for quiet reflection. The last few days had been crammed with social events, and while many things had happened, her mind always wandered back to the times when she was allowed a precious moment alone with Fitzwilliam. Her favorite reflection occurred among a crowd of people at church, but recalling the intimacy of the moment always brought a smile to her face. During the service, Darcy had offered her the use of his prayer book, holding it in front of her and leaning toward her so that he could read along. She had to admit that their close proximity made any concentration on what was being said almost impossible.

To steady herself and, in part, to distract herself, she held the other end of the book. All attention to the service was totally lost when he moved his index finger to graze hers under the cover of the book. She attempted to look straight ahead and remain composed, but soon found herself not up to the task. Seeing her reaction, he began to draw teasing circles on the back of her hand. Despite her resolve, she discreetly turned toward him, in the hope of imploring him to stop, but to her surprise, he returned her gaze with a look of such intense emotion that she was unable to look away. They seemed locked in the moment, the reality of the commitment they had made to each other, and the sweeping changes that it would bring, taking tangible form. The connection between them, so appropriate in this church, seemed a testament to the life they had agreed to form together.

Eventually, the spell was broken by the rustling of pages indicating that the service had moved on without them. Both participants seemed embarrassed by their lack of control and attempted to return to their places, but the solemnity of the moment had left its mark. By the end of the service, she was hard-pressed to remember anything of the minister's message.

After church, she accepted his extended arm as they stood to receive the good wishes of many of her neighbors. As the Lucases made their way toward them, she felt him stiffen. After Sir William noted Mr. Darcy's good luck at having won such a local jewel, John Lucas extended his hand. "Miss Elizabeth, Mr. Darcy, may I congratulate you both on your betrothal. I wish you every happiness."

Darcy nodded crisply and formally shook his hand, adding a curt, "Thank you."

Elizabeth curtseyed her acceptance, and warmly said, "Thank you, sir, we have received many good wishes today, but the sentiments of old friends are always the most treasured."

Before more could be said, Mrs. Lucas excitedly exclaimed,

"My, my, Elizabeth, I had no idea. I wish you both joy. It all seems so exciting, to have become engaged so suddenly. I believe no one in the neighborhood had any idea of it."

John Lucas immediately looked to Darcy to see his reaction, but it was Elizabeth who answered first, stating that their courtship was not as sudden as it seemed. But, before she could elaborate further, Mr. Darcy replied in a definitive tone, "Thank you, madam, for your good wishes," and then made their excuses.

Afterward, she asked him if his retreat was on account of Lady Lucas's statement or John Lucas's presence. He replied that it was a little of each. While she understood his feelings in both regards, she wondered if he wished the full story of their engagement to remain only between themselves. She thought it natural that he would feel that the details of his first proposal might reflect poorly on his character, but the full arc of their courtship actually demonstrated that he possessed a generous and forgiving heart. Given that she could not reflect on her own conduct at the beginning of their relationship without reproach, she understood that it was not too much for him to ask that their history remain private and resolved to do as much.

After church, the Netherfield party was invited to Longbourn, but to Elizabeth's relief, both of Mr. Bingley's sisters expressed their regrets. Once at Longbourn, the engaged couples met to discuss wedding dates. Jane thought the idea of a double ceremony lovely, and the plan was presented to Mrs. Bennet, who after much consternation eventually saw the wisdom of the idea. Despite Mrs. Bennet's constant interruptions seeking clarification of various wedding details, the couples were left to talk among themselves in a most agreeable manner until long after dinner. For Darcy, the evening would have been perfect had not Mr. Bennet's presence at their farewell again thwarted his attempt at a more personal adieu.

After having spent such a pleasant day with him after church on Sunday, Elizabeth was surprised to find a parcel from Fitzwilliam awaiting her at breakfast the following Monday morning. It contained a note from him indicating that he had to attend to some business until after lunch. He did not want her to be disappointed when Mr. Bingley called without him. Accompanying the note was a beautifully bound edition of *Hero and Leander* that he had inscribed, "To my dearest, loveliest Elizabeth, To have won your admiration seems an unobtainable feat. You have made me the happiest of men. Never doubt my devotion. Yours always, Fitzwilliam." After reading the inscription, she flushed with excitement and longing. She was temporarily mortified when her mother eagerly grabbed the book and letter, assuming that a gift of greater value must have been included in the box. Luckily, she discarded both items without further perusal when she discovered that was all he had sent. Elizabeth smiled to herself, as both Lydia and Kitty expressed their dismay that anyone would send his fiancée a book, arguing that they would expect something much more romantic when they became engaged.

Her mother's disappointment over the meager value she placed on Elizabeth's first gift was assuaged the next morning when Mr. Darcy called on Mr. Bennet. He had asked Elizabeth to accompany him so he could acquaint them both with the details of his settlement, the terms of his new will, and his intentions regarding Elizabeth's household accounts and pin money. She sat in stunned silence as he explained, in a matter-of-fact manner, the large sums of money that would be at her disposal.

When she complained stridently that it was all unnecessary, he earnestly replied, "Madam, I am fully aware of your desire to be included in the various decisions regarding our future life together, but as to this matter, I cannot respect your wishes. You are not familiar with my finances or how such dealings are determined. I assure you, I have given this matter a great deal of thought. My father and I even discussed many of these details before his death; it is how the mistress of Pemberley is to be treated. Consequently, regardless of your objections, I will not change this. I asked you to join me today while I discussed this with your father, because in your new position you will need to be aware of these details, but I am only seeking your father's approval, not yours."

Mr. Bennet quickly acceded that it was more than he had imagined and thanked him for his generosity. Mr. Bennet watched in amusement for Lizzy's reaction, thinking it an interesting test of their suitability. As they both awaited her response, Mr. Darcy added, "Elizabeth, if you intend to marry me, this is one of the few things I expect you to accept silently. Do I ask too much?"

Mr. Bennet watched both of them closely as Lizzy curtly replied, "Sir, I will indeed relent, as long as you understand this may be the very last time I grant you such a courtesy."

To Mr. Bennet's surprise, Mr. Darcy simply laughed at her impertinent reply and said, "Oh, yes, I am more than forewarned," and then offered her his arm.

Elizabeth's reflections were interrupted by the sound of Mrs. Hill entering the breakfast room with a very large parcel. "Miss Elizabeth, Mr. Darcy's footman just brought this for you. There is a letter that goes with it." As Elizabeth read the note, she could not help but smile. His sister and cousin were due to arrive later that afternoon, and she was expected for tea at Netherfield to receive them, but he was requesting that they see each other beforehand. She opened the box to find a very fine saddle and another note stating that the saddle came with a horse so they could begin a habit of riding out together. She did not know whether to smile at his thoughtfulness or find his domineering manner offensive.

At the appointed hour, Elizabeth had not yet decided whether she should don a riding outfit or explain to him that the gift was unnecessary and somewhat presumptuous, given that she had already indicated to him that she had no desire to ride more. Part of her worried that this was a harbinger of their life together. She did not want to start their marriage by setting a precedent that she would agree to act in a manner contrary to her desires simply because he wished it. On the other hand, his eagerness to share with her an activity that he enjoyed was endearing. As she heard his arrival in the hall, she decided to meet him halfway and go riding. The horse and saddle she would return. She felt uncomfortable that her actions might give him pain, but she thought the principle at stake too important to ignore.

After the formalities were dispensed with, they found themselves momentarily alone. "Elizabeth, I was happy to find that you were available to receive me this morning. I hope I have not interrupted your plans for the day."

"No, your timing is quite convenient. I have no commitments beyond my visit to Netherfield, and once my mother learned of your intention to visit, she spared me the ordeal of another shopping trip to Meryton."

Laughing at her description of an outing with her mother, he replied, "Well, then I am happy to have been of service."

She was torn. He seemed in such high spirits that she hated to bring up her concerns about his gift, but saw no other option.

Before she could, Darcy said, "Elizabeth, may I tell you how very fetching you look in a riding outfit?"

Smiling archly, she replied, "Is it not rather early for such pretty words?"

Eyeing her intently, he asked, "Have I done something to displease you, Elizabeth? You seem unhappy to have my company this morning."

Trying to act casually but failing in her attempt, she replied, "Not at all, sir. Your visits are always welcome."

"Now I am sure you are displeased. You have not called me by my name, and while I do not know your every mood yet, I do have some experience with your displeasure. I once mistakenly took it for something else, and I will not make that mistake twice." His words could not help but evoke a small smile from Elizabeth. "Well," he added, "since you seemed to enjoy my company last night and I have not seen you since that time, I must deduce that either someone said something to you in the interim to give you pause or you do not like my gift. I am inclined to think it the latter."

"If you think it likely, then you must have had some idea that I might not appreciate your gift. I might wonder why you would send something that you had reservations about."

"Ah, so it is the gift." He grinned. "May I be so bold to tell you why it is that I think you are upset?"

Surprised by his cavalier attitude to her obvious concern, she simply replied, "By all means."

He proceeded to explain his answer in a calm and jovial manner that Elizabeth found particularly annoying. "I believe you have convinced yourself that you are displeased with me because I did not ask you if you wanted to take up riding for pleasure before I gave you a horse for that purpose. I think, though, if you reflect on this more deeply, you will find that your concern stems from something much simpler. You are afraid and using me as an excuse to avoid your fear."

"Fitzwilliam! May I suggest you rethink your assumption? I cannot believe that you have truly considered what you are saying or, for that matter, the manner in which you are saying it."

"But it is the only rational explanation for why a woman of your temperament would not want to ride."

"Sir, I do not have the pleasure of understanding you."

"Elizabeth, we have spoken many times about our mutual appreciation of the natural world, and your frequent walks attest to the fact that you are very comfortable outdoors. Riding is a natural complement to those interests. The ability to travel freely beyond your immediate surroundings is a pleasure I know you would appreciate. While walking does allow you to explore the various natural beauties of the countryside in more detail, there are places you cannot access on foot that you can with a horse. You cannot tell me that you have never explored a woods and been disappointed to come across a small stream that you wish to transverse but cannot on foot. Moreover, the freedom a horse affords a rider, to travel at both speeds and distances inaccessible to even the best walker, cannot compare. The only reason a woman of your interests and disposition would not ride out often is because she has not sufficiently mastered the art."

"Fitzwilliam, I think you might be overlooking the fact that as a woman who, as you yourself say, values her independence,

I might not appreciate being put in a position where I have no say over how and when I would engage in an activity that I have previously expressed a desire not to undertake."

"But if I am correct, and you are simply afraid, then you will never find an opportune moment to try to overcome your fear. Besides, I am not putting you in a position where you have no say over what you will or will not do. The decision is still yours to make. I simply sent you a horse so you would not have an excuse not to try."

She looked at him in exasperation. "Sir, I believe we are at an impasse."

He smiled kindly in return and gently said, "We should not be! I will be satisfied to take a walk with you instead. Riding is something I greatly enjoy, and I will be honest with you that it is something I hope one day to share with you. If you do not choose to attempt that today, I will understand, but I want you to consider it in the future."

"Fitzwilliam, I do not want to seem ungrateful, but you are trying to change me into something that I am not."

After thinking a moment about his response, he carefully said, "But, in a manner of speaking, we are both changing each other in subtle ways all the time. Knowing you has changed my behavior in so many ways. I hope by sharing our life together I will change you as well. I want to show you the world. I want you to share in the things I enjoy, and I hope that you will do the same for me. If you truly feel that riding is something you would never be interested in, then I apologize for my actions. I just thought that maybe you were simply anxious about the endeavor and needed a push to get started."

As he waited for an answer, she knew her response was of

some import as it seemed to foreshadow how they would resolve their disputes in the future.

She briefly thought how another couple would handle such a dilemma. She could not even imagine her parents being confronted with such a question, as they had apparently long ago resolved never to attempt to include each other in their private pleasures. She tried to picture Jane's response if Mr. Bingley were to press her in such a manner, but she could not envision Mr. Bingley doing more than simply asking. Then again, she could not imagine Mr. Bingley being able to ever persuade her to do something that she was not inclined to do.

She knew she had a strong personality and that she would never waver from her position without being challenged to do so. Maybe that was what she found so infuriating about Fitzwilliam's actions. He had outmaneuvered her—a feat not often accomplished. She was now left with only two alternatives: admitting to a fear or looking as though she was rejecting his request because she was petulant and unwilling to participate in an activity that he held dear. Reluctantly, she began to smile and finally asked, "Exactly how big is this horse?"

Her response made him break into a smile that exposed his dimples. Sweeping her into his arms, he said, "I promise you will not regret this. It is wise to be cautious around horses. They are proud and independent animals, but you need not fear them. You simply need to understand them and then make sure that they respect you in return. We should start by meeting your horse. His name is Fleece. I think you will like him."

"Why is that?"

"You share common attributes: You are both beautiful to look at, gentle, and, apparently, neither of you startle easily."

As Elizabeth approached the stable, she watched Darcy talk to her father's steward. She noted that he seemed much more at ease in this setting than he did moments ago with her sisters and her mother in Longbourn's drawing room. She could not help wishing that he were more comfortable with her family. As she looked at her horse and began to wonder why it was that she had agreed to this feat, she thought that her one consolation was that it would give her an opportunity to talk with Fitzwilliam away from her mother and the confines of her house.

As she neared, Darcy looked up at her and smiled warmly. He then said, "I am glad you have come. I must say that it did cross my mind that you might have sought the opportunity to be apart from me in order to flee."

Taking his hand to stand across from him, Elizabeth returned his smile in an unrestrained manner and replied archly, "Not at all. As a matter of fact, I must confess I did in fact consider escaping, but I knew from past experience that you would probably just follow me. I know you have trouble taking no for an answer."

Laughing again, he replied, "Well, then, I am happy to see that my persistence has served me so well." As they stared at each other, smiling, Darcy was inclined to lean down and kiss her, but he soon recollected his surroundings and the workers about on the property. "I think for now we should get to the task at hand."

As they approached, Fleece backed up ever so slightly. His movement gave Elizabeth reason to pause. Embarrassed that she had let it bother her, she said, "It might be worthwhile to remind me once again why I am learning about riding a horse."

"I told you before, because it is one of life's pleasures."

"And do you, sir, feel that it is your responsibility to familiarize me with all of life's pleasures?" As Elizabeth waited for a reply, she understood how her question could be taken and wished she could retract it.

Taking his time to answer, Darcy eventually looked at her with his eyebrows raised and replied, "As a matter of fact, yes I do," adding with a mischievous smile, "If you must know, I spend an inordinate amount of time contemplating that very subject. I thought riding seemed a safer avenue to explore, but I hope our lessons will not end with that."

"Mr. Darcy, I believe your real interest in taking me out to ride is to orchestrate time alone with me so that you can attempt to frighten me with your provocative suggestions."

"May I take it then that I am only attempting to frighten you, that I have not yet actually succeeded?"

"Is your goal to frighten me?"

"Not at all. My spirits are greatly buoyed by the possibility that my words have given you no concern at all. But Fleece is waiting. I know that you are nervous, and that is natural. But please trust me. I would never allow any harm to come to you." He determined, however, that much like her riding lesson, he should also follow a natural progression in the course of their relationship, and this morning was devoted to teaching her to enjoy riding.

As Elizabeth's carriage took the short trip to Netherfield, she sat within it fidgeting with her new gown. Her mother had insisted that she wear it to tea to meet Darcy's sister. At the time, she thought it silly, but as she became more nervous, she had to admit that she wanted to make a good impression on his sister, and with Miss Bingley acting as their hostess, she wondered if she would be given the opportunity. As the carriage pulled up, Darcy was outside, pacing in front of the entrance, clearly awaiting her arrival. As they entered the main drawing room of Netherfield together, Miss Bingley's voice could be heard. "Colonel, then you have met Miss Bennett."

"Yes, I had the pleasure last spring in Kent."

"Oh, I did not realize. Forgive me for asking, but having had the benefit of her acquaintance, you must have been as surprised as we were to hear of their engagement. We were all quite stunned."

The colonel replied in a curt tone, "I was indeed surprised, but I think it was for reasons other than yours."

As Darcy entered, he cleared his throat and said in a formal manner, "Fitzwilliam, Georgiana, let me present my fiancée, Miss Elizabeth Bennet." As the introductions were made, Elizabeth took solace in Darcy's kind words, but she could not help but feel disappointed that he continued to show Miss Bingley every civility. She knew there was nothing to be done about the slight they had overheard Miss Bingley make, but she could not comprehend how Darcy could keep his temper so even as to make his emotions unreadable. Before Elizabeth could give it more thought, she was drawn into a pleasant conversation with the colonel, who welcomed her unreservedly to his family.

Elizabeth and Georgiana were just beginning to become acquainted when Miss Bingley announced the arrival of the tea and took the opportunity to inject herself into their conversation. "Georgiana, darling, this must be so exciting for you. I am sure Eliza would agree that it must be quite an event to hear of your brother's betrothal by post. I know that Eliza had the pleasure of making the colonel's acquaintance on a previous occasion, but am I not correct that you two have never had the opportunity to meet before now?"

"Yes, Miss Bingley, that is true," replied Elizabeth.

"But I suppose that is easily explained," replied Miss Bingley with mock solicitude. "After all I can hardly imagine when your paths might otherwise cross."

"And yet I do feel," interjected Georgiana in a meek voice, "that I know Miss Bennet. My brother first mentioned her in his letters to me last November. He had never before referred to any woman of his acquaintance in any of his correspondence, other than, of course, to say that someone sent their regards. I therefore took great notice of the fact that he would often relate to me what she had said or her specific opinion on a given subject. Consequently, when he wrote to say he had secured her hand, I cannot say I was really surprised."

"He sounds a very loyal correspondent, then?" inquired Elizabeth in an attempt to steer the conversation to safer ground.

"Yes, he has always been. He has been a very devoted brother. I could not be more fortunate."

As Elizabeth went on to tell Georgiana about her family, they soon fell into a comfortable discourse and the afternoon passed as pleasantly as could be expected.

Before long, Elizabeth soon found that it was time to prepare for dinner and the arrival of her family. The idea gave her some initial discomfort. She knew that her family was an acquired taste, and while Georgiana and Colonel Fitzwilliam had been nothing but cordial since their arrival, she felt that the mixture of their personalities under Miss Bingley's indifferent hand might prove awkward given that that lady had no incentive to make the evening a success.

Her family soon arrived with much more noise and fanfare than she would have liked. Her mother seemed intent on asking Georgiana a series of questions without waiting for her to answer before proceeding to the next. Luckily, Mr. Bingley and Colonel Fitzwilliam were able to provide enough liveliness for the group in general.

The evening began well enough. Mr. Darcy and Elizabeth quickly fell into a discussion of their upcoming trip to London. After several moments had passed in this pleasant manner, Mr. Darcy said, "I know there is much to be done while we are in London, but Georgiana has expressed the hope that there might be enough time to attend the theater or perhaps even the opera. My steward tells me there is presently a grand production at the opera house that I think you would enjoy."

Before Elizabeth could respond, Miss Bingley spoke. "Mrs. Bennet, have you been to the opera in London? Mr. Darcy has an exquisite box there. If your family party is destined to attend, I would highly recommend it."

Mrs. Bennet, who had been talking to Lydia about the latest fashion, replied in a flustered tone, "Oh, yes… what? I am sorry, dear, I did not hear what you asked."

"I was just noting that Mr. Darcy was discussing the plans for your upcoming visit to London. A trip to his box at the opera would be a delightful diversion."

"Oh, yes, my Lord, yes! What a good idea! I have not been in years," cried Mrs. Bennet. "But I will need something new to wear. You will too, Lizzy. I am sure Mr. Darcy would not want you to be seen in the same old gowns. We will have something made. You must remember, dear, that you need to look the part."

Unsure who was more vexing, her mother or Miss Bingley, Elizabeth directed her response to the woman whose behavior she thought she might have some small ability to control. "Mother, I am sure I have many acceptable gowns to wear, but I do not think any definite plans have been fixed. We should not assume."

"Oh, but why should we not go? Now that it has been mentioned, I have my heart set on it. And besides, Lizzy, you need to start thinking of such things. In your new position, it will be important for you to be seen about the *ton*. Moreover, we could bring some of your sisters with us. It would be a wonderful opportunity for Lydia to be seen in such a refined setting. Just because Jane's and your futures are set, we cannot forget your younger sisters."

But Lydia's assent was much harder to come by. "Mama, I don't want to go to some stuffy old opera. I'll never understand what they are saying. I would much rather go to a party. There must be lots of parties in London. Why can't we have a ball? That would be far more fun. Lizzy, your fiancé's house must be big enough to host a ball. And if it is not, Mr. Bingley's house must be. He probably knows more people who like to dance anyway. I am going to ask Mr. Bingley about it the first chance I get."

Elizabeth sat in mortification. Lydia's refusal of an invitation that had not yet been offered seemed rude in more ways than one could count, and her unfeeling insult to Darcy made her blush from head to toe. To make matters worse, Elizabeth knew her mother would be oblivious to both the insult and the impropriety of Lydia's suggestion. She looked to Darcy for both his reaction and guidance, but he seemed suddenly engrossed by his watch. Attempting to dissuade her mother from either of the topics at hand, Elizabeth tried a different approach. "Mother, I do not believe our Aunt Gardiner has sufficient room for all my sisters to visit at the same time. We have never discussed them coming. I thought it was decided that only you would accompany Jane and me to London."

Before her mother could object, Miss Bingley offered, "If it would help with your family's arrangements, dear Jane could stay at our townhouse. Then, perhaps there would be more room for your other sisters at your relations' home in, where is it... oh, yes, Cheapside."

Elizabeth looked at Miss Bingley with surprise and saw a glint in her eye that showed how much she was enjoying the discomfort she was inflicting. She suddenly understood why Miss Bingley had initiated a conversation with her mother. She had obviously anticipated Elizabeth's weakest side and hoped to play on it.

"Oh, Miss Bingley," squealed her mother, "what a very thoughtful invitation. How can I thank you? I am sure Jane will appreciate such generosity, and it would indeed give us more room at my brother's house. That way, we could squeeze in Lydia and maybe, if possible, Kitty as well."

Seeing that her mother had no intention of stopping, Elizabeth attempted to interrupt. But her mother continued on without pause. "Mr. Darcy, perhaps if your sister were inclined to extend the same invitation to Elizabeth, we could fit Mary in as well. Mary will never find a husband with her nose in a book, and while she will no doubt be a trial to me during her entire visit, I suppose it is my duty as her mother to endure it the best I can."

Mortified, Elizabeth began to plead, "Mother, please, I am sure…"

"Mrs. Bennet," interrupted Darcy, "Georgiana and I were just discussing this morning how much she would enjoy an opportunity to spend more time with Miss Elizabeth. She wanted to invite Miss Elizabeth to stay at our house in London but was unsure if she would want to be separated from her family party. If I may be so bold, perhaps both Miss Bennet and Miss Elizabeth could stay at our townhouse. That way, there would be more room at the Gardiners' house and your party would not be quite so scattered."

Elizabeth looked at Darcy, wondering if he knew what he was about by making it easier for her younger sisters to come with them to London. Elizabeth might have been shocked to know that Darcy knew exactly what he was about. He wanted Elizabeth near him, and all other considerations were beside the point. He thought it unlikely that her father would let her stay at his townhouse all by herself, and thought that the addition of Jane would be most to Elizabeth's liking. Bingley might be disappointed at his opportunism in snatching Jane away, but he sincerely believed that Bingley would have more opportunity to spend uninterrupted time with Jane if she were not at Bingley's home, where his sisters would also be in residence.

"Oh, Mr. Darcy, you are so gracious," cooed Mrs. Bennet. "It would be such a comfort to have all my daughters in town."

Nodding at Mrs. Bennet, Darcy smoothly turned his attention to Caroline and intoned, "Miss Bingley, I hope that you will forgive me for stealing Miss Bennet away. I know that you would want both ladies to stay with you, but this will give Miss

Elizabeth an opportunity to familiarize herself with what will eventually be her new home."

"Not at all, sir," replied Miss Bingley coolly. "This way, Eliza and Jane will be together when you and Charles call on them, and it will spare you the need to travel to Cheapside on a regular basis."

Darcy bowed slightly. If he was fazed by Miss Bingley's comment, Elizabeth could not tell from his demeanor. After a pause, he looked up at Elizabeth and stated, "I think you will like our housekeeper in London. She has been with our family for many years, and she is very capable. I hope she meets with your satisfaction."

As she and Darcy continued to talk, she could feel Miss Bingley's frosty stare. At the first lull in the conversation, Miss Bingley cleared her throat and spoke in a voice meant for all, "Mrs. Bennet, I think you were just saying how lucky you are to have two daughters engaged. It must be quite a comfort to you."

"Oh, yes. You cannot know. I only hope that my other daughters are as fortunate."

With a condescending smile, Miss Bingley replied, "Yes, I am sure they will be, given that you will be there to oversee their futures."

"Oh, you are too kind," twittered Mrs. Bennet. "Not everyone understands what a heavy burden a mother carries in this regard. A daughter's future is made by her marriage, and it is up to a mother to ensure that she secures the best place she possibly can."

"I had never thought of it that way before," replied Miss Bingley with fake sincerity. "Then you are careful to ensure that your daughters take serious account of financial considerations when they consider a marriage proposal."

"Oh, yes, my dear, we must be practical too," beamed Mrs. Bennet.

With a triumphant smile, Miss Bingley replied, "Yes, Mrs. Bennet, I suppose some people must."

Elizabeth sat in mortification. Miss Bingley had clearly won her point. She had always known in the back of her mind that some would think she had accepted Darcy's proposal for mercenary means, but it had never hit home as forcefully as it did now.

Before she could think how to react, Elizabeth heard Darcy addressing Miss Bingley. "While it is true that both partners in a marriage often look to more material considerations when selecting or accepting a spouse, it is not the foremost concern of every individual who anticipates marriage."

"Oh, yes, Mr. Darcy. I am sure that men of a certain means need not take such issues into account. I was simply agreeing with Mrs. Bennet that it is something a woman may need to consider if she is not of... independent means."

Darcy cleared his throat and looked closely at Miss Bingley before speaking. If his intent was to unnerve her, he succeeded. "You may be right, Miss Bingley. You are, of course, more familiar with what a woman considers important in seeking a husband than I. But I am roused to defend my sex. I think some would consider attention to such considerations, to the exclusion of all else, an insult to the virtues of all men since a man's worth in the matrimonial state might be misconstrued as tantamount to his worth in a material sense."

"Yes, of course, Mr. Darcy," cooed Miss Bingley, "I am in complete agreement. But I think Mrs. Bennet was simply saying that it is something that she has been careful to instill in her daughters as it is a concern that will obviously affect their futures more than others."

Elizabeth could not believe that Miss Bingley had so openly questioned her motives. She wanted to reply—at least to defend her attachment to Darcy—but every approach to the subject seemed blocked. Miss Bingley's cruel innuendo seemed extreme, as it was done directly to her face, but she knew that similar gossip would follow them wherever they went. As she struggled for a reply, she heard Darcy casually state, "I am particularly relieved, then, that such ideas held little sway over my fiancée, as I know that did not motivate her to accept me." The silence in the room was deafening.

Miss Bingley could not help but offer one more barb. "Luckily, most men feel the same as you do, sir."

"Yes, Miss Bingley, I am sure you are correct. But there is a difference between hoping something is true and knowing something is true. I know that I have been blessed in choosing a wife who possesses superior beauty, intellect, and character. While she may not be receiving similar advantages in accepting me, I know that she has done so because she believes our temperaments are particularly suited for each other and because I have been lucky enough to win her affections. I know not all men can make such a boast, but I do so sure of its veracity."

Elizabeth had watched this exchange with growing concern. In an attempt to dissuade him from what she feared was his intended course, she quickly interjected, "Mr. Darcy, I do not think…"

But Miss Bingley was quicker, stating sweetly, "Your faith in womankind is clearly a testament to all women. I thank you on all our behalf."

Instead of letting the issue drop or heeding Elizabeth's hint, Darcy offered, "But I did not intend to compliment all women, for I certainly cannot attest to the motives of your entire sex. Of Miss Elizabeth's intentions, I have no doubt. For you see, if she had wished to accept me for the material advantages that I can obviously supply, she would have accepted me the first time I proposed. At the time, though, she did not hold me in high regard, and consequently she appropriately rejected my offer and whatever advantages such a union might provide her."

While his words sunk in, Mrs. Bennet sat in stunned silence, blinking. Miss Bingley fared no better as she unsuccessfully attempted to formulate a reply. Bingley abruptly laughed but then quickly looked down, afraid that his sister might attempt to catch his eye. Jane looked to Elizabeth with concern and found her head bowed and her cheeks bright pink. Georgiana and Colonel Fitzwilliam stared at Darcy with open astonishment. Mr. Bennet observed Darcy in what appeared to be thoughtful consideration. It was therefore to the surprise of everyone in attendance that Kitty's voice was heard to reply in a dreamy tone, "How romantic. You proposed twice. How? When?"

Darcy smiled indulgently at Kitty, and she seemed to look back at him as if seeing him for the first time. He then answered slowly, "I asked Elizabeth to marry me in April when we were both in Kent."

Replying as if they were the only two people in the room, Kitty quickly asked, "But she said no?"

"Yes, she rejected my proposal out of hand."

"Were you heartbroken?"

"Yes, I suppose so. I thought she would accept me when I

first asked, and when she did not, I found it very difficult to live with the results."

"So, you came to Meryton to win her back."

"Yes, it was one of the reasons I returned."

"And how did you succeed in getting her to accept your second proposal?"

He looked quickly at Elizabeth, but she continued to keep her gaze down. "I attempted to court her, as I had failed to do in Kent. I persuaded her to give me a second chance to prove myself. But maybe it would be best if you asked your sister the details yourself. I am sure this is of very little interest to the rest of the room, and I have monopolized the conversation long enough."

When he looked up again, he saw that most of the party was still staring at him. He looked to Miss Bingley and said, "Miss Bingley, I am so looking forward to dinner. You always set the most sumptuous table."

HONESTY AND DESIRE

DARCY ARRIVED AT LONGBOURN the following morning to find all of the Bennet women assembled in the parlor. After his confession at dinner, there had been little opportunity to speak to Elizabeth alone. As the carriages were called, he had hoped to say his good-bye to Elizabeth in private, but her father once again seemed omnipresent. He almost thought that Mr. Bennet wanted to say something to him, but in the end, he simply departed with a nod. Remembering the charge that Bingley had given him at breakfast, Darcy turned to Jane. "Miss Bennet, Mr. Bingley asked me to make his apologies for not coming to call this morning."

"Oh, I hope he is well?" asked Jane with concern.

"Yes, very," replied Darcy. "It seems that Miss Bingley and the Hursts have decided to return to London a little earlier than planned. He will be detained while he sees to their traveling arrangements. He intends to call later today.

"Mrs. Bennet," continued Darcy, "I was hoping to take Elizabeth riding this morning. With your leave, I thought we could start off directly."

Mrs. Bennet did not seem to be following the thread of the conversation. Instead, since his arrival, she had been eyeing Darcy with an odd look on her face. Remembering herself, she said, "Oh, a ride? Yes, yes, by all means."

After they made their way to their awaiting horses, Darcy helped Elizabeth to mount, happily noticing that she seemed much more relaxed on Fleece. He seemed to be formulating a question and then abandoning it, when he finally asked, "Elizabeth, I hope I did not put you in an uncomfortable position last night. I did not mean to make public something that you intended to keep private."

Surveying him thoughtfully, she replied, "No. I am no longer uncomfortable on that account. I understand that you were trying to defend my honor. But I must say, I am surprised that you would attempt such an undertaking without consulting me first." She then raised one brow and added, "I believe I can recall being called to task by you not so very long ago when you mistakenly thought I had divulged the same information. I wonder how it is different now, other than, of course, that the shoe is now on the other foot?"

He looked at her seriously, struggling with a reply. "I have no defense. I suppose I was moved by my emotions to act." Looking earnest, he added, "I am truly sorry if I embarrassed you."

Content with his honest answer, she smiled. "I doubt there was any other way in which to silence Miss Bingley." The slightest of smiles graced his lips, as he acknowledged her compliment. "It did," she continued, "make for quite a long evening, though. It took my mother rather a long time to understand the matter."

"Yes, Georgiana and my cousin were quite adamant about knowing all the details of our courtship. I can only imagine that if

Georgiana was so difficult to placate, your mother, with her more direct style, would not rest until she felt completely satisfied."

"I think the problem is that my mother finds the both of us so baffling. She cannot imagine why you would want me after I had rejected you and why I would not have accepted you in the first place. I think we defy her closely held precepts as to how marriage should be approached. I do not believe the three of us will ever fully understand each other."

As they approached the bank of a small stream, Elizabeth showed him a clearing she admired and he dismounted in order to help her down and secure the horses. As he worked, he asked, "But she is at least content with the result?"

"Oh, yes, just confused by the process by which we got there. She just needs time. In the meantime, I can well understand your reluctance to spend too much time in my family's company."

Darcy looked at Elizabeth with an unreadable expression and then looked to the stream. After several moments, he asked, "Do you feel that I do not want to spend time with your family?"

Seeing his serious expression, she regretted the slip of her tongue. "I did not mean to imply that you have not acted properly in regard to them. It just seemed that you prefer to see me away from Longbourn." She added in a light tone, "Truly, I understand. All together, they are quite a disconcerting lot. It makes perfect sense if you wish only to see them in small doses."

"Do you think that is why I suggested riding today?"

"Well, to be honest, yes."

Darcy sat next to her in contemplation. He then spoke. "Elizabeth, you misinterpret me. I must say I am unsure how to proceed. I do not want you to labor under a misconception about my feelings toward your family, but I am also at a loss as to how to explain." As he twisted his signet ring, he continued, "I do not like disguise, but I have also erred before as to what level of honesty is required or, for that matter, wise... I have never been engaged before."

Elizabeth laid her hand on his arm and said, "I do not think we have erred before by being honest, just in the level of understanding we have been willing to extend each other for our honest opinions."

"Very well, then. I will tell you. Although I think it would be obvious..." Looking slightly away from her, he said, "When you accepted me, I understood that we both were also accepting each other's families. I know I am to be a brother to your sisters, and I hope I have made some progress in that regard. I think Jane and I are content in each other's company, and today I thought Kitty was much more comfortable in my presence. I do not always know what to say to Mary or Lydia, but I assume that will come with time." After a pause, he squared his shoulders and looked intently into her eyes. "It is not that I want to be away from your family. It is that I want you to be away from them—from everyone. I want to marry you because I love you. But I would be lying if I did not confess that what I anticipate most about our marriage is being able to be alone with you—completely alone. Sometimes, it is all I think about. I have been in love with you for a very long time."

As Elizabeth listened, her cheeks flushed. Seeing her discomfort, he continued to speak. "It is just that your father has taken to the habit of accompanying us at the end of each evening and I wish... I wish to have some time alone with you. After our first ride, I saw that I had you to myself, since your sisters do not seem inclined to join us as they might on a walk to Meryton."

Elizabeth stared at her hands and quietly replied, "I see."

Forlorn, he said, "I have made you uncomfortable. I am sorry. I just did not want you to have the wrong impression. But now I wonder whether you have a worse impression of me...." Resolute, he added in a formal tone, "We can return. We should return. You need not fear that I will not act as a gentleman."

Looking up, concerned about his tone, she replied timidly, "No. That is not necessary. It is not that I am uncomfortable here with you. I am just embarrassed that I did not understand... You must think me very naïve."

Staring at her with great intensity, Darcy replied, "No, I think you lovely."

As they gazed at each other, Elizabeth felt she could hardly breathe. His honesty had moved her. She suddenly realized that they were at another crossroad. They had always challenged social convention by saying what they meant. She regretted that he now obviously felt ashamed for having done so. She wanted to tell him, that while she misunderstood his primary reason for seeking to be away from her family, she did not regret that they were now alone. Why was it so hard to say something, anything? *Because I also risk myself*, came the answer in her head.

"Fitzwilliam, I have been foolish. I do not know how I could have confused your desire for us to be alone with anything else. I should have known better..." She watched as her words seemed to give him some comfort, but he maintained a rigid air that betrayed his unease. Gathering her resolve, she said, "I should have known better because I feel the same way. Perhaps I was just too embarrassed to acknowledge it. But each time you have kissed me, it has made me long for more. I know that I should not say this, but... I am glad you have brought me here and with the intent of being alone. I welcome it." With her voice now only a whisper, she added, "I only… I do not know what you expect. What I should do."

Confusion and then relief crossed his face. Ultimately, he smiled. "I expect nothing, but I wish many things."

She reached up to run one finger down his cheek and then across the line of his jaw. He closed his eyes for a moment as he held his breath. As she moved her finger across his lips, he watched her intently. She then asked in a very quiet voice, "Do you wish a kiss? A touch?"

She watched as his eyes darkened with pleasure. He reached up and held her wrist in order to still her hand at his mouth. Breathing heavily, he responded in a slow, deep voice. "Yes… Each… Both." He turned her wrist to give his mouth access to its length. He gently, but with steady pressure, dragged his teeth down it and then began to lightly kiss his way back. He then took each fingertip in his mouth in turn. She watched him with her mouth slightly parted, her breath coming quick.

When he had finished, he cupped his hand behind her head to bring her slowly to him. He stopped when she was just inches from him and looked deeply into her eyes, murmuring, "Dearest, loveliest Elizabeth, I cannot tell you the ardor I feel for you. I… I… I am simply bewitched." He then brought her mouth to his.

She could feel his shudder as they touched. He had kissed her before, but there had always been a rushed quality to it—as they each feared an interruption. This kiss began slow and teasing, but soon turned intense as he sought access to her lips and then her mouth. His other hand came around her, and he pulled her to him. Her arms slipped around his waist and she began to explore the taut planes of his back. As his mouth moved from her lips to behind her ear, she closed her eyes to savor the exquisite feeling he was eliciting, a feeling that spread to her neck and then to her shoulder until her whole body began to tingle. Awash in her own passion, she tangled her fingers in his curls and brought his head to her mouth, seeking to claim him. Surprised by her intensity, he moved his head back so that he could look at her, his eyes crinkled in a smile. She seemed to sway ever so gently as she opened her eyes to look at him, silently inquiring as to why he had stopped. "You are so beautiful," he whispered. "I am so lucky to have found you."

She broke into an infectious smile that made her eyes dance. "No more than I."

He looked deeply into her eyes, and their smiles soon turned serious. He began to kiss her again and eventually surrendered to his need to hold her ever closer. Pressing himself against her, he began fervently to kiss her neck, dipping down to her collarbone and then returning to her lips. She soon felt his hands move from her back to either side of her waist. He held his hands there for a moment while they continued to kiss. He seemed to be measuring how small it was around the whole of her. He then slowly moved one of his hands along her side until it gently rested beneath her breast. He dipped his mouth lower until he was exploring the bodice of her dress, gently edging his mouth toward the lace that marked where he was allowed to look but not touch. As she became more and more mesmerized by his ministrations, she moaned ever so softly, unaware that any sound had escaped her lips.

The noise seemed to bring him back to the reality of their situation. He looked confused and then embarrassed. His brow furrowed. "Elizabeth, I am sorry. I did not mean to... to go so far. I would not risk..." Squaring his shoulders, he said in a formal manner, "I have forgotten myself. Please forgive me. We should go."

Bewildered, Elizabeth asked, "I do not understand I... I thought we both..."

"No," he interrupted, "I alone am responsible... Please forgive me. I should have known better. I am not sure how I let things get out of control so quickly. When I said that I wanted to be with you alone, I did not mean... I do not want to take advantage of your generosity. I promise you it will not happen again."

She studied him, trying to understand his complex nature. There was much she could say, but she was uncertain how to say it and unsure that it would do any good at this moment. Instead, she raised her eyebrows and said, "Very well, then, we shall leave. It is getting late, and Jane will be expecting us. But, Fitzwilliam, may I caution you, do not make promises you cannot keep."

❧

When Darcy arrived the next day, Elizabeth could see his troubled countenance. He wasted no time in seeking her out. "Elizabeth, I received an express this morning from my uncle. He has reminded me of some business matters that exist between our two families that I will need to resolve before we marry. Inasmuch as we are all planning to go to London soon, I cannot see putting off the trip to see him. I do not want to go now, but I know I will be even more disinclined to undertake the journey once we are in London and you and your sister are guests in my home. I am afraid that if I leave the trip until after you leave

London, there will be insufficient time to resolve everything that needs to be done."

Hiding her distress at the idea of their separation, Elizabeth asked, "How long of a journey do you think is required?"

"I am still uncertain. If I leave right away, we could attempt to settle the matter as soon as possible and set into motion whatever contracts will be required. Perhaps I could return in time to accompany you to London. Colonel Fitzwilliam has also said that he needs to see his father. If I can convince him to take the journey with me, he could stay on with his father until after the contracts are copied. Then he could bring them with him to London for me to sign."

"Wouldn't that require you to spend a great deal of time in travel with very little time for rest?"

"It will be a strenuous schedule but I am up to the task. My greater concern is leaving at all."

Seeing the tenderness in his eyes, Elizabeth leaned toward him to place her other hand on his arm. "I will obviously miss your company, but I understand that you have responsibilities you must fulfill."

"If you are sure it will not be too much of an inconvenience." Seeing her nod her consent, he added, "I loathe saying it, but I believe I should go tomorrow. But I promise to return as soon as humanly possible."

"That is not necessary; simply undertake the journey in whatever manner will keep you safe," she said, adding with a warm smile, "I will be here awaiting your return."

ᴄ⚬ᴆ

Once Darcy left, time passed quite slowly for Elizabeth. She endeavored to keep herself busy by spending as much time as possible with Georgiana. Her efforts proved fruitful, as their bond of friendship grew daily. Elizabeth also resigned herself to spending more time with her mother in the hope that they could complete most of the wedding preparations. She thought that if she gave in to her mother's demands now, she might be spared her entreaties when Darcy returned.

After a few days, Elizabeth was delighted to receive a letter and a small box from Darcy. The missive contained Darcy's warmest affections and news of his progress; the box held a beautifully crafted pair of opera glasses that he hoped she might use during their time in London. While his letter was brief, the sentiments it contained gave Elizabeth secret comfort. She was embarrassed to admit she began to keep the letter in her pocket each day.

True to his word, Darcy returned the day before their departure to London. At Georgiana's invitation, Jane and Elizabeth were dining at Netherfield with Bingley when they heard a rider approach. Elizabeth quickly looked down the hall and saw Darcy as he entered. His hair was tousled, and his riding pants and boots splattered with mud. Elizabeth's heart quickened. She knew she must have been blushing with the anticipation of seeing him again. But before she could think to move forward to greet him, Georgiana had swept down the hall to welcome him with open arms. As his sister attempted to hug him fully, Darcy pulled away, laughing, "Georgiana, I am not fit to be touched," and instead leaned forward to kiss her on her cheek.

Darcy bowed to the rest of the party in turn, letting his gaze come to rest on Elizabeth. Remembering himself, he said to the group in general, "Please, pray, excuse me. I am interrupting your meal. I intended to slip in and make myself presentable before I sought you out."

Bingley smiled easily at his friend. "When we heard a rider approach, we thought it was the post with news of your travels. We would have waited the meal for you, but thought it far too late for you to arrive at this point. We are all certainly pleased, though, that you are here. But we are keeping you. Go and dress; we will wait dinner for you."

"No, I could not ask you to," declared Darcy. "You were clearly about to go in. With your leave, I will take something on a tray in my room while I change and be down once you are finished."

"But, Brother," Georgiana quietly interrupted, "you must be exhausted. Perhaps you should get some rest."

"No, I am fine. While I know I look the worse for wear, I am actually quite eager for company. I will just change and join you after your dinner."

Darcy retired to his room, where Bingley's valet began to prepare a bath. He was so sore and tired; he knew the warmth of the bath would do him a world of good. Despite his weariness, he knew he still had more than enough energy to visit with the guests assembled in the dining room. He had ridden all that way in one day so that he would be able to escort Elizabeth to London in order to maximize his time in her company. That Fortune had smiled on him to such an extent as to have Elizabeth here when he arrived was a gift too great to pass up.

As dinner ended, Darcy arrived looking much improved, though his hair was still wet. He immediately went to Elizabeth and took her hand in his to kiss it. As he looked into her eyes, he felt that his journey was now over.

To quell the various inquiries, Darcy told the assembled party of his travels, minimizing any discomfort he endured by focusing instead on his cousin's exploits on the way. Despite finding his tales amusing, both Elizabeth and Georgiana questioned Darcy's intention to ride with them tomorrow, so soon after riding all day. He shook his head and said he had no reservations about his decision, making it clear that the subject was closed. As the evening drew to a close, Darcy was thrilled to hear his sister announce her intention to retire before he walked Jane and Elizabeth out to their carriage. Bingley and he seemed to be of one mind on the subject and silently varied their pace so that both couples were able to say their good-byes in the hall out of view of the servants and each other.

Once they were in relative isolation, Darcy pulled Elizabeth to him and encircled her in his arms. For a moment, he just held her close, relishing in the comfort her warmth provided. He then tilted her chin so that he could gaze into her eyes. "I have missed you so very much. I am almost ashamed to admit it. You have such power over me."

Smiling slowly at him, she replied, "I feel the same is true for me. I found it very difficult to keep you from my mind the whole length of your absence. I am so very glad to see you, but I must say, I am still worried that you are not sufficiently rested to undertake the journey." Holding his face in her hands and carefully surveying his features, she added, "On such close inspection, I can see how tired you are."

"That is hardly the reaction I seek when holding a woman so close."

"I do not mean to imply that you are not handsome, just that you are in need of rest."

"I can assure you, madam, I know what I need at this moment, and it is not sleep." That said, he slowly brought his lips to hers and began to kiss her in a manner that left no doubt of his enthusiasm for the endeavor. They separated when they heard Bingley's voice indicating that the carriage had arrived. He rested his forehead on hers and asked, "So, does that mean that you find me handsome when I am rested?"

Laughing, she replied, "What an insufferable question! Are you so unsure of my regard that you need such assurances after I have already agreed to be your wife?"

While attempting to restrain a chuckle, he replied, "One would think not. But your unwillingness to answer does not bode well either."

"If you must hear me say the words, then I think your only option is to get some real rest and see my reaction."

Openly laughing at her reply, he reluctantly led her to the carriage.

THE MISTRESS OF PEMBERLEY

Despite Darcy's promise to obtain rest, he was at Elizabeth's door with Georgiana at daybreak, prepared to depart. Like Bingley, Darcy had opted to ride alongside the carriages to provide more space for the ladies. When they arrived in Cheapside, Elizabeth had hoped to introduce Darcy and Bingley to her aunt and uncle without fanfare, but the transition was too much for her mother to bear silently, and Elizabeth was relieved when she was back in Darcy's carriage with only Georgiana and Jane.

As they arrived at Darcy's townhouse, Elizabeth was astounded at how nervous she was. She had attempted to prepare herself for the grandeur of his home—trying as she might to envision it someday as her own. Once inside, her fears subsided. Darcy's housekeeper, Mrs. Larsen, was such a sensible and kindly woman that Elizabeth immediately felt relaxed in her company. Refreshment magically appeared, and before she knew it, Elizabeth was feeling renewed and content. Darcy seemed eager to show Elizabeth and Jane around, and after Mrs. Larsen quietly confirmed in which rooms the women were to be settled, he began the tour with Bingley escorting Jane.

Elizabeth listened intently as Darcy explained the history of the house. He spoke well, and she soon felt the tangible impact of the prior inhabitants on the evolution of the house. Darcy told Elizabeth that he wanted her to feel free to redecorate any room she wished without concern for the cost and that the same would be true at Pemberley. She immediately told him that she sincerely found nothing wanting in all that she had seen. After debating the issue, Darcy relented, saying, "Well, you will at least want to refurbish the suite you will occupy when you are mistress of the house? Let me bring you there next." As they examined the spacious and well-appointed master suite, Darcy opened the various doors leading off it, including what would someday be Elizabeth's dressing room and her private sitting room. As he opened the door to his adjoining room, she did not resist the temptation to glimpse his private sanctuary. She could not see much, other than to get a sense that it had a warm, masculine air. She and Jane were then brought to their rooms in order to freshen up for dinner, which was a quiet affair given the lateness of the hour.

As Elizabeth dressed the next morning, Mrs. Larsen arrived with a breakfast tray containing fresh fruits, cream, and tea. Elizabeth thanked her for her thoughtfulness.

"It was the master's idea. He too is an early riser and thought you might appreciate some tea while you dressed. Your sister and Georgiana are not yet up, but he thought you might be."

Smiling at his thoughtfulness, she asked, "Has Mr. Darcy had breakfast?"

Shaking her head, Mrs. Larsen replied, "No, he needed to meet with his steward over several pressing matters, and they began very early this morning. He asked that he be told when you came down though, as he hoped to see you before you left to shop with your mother."

"That would be lovely. I think I will see my sister after I finish here and then go down."

"Miss Bennet," added Mrs. Larsen, "the master also asked that I make an appointment with you, at your leisure, to go over the running of the house. We both want to ensure that everything is to your satisfaction."

"Mrs. Larsen, I would be delighted to have you show me how the house is managed, but only so that you can tell me if there is anything I can do to help you. I know that you have been taking care of Mr. Darcy and Miss Darcy for a very long time, and I would never imagine that I could attempt it with better results."

With sincere appreciation in her voice, Mrs. Larsen said, "Thank you, miss, you are too kind. But it is soon to be your house, and it is my job to make sure you are happy here."

Smiling, Elizabeth replied, "I know that I will be. We can meet, but only so that you can show me what to do, not the other way around. Would today before tea be convenient?"

It had been decided that Bingley would host the entire Bennet party and the Darcys on their first full night in London. Elizabeth felt all the discomfort attendant in having to see Bingley's sisters again. Her mother's fawning over Mr. Bingley's furnishings did not help the matter, but her real concern was for Darcy, who looked even more tired. She had only seen him for a few minutes at breakfast and then later at tea, apologizing on both occasions for not being able to stay and explaining that several estate matters he had put off during his trip now needed immediate attention.

As Elizabeth watched him discreetly rub his forehead as her mother went on about the purchases they had made that day, she wished she could give him some form of comfort but understood it was impossible. Elizabeth knew that he had never really rested from his trip and could not help but notice the change in him since his arrival. His time here did not seem to be his own, and the weight of his responsibilities was a tangible force. She suddenly understood how lucky they both had been to have had so much uninterrupted time together in Hertfordshire. She wondered how often in his life he had allowed himself such pleasure. However infrequent, he now seemed intent on paying a penance for having enjoyed himself so freely. Despite his fatigue, she was happy to see that he seemed to have genuinely enjoyed making the Gardiners' acquaintance, and she was glad she had at least some members of her family for whom she need not blush.

The next day Darcy was to host her family for dinner after they finished shopping in the late afternoon. To accomplish this, Darcy had arranged for his business to be commenced at first light so that it might be concluded before tea.

Elizabeth used the time to meet with Mrs. Larsen again. The more time she spent with her, the more Elizabeth was impressed with the older woman's organizational skills and her attention to detail. While Elizabeth had some minor suggestions, she came to realize that even though she would assume responsibility for the running of the household upon her marriage to Darcy, the staff was so adept at seeing to his needs that her oversight was hardly necessary. Before she finished her interview with Mrs. Larsen, Elizabeth quietly asked a question that had been on her mind. "Does Mr. Darcy always keep such hours? He seems to be busy almost around the clock."

The older woman surveyed the younger woman's worried features for a moment before speaking. "There are times when his schedule is very regular. But when there is a problem that needs his attention, like the one that is now occupying his time, he devotes himself to its resolution with all his energy while still seeing to his other responsibilities as well. Rather than renege on any of his commitments, he simply works longer hours so that he disappoints no one. During those times, his schedule is very erratic and the staff attempts to help him the best they can. I sometimes think he takes on more than he should, but it is not my place to make such judgments. He is the master of the house."

Elizabeth nodded her understanding as Mrs. Larsen continued on to review the plans for the next two days. Elizabeth's mother, sisters, and the Gardiners were to arrive by teatime. The Bingley party was expected before dinner. The following day, Darcy was to meet with his solicitor by breakfast, and then join Georgiana and Elizabeth in the afternoon when the colonel was scheduled to arrive. Thereafter, Mr. Darcy had arranged for the entire party to attend the opera and dine together afterward.

Later that day, as Elizabeth walked by Darcy's door on the way to tea, she was startled to see the door open and its owner emerge. Upon seeing Elizabeth, Darcy broke into an unreserved smile. He immediately looked both ways and, seeing no one else in the hallway, pulled her in through a door that was clearly designed to blend into the pattern of the wall. Once the door was shut behind them and she had stopped laughing at his impetuous behavior, she asked, "Where have you taken me?"

Slowly smiling at her, he deeply intoned, "Away from everyone else."

With her eyes dancing, she asked, "I can see that, but where exactly is this, and what do you hope to accomplish?"

"It is just the servant's entrance to my room. Only my valet uses it, and I just sent him on an errand. What I hope to accomplish is a moment alone with you. It has been all I have desired since we arrived, and it seemed that I was destined to be denied it."

As she looked at him, about to give an impertinent reply, his serious look stopped her. Instead of kissing her, he held her tenderly and exhaled deeply. She intuitively understood that, at that moment, he seemed to need her warmth and support more than anything else. She put her hand behind his head to hold him close and inhaled his scent. She could feel the stress in his body as he seemed to hold her ever tighter. After a moment though, he reluctantly let her go. The strain of the last few days was evident on his brow. With a sad smile, he said, "I suppose we must leave before we are missed. I will go back to my room. Elizabeth, you should go back out the way you came. No one will see."

"Certainly, but, Fitzwilliam, you do not seem yourself. Are you feeling well?"

With a weary smile, he replied, "I am fine. I just have a lot to accomplish in the next few days. Once that is over, I will have more time to be with you. I hope I have not been neglecting you."

"Hardly, my mother and both of our sisters have kept me so busy, I could not have seen you had you been free. But I am concerned about you. Could you not rearrange your schedule so that you have a little more time to rest?"

"No, I am afraid not. I need to solidify things with my solicitor within a day or two, and we have the opera tomorrow night."

"Could we not reschedule it?"

"No, everything is set, and I think both our families would be disappointed if they did not have the opportunity to attend. There is no reason for concern. I am just a little tired. There will be time to rest later."

The dinner at Darcy's townhouse was truly an elegant affair. As Elizabeth watched the staff work in unison to present a seamless meal, she was again impressed with Mrs. Larsen's capabilities. The evening was such a success that the guests seemed in no hurry to leave. While Elizabeth normally would have felt immense relief over how well the evening was received, her thoughts were centered on Darcy.

When he had escorted her into dinner, his hand was clammy, and she noticed he hardly ate his meal. When he walked her out after dinner, she could see how pale he was and that there was a light sheen of perspiration on his brow. Despite the obvious toll that the evening was taking on him, he executed his duties as host without any indication of his distress.

As the evening continued on without any sign of abating, it was Elizabeth who rose to declare her intent to retire. Her announcement was received with a raised eyebrow from Miss Bingley, but it had the desired effect. Soon everyone began taking their leave. Rather than going to her room, however, Elizabeth discreetly sought out Mrs. Larsen and then her aunt.

Darcy lay back in his bed and pulled the covers close around him as he attempted to read one of the documents his solicitor had prepared. He knew there was no use. He was far too sick to read anything. He had felt a slight fever coming on before dinner and had attempted to ignore it, but it had only gotten worse. He could barely wait to return to his room so that he could lie flat. If his valet had not helped him undress, he would have slept in his clothes. He knew that he was so exhausted that he needed to give in to the call of sleep if he was to make his morning appointment with his solicitor and steward. As he heard his valet reenter again, he called to him without opening his eyes, "Thank you, Robert, but I require nothing further this evening. I think all I need is some sleep."

"I am glad to hear that you still have enough sense about you to know that at least. One might wonder why it has taken you so long to realize it." Upon hearing her voice, Darcy sat bolt upright in his bed, trying to see into the far end of the room, where the candles shed very little light. He was unsure if his fever was making him hallucinate.

As Elizabeth walked forward holding a tray, his question was answered. As he beheld her, his mind was full of so many conflicting thoughts. He had fantasized about her coming to his room so many times that her presence now almost seemed natural, but the circumstances of this reality rang a note of discordance. In his dreams he was not sick, and the worry of their being discovered had never crossed his mind. He was surprised to realize that, besides desire, he also felt a strong surge of protectiveness for her, knowing what she was risking by coming, and he struggled to understand her purpose. Unable in his current state of exhaustion to coherently voice his thoughts, he confusedly asked, "Elizabeth, what are you... Why...?"

"Am I here?" she answered for him in an arched manner. "An excellent question, and since I am clearly trespassing in a most inappropriate manner, I promise to explain it to you in full.

But before I do, will you tell me how you are feeling? How you are truly feeling?"

"I am fine," he replied quickly. Seeing her look of impatience, he relented. "I have a slight fever and it has made me tired, but I am otherwise fine."

Coming to rest on the edge of his bed, Elizabeth set the tray down with a furrowed brow. He was hot to the touch, and his hair felt damp. She began to push his curls off his brow and gently massage his temples. Her ministrations were so soothing that he immediately gave in to them and laid his head back on his pillow and closed his eyes. After resting a minute, he felt some of the tension leave his body, and he instinctively moved his head to kiss her hand. The tinge of excitement he felt when he found his target suddenly brought him back to the present—and all of his questions back to the forefront of his clouded mind.

Looking at her with a puzzled gaze, he tried to formulate what to say or even ask. Seeing his struggle, she volunteered an answer. "I came because I am worried about you. As you can also see, I brought you some wet cloths to help with your fever, and I asked Mrs. Larsen for some broth. I noticed at dinner that you hardly ate. I told her it was to settle my own stomach. I think you should eat some. I also brought some tea with a little brandy mixed in. I would often prepare such a drink for my father when he felt an illness coming on, to help him get a good night's sleep."

Beholding her with the most tender gaze, he slowly said, "Elizabeth, while I truly appreciate your thoughtfulness in coming here and all of this," indicating her tray, "it is not necessary. I am just feeling a little under the weather. I will be fine tomorrow. Also, you must know that I have people to take care of such things. You need not wait on me. Besides, if your goal is to help me rest, I think your plan ill-advised. Your presence here is quite provocative, and I am suddenly feeling anything but sleepy. I know that your intentions are pure, but mine may not be so."

Laughing at him, she gently put the cloth on his head and said, "I felt certain enough of the state of your health to know I have nothing to fear. In your condition, I doubt you could lift your head from the pillow."

Slowly smiling, he replied, "I would not be so sure."

"But yet I am," she gently laughed as she looked down at him. Turning serious, she added, "But you are right, I know you have people who can bring you soup if you desire or need it, and I would not risk coming here simply for that. I needed to speak to you, and I knew this would be the only opportunity I would have. If you are willing to listen, may I explain?"

Nodding for her to continue, he watched her attentively.

"As you know, I have been learning about the operation of your household. Having observed the staff these last few days, I have come to the conclusion that there is really very little for me to do, and I assume I will find Pemberley run in the same competent manner. I could add a touch here or there, but your staff is so proficient that no real improvement is possible. It has, however, made me think a great deal about what my role as the mistress of your estate will entail. While I have found no flaw in the operation of this household, there has been one matter that has given me pause during my visit. It is your behavior, as it impacts upon your own well-being. While your staff provides you every comfort and willingly pledges you their support, it is not their place to tell the master when he is not taking proper care of himself. I have come to the realization that no one is in such a position, except perhaps me. So I am taking this opportunity to tell you in private that you are acting inappropriately."

As he attempted to interrupt, she frowned at him and continued on in an even and solicitous voice. "You have been working far too hard, and it is making you sick. You seem unwilling even to consider rearranging your schedule to allow yourself some time to improve your health. I know you feel the weight of obligation, and I very much respect that about you, but you must be realistic as well. You will do no one good by getting seriously ill, and I believe you owe it to Georgiana and, to be frank, me, to safeguard your health. So, while this household can obviously look after itself, you apparently cannot. Consequently, I have taken it upon myself to tell my aunt and mother that estate business prevents you from attending the opera tomorrow evening and that I will not be going either. Mr. Bingley has agreed to escort Georgiana with Jane, and my family will otherwise attend the performance as planned. Bingley will host them at dinner. I have talked to your steward, and he will reschedule your meeting with your solicitor until dinnertime. That way you will be allowed to rest uninterrupted until that time. If the colonel arrives tomorrow, I will host him with Georgiana. If you have rested all morning and are feeling better, perhaps we will let you join us."

"Elizabeth," he declared in bewilderment.

Smiling sweetly in return, she patiently replied, "Yes?"

Seeing her kindly countenance, he said her name again, though this time in a defeated voice, "Elizabeth, I truly do appreciate your thoughtfulness, and I want you to know that I also understand the risk you took in coming here. Seeing you has lifted my spirits immeasurably." Taking her hand in his and holding it tightly, he added, "I know how lucky I am to have found someone who cares for me in such an unselfish manner. But, Elizabeth, you do not comprehend the pressing nature of the dispute I am trying to resolve. You should not have interfered in my business concerns."

Smiling at him, she explained in a measured and patient manner, "Truly, I understand that I cannot, and I have not. You told me that you needed to resolve matters with your solicitor within the next day or so. You will see him tomorrow night without fail. I have simply changed your plans for the opera in order to make it possible for you to see your solicitor later in the day. That way, you can get some uninterrupted rest before your meeting. It was gracious of you to invite my family to the opera, but I cannot believe you really care if you attend tomorrow night, other than out of a sense of obligation to my family. I have sent your regrets, and they understand. For better or worse, you will have many opportunities to take my mother and sisters to the opera. While my mother would have preferred your company, she is ecstatic that she will be sitting in your box. By rescheduling this social commitment, I am actually attempting to ensure that your business concerns take precedence. You will not be able to handle important decisions properly if you are exhausted and ill."

Darcy sat there looking at her for a long moment. He then reached up to wrap one of her errant curls around his finger, and slowly said, "I now see why you came; you understood the tactical advantage of presenting your arguments while I am lying here."

"Well," she laughed, "it is an added advantage, but I also wanted to bring you the soup." Smiling at him, Elizabeth felt his forehead again and told him, "You should eat it before it gets cold and then drink the tea too."

"Will you stay?"

"I suppose I will not risk anything further if I stay for a few minutes more. Everyone had already retired before I came." Elizabeth helped Darcy with the soup, got him to drink a little tea, and then kissed him reverently on the forehead. She then returned to her room without incident.

❧

Despite his weakened condition, Darcy awoke out of habit at daybreak. He began to rouse himself before he remembered the details of his late-night visit with Elizabeth. While he treasured her concern for his well-being, his first impulse was to disregard her entreaties and conduct his day as he had planned.

As he felt the persistent throb of his headache, he began to reconsider. He had to admit that her modifications to his schedule made abundant sense. Sleeping late would do him a world of good, and it would not matter if he met with his solicitor later in the day. But if Elizabeth's plan was superior to his, why did he feel so uneasy taking her advice? He felt, for want of a better word, weak. He had always prided himself on fulfilling all his commitments no matter what the cost. Giving in to his body's needs seemed at odds with that precept.

Then again, he was reluctant to ignore Elizabeth's wishes and did not look forward to her eventual disapprobation. Most women would not feel free to question his choices and would hardly feel confident challenging him. But that was a lesson he had already learnt: She was not like other women. Her opinion mattered, and not just because he did not want to awaken her ire. If she thought he was acting inappropriately, he needed to listen to her. What was holding him back from accepting her advice was concern over how someone else might view his actions if he did. His pride was at stake, even if only he thought so.

He knew full well what Elizabeth would think of such an argument. He thought it ironic that Elizabeth held concern for his pride in so little regard when she was not without a certain amount of pride herself. As he recalled their exchange over his efforts to get her to ride, the memory of it convinced him to take her advice now. Despite her reluctance to undertake that endeavor, she had trusted him enough to resist the temptation to adhere to her position out of stubbornness. Perhaps that was what was required to forge a strong union between two opinion-ated people: a willingness to put aside one's pride and listen to another's advice. If she had been willing to do it for him, he owed her as much. With a mixture of exhaustion and resolve, he called his valet in.

"Good morning, Robert. I am not feeling particularly well today, so I have decided to take the morning to rest." Ignoring his valet's questioning look, Darcy continued on. "Would you please let Miss Georgiana know that I will not be down for breakfast? Before I return to sleep, I need to send Mr. Bingley a note. I will not be attending the opera. Mr. Bingley will escort my sister and both of our guests. Wake me when Colonel Fitzwilliam arrives, but otherwise, only disturb me if there is a pressing matter."

❧

Elizabeth and Georgiana were in the parlor when Colonel

Fitzwilliam was announced. Elizabeth had been relieved to hear from Georgiana at breakfast that her brother had sent word that he would not be attending the opera that evening. It was clear from Georgiana's comments that she was concerned that Elizabeth would be disappointed by the turn of events. Elizabeth did her best to reassure her sister-to-be that she completely understood Darcy's decision. Elizabeth could see, however, that her words failed to gain Georgiana's confidence. It may have been a testament to Georgiana's intuition that she doubted Elizabeth's professions of serenity. A keen observer could see that Elizabeth was not as sanguine as she claimed. What was not clear was that her discomfort stemmed from her own behavior and not from Darcy's conduct.

Her reunion with Colonel Fitzwilliam was marked by an ease of conversation that made Elizabeth feel more a member of the family than a guest. As the threesome made their way to the dining room, their progress was interrupted by the appearance of Darcy at the door. After welcoming his cousin, he turned his attention to Elizabeth.

"Miss Bennet, good afternoon. I was hoping to have a moment of your time if you were not too busy?"

As the colonel and Georgiana departed, Darcy took Elizabeth's her hand and kissed it. "It appears it is much easier to get time alone with you than I imagined. I simply need to be direct."

With a nervous laugh that expressed both her amusement and relief, Elizabeth replied, "I somehow doubt that such a tactic will suffice in the long run, but I am happy to see that it has worked so well now." She added in a more tender tone, "How are you feeling?"

"Much better, thank you. As a matter of fact, I am feeling well enough to join you. I have come to seek your permission."

Elizabeth studied his demeanor to see the intent of his words, but he was unreadable. She paused for a moment. She had been worried over whether she had overstepped her bounds, both by being so forward in coming to his room and by interfering in his affairs. She knew that when they were married, she would have no qualms. But she was not yet his wife, and that thought had disrupted her sleep. She had woken up to pangs of unease over whether her actions would seem as presumptuous to him as they now did to her.

"Sir, I… this is your home. I am your guest. You hardly need my permission to move within your own rooms."

"Really? I thought I was told last night that I could only attend with your permission."

His earnest expression unnerved her. Speaking rapidly, she said, "While I am quite thankful that you took some time to rest, and I can see from your countenance that it has indeed helped you… it was not my place. I see now that I should not have presumed. I know I am not yet your wife. I did not mean to…"

"Elizabeth, what has gotten in to you? I was teasing you. I very much appreciate your concern for me. I am not used to being taken care of, and I have shown my gratitude poorly." Placing his hand gently under her chin to direct her to look at him, he added, "I love you, and I am pleased that you would take my concerns so wholeheartedly as your own. I did not seek you out to offer a rebuke. I wanted to thank you."

"But I see now that telling you how you should conduct yourself seems more the duty of a wife than of a fiancée, and I want you to know that I do know the difference."

Smiling, he encircled her in his arms and gently kissed her. Resting his head against her hair and breathing in its scent, he quietly replied, "I understand that, but I… have no problem with the distinction. All I want is to actually be your husband. I have no value for this interminable waiting. In my heart you are already my wife. If you feel the same for me, even a little, I am immensely pleased, not upset."

With relief evident on her face, she looked up at him and replied, "Sir, you seem intent on being nothing but generous with me," adding in a more playful tone, "Though I should at least refrain from telling you whether or not you can dine in your own home."

"Quite frankly, madam, you underestimate your power over me. If it means that you would have to come to my room, I believe I would agree to most anything that you were to propose there."

Blushing at his words and feeling her pulse quicken, she attempted to reply nonchalantly. "I see that you are indeed feeling much better."

"Yes, having some uninterrupted time to myself not only gave me some much needed rest, but it also allowed me to see more clearly the issue my steward and I have been attempting to resolve. I see now that some of my previous haste sprang from my desire to spend uninterrupted time with you. I now realize that I will always need to balance my obligations with my personal commitments and that it would be folly to pursue either to the exclusion of the other. You were right last night to remind me of that."

"Sir, you seem in a remarkable mood today. I cannot imagine my suggestion has worked such an improvement."

"Well, while I have been able to clear my head and therefore improve my disposition, I am still tired and feeling the slight effects of the fever. I will retire after I eat. I would like to visit with you, though, at tea before you leave for the opera."

"But I told you last night, I will not be attending it either."

"Yes, you did say that, but I will not have it. You will go. I wrote to Bingley this morning to arrange it. He will be by to escort all three of you in his carriage."

"But I intend..."

"Yes, I am sure you have many intentions. But as to this, you will oblige me. I see no point in your not going. After Mr. Lynch leaves me, I will do just fine with Colonel Fitzwilliam," he said, adding with a mischievous smile, "Unless, of course, you had something else in mind? Are you attempting to arrange things so we have more time alone together? If that is the case, rest assured, I will insist that the colonel go in your place."

"Fitzwilliam, I did not mean..."

Smiling, he raised his hand. "Yes, of course you did not. But if that is the case, I can see no other benefit in your staying behind. You cannot possibly think that I would get any rest if you were here. The mere possibility that you would check on me in my room would keep me up the entire night in sheer anticipation and hope."

Unsure how to respond, she stammered, "Sir, I..."

Smiling at her broadly and barely refraining from laughing, he replied, "I can see that you are shocked at my behavior. As I said, I am still feeling the effects of the fever. If you ask me tomorrow, I will claim no memory of this conversation." Turning more serious, he added, "But I hope that I at least have your assurance that you will attend the opera. I would not be able to rest thinking that I had caused you to forgo an entertainment that I am sure you would take pleasure in."

As she nodded her assent, he said, "Thank you. I promise that I will make amends for failing to escort you there myself."

"You need do no such thing, but I will look forward to the time when we can attend together. I think I will enjoy it very much."

✦

The following morning, Darcy arrived at breakfast feeling significantly better. After learning the details of the quality of the performances at the opera of both the players and the attendees, he inquired of the ladies' plans for the day. In response, Jane explained that Miss Bingley had invited all three of them to go shopping with her and Mrs. Hurst.

Hiding his disappointment, he casually asked, "Will you be available to dine here afterward?"

Smiling warmly at him, Elizabeth responded, "Yes, I believe we shall."

Gazing at her intently as a slow smile came to his lips, he replied, "Wonderful. I will look forward to it." Their eyes locked as they shared a private smile. Their reverie, however, was interrupted by his recollection that his sister and Miss Bennet were still present. After he regained a more somber expression, he asked, "Will your mother and sisters be going as well?"

With subdued mischievousness, Elizabeth replied, "No. My mother had planned to focus on getting fabric for some new gowns for Lydia today, and Lydia prevailed on her to keep our parties separate. It seems that my youngest sister gets quite taxed if she has to shop for anyone other than herself."

"But," Jane interjected, "we do plan to have tea with our

409

aunt. Speaking of her, sir, at the opera last evening my aunt and uncle invited the entire party to dine at their home tomorrow evening. I know they will be sending you a note, but they specifically asked me to mention it to you this morning."

After Georgiana expressed her own wishes that they attend, it was settled.

❧

As Elizabeth awoke the next day, she was startled to realize that she had only three more days before returning to Longbourn. She thought how different she now felt about her childhood home. She was not yet married and could not claim either Darcy's townhouse or Pemberley as her home, but she could also no longer name Longbourn by that term either. As her maid arrived with a tray of her favorite breakfast foods, she felt the separation all the more.

It was not that Darcy's house provided more comforts, although it certainly did; it was more that the rhythm of the household was more attuned to her disposition and tastes. Rising early and then taking a brisk walk was an expected activity and not a peculiarity that had to be borne. The house was designed to provide an abundance of areas where one could quietly read and reflect or pursue musical accomplishments. At Longbourn, only her father's study provided that sort of haven, and admittance into that room was always subject to her father's whim. The style of Darcy's household was understated, and there was a pervasive calmness throughout. Longbourn was in constant disarray, and her mother prized restless activity over all else. The bustle of commotion at Longbourn was sometimes diverting, but it lacked substance, and Elizabeth could not help but feel alienated at times. In the past, she experienced similar sentiments after returning from a visit to her aunt and uncle's house in Cheapside. Knowing that she would be leaving Longbourn for good meant that the time she had left there would be bittersweet at best. With such thoughts, she decided to seek out Jane to convince her to spend an uninterrupted morning together, as Elizabeth doubted whether there would be many more occasions for a tête-à-tête.

Elizabeth and Jane entered the dining room after having spent a pleasant morning together. Any of the remorse that Elizabeth had experienced about feeling so unconnected to her family dissipated on seeing Darcy's welcoming smile. She wondered if the giddy sensation she felt whenever they were reunited after an absence of any length would cease once they were married. She hoped not. While the feeling was disconcerting, it was also exhilarating.

After lunch, Darcy and Georgiana arranged to take Elizabeth on another tour of the private rooms. As they made their way upstairs, Georgiana lagged behind. With Elizabeth on his arm, it was clear that her brother was enjoying a private conversation with his fiancée. Feeling both intrusive and invisible, she opted to let them slowly leave her behind.

As Darcy finished explaining the history of the recent renovations the house had undergone, they entered into what would be Elizabeth's suite as the mistress of the house. "I at least thought you would want to change the decor in this room and your private sitting room. The suite has not really been touched since my mother used it."

Unsure how to broach the subject, she tentatively asked, "You must have very fond memories of her?"

Wistfully he responded, "Yes, I do, but they are the memories of a child. I wish I had known her as an adult. I wondered about her life with my father, how the two of them came to accept one another. When I first fell in love with you, I would have liked to talk to her about it. You may not have known from our history, but I found the working of a woman's mind impenetrable."

Laughing, she quickly replied, "But as to your mother, you have said she was quite content. I think that even if you cannot know how she obtained her happiness, it does not diminish that she was in fact happy. There must be some comfort in that?"

"Yes, that is very true. I do remember her in these rooms, though. When I was very little, she used to let me come in first thing in the morning and sit in bed with her. She would tell me of her plans for the day."

"Your father did not mind?"

With a furrowed brow, he replied, "I am not sure he even knew about it." After a shrug, he continued to speak. "I hope you will redecorate these rooms to your taste. I am looking forward to seeing the result."

"But, Fitzwilliam, even if I were inclined to do so, are you sure you would want me to? If these rooms remind you of your mother, perhaps they would be better left as they are."

"You are to be the new mistress of the house, and these rooms should reflect your taste and no one else's. Here and at Pemberley, I have many things to remind me of my mother. Besides," he added with a twinkle in his eye, "although I love the memory of my mother very much and will always keep it dear to me, this is to be your bedroom. I cannot think you naïve enough to hope that I will be reminded of my mother when I am in residence in these rooms with you."

Blushing, Elizabeth could only meekly reply, "Yes, I see."

Concerned over her reaction, he quickly stated, "Elizabeth, I see that I have made you uncomfortable, and I fear it is not the first time. I apologize."

"No, there is no need to apologize. This is all just very… new to me. My father would call me missish and I hope to be more sensible than that. I would rather that we speak our minds openly and without disguise." With her own twinkle in her eye she added, "But to answer your question, sir, no, I am not that naïve, and your point is well taken."

With a nod, he said, "I am happy to hear it. I look forward to the results."

As he beckoned her to follow him to his adjoining suite, he said, "You should also decide whether my own rooms meet with your approval. I would welcome any suggestions you may have. I will leave such decisions in your capable hands."

After she stepped over the threshold, she could not resist looking about thoroughly. She had seen his room in candlelight the night before the opera, but she now had an uninhibited view. His large sleigh bed dominated the room, covered in a rich burgundy velvet coverlet with a matching upholstered bench at its foot. On either side of the bed were recessed bookshelves that clearly held his favored collection. Placed in front of the fireplace were two comfortable chairs with a table between them, where some of his work rested in a scattered fashion. Recalling herself, she replied, "Fitzwilliam, I hardly think that is my place to dictate the style of your own private rooms."

With an unreadable look on his face, Darcy simply smiled.

"Fitzwilliam, do you not agree?"

"Madam, are you tempting me to say something provocative? I do not wish to get myself in trouble again."

"Well, now you must oblige me. I am all curiosity."

"Very well, but remember that you asked. While I agree that my suite is, of course, my own, I hardly think it likely that you will have no interest in its comforts. You have already spent more time in it than you have in the rooms you will one day occupy. I was hoping it was a trend."

Laughing despite herself, she replied, "I see, sir, that it is your plan to never to let me forget my breach of propriety the other evening. I suppose it will be my cross to bear."

Taking her hand, he said, "If my teasing bothers you, I will stop right away."

"No, I will not hear of it. Given that I once thought you too solemn, I am now in no position to complain about your attempts at levity, even if I am the victim of your wit."

"I would hope that you would know that I would never knowingly cause you any pain." He fell silent and pensive. After a pause, he continued to speak. "Elizabeth, in any regard, I did want to say… I… I know that I should probably wait until after we are married to speak of such things, but since the issue is before us now, I will rely on your assertion that you value our honesty and forge ahead, even if discretion might be more prudent."

After receiving her assent, he continued on awkwardly. "I want to ensure that my rooms are to your liking. I hope you understand that once we are married, I would not wish for such artificial boundaries to come between us. I am not sure what you would expect… how your parents… and I will of course respect whatever distinctions you feel we should preserve between us, but I have been alone for a very long time. I have had my fill of solitude. I see no reason to divide our living quarters between us simply because convention calls for such a device. I would hope that we would occupy the rooms together—as a couple. I know myself well enough to know that once I have you, I will not want to let you go. So unless you disagree with me on this fundamental point, you should be comfortable in either set of rooms because, one way or another, I think you will become quite familiar with both."

Having spoken for so long, Darcy suddenly felt the enormity of what he had said. As he looked to her for a reaction, she stood silent for a moment and then stepped forward, placing her hand behind his neck to pull his lips to hers. Before she kissed him she said, "I am very lucky to have you. I cannot believe I almost lost you once by my own foolishness. If I had any doubts about the efficacy of our talking plainly with each other, they have been put to rest. I would not trade the words you have just said to me for anything. You have both reassured my peace of mind and shattered my composure. I believe our life together will be quite wonderful."

As they began to kiss, she was not prepared for the torment of passion their contact released. Darcy quickly moved his hands to cup her face and began to seek her mouth with such fervor that she began to tremble. He slid his hands down her back in order to draw her body ever closer. She could not help but respond in kind and wound her hands about his waist. As they continued to kiss ever deeper, boldly exploring each other's mouths, she could barely register a thought.

Through the haze though, she could feel how rapidly they both were breathing and felt herself slightly dizzy. Seemingly understanding her sensations, he held her even tighter and then suddenly, fluidly, turned to sit in the chair, pulling her onto his lap as he did. He momentarily seemed shocked by his own actions, but was drawn to her mouth again. As he kissed her, he slowly brought one hand to her shoulder and began to lightly trace his finger along the neckline of her dress. His mouth soon followed as he let his lips, and then tongue, slowly explore the contours of her neck and exposed shoulder.

As Darcy continued his ministrations, he felt consumed by his desire. The culmination of so many fantasies and the reality of her responsiveness made rational thought impossible. He soon, however, found the confines of the chair too restrictive and, out of sheer animal instinct, slid off the chair and onto his knees, taking Elizabeth with him. As they knelt before each other, he gave her a fiery look before he began to kiss her again, all the while slowly pulling the sleeve of her gown down to reveal one of her shoulders.

Darcy was forever grateful for the fact that his passion-induced stupor did not stop him from hearing Georgiana talking to Mrs. Larsen in the hall. He knew it would be a matter of minutes before his sister would see the open door to his chamber and discover them. His alarm at such an image forced him into action. As he awkwardly attempted to pull Elizabeth up, she suddenly stiffened, making it clear that she had heard his sister's approach as well. As they both attempted to recompose themselves and straighten their clothing, Darcy called out, "Georgiana, is that you? Miss Bennet and I were just looking over the suite of rooms." Giving Elizabeth a quick, contrite frown, he strode from the room to delay Georgiana for as long as possible.

Elizabeth had retreated to the mistress's bedroom by the time Darcy and Georgiana joined her. Georgiana's easy manner made it apparent that she did not suspect anything unusual had occurred. Despite this, Elizabeth could not help but feel the awkwardness of the situation and barely knew how she replied in response to Georgiana's questions about redecorating the suites. Mercifully, the encounter did not last long, as Georgiana's main goal in coming to find them was to announce that Mr. Bingley had arrived with his sisters.

That visit seemed to drag on interminably. As the party broke up to prepare for dinner at the Gardiners' home, Darcy hoped to draw Elizabeth aside, but Miss Bingley resolutely stood by him until her carriage was called. Elizabeth attempted to wait her out, but was forced to excuse herself when Jane and Georgiana announced their intention to dress for dinner.

As Darcy readied his own appearance, he resolved to find a private moment to speak to Elizabeth. He was mortified that he had almost compromised the woman he loved on the floor of his room in a manner that would have allowed his younger sister to walk in on them. He could not believe that he had acted so brutishly. Yet, he had to admit that making love to Elizabeth was his heart's desire. Even when he had been trying to convince himself that she was an unsuitable match, he had never attempted to deny how very much he wanted her. But the fact that his interest in her was long-standing could hardly mean that he had license to act on his passion. He simply needed to exercise some self-control. He would apologize to Elizabeth and tell her that while her willingness to indulge him was a joy he would cherish, he could not be trusted with her generosity.

Despite Darcy's resolution, he could not find an opportunity at the Gardiners' to speak privately with Elizabeth as their drawing room was considerably smaller than his. He did try to catch her eye to convey his remorse, but she seemed shy with him as well, and in the end he felt nothing had been resolved.

When they returned home and Darcy bid Elizabeth good night at the foot of the staircase in Jane and Georgiana's presence, she seemed so tentative that all of his anxieties over his conduct returned in full bloom.

◈

Elizabeth attended breakfast the next morning feeling just as awkward as she had the night before. Darcy's eyes were often upon her, but she did not know how to resume their previous intimacy without recalling her blunder in his room. Instead, Elizabeth fell as silent as Darcy. At the end of the meal, Darcy broke his silence. "Miss Bennet, the weather seems quite pleasant. I was wondering if you might consent to a walk with me?"

With a nervous smile, Elizabeth responded, "Yes, yes, that would be quite nice."

After entering the park, Darcy spoke first. "Elizabeth, I... I am sorry that we have not talked sooner, but there seemed no appropriate opportunity. I beg you to believe that I do understand the gravity of my mistake. I have barely been able to think of anything other than my need to speak to you—to seek your forgiveness. I can offer no excuse. I know I put you in a most embarrassing... It was so improper of me and to place you in a situation where my sister... I am so sorry. In saying it out loud, I do not know how you can forgive me. But whether you can find it in your heart to do so or not, I want you to know that it will never happen again. I can promise you that."

Elizabeth barely knew how to respond. But after a moment, a faint smile graced her lips, and with an arch brow, she asked, "Never, Fitzwilliam? Even after we are married?"

Her words had caught him off guard. He stared at her,

blinked, colored, and then stammered, "I might have been slightly zealous in my choice of words, but I had hoped that you would understand… that I meant to convey that I would not place you in such a position—I mean, in such unacceptable circumstances—again before we are married."

Smiling, she said, "Ah, I see."

Her smile helped to dissolve the tension between them, and despite his feelings of remorse, he could not help but return the smile. "Elizabeth, I must say, you seem in a better frame of mind than I expected. I am of course grateful for it. I knew that you would be upset, and I was worried at the extent of your distress. Last night, you seemed… so uncomfortable in my presence. Having disappointed you has been the greater part of my self-reproach."

"Fitzwilliam, I will be honest with you. I am a little surprised myself. After yesterday's… indiscretion, I was distraught. I spent a fitful night of sleep reproaching myself over my conduct. I have reviewed the events of yesterday afternoon many times, cataloguing all of my missteps…"

"But, Elizabeth, you were not to blame, I was the one…"

Gently interrupting him, she said, "Fitzwilliam, please, I understand that you blame yourself, but I also know that I did not act as I should. I also wanted to apologize to you today for my provocative behavior. But in hearing you berate yourself, knowing that I intend to do the very same thing myself, I suddenly saw the encounter in a different light. I could apologize to you for my lapse in behavior, as it was my duty to set the boundaries between us. You could apologize to me, as you have already tried to do twice, because it was your duty to guard my respectability. But I cannot help but admit that I understand your temptation. I felt it too, and I would be a hypocrite to argue otherwise. If you can understand my behavior and I can understand yours, perhaps both of our behavior was understandable given the circumstances. I have chastised myself, thinking myself wanton and immoral for my conduct yesterday. But when I think of your behavior yesterday, all I see was a man in love who desires me. I cannot help but value that in you. I know we must not act on such feelings, but I cannot condemn them. They are natural. If such feelings are appropriate within our marriage, then the feelings themselves cannot be condemned, just the timing of them."

"Elizabeth, I do not know what to say but that you are a remarkable woman."

"I am not sure if that is so. I think it more likely that I am just in love."

"Elizabeth, while I appreciate all that you have said, and I am so exceedingly grateful for both your love and understanding, I do not think our agreeing on the cause of the problem changes what must be done about a solution."

"No, as to that I think you are correct."

"Elizabeth, our wedding is slightly more than three weeks away. Despite the temptation you present, I know that I can act honorably until we are wed. I think, though, that we should not tempt fate by spending too much time alone together in private. My judgment seems to fail me when you are in my arms."

Embarrassed but unwilling to look away, she nodded. "That seems wise."

Taking her hand in his and caressing it absentmindedly, he looked down at it as he spoke. "Elizabeth, I would be remiss in not telling you how grateful I am to have found you. I have been dreading this conversation. To speak of such things... but you somehow seem to make what I fear is impossible to discuss a source of communion between us." Looking up at her, he continued, "I have long thought your beauty, disposition, and intellect unsurpassed by any other woman. I knew when you accepted me that I would be happy simply to be in your company for the rest of my life, but to be able to talk to you—to tell you of my concerns, apparently whatever their nature—is a gift I cannot measure. I love you so dearly. I have often thought that the poets invented the idea of a soul mate, but I now know better."

Overcome with emotion, Elizabeth tenderly replied, "My Fitzwilliam."

Smiling at her in gratitude, he added, "Let us not waste this fine day. Would you care to take a turn about the park?"

As Darcy undressed, he looked back at the evening with both regret and satisfaction. He had enjoyed his time with the Gardiners and was touched to see Mrs. Gardiner's successful attempts at drawing Georgiana into conversation. He had even enjoyed a lively discussion with Mr. Bennet. While his interactions with Mrs. Bennet were indirect, he was more concerned with the substance of her discourse than its delivery. She had catalogued the social calls Elizabeth would be required to make upon their return to Hertfordshire in preparation for taking her eventual leave of the neighborhood and the various dinners he and Elizabeth and Bingley and Jane were expected to attend as their wedding day approached. It seemed clear that the next day and a half in London with Elizabeth would be the calm before the storm and that he should expect no relief or privacy with Elizabeth once he returned her to her home.

He signaled for his valet to stop fussing with his clothes and walked away wearing just his shirt and breeches. "Robert, I will retire now. Maybe I will have a glass of brandy while I read to help me get to sleep. Would you please?" With an efficient nod, his valet complied and left.

Standing by his bed, Darcy scanned the shelves near it for a book that might pique his interest. Having found one, he flopped on the bed. Elizabeth's vibrancy had always drawn him to her, and her teasing manner and quick wit made him feel the strength of his attachment all the more. His longing for her tonight was tempered by the fact that he knew, after the discussion they had had in the park, that she loved him, understood him, and could accept him despite his flaws. That knowledge gave him a sense of intimacy with her that he could not explain, other than to say that he finally felt that she was his.

Darcy had long finished his brandy when he heard the servant door open. As he leaned forward on an elbow to see who it was, he was stunned to observe Elizabeth standing inside his room, in what appeared to be her nightgown. "I was wondering, sir, if I might come in."

Awkwardly standing up, Darcy exclaimed, "Elizabeth, what are you doing here?"

"I see that you are intent on starting with the most difficult question first. How singular. Would it not be more polite to simply invite me in and inquire after my health?"

"Elizabeth, I do not understand... Of course, come in, but... what..."

As she walked toward him, he could see that she was

confused about where to sit. After a moment, she said, "Your fireplace has such a lovely blaze; perhaps we could rest by it." To his surprise, she sat on the rug directly in front of the fire and not on the chairs placed there. He sat beside her, trying not to crowd her, but needing to stretch his legs to fit.

She had carefully organized her reasons for coming and had rehearsed her speech several times in her room, but as she sat there next to him, her mind was foolishly preoccupied. He was barefoot, and she realized that she had never seen him in such a state before. When she had attended to him when he was ill, he had been in bed and covered. His unexpected appearance threw her off her intended course of action and made rational thought impossible.

Eventually, it was Darcy who spoke. "Elizabeth, I do not mean to be rude, but I must ask you again why are you here? I thought we had agreed this morning that we should not be alone together in private."

"Ah, yes, the purpose of my visit. Of course... This all made so much more sense, before I arrived." Turning to him, she smiled in a nervous fashion. She took a moment to collect herself before she added, "Earlier this evening, when everyone was here, you were discussing politics with my uncle and Bingley and I had a feeling, a sort of vision, that this is how our life would be once we are married—that this is the manner in which we will entertain. I looked around, and I could envision us here spending quiet evenings together, and I began to pretend—or imagine—how it would feel if we were in fact married. It felt so very natural to think of us that way. It was not very difficult for me to imagine that I was your wife; that I am your wife. But I know that we are not husband and wife. I know it, not because

I do not feel it, but because it has not been proclaimed in public. As a result, we are not allowed all of the rights that exist between a husband and wife. We are not free to speak privately whenever we wish, and we cannot be together at night as we are now. But as to the rest—as to the feelings that exist between two people when they agree to face the future together and to take each other's happiness into account before acting—that is something we have already experienced. Being in your house has allowed me to envision being here with you forever. But that thought made me realize that my time here will soon end and that I will have to go back to Longbourn in a matter of days. I know when I do leave, my heart will stay here. It will stay with you wherever you are. It will be the time when we are in Hertfordshire that will be the illusion. We will have to pretend that we are still practically strangers attempting to get to know each other, when we are already so much more. The thought of that made me realize that I do not want to waste any of the time that we still have here together. So I decided to come to you. So that we can talk of whatever we wish, so that we can hold each other, and I can lie in your arms until the servants wake up and I need to return to my room."

For a moment, all he could do was whisper her name. He had listened to her in growing amazement. She had captured the way he felt, but he could scarcely credit that she was saying it to him in this manner. Finally, he said, "But, Elizabeth, are you sure?"

"I suppose I could ask you such a question, and it would serve as my answer. Are you sure, Fitzwilliam? Are you sure that you love me? That you want to be my husband? That you will always love me?"

"Oh, yes," he murmured, raising his hand to her hair, "I have no doubt. I have known it for so long that it is now a part of me."

"Then I am sure of everything else."

He looked at her for a long moment. She could see that his breathing was erratic. Slowly a small smile came to his lips, and he swept his eyes up and down her. She was amazed that his one look seemed more forward than all of his previous caresses. In a low, deep voice, Darcy asked, "Then you are to be mine for the evening?"

Mesmerized by his gaze, she nodded, keeping her eyes upon him.

As his face registered her answer, he said, "Then we must have your hair down. I have wanted to see it loose on your shoulders since the day you walked to Netherfield and I saw you on the lawn."

"Even then?"

"Oh, yes."

Wetting her lips, she slowly reached up and undid the pins in her hair. Her full, brown locks cascaded down her back and framed her face to enhance her natural beauty. Once her hair was down, he reached over, pulled some of the curls apart, and carefully arranged them on her shoulders. He then ran the tip of his index finger down her jaw and traced a line from under her chin to her collarbone. "You are so very beautiful," adding in a whisper, "You take my breath away." He then leaned forward until his lips met hers. The sensation was exquisite.

As they kissed, she became lost to all other sensations. His mouth began to tease her, moving from her lips to her neck and back again. He then returned to her lips and explored her mouth with his tongue in a manner that was both delicate and overpowering. He stopped for a moment to look at her. Her eyes were half closed, and her lips full and glistening. "I need to make sure that I am not dreaming," he confessed.

"As do I," she replied.

He waited for a moment and asked, "Elizabeth, may I bring you to my bed?"

While she knew that this was where they were headed, she suddenly felt overwhelmingly nervous. "Yes," she whispered, "but I do not know…"

"Elizabeth, I will expect nothing. Your presence here is a gift." He then buried his fingers in her hair and pulled his hands through its length. Engrossed by the silky texture of her curls and the colors that were reflected in it from the fire, he continued for a moment to examine her tresses in the light before returning to her mouth, lightly brushing his lips back and forth. He then rested his gaze on her again and whispered. "We need not do anything that you are not comfortable with, but if you are willing, we could begin by discovering each other. We will touch each other, in order to feel all there is to feel of each other's bodies. Have you not had some curiosity about me? I will admit to having an overwhelming curiosity about every part of you. I would like to see all of you, to touch you everywhere, but if you are not ready, that is fine, too."

Her breathing was so rapid that she struggled to reply. In a gesture of embarrassment, she looked down as she quietly said, "I would like to touch your curls, to feel them in my hands."

Darcy put his hand under her chin and tilted her head back so that she was now looking at him. With a smile that fully displayed his dimples, he said, "Then please do."

As she reached up to run her hands through his hair, he

closed his eyes and swayed under her ministrations. He eventually opened his eyes and asked, "Is that all you have wondered?"

Their gazes locked, and his intense stare emboldened her. "I suppose I would like to see you without your shirt on."

At her words, he smiled ever so slightly and moved to stand up. He then reached down and pulled her to her feet. As they stood facing each other, he leaned down to kiss her. When they broke apart, he led her to his bed. As she stood looking at it, he slipped his arms around her from behind and began to kiss the sensitive area behind her ear. It was now her turn to sway as he continued his assault on her neck. He then circled around her and sat on the bed, pulling her to stand between his knees. She rested her hands on his shoulders and surveyed the fine features of his face as he looked up at her. Without breaking their gaze, he began to untie the top of his shirt and then pulled it off over his head.

As he sat there with his chest exposed, he gently pulled her onto his lap, and they began to kiss. Her hands were tentative at first, but soon began to caress the taut planes of his shoulders and back. She could not help but be fascinated by his masculinity and began to trace the pattern of his hair on his chest. Passion soon ruled them, and their kisses turned all-consuming. She felt bereft of his lips when he pulled away to whisper, "Elizabeth, may I see you?"

Darcy saw her nod imperceptibly and kissed her with renewed fervor. He then slowly began to untie her nightdress. The anticipation of his exploration washed Elizabeth in desire. When he had her dress open, he slowly slid his hand inside it and began to caress her breast. Upon contact, they both sighed, and the sound of it made them look up at each other in surprise.

Elizabeth could not help but smile at their mutual shock in finding themselves thus engaged. Her infectious expression, in turn, made him smile, and his smile made her laugh.

"Elizabeth, I think you are the only woman in the world who could drive me wild with passion and laugh at me at the same time."

"It is not that I find you amusing at this moment, quite the contrary. It is just that while I know how we got here, I cannot but be amazed at the voyage."

"Yes, I understand. I cannot tell you... This is so... Having you here is a dream come true..." Adding in a more playful tone, as he began to gently bite her earlobe, "But... if you do not mind... I have many more destinations I would like to navigate... So if you must laugh at me, be forewarned that I will exact my revenge one way or another." With that, he slid her nightdress off her shoulders and let it fall to the ground. He then began to tease her breasts in the most exquisite manner.

Despite the rapturous feeling he was producing in her, her exposure made her uncomfortable, and she instinctively moved up against him to hide herself. Darcy would have none of it and leaned back to get a better view of her. With his eyes alight with passion, he said, "Do not be ashamed, Elizabeth. You are so beautiful. I want to look at you. We must have no embarrassment. It should be just you and me with no boundaries between us. I want to worship you. But you must share yourself with me first."

His words had a dizzying effect on her. The feel of his hands on her and his mouth on her neck was too much to resist. At that moment, she surrendered herself to him. She moved back off his lap to lie on the bed in full view. He followed her as a man possessed. Kneeling over her, he murmured, "Elizabeth, oh, Elizabeth," and looked upon her with reverence. "I love you so completely."

By the rooster's first crow, he awoke alone with only a hint of her scent and a set of discarded hairpins to confirm it was not a dream.

PEMBERLEY AND BEYOND

ELIZABETH AWOKE AND INSTINCTIVELY reached toward the other side of the bed to find the source of warmth that had given her profound joy since her marriage. To her consternation, she found the bed empty. She rose and, after donning a robe, walked to the center of the room where she found a breakfast tray with her favorite fruits and a note written in an elegant hand. Darcy had awoken early to see that everything was prepared for their trip to Hertfordshire and was hesitant to wake her given the long journey before them. She smiled at his thoughtfulness and was reminded of the first time she had awoken to a similar sight.

It had been almost five months ago. Elizabeth had returned to her room after that fateful night in London where they had anticipated their wedding vows. Despite her exhaustion at having returned only moments before dawn, sleep would not find her. She tossed and turned with regret. Before she had entered Darcy's room, it had seemed the right thing to do, and once there, their time together had been exquisite. The night had been one of slow discovery. As they made love for the first time, she realized how very little she actually knew of marital relations, but it was afterward, as they lay contentedly together, gently caressing each other, that she came to understand how limited her knowledge was of a man's body and, more importantly, how little she knew of her own. The surprising combination of his gentle regard for her feelings and his eagerness to have her experience everything left her satiated and dizzy with admiration of him—his beautiful body, his piercing gaze, his exquisite touch, and his refusal to let them be anything but open and honest with each other despite her moments of awkwardness and reserve. Her astonishment was all the more complete when he made it clear that he intended to repeat the act with even greater attention to detail.

As sunrise approached, they alternately reminded each other that it was time for her to go. After another round of kisses and murmured endearments at his door, Darcy took both her hands in his and kissed them reverently. After he finished, he held her in such a steady and intense gaze that it gave her the courage to leave. She smiled tenderly in return, held her head up, and nodded her adieu.

Once in her room and devoid of his reassurances, she began to feel an overwhelming sense of panic over her actions. Years of being taught that what she had just done was never to be done could not be ignored. Her dismay over her actions rapidly led to anxiety over what Darcy thought of her coming to his room in the first place. She knew that, presented with such an opportunity, it was not unexpected that he would be willing to follow her into folly, but she wondered how he would judge her provocative behavior in hindsight. She drifted into a fitful sleep and awoke feeling worse. As her eyesight focused on the table beside her bed, she saw that it held a breakfast tray with a note addressed to her. Recognizing the handwriting, she eagerly broke the seal.

My Dearest Elizabeth,

I wanted this letter to greet you when you awoke, since I will not be able to perform that most enviable task myself. Watching you leave this morning was one of the more difficult things I have ever done, yet I would not change an instant of our time together. You have made me the happiest of men. While I learned long ago that I should cherish every moment I am able to spend with you, I cannot but hope that the next few weeks will somehow pass quickly so that we need never be separated like this again. I know what you think of poets' pretensions, but you must allow me to tell you how deeply I love you. I have never in my life before felt so affected. The communion we shared seems to have relieved me of what feels to be a lifetime of loneliness. I knew that our life together would afford us an intimacy that would bind us as a couple, but I underestimated the depth of the attachment. I will never again think of my future except as it is intertwined with yours. My separate life has ended, and our future together has begun. Your happiness will always be paramount to me, as you have already shown me how important mine is to you. Of this you have my pledge.

After you left, I felt bereft without you. I craved your touch, your smile, and your tenderness. As I waited here for the morning to come so that I could see you again, I began to worry that you would regret our conduct. But then I thought of your strength of character and the wisdom that you have

*always shown regarding the honesty upon which we have built
our relationship. You have taught me through your actions
how to love without reserve or concern for oneself, and that
has been your greatest gift to me. I can only hope that over
time I can prove to you that my love is worthy of your recipro-
cation. For now, I must simply wait here for time to tick more
rapidly so that I may see you again.*

    Yours in every way, F.D.

Elizabeth put down the letter with her heart full. His belief
in her—his belief in her love for him—gave her strength. Their
journey together had taken many twists and turns, and last night
was one more change of course, for better or for worse. What
mattered though was that she loved him and that he loved her.
They would always be together, and if their love for each other
had developed in an unconventional manner, she could never
regret the results. However they had gotten to this moment in
time did not matter as much as the fact that they were here now
together. She suddenly felt able to face the day, no matter what
it would bring, and rang for the maid to prepare her bath.

She soaked for several minutes, comforted and buoyed by his
letter, now free to recollect all of the feelings and emotions that
he had elicited from her during their night together, and bask
in the sensations that he had created. Given her lack of sleep,
she could not help but close her eyes and let her emotions wash
over her.

Elizabeth was startled from her musing by the sound of
her maid answering a knock on the door. If the maid thought
it irregular, she kept it to herself and returned with a letter
addressed to Elizabeth.

"Excuse me, miss, but Mrs. Larsen just brought this for you. The master wanted to let you know of a change in plans and asked that it be delivered to you immediately."

"Thank you. I... Thank you."

If Elizabeth was surprised and comforted by Darcy's first letter, his second letter left her confused.

My Loveliest Elizabeth,

As I listen to the sounds of the house awakening, ever anxious for the time when you will be able to join me, I cannot help but be concerned. While I cherish every moment I have spent with you, I cannot help but see how selfish I have been. I hope that you do not regret too dearly what I have done. I realize now that you may view my actions very differently in the cold light of day and that my first letter may have presumed far too much. I know how generous your nature is and how willing you have been to forgive my transgressions in the past, but I fear that I have overstepped the bounds from which even your charitable heart can forgive. Nonetheless, I must ask, no, beg your forgiveness. As I humbly await you, I promise that in the future I will do everything in my power to make myself worthy of your love and your respect.

Yours in every way, F.D.

As Elizabeth dressed, she could not help but wonder at his letters. His previous reassurance had calmed her and given her strength. His sudden concern over her reaction unnerved her. While she was touched by his distress, she was more alarmed about what the loss of his resolve augured. As she tried to understand what had caused his change of heart, she was struck by the realization that he was simply as nervous as she was and as unsure over how to proceed as she had been. Rather than let his confusion spread to her or make her rethink her own resolve, his insecurity made her smile.

As she resumed dressing, she tried to rehearse what she would say to him. Her responses would, of course, depend on who was present. If Jane or Georgiana were already in attendance, perhaps she could ask him to take a stroll with her after they ate. It would be a little forward of her, but she did not think that either lady would hold her informality against her. As she looked at the hour, she became fearful that he might already have finished his breakfast and become occupied with appointments. Rushing to finish, she was preparing to go downstairs when she heard another knock at the door. It was a footman with yet another letter.

My Loveliest Elizabeth,

I am sorry to bother you again, but I cannot help but wonder when you will be coming to breakfast. I do not mean to rush you. I am just so concerned and will not rest until I am able to see you again. Please forgive me.

Yours in every way, F.D.

After reading his last letter, Elizabeth could not help but laugh out loud. The sway of her own emotions had greatly troubled her, but in seeing the tumult of his thoughts through the progression of his three letters, she had to laugh at the circumstances they both found themselves in. Apparently, he was in more turmoil than she.

As she came to the bottom of the stairs, she heard Mr.

Bingley, Miss Bingley, and Mrs. Hurst being announced. The hope of a private tête-à-tête was dashed. As she entered, she saw Darcy standing at the head of the table, greeting his guests. He turned immediately to her. His gaze felt as intense as she had ever experienced, but to someone less attuned to his mood, his words sounded controlled and easy. "Miss Bennet, good morning. I hope you slept well."

"Yes, sir, thank you." After Elizabeth made her acknowledgments to the rest of the party, she moved to the far end of the table. When she had entered, there had been an unoccupied seat to Darcy's right, but Miss Bingley had quickly usurped that station. Seeing that Elizabeth intended to sit at the other end of the table where the only remaining seats could be found, Darcy moved with alacrity to pull her chair out for her. As he leaned close to her to push it in, she felt the tickle of his breath on her neck. She looked up at him, and he returned her gaze with a faint contrite smile. As their eyes met, he seemed to be communicating his regret, his adoration, and his concern. Having tarried longer than was appropriate, he then, to her surprise, took the seat next to her, despite the fact that he already had a place setting at the head of the table. Whether his actions were consciously done or not, he now seemed to slowly comprehend the import of his position and awkwardly looked to where he had left his plate.

Before he could react, Elizabeth rose to the sideboard and returned with two cups and saucers. She then brought the coffeepot. "Mr. Darcy, would you like some coffee?"

"Thank you. Indeed I would." His reply was innocuous, but the real gratitude that the tone of his words conveyed was not lost upon her. As she gracefully poured his cup and then her own, she smiled at him with such genuine warmth that he became transfixed. As he watched her performing such a domestic task intended solely for his comfort, his anxiety began to melt and he was able to see her as she was last night: giving, intensely beautiful, and his own.

After exchanging a knowing glance, she asked with an impertinent smile, "I saw when I arrived that you had the paper. What news is there of the troubles in France?"

As Elizabeth sat at Pemberley, with the note Darcy had placed on her breakfast tray that morning, she could not help but think of all of the thoughtful letters he had left her since they had married. It had become his habit to do so whenever he was unable to be with her when she awoke. Over time, their mornings together had come to hold a special significance, and he always regretted when circumstances forced his absence.

On the eve of her wedding, Elizabeth had worried that, having already consummated their relationship on two separate occasions, their wedding night might be anticlimactic. She now had to laugh at her naïveté. She had found that marital relations improved with practice, not diminished. The wedding had been beautiful. Sharing it with Jane and Bingley had made it all the more joyous.

Darcy and Elizabeth had spent their first night as husband and wife at his townhouse in London. In the morning, Elizabeth lazily awoke as Darcy answered the discreet knock at the door. He quickly instructed the maid to give him the breakfast tray that he had ordered and dismissed her. She seemed momentarily confused that he did not want her to enter the room to set out the contents of the tray, but then blushed in understanding, curtseyed, and departed. As Elizabeth wrapped herself in a sheet, she inquired as to his intentions.

"This was very thoughtful of you, Fitzwilliam, but will we not be going downstairs for breakfast, or do you plan to serve me yourself?"

With a mischievous smile that she had come to adore, Darcy prepared her a cup of tea and replied, "Perhaps I could serve you, and then you could serve me?" Lying on the bed, he then leisurely explained, "After having to endure the good wishes of so many people yesterday, I do not intend to share your company with even the servants, and I see no reason to leave this bed so impetuously. Having previously been deprived of waking with you, I do not intend to squander any of our first morning together."

Raising her eyebrows innocently, she asked, "Am I to have no say in the matter?"

With a challenging smile, he replied, "As to this, none. I have quite set my mind on the course of the day. I thought we would both need some sustenance, so I ordered this food. We will, of course, periodically need more nourishment, but I think that anything that we would require could easily be fetched here for us. Otherwise, we are to see no one and do nothing in particular, other than that which inspiration provides." He then swept an appreciative look over her sheet-draped body.

Laughing, she asked, "Are we not to bathe or dress?"

"Dressing seems foolish, but, yes, we are to bathe, and I have a specific plan as to that as well. But we will come to that in good time. For now you should eat. Let me feed you a scone. I made sure that we had your favorite preserves. I think you will find it more than satisfactory."

As he moved to her side to serve her, she began to laugh at his earnest attempts to feed her little bits of scone and jam.

He was so serious in the performance of his task that it made her giggle, which in turn made his job all the harder. After a moment, he stopped, looked at her appraisingly, and in a voice deep with passion said, "Elizabeth, you have a tiny drop of jam on your lip; let me attend to it." As he began languidly to nibble her lip, her scone was quickly forgotten.

Later when Elizabeth awoke from the slumber they had both drowsily fallen into after their lovemaking, she found herself in Darcy's arms with her back resting against his chest. Upon seeing that she was no longer asleep, he began to trace circles on her exposed hip. Once his ministrations began to tickle, she took his hand and wove his fingers in hers. "I cannot believe we are still abed. What time is it?"

"It is barely eleven o'clock, and we have no plans." After furrowing his brow for a moment, he added, "Unless, of course, you wish to go somewhere? Or need some time on your own?"

Hearing the apprehension in his voice, she quickly replied, "No, there is nowhere else on earth that I would rather be. This has been bliss, rest assured. But I cannot help but wonder what the staff must think. I am the new mistress of the house, and I have not even risen from my bed."

"Elizabeth, the staff thinks that it is your honeymoon and most likely properly believes that I am holding you hostage. If there was talk, and Mrs. Larsen takes prodigious care that there is none, the staff would simply blame me, and quite frankly, I couldn't care less. At worst, they will whisper that I am besotted with you, and nothing could be truer."

"I suppose you are right. I think that I am probably just feeling guilty. This has all been so glorious. I cannot imagine that I should be allowed so much happiness."

"Elizabeth, you deserve all the happiness in the world, and I want nothing other than to make your life perfect."

"Dearest, that is hardly possible, but I appreciate that you would wish it so." After a pause, Elizabeth said, "Fitzwilliam, earlier you expressed some discomfort over the events of yesterday. I know that such a prolonged social gathering was not to your tastes, but I do hope you enjoyed yourself somewhat."

"Madam, I have sorely misrepresented myself if you can think that I thought yesterday anything other than the most important day of my life. We were married yesterday. Therefore, the day was perfection."

"I appreciate the lovely sentiment, but I cannot believe that you enjoyed being so much on display. I think I feel far more at home in social gatherings than you do, especially one held in Hertfordshire, and yet the day was too much even for me."

Darcy turned on his side to face her and said, "No, you are right, my dear. I was anxious to leave, to have you here to myself, but I still enjoyed the day. I particularly found Reverend Fischer's words a comfort. I thought his message about the ties our marriages were creating between and amongst our families was a very important one. However, it was his admonition that we were also creating a new family for which my primary responsibility lay that made me understand the solemnity of the ceremony and helped me to put some of my family's actions into perspective. His words captured how I felt and gave me strength throughout the day to make small talk with absolutely anyone who sought to remind me how lucky I was to have wed you."

"Sometimes, sir, I am not sure if you are teasing me or not."

"It is a skill I learned from you, my dear. I hope to remain an enigma so that you might always be interested in me."

"I think it is safe to say that I will remain interested even if, by chance, I should somehow come to understand you."

With a gentle kiss, he replied, "Then that shall be my comfort."

Smiling sweetly, Elizabeth replied, "I am glad. But, sir, I do think that it is time for us to rise, or am I still being held hostage?"

"I see no reason why both cannot be true. Let me see about a bath, and then I will apprise you of my plans."

While they did remain in their room for most of the first day, they eventually emerged for dinner. As they sat at their table, which had been formally outfitted for a special meal, they were free to discuss whatever they wanted and to lean ever closer or touch hands whenever the whim moved them. The realization that once their dinner was over he could take Elizabeth with him back to their room made it the most enjoyable meal Darcy had ever spent.

Despite his newfound appreciation for the dining room, Darcy insisted on having breakfast delivered to their bedroom all week. The practice allowed Elizabeth to begin to understand her husband's tastes. Mornings tended to make him ravenous both for his breakfast and for her.

Once the week was up and visiting could begin, their time no longer seemed their own, as an unending stream of guests began to descend upon them. At first, Darcy took it in stride, but he soon resented the interruption. Propriety required Elizabeth to accept the calls and even return several of the visits. Moreover, Darcy's business and estate concerns soon needed his attention as well. Elizabeth could no longer recall whether it was by design or circumstance that they began to make their mornings together their private sanctuary. Calls were never accepted before eleven, and visitors soon realized it was futile to try. Darcy's steward quickly learned that while his master would spend long hours on the care of his estate, he was not to be bothered before mid-morning unless it was an emergency.

This demarcation of time gave Darcy a better way to manage his duties and also an opportunity to discuss his business with Elizabeth before his appointments. Her insights often gave him clarity and helped organize his thoughts. Their discussions sometimes led to disagreements, but none ever lasted for very long.

After they arrived at Pemberley, at Darcy's prodding Elizabeth ordered the refurbishing of several rooms. It was then that Darcy suggested a novel use for his bedroom. He argued that it could be more efficiently used as a private sitting room with a small dining table than a suite where he would never sleep. He wanted to continue their morning interludes, but he was tiring of breakfast on trays. Pemberley was a vastly larger house than their home in London, and the dining room was too far to go to before dressing. Because he wanted to eat breakfast in the leisurely manner they had done in London, but wanted a larger variety of hot foods, he suggested that his room be transformed into a small dining room with a sideboard where hot foods could be left warming. That way, when they wanted breakfast, the food would be there and they could wait on themselves.

At first Elizabeth simply laughed at his idea. She could not believe that she had once thought Darcy formal and stiff. He was more at home defying convention. She thought his idea had merit but could imagine the gossip it might cause. Darcy pointed out that no one would ever be invited into the master's bedroom. Therefore, no one would ever know of the renovations except his trusted staff, and they knew better than to gossip in such a manner. In the end, Elizabeth acquiesced, and his suite became their private breakfast room, with a settee and two writing desks.

Elizabeth was roused from her thoughts by the arrival of her maid with another missive.

After she had finished dressing, Darcy entered. "Elizabeth, everything is prepared. We can depart at your leisure. I know you must be looking forward to seeing your family again."

"I am," she brightly replied. "I was just thinking about our wedding and the last time I saw them all together. Since then, Jane and Bingley's visits have been such a comfort, and my father's sojourn last month was as enjoyable as it was unexpected. But I must admit to wanting to see Longbourn again and my whole family. It will be odd, though, to visit as a guest."

"I imagine it might be, but I suppose that is to be expected."

"Yes, but it has made me wonder if you might also be feeling some apprehension. I know my family can sometimes be overwhelming, and to be honest, I fear that they might not all value you as they should."

Sitting next to her, he took her hand and said, "If that is true, it is most likely the results of my prior actions." After pausing to think, he added, "In returning to Hertfordshire, I cannot help being reminded of my trip there last year, when I came to speak to Jane. I was also worried over what reception I might receive, but by finally focusing on someone else's concern over my own, I was able to begin to fulfill my obligations as a gentleman, and that ultimately led to your reevaluation of my worth. I cannot hope for similar transformations, but my goals this trip are more modest. I would simply like your family to understand our devotion and begin to forge friendships where I have previously been unsuccessful."

Smiling, she took his face in her hands and kissed him. "While I will be forever grateful that you did in fact return to Hertfordshire, and despite what I might have improvidently once said, I think that in essentials you have always acted the gentleman." Smiling, she added, "At different times, it has just been easier for others to see."

Laughing, he replied, "Your defense of my earlier behavior may actually serve as the basis for its indictment. But I appreciate the sentiment all the more." Pulling her to stand in his embrace, he added, "But whatever apprehension either of us possess, delaying the start of our journey will not improve its ultimate success."

"Yes, you are, of course, correct, and I will prepare to depart directly, but you must promise to let me know if my family proves disconcerting. We have both come to value our time alone, and being so much in company may be a difficult accommodation."

"I appreciate that, but as long as we can retire to the privacy of our room together at Netherfield, I think I will be able to bear the change sufficiently well."

Elizabeth suddenly frowned. "I trust that will be true, but I just received a letter from Jane saying that our visit may coincide with Bingley's sisters'. It is not yet certain, but if it is, I fear that Netherfield may not be quite the refuge we may have imagined."

"Oh," he stammered, considering the implications. "That is... I did not realize."

Smiling at his unease and the value he obviously placed on their time alone together, she said, "But do not be overly concerned. It is not certain, and in any regard, this entire trip is of limited duration. We will enjoy the company of our friends and family, and then we will return to the comfort of Pemberley.

Whenever I feel some impatience over a social obligation because I would rather have you all to myself, I endeavor to remember that we have a full lifetime together. Inconveniences, joys, sorrow, absurdities, and tribulations will all come and go, but we will remain. No matter what comes, we will have each other, and that is our blessing. And now, I think, we should begin the journey."

THE END

Acknowledgments

I want to thank Marsha Zierk for encouraging me to write before I even started and thereafter always offering her support and encouragement without reserve. I want to thank Abigail Reynolds for inspiring me to write by sharing her own wonderful books and for introducing me to my talented editor, Deb Werksman. I want to thank everyone at Sourcebooks for being supportive and helpful, and for being a wonderful place to grow in creativity. And, finally, I want to offer my ultimate thanks to Jane Austen for offering us all such a vivid world between the covers of her books that our imaginations can live a lifetime within them.

About the Author

Maria Hamilton is a graduate of Harvard Law School and is an attorney in Boston. Her interests include travel, politics, the Red Sox, bicycling, and a random succession of hobbies that allow her to express her creative passion. She is perpetually learning Italian and hopes one day to attempt a complete conversation. She lives in New Hampshire with her husband and two children.

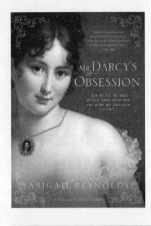

MR. DARCY'S OBSESSION

~

ABIGAIL REYNOLDS

The more he tries to stay away from her, the more his obsession grows...

"[Reynolds] has creatively blended a classic love story with a saucy romance novel." —Austenprose

"Developed so well that it made the age-old storyline new and fresh... Her writing gripped my attention and did not let go." —The Romance Studio

"The style and wit of Ms. Austen are compellingly replicated... spellbinding. Kudos to Ms. Reynolds!" —A Reader's Respite

What if... ELIZABETH BENNET WAS MORE UNSUITABLE FOR MR. DARCY THAN EVER...

Mr. Darcy is determined to find a more suitable bride. But then he learns that Elizabeth is living in London in reduced circumstances, after her father's death robs her of her family home...

What if... MR. DARCY CAN'T HELP HIMSELF FROM SEEKING HER OUT...

He just wants to make sure she's all right. But once he's seen her, he feels compelled to talk to her, and from there he's unable to fight the overwhelming desire to be near her, or the ever-growing mutual attraction that is between them...

What if... MR. DARCY'S INTENTIONS WERE SHOCKINGLY DISHONORABLE...

978-1-4022-4092-8 • $14.99 U.S./$17.99 CAN/£9.99 UK

Mr. Fitzwilliam Darcy:
THE LAST MAN IN THE WORLD
A *Pride and Prejudice* Variation
ABIGAIL REYNOLDS

What if Elizabeth had accepted Mr. Darcy the first time he asked?

In Jane Austen's *Pride and Prejudice*, Elizabeth Bennet tells the proud Mr. Fitzwilliam Darcy that she wouldn't marry him if he were the last man in the world. But what if circumstances conspired to make her accept Darcy the first time he proposes? In this installment of Abigail Reynolds' acclaimed *Pride and Prejudice* Variations, Elizabeth agrees to marry Darcy against her better judgment, setting off a chain of events that nearly brings disaster to them both. Ultimately, Darcy and Elizabeth will have to work together on their tumultuous and passionate journey to make a success of their ill-timed marriage.

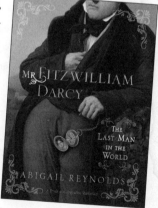

What readers are saying:

"A highly original story, immensely satisfying."

"Anyone who loves the story of Darcy and Elizabeth will love this variation."

"I was hooked from page one."

"A refreshing new look at what might have happened if…"

"Another good book to curl up with… I never wanted to put it down…"

978-1-4022-2947-3
$14.99 US/$18.99 CAN/£7.99 UK

In the Arms of Mr. Darcy

SHARON LATHAN

If only everyone could be as happy as they are...

Darcy and Elizabeth are as much in love as ever—even more so as their relationship matures. Their passion inspires everyone around them, and as winter turns to spring, romance blossoms around them.

Confirmed bachelor Richard Fitzwilliam sets his sights on a seemingly unattainable, beautiful widow; Georgiana Darcy learns to flirt outrageously; the very flighty Kitty Bennet develops her first crush, and Caroline Bingley meets her match.

But the path of true love never does run smooth, and Elizabeth and Darcy are kept busy navigating their friends and loved ones through the inevitable separations, misunderstandings, misgivings, and lovers' quarrels to reach their own happily ever afters...

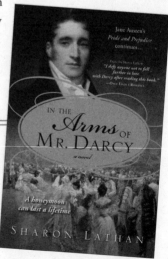

"If you love *Pride and Prejudice* sequels then this series should be on the top of your list!"
—*Royal Reviews*

"Sharon really knows how to make Regency come alive." —*Love Romance Passion*

978-1-4022-3699-0
$14.99 US/$17.99 CAN/£9.99 UK

My Dearest Mr. Darcy

Sharon Lathan

Darcy is more deeply in love with his wife than ever

As the golden summer draws to a close and the Darcys look ahead to the end of their first year of marriage, Mr. Darcy could never have imagined his love could grow even deeper with the passage of time. Elizabeth is unpredictable and lively, pulling Darcy out of his stern and serious demeanor with her teasing and temptation.

But surprising events force the Darcys to weather absence and illness, and to discover whether they can find a way to build a bond of everlasting love and desire…

Praise for *Loving Mr. Darcy*:

"An intimately romantic sequel to Jane Austen's *Pride and Prejudice*…wonderfully colorful and fun." —*Wendy's Book Corner*

"If you want to fall in love with Mr. Darcy all over again…order yourself a copy." —*Royal Reviews*

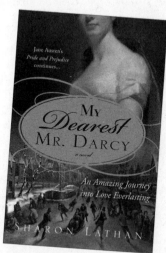

978-1-4022-1742-5
$14.99 US/$18.99 CAN/£7.99 UK

Mr. Darcy's Diary

AMANDA GRANGE

"A gift to a new generation of Darcy fans
and a treat for existing fans as well." —AUSTENBLOG

The only place Darcy could share his innermost feelings...

...was in the private pages of his diary. Torn between his sense of duty to his family name and his growing passion for Elizabeth Bennet, all he can do is struggle not to fall in love. A skillful and graceful imagining of the hero's point of view in one of the most beloved and enduring love stories of all time.

What readers are saying:

"A delicious treat for all Austen addicts."

"Amanda Grange knows her subject...I ended up reading the entire book in one sitting."

"Brilliant, you could almost hear Darcy's voice...I was so sad when it came to an end. I loved the visions she gave us of their married life."

"Amanda Grange has perfectly captured all of Jane Austen's clever wit and social observations to make *Mr. Darcy's Diary* a must read for any fan."

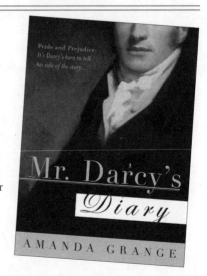

978-1-4022-0876-8 • $14.95 US/ $19.95 CAN/ £7.99 UK

WICKHAM'S DIARY

AMANDA GRANGE

Jane Austen's quintessential bad boy has his say…

Enter the clandestine world of the cold-hearted Wickham…

…in the pages of his private diary. Always aware of the inferiority of his social status compared to his friend Fitzwilliam Darcy, Wickham chases wealth and women in an attempt to attain the power he lusts for. But as Wickham gambles and cavorts his way through his funds, Darcy still comes out on top.

But now Wickham has found his chance to seduce the young Georgiana Darcy, which will finally secure the fortune—and the revenge—he's always dreamed of…

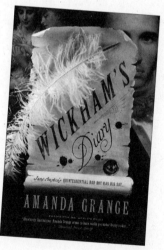

Praise for Amanda Grange:

"Amanda Grange has taken on the challenge of reworking a much loved romance and succeeds brilliantly." —*Historical Novels Review*

"Amanda Grange is a writer who tells an engaging, thoroughly enjoyable story!" —*Romance Reader at Heart*

Available April 2011
978-1-4022-5186-3
$12.99 US

Mr. Darcy Takes a Wife

LINDA BERDOLL

The #1 best-selling Pride and Prejudice sequel

"Wild, bawdy, and utterly enjoyable." —*Booklist*

Hold on to your bonnets!

Every woman wants to be Elizabeth Bennet Darcy—beautiful, gracious, universally admired, strong, daring and outspoken—a thoroughly modern woman in crinolines. And every woman will fall madly in love with Mr. Darcy—tall, dark and handsome, a nobleman and a heartthrob whose virility is matched only by his utter devotion to his wife. Their passion is consuming and idyllic—essentially, they can't keep their hands off each other—through a sweeping tale of adventure and misadventure, human folly and numerous mysteries of parentage. This sexy, epic, hilarious, poignant and romantic sequel to *Pride and Prejudice* goes far beyond Jane Austen.

What readers are saying:

"I couldn't put it down."

"I didn't want it to end!"

"Berdoll does Jane Austen proud! ...A thoroughly delightful and engaging book."

"Delicious fun...I thoroughly enjoyed this book."

"My favorite *Pride and Prejudice* sequel so far."

978-1-4022-0273-5 • $16.95 US/ $19.99 CAN/ £9.99 UK

THE OTHER MR. DARCY

PRIDE AND PREJUDICE CONTINUES...

MONICA FAIRVIEW

"A lovely story... a joy to read."
—*Bookishly Attentive*

Unpredictable courtships appear to run in the Darcy family...

When Caroline Bingley collapses to the floor and sobs at Mr. Darcy's wedding, imagine her humiliation when she discovers that a stranger has witnessed her emotional display. Miss Bingley, understandably, resents this gentleman very much, even if he is Mr. Darcy's American cousin. Mr. Robert Darcy is as charming as Mr. Fitzwilliam Darcy is proud, and he is stunned to find a beautiful young woman weeping broken-heartedly at his cousin's wedding. Such depth of love, he thinks, is rare and precious. For him, it's love at first sight...

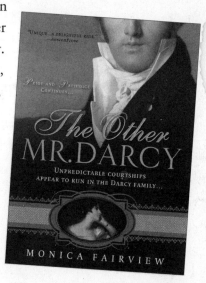

978-1-4022-2513-0
$14.99 US/$18.99 CAN/£7.99 UK

"An intriguing concept...
a delightful ride in the park."
—*Austenprose*

A Darcy Christmas

Amanda Grange, Sharon Lathan, & Carolyn Eberhart

A Holiday Tribute to Jane Austen

Mr. and Mrs. Darcy wish you a very Merry Christmas and a Happy New Year!

Share in the magic of the season in these three warm and wonderful holiday novellas from bestselling authors.

Christmas Present

By Amanda Grange

M

Praise for Amanda Grange:

"Amanda Grange is a writer who tells an engaging, thoroughly enjoyable story!"
—*Romance Reader at Heart*

"Amanda Grange seems to have really got under Darcy's skin and retells the story with great feeling and sensitivity."
—*Historical Novel Society*

Praise for Sharon Lathan:

"I defy anyone not to fall further in love with Darcy after reading this book."
—*Once Upon a Romance*

"The everlasting love between Darcy and Lizzy will leave more than one reader swooning." —*A Bibliophile's Bookshelf*

978-1-4022-4339-4
$14.99 US/$17.99 CAN/£9.99 UK